"I never said I
D..... .... a low, rich voice that
...ed testosterone.

... their madcap embrace was a
...med. "How dare you!"

....d and further invaded her space.
"How dare you?"

With effort, Emily ignored the sexual tremors starting deep inside her. Determined to get command of a situation that was fast escalating out of control, she extended her index finger and tapped him on the center of his rock-solid chest. "Let's get something straight, cowboy." She waited until she was certain she had his full attention. "My request for help did not include anything sexual."

He winked at her facetiously. "Too bad, 'cause if it had, I might have said yes."

Dear Reader,

We hope you enjoy the Western stories
One Wild Cowboy and *A Cowboy to Marry,* written
by bestselling Harlequin American Romance author
Cathy Gillen Thacker.

The Harlequin American Romance series is a
celebration of all things Western! These stories
are heartwarming contemporary tales of everyday
women finding love, becoming part of a family or
community—or maybe starting a family of her own.

And don't miss an excerpt of *Home to Wyoming*
by Harlequin American Romance author
Rebecca Winters at the back of this volume. Look
for *Home to Wyoming,* available September 2013.

Happy reading,

The Harlequin American Romance Editors

One Wild Cowboy
&
A Cowboy to Marry

———

CATHY GILLEN THACKER

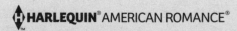

HARLEQUIN® AMERICAN ROMANCE®

ISBN-13: 978-0-373-68915-6

ONE WILD COWBOY & A COWBOY TO MARRY

Copyright © 2013 by Harlequin Books S.A.

The publisher acknowledges the copyright holder of the individual works as follows:

ONE WILD COWBOY
Copyright © 2011 by Cathy Gillen Thacker

A COWBOY TO MARRY
Copyright © 2011 by Cathy Gillen Thacker

Recycling programs for this product may not exist in your area.

Printed in U.S.A.

www.Harlequin.com

CONTENTS

ABOUT THE AUTHOR

Cathy Gillen Thacker is married and a mother of three. She and her husband spent eighteen years in Texas and now reside in North Carolina. Her mysteries, romantic comedies and heartwarming family stories have made numerous appearances on bestseller lists, but her best reward, she says, is knowing one of her books made someone's day a little brighter. A popular Harlequin author for many years, she loves telling passionate stories with happy endings, and thinks nothing beats a good romance and a hot cup of tea! You can visit Cathy's website at www.cathygillenthacker.com for more information on her upcoming and previously published books, recipes and a list of her favorite things.

ONE WILD COWBOY

Chapter One

This is not good, Emily McCabe thought as she led her beloved mare, Maisy, toward the Circle M Ranch stable. Standing just inside the entrance to the barn were all three of her older brothers. Their postures were as inflexible as the set of their jaws, and they appeared to be waiting on her.

The relaxation she'd felt after her Monday afternoon ride was fading fast as Emily studied the trio of determined expressions. "What's going on?" she asked warily. It had to be something. Otherwise, Jeb would have been looking after his rodeo livestock, Hank would have been tending his cattle, and Holden would have been caring for his quarter horses. Instead, all three ranchers were gathered here on her parents' property.

Awkward glances were exchanged—the kind that told her this was not an actual emergency. Great, Emily thought. Just what she needed—her wildly overprotective clan butting into her life again.

Looking less rambunctious than usual, Jeb squared his shoulders. "We wanted to talk to you."

Emily sighed, bored already. She patted Maisy's silky black mane and led the big bay mare past her brothers, toward her horse's stall. "About what?"

"Mom and Dad are worried about you." The always-gallant Holden kept pace. "You've put everything you've got into the café for two years now. And with the new diner opening…"

They were all acting as if she was about to have her heart broken. "I have a very loyal customer base. It's not going to cut into my business."

To her annoyance, her brothers stood their ground.

"On top of that," Holden continued, "it's been over a year since you had a date."

Uh-oh. Now that had an ominous ring. Emily knew her brothers could be ridiculously sexist where she was concerned. They had been that way since she was a kid, something that happened when there was only one girl in a family. It didn't mean she had to like it.

"So?" Emily unfastened the girths on Maisy's saddle and lifted it off. She set the saddle and blanket on the cement floor outside the stall. "Since when do you-all care about my social life?" she demanded, aiming a disparaging look their way.

Ignoring her Hank replied pleasantly, "Since we've taken it upon ourselves to do you a big favor and help you out."

Emily liked the sound of that even less. Wordlessly, she removed the rest of Maisy's tack and heaped it on top of the leather riding gear. She ran an affectionate hand down Maisy's neck and rubbed her face against her beautiful horse in silent thanks for a great canter across the meadow. Then she stepped outside the stall, shutting the door behind her. While Maisy quenched her thirst from the stall water trough, Emily confronted her three well-meaning but totally idiotic brothers. "Didn't you learn anything from the last time you guys tried to fix me up?" What an unmitigated disaster that had been! The longest evening on record, followed by an impossibly awkward good-night. She propped her hands on her hips and glared at them. "No more!"

"Normally we'd agree." All three nodded vigorously. "But that was before Mom figured out who you *should* be seeing," Hank explained.

Emily's heart sank.

She had no doubt her mother meant well, too.

Thanks to more than thirty-six years of happily wedded bliss with the love of her life, there was no one more romantic than her mother. Her father, in his own way, was just as bad although her dad had yet to actually approve of any man she'd dated.

"Tell me you're pulling my leg here," Emily pleaded.

"Nope." Jeb flashed a grin. "Mom's planning to play matchmaker at tonight's charity dinner for the Libertyville Boys Ranch."

There was no way Emily could avoid the fund-raiser. Her Daybreak Café was one of a handful of restaurants in town providing food and beverage for the outdoor event. Plus, it was a worthy cause.

Emily picked up the reins and bridle while Hank carried the saddle and blanket to the tack room. She put the riding equipment away, then turned back to face her brothers. She swept off her flat-brimmed hat and slapped it impatiently against her thigh. "Surely Dad isn't going to sign on for this foolhardiness."

If there was anyone who could talk sense into Greta McCabe, it was her husband....

Her three brothers watched as she went to the fridge in the corner and took out a bottle of blackberry-flavored water, kept on hand just for her.

"Actually," Holden recounted, serious as ever, "Dad thinks Mom might be onto something. You have to admit, you have been one heck of a bum magnet on your own."

Emily narrowed her eyes. "Thanks, heaps."

Jeb chuckled. "It's true, little sis. Who knew there were so many losers in the world till you dragged them all home?"

Emily recalled with startling clarity why she'd had such a hard time with her love life. Part of it was her ability to see the "potential" in just about everyone. The only problem was, most men did not want to be "improved" and certainly not by the woman they were dating. So she constantly had to shelve her need to help. The rest had to do with the fact that all the truly successful men she had met seemed to want a woman who'd be content to tend to *their* needs and live in their shadow. Few wanted a woman who was already successful in her own right.

But not wanting to get into any of that with her brothers, she turned to the third and most annoying reason her love life remained a bust.

"My lack of dates this past year is because no guy in his right mind has wanted to come near me knowing he would have to put up with you-all constantly breathing down our necks."

Hank refused to apologize. "We were just trying to protect you."

Emily glared at her three tall, brawny brothers. "Well, stop!"

Holden looked her in the eye and held the line. "No can do. Now, here's the plan. We're sure we know better than Mom and Dad who you should be dating. So… we have each picked out a guy for you to meet. All of them understand the restaurant business—so you should have something in common—and all of them already get along with us." He smiled confidently. "And as a bonus, none of them are from around here. So it won't be anyone you've already met and rejected."

Emily didn't care where these potential suitors hailed from. "I'm not going on any blind dates!" she warned. "And especially not with any men that have already received the McCabe Men Stamp of Approval!" That would simply confirm they were the type who would bore her to tears.

Jeb grinned, mischievous as ever. "That's the beauty of our plan, baby sis. You won't have to go out with them, 'cause we're bringing them to you at the cafe. You can scope them out while you're serving them breakfast or lunch and then decide who you want to go out with—and then we'll set it up for you."

This was insane, Emily thought. Like some sort of reality show she never would have signed up for in a million years. "These three guys agreed to be looked over by me, like hunks of prime beefcake?"

For the first time, her brothers looked uncertain. Aha, Emily thought, this plan did have a hitch! And a possibly insurmountable one, at that...

Grimacing, Holden said, "They all agreed to have breakfast or lunch with us at your place. The meals themselves are going to be more like business meetings, with a little socializing thrown in."

"And during said meeting, I'm supposed to come over, make nice and flirt a little," Emily mused sarcastically.

Jeb shrugged and regarded her as if she were overreacting. "Couldn't hurt."

Oh, yeah? Emily drained the rest of her water in a single gulp and tossed the empty bottle in the recycling bin. "You're making it oh so tempting," she drawled in her Scarlett O'Hara imitation, batting her eyelashes for effect, "but no. Besides, I already have a date," she fibbed with as much bravado as she could muster. "It's tonight, at the benefit for the boys ranch, as a matter of fact. So you might want to pass that on to Mom and Dad, because I know they wouldn't want to interfere in a date I already lined up."

"Is that right?" Hank prodded, clearly not believing a word of what she'd just said. "With whom?"

Emily mentally ran down the list of eligible men in Laramie, Texas, and quickly centered on the one who would be the least desirable, at least by her family's standards. The one man who had sworn he would never be tamed by any woman...

She beamed at them proudly. "Dylan Reeves."

"No."

Emily stared at the sexy rancher in front of her, sure she hadn't heard right. Especially, since she had just offered the town's most notorious bachelor the kind of deal he couldn't possibly resist. "No?" she repeated, stunned.

Dylan Reeves swept off his hat, ran an impatient hand through his thick, wheat-colored hair and stepped out of the round training pen. His golden brown eyes lasered into hers with disturbing accuracy. "That's what I said."

Emily cast a glance behind Dylan at the once-wild gelding who was now mooning after his momentarily distracted trainer like a little puppy awaiting his return. Then she returned her attention to the ruggedly fit cowboy who was scowling down at her.

Dylan wasn't just an incredibly attractive man with a towering build that dwarfed her own five-foot-seven frame. He was a horse whisperer who had moved to Laramie five years before and, through sheer grit and hard work, founded the Last Chance Ranch.

Dylan took on the horses everyone else had given up on, and transformed them.

That being the case, Emily reasoned, he had a heart in

there somewhere that would allow him to participate in yet another worthy cause. "It's a fund-raiser for charity."

His lips formed an uncompromising line. "It could be a dinner for the Crown Prince of England for all I care." He lounged against the metal rails of the round training pen and folded his arms in front of him. "The answer is still no."

Emily ignored the way the tan twill shirt hugged his broad shoulders and molded to the sculpted muscles of his chest before disappearing into the waistband of his worn, dark blue denim jeans. She forced her gaze away from the engraved silver-and-gold buckle on his belt. "Look. You know we have nothing in common," she said as a shimmer of awareness shifted through her, "so there's no possibility this will be a real date. That's why I asked you to go with me tonight."

Dylan narrowed his eyes at her. "*Asked* being the operative word. You asked…I declined. As, I might point out, I have every right to do. End of story."

"Fine." Emily stepped closer and tilted her head toward him. "Then what's it going to take?"

He looked her up and down suspiciously, from the top of her flat-brimmed hat, to the toes of her favorite burgundy rattlesnake boots. "What do you mean?"

"How many free meals at the café?" she bartered.

Initially, she'd thought two was fair. Evidently not, in his opinion.

Dylan flashed her a crocodile smile that didn't begin to reach his life-weary eyes. He rubbed his jaw with the palm of his hand. "What makes you think I want to eat at your restaurant?"

"Oh," Emily looked him up and down just as impudently and mocked his condescending tone to a T. "Perhaps the fact that you're there every morning when I open—and sometimes lunch, as well. And you've asked more than once why I don't serve dinner at night!"

That alone conveyed that either he couldn't cook, or he was too unmotivated to do so. He also had a penchant for the cowboy cuisine she had perfected.

Poking the brim of his cowboy hat up with maddening nonchalance, he leaned toward her and whispered conspiratorially, "It's a good point, sweetheart. You'd make more money if you did stay open through the dinner hour."

She would also be competing with her mother's restaurant, which was a Laramie institution and had a dance floor and lively music every night.

"I would also have to work much longer hours," Emily replied, suddenly flustered by his blatant nearness.

He smirked in a way meant to infuriate. "Or—" he prodded "—hire more staff."

Emily harrumphed. The last thing she wanted was anyone telling her how to run the restaurant she had dreamed up and started from scratch. "I don't want to hire more employees. I like my café the way it is—open for breakfast and lunch six days a week. Now," she said, peering at him sternly, "back to what we were saying…."

Dylan chuckled and released a long-suffering sigh. "Goodbye, I hope?"

She ignored his stab at a joke and stepped even closer, not caring that the move left mere inches of empty space between them. She felt the heat emanating off him, stronger and warmer than the April sunshine overhead. "Just tell me your price, cowboy." *To keep me from being thoroughly humiliated in the wake of my premature claim to have a date with you.*

Emily stood and propped both hands on her hips. "How many meals is it going to take for you to pretend to be my date for the evening? I need you just long enough to scare away the man my parents have picked out for me—and to disabuse my brothers of their own lame-brained matchmaking idea."

"None." Dylan gave her a steady look, then straightened and moved behind her. Taking her by the shoulders, he pivoted her in the direction of her car. As abruptly as he'd taken hold of her, he dropped his firm but gentle grip and stepped away. Her shoulders tingled as badly as the rest of her. "'Cause I don't do family drama," he said flatly.

Temper boiling, Emily whirled back around to face him.

He lifted one work-roughened palm. "And I don't tame women, either."

Tame! Had he actually used the word *tame*? "Excuse me?" she fumed, daring him to say that again!

The corners of his lips twitched in barely checked amusement. "Your family is right. You are a woman in need of 'assistance' when it comes to dealing with the opposite sex." He paused, wearing a self-assured, faintly baiting expression, then returned to the pen and the magnificent horse he'd been training when she arrived.

He closed the gate behind him and let his glance drift lazily over Emily before deliberately meeting her eyes. "Luckily for both of us, darlin'…that schooling is *not* going to come from me."

"WELL, IF YOU ASK ME," Simone Saunders said two hours later, "I think you should just relax about the whole thing."

"Easier said than done," Emily murmured, arranging trays of fruit cobbler and pecan-pie bars on the banquet tables set up on the town square.

"You never know," the Daybreak Café's assistant chef teased. "The guy your parents want you to meet could be a real hottie."

Emily regarded the petite dynamo with the copper-colored hair. Simone was not only her trusted employee but also a close friend. "Don't you start! Besides, aren't you the one who has been extolling the virtues of freedom since your divorce?"

Simone cast a worried look at her increasingly rebellious fifteen-year-old son, Andrew, who was hanging out with a group of friends on the other side of the green. "My situation is different. My husband was a crook."

Who was now in jail, Emily thought.

"Any guy your parents want you to meet would at least be honorable."

True. Emily shrugged. "I like nice guys, but there has to be chemistry." It couldn't just be conjured up on demand because her parents wanted it to be.

With Dylan Reeves on the other hand… Emily still couldn't believe the audacious cowboy had turned her down, and so rudely! Put his hands on her shoulders and invaded her space.

Simone glanced at the fast-growing crowd, then reached for another tray of brownies off the pastry cart. "How are you going to explain not having a date with the horse whisperer after you told your brothers you did?"

Good question. Emily added apricot scones to the table. "I could always say something came up, that Dylan wanted to attend but just couldn't."

"Uh…no…you can't."

Emily brought the buckets of fresh churned ice cream out of the portable cooler, and set them in tubs of ice on the buffet table. "Why not?"

"Because Dylan's here. Talking to Holden and Hank right now."

Heat flooding her cheeks, Emily turned around. Sure enough, Dylan Reeves *was* here, looking mighty fine in a starched white shirt, a clean pair of jeans and a black Resistol hat. It was all she could do not to wring her hands in dismay. "Holden and Hank are probably grilling him on why he didn't accompany me. If Dylan tells them I asked him for a date and he turned me down, I'll just die of embarrassment."

"Maybe he won't."

And maybe, Emily thought, already tossing her chef's apron aside, there was only one way she could stop this. She hoped it wasn't too late. "Are you okay here?"

Simone nodded, her expression as resolute as Emily's mood. "I'll handle this. You go do damage control. And from the looks of it," Simone said softly, as the men's faces grew serious, "you better hurry."

"So what's going on with you and my sister?" Holden McCabe asked.

Didn't Emily's brothers ever lighten up? Dylan wondered, resenting the polite chitchat that was fast turning into a McCabe family inquisition.

Dylan folded his arms in front of him. "I make it a policy never to discuss my personal affairs." Not that there was anything to report.

Hank McCabe paused. He exchanged confused looks with his brother, then turned back to Dylan. "So the two of you are dating?" he asked finally.

Dylan was still contemplating how best to respond when Emily rushed up, looking gorgeous, flushed and a bit disheveled. Not that he was noticing the way the sunshine-yellow sundress hugged her slender waist and feminine curves. Or how sexy her legs looked when not encased in the usual jeans.

"Holden...Hank, for heaven's sake!" she scolded.

Predictably, her ridiculously overprotective brothers refused to back down.

"What's the problem?" Hank asked.

Holden added innocently, "We're just talking to your 'date' here."

Emily swirled around in a drift of jonquil perfume he found amazingly enticing. She shot Dylan a beseeching glance that only he could see. Her soft-as-silk hand curved possessively around his biceps, compelling him to remain silent.

Curious as to how she was going to get herself out of this mess, he merely smiled.

The panicked look in her blue eyes fading, Emily released her grip on him and turned back to her brothers. "*Dating* is for teenagers, guys."

More skeptical glances. "What does that mean?" Holden demanded.

"It means she doesn't like to put a label on things any more than I do," Dylan intervened.

"And neither of us like answering nosy questions," Emily added.

Holden shrugged, unrepentant. "You're the one who brought it up." He turned to Dylan. "Emily told us earlier that the two of you had a date tonight."

Jeb sauntered up, a typical know-it-all grin on his face. "I've got to say, we didn't believe her then and given the fact the two of you arrived separately now..." He regarded his little sister suspiciously. "Now you wouldn't happen to be pulling one over on the whole family just because we're trying to set you up, would you?"

The only thing Dylan liked less than being put on the

spot was seeing a strong, independent woman like Emily reduced to making up stories simply to get her interfering family out of her business.

"I can't believe you would even think that!" Emily sputtered.

Something about her vulnerability got to Dylan.

He'd never been prone to rescuing damsels in distress—because that could only lead to trouble. But this was different.

So he did the only thing that he knew would shut everyone up.

He wrapped his arm around Emily's slender shoulders, pivoted her slightly and brought her all the way against him.

Chapter Two

Shock rendered Emily completely still. She couldn't believe Dylan was about to kiss her, but she could not deny the electric jolt of the first brush of his lips. Suddenly breathless, she found herself closing her eyes and parting her lips. Darn it all, this reckless cowboy was one fine kisser. And she was susceptible as could be to the seductive heat of his mouth, combined with the masculine certainty of his tall, strong body pressed against hers. Despite her efforts to remain immune to this ridiculously false display of affection, she impulsively wound her arms around his neck. And still he kept on kissing her, until she shivered with sheer pleasure and the rest of the world literally fell away...

Dylan hadn't meant to get so caught up in the moment. And maybe he wouldn't have, had Emily's lips not been so incredibly sweet, her body so warm and womanly.... This was *supposed* to be his chance to put the audacious heiress in her place and make sure she never made false claims about the two of them again.

And yet, the kiss that had started out merely as a way to knock her off balance and show her who was boss swiftly turned into much, much more. It was an invitation to delve further into the chemistry between them.

A lightning bolt of desire that instinct told him neither of them would soon forget.

He might not be the right kind of guy for her, or she the right kind of woman for him, but the passion between them was potent. Too potent, Dylan decided, for the kiss to continue.

It took everything he had to let the passionate embrace come to a halt. And a second after that he was reminded that they had an audience.

All three of her big brothers looked at him as if they wanted to clock him.

Dylan could hardly blame them.

Had Emily been *his* wildly impetuous baby sister...

Blushing, Emily stepped back slightly, grabbed Dylan's sleeve and held on tight. "You know," she said, seemingly making up words on the fly with the same impetuousness that had him kissing her, "that wasn't the smartest move either of us has ever made, Dylan. But," she continued before any of the four males around her could interrupt, "that's what happens when you're in love." She paused to beam at him. "Right, Dylan?"

Once again, he had a chance to put her in place. All he had to do was disavow having any feelings at all for her. Tell the truth about their "date."

Certainly, it would have been the wise thing to do—if he wanted to end this craziness.

For some reason, he didn't.

Dylan rocked back on his heels, braced his hands on his waist and shrugged in the direction of her outraged brothers. "I'm not sure there are words that would ever adequately explain this situation," he said.

"You've got that right," Emily concurred. "Besides, we should get a move on. We have to go back to the café and pick up the rest of the desserts for the buffet."

She dropped her grip on his sleeve, clasped his hand in hers and tugged Dylan away from her still-scowling, perplexed brothers. "See you later, guys!" She tossed the dismissive words over her shoulder.

Seconds later, Dylan felt Emily begin to disengage her hand from his.

Loath to let her go—because that would have meant he was letting her call *all* the shots, which was not a good precedent to set—Dylan held tight.

She turned, flashed a smile that did not reach her pretty eyes and then whirled around and kept going.

Half a block of historic downtown buildings later, she had unlocked the front door to the Daybreak Café, stormed inside and shut the door behind them. Still fuming, she promptly wrested her hands from his. "All right, cowboy!" she snapped, pausing only to give him a long, withering glare. "You have one heck of a lot of explaining to do!"

EMILY EXPECTED AN APOLOGY. It was, after all, the only decent thing to do, given the outlandishly passionate way Dylan had just kissed her. In front of an audience of her family and countless others, no less!

"Hey." Dylan mocked her impudently. "I'm not the one still claiming to have a date with a person who's already rejected me!"

Indignation warmed Emily's cheeks. "Claim what you like, cowboy, if it soothes your ruffled feelings, but there was nothing 'rejecting' about that kiss you just gave me."

"I never said I didn't *desire* you," Dylan volleyed back in a low, rich voice that practically oozed testosterone.

He was acting as if their madcap embrace was a *good* thing. "How dare you, anyway!"

He stepped forward and further invaded her space. "How dare you?"

With effort, Emily ignored the sexual tremors starting deep inside her. Determined to get command of a situation that was fast escalating out of control, she extended her index finger and tapped him on the center of his rock-solid chest. "Let's get something straight, Dylan." She waited until she was certain she had his full attention. "My request for help did not include anything sexual."

He winked at her facetiously. "Too bad, 'cause if it had, I might have said yes."

Emily curtailed the urge to deck him for that remark. She didn't know what he was up to now, but she did not like it one bit. "Furthermore, you are incredibly ill-mannered."

"Never claimed to be otherwise," Dylan said with a careless shrug.

Emily arched her eyebrows and ignored his pronouncement. "And you owe me an apology for that kiss."

"You owe *me* an apology for that kiss!" he countered just as emphatically, even as her knees grew weaker still.

"Really." She lifted her chin, drew a deep breath. *"Really?"*

Dylan looked at her as if he already knew what it felt like to make love to her. "You bet your hot temper you do!"

"Listen, cowboy, I did not start that!"

He moved closer, once again towering over her. "You sure continued it enthusiastically though, didn't you?"

Darned if he hadn't made her flush all over again.

Emily's spine stiffened. "Only because I didn't want to make my brothers suspicious," she retorted, hanging on to her composure by a thread.

"Yeah, well," he pointed out glibly, "you sure failed on that count."

Emily blinked. "Are you kidding? They thought our embrace was so genuinely hot they wanted to punch you out."

And whether Dylan wanted to admit it or not, their clinch *had* been genuinely hot. As well as definitely misguided, Emily thought, pushing aside the potent fantasy this discussion was evoking.

The last thing she needed to be thinking about was kissing him again, she reminded herself firmly.

And she certainly didn't need to be imagining Dylan's beautifully muscled body stretched out alongside her own.

Or fixate on the fact that everywhere she was soft, he'd be hard. Everywhere he was male, she'd be female....

He regarded her with a devil-may-care glint in his eyes. "Your siblings wanted to throttle me because they suspected it wasn't a real date and therefore felt I had no place making out with you—on the town square no less."

"They had a point about that, Dylan. You did not have a right to haul me into your arms and plant one on me."

Dylan exhaled. "You reap what you sow, sweetheart."

The warning in his tone sent a chill down her spine. "What's that supposed to mean?"

Dylan narrowed his eyes. "I'm not interested in being one of your little projects."

Despite her desire to stay cool, calm and collected, Emily's heart beat faster. "Excuse me?"

Dylan eyed her seriously. "I wasn't in town five minutes before I heard all about how the beautiful Emily McCabe likes to bring home 'strays' and fix 'em up... and then gets them to fall in love with her before she dumps them."

More like the guys dumped me, Emily thought glumly.

But not about to correct Dylan on that, she let the misconception stand.

She gave him an arch look and started to turn away. "I don't deny I was trying to help you, too." *My mistake!*

He caught her by the elbow and reeled her back. "By ensnaring me in your web so you could make me over, too?"

"You could use a few more manners, not to mention a haircut and a decent shave," she said tartly. "But that's hardly the point."

He snorted in exasperation. "Then what is?"

"Your horse-training business here in Laramie is only a couple of years older than my business." Searching for a theory he might accept as plausible, she continued making it up as she went. "I know you're constantly trying to improve the facilities and equipment on your ranch, and I thought free meals here might help your bottom line."

He glared at her. "First of all, I'm paid very well for the problem horses I diagnose and train—and I have no shortage of work coming my way. So my bottom line is fine, thank you very much."

And yet, Emily noted, she had somehow struck a nerve with her mention of money....

Her pulse inexplicably picking up, she angled her head at him. "If business is so good, why don't you hire some cowboys to help you?"

Dylan grimaced. "I like working alone. I don't want to be responsible for anyone else's livelihood. And most important of all, I don't ever want to invest so much in a piece of property that I can't pick up and move the whole operation if—and when—I feel like it."

Emily had the feeling he was talking about much more than just his ranch now. She shook her head in mocking censure. "That's a crying shame, cowboy. You'll never put down roots that way. Never belong. Probably never marry and have a family, either!"

Although why that should bother her, she did not know. It wasn't any of her business!

Dylan's broad shoulders stiffened. "I don't want roots. Or marriage. Or any of the happily-ever-afters you're peddling, because that's never been for me, either. I want my freedom. Which is why I would never—and I repeat, *never*—hook up with a down-home family gal like you."

Emily inhaled the sandalwood-and-spice fragrance of his cologne. "I don't deny I love my family, but I am my own person."

A victorious light gleamed in his golden brown eyes. "Then how come they all feel they need to find your boyfriends for you?"

Emily bit down on a most unladylike oath. She threw up her hands in frustration, hating the fact she had to practically beg this temperamental cowpoke to cooperate. But the fix-up currently being engineered by her parents—not to mention those of her three brothers' machinations—remained a very big problem. One she was determined to solve.

Hopefully, with his help.

Emily inhaled deeply and said in the softest, most feminine voice she possessed, "Look, Dylan, all I ask is that you pretend for just a *little* while longer that you and I are an item." She added persuasively, "It shouldn't be that hard, after the way you just kissed me."

He lifted an eyebrow, said nothing.

"My offer for free meals at the café still stands." Telling herself the end justified the means, *this once,* Emily lifted a hand airily and recklessly gave herself permission to go crazy. "You can have as many breakfasts and

lunches as you like…as long as you cooperate with me."
There, that ought to do it. A gal couldn't get more magnanimous than that.

He hooked his thumbs through his belt loops and rocked forward on his toes. "That's very generous of you, Miss Emily."

Emily flushed at the sudden moniker of respect. "Thank you."

He lowered his handsome face until they were nose to nose. "But if I were to agree—and that in itself is a long shot—that is not the payment I want."

Oh, dear heaven.

How was it he knew just what buttons to push with her? "Then what compensation do you want?" she asked sweetly, fearing she already knew.

"This."

Bringing his lips even closer, he cupped a hand beneath her chin. Emily could not believe he was about to kiss her again. Or worse, that she was welcoming his attentions! What kind of fool did that make her? She knew this didn't mean anything to him. Not what it should have anyway, for someone kissing her with this much passion.

Behind them, a bell rang.

Abruptly aware they were no longer alone, Emily turned her head slightly without actually stepping out of the circle of Dylan's arms. To her dismay, her parents walked in the door.

DYLAN STEPPED BACK as Shane and Greta McCabe stared at him in mute amazement. He could hardly blame them. What had gotten into him? He was usually so controlled.

Whenever he was around Emily, he acted like a hormone-driven teenager—and she was behaving just as badly. Except right now, she looked as if she wished a hole in the floor would open up so she could sink right through it.

He felt the same.

This was not the way he wanted the respected horse rancher and his accomplished wife to see him. Especially given all he now had at stake, with a soon-to-be-announced deal Emily apparently knew nothing about. Otherwise, Dylan was sure she would have mentioned it.

Not about to apologize for kissing Emily—even if it would smooth over what was an incredibly awkward situation—Dylan nodded at the older couple. He said formally, "Mr. and Mrs. McCabe. Nice to see you."

"Good to see you, Dylan," Shane and Greta McCabe replied, in unison.

"Emily." A cautioning lilt was in Greta McCabe's tone as she took in her daughter. "Your father and I just met the proprietor of the new restaurant."

"I hope he's not the guy you're planning to fix me up with," Emily said.

For some reason, Dylan noted, that notion seemed to amuse them.

"Ah—no," Shane said finally.

Unconvinced, Emily narrowed her eyes at her parents. "You're sure?"

"Absolutely," Greta said, her tone definitive.

"Because I can see how that would seem to make sense to you," Emily continued, working up a head of steam. "Me and the new diner owner, becoming a thing."

"Believe us," her mother said firmly, "the two of you are *not* a match your father and I would ever try and make."

"That's too bad," said a smug teenager with trendy, bleached-blond hair, catching the tail end of their conversation as he sauntered in to join them.

He was just under six feet tall, wearing a burnt-orange Cowtown Diner T-shirt, jeans and the most ridiculously expensive and ornate pair of ostrich boots and gold belt buckle Dylan had ever seen.

Ignoring him, the kid grinned at Emily and extended his hand. "Because I would very much like to get to know…and date…you!"

EMILY'S JAW DROPPED even as she did the polite thing and accepted the proffered greeting.

"Xavier Shillingsworth, owner of the soon-to-be-open Cowtown Diner." The teen continued holding her hand long after it would have been polite to let go. He leaned in even closer, inundating Emily with expensive cologne. "And you must be the Emily McCabe, head chef and owner of the Daybreak Café, that I've heard so much about."

Emily forced a smile and wrested her hand from the young man's grip. "Yes. I am."

Xavier continued sizing her up with undisguised interest. "I hear we're going to be in hot competition with each other—since our two restaurants are the only table-service establishments in Laramie that serve breakfast."

Emily had been brought up to be courteous, even to those who were pushy and borderline rude. And that rule went double in business situations. "I'm sure there is room for both of our establishments," she said pleasantly, injecting the situation with the down-home hospitality for which Laramie, Texas, was known.

"If not, may the best restaurateur win," Xavier taunted. Grinning confidently, he aimed a thumb at his chest and proclaimed, "I know who my money's on!"

The look in his eyes briefly telegraphing he'd had enough, Dylan stepped forward, putting his tall body between Xavier and Emily. "I don't believe we've met. I'm Dylan Reeves. One of the ranchers in the area. And I know a lot of people here tonight who would like to meet you, too. Especially Emily's three brothers. So why don't we go—" Dylan slapped a companionable hand on Xavier's shoulder and spun him around toward the door "—and talk up your new establishment."

Quick steps were made, and the door shut behind them.

"That was nice of Dylan," Greta said.

"No kidding." Emily breathed a sigh of relief.

Shane shook his head. "Shillingsworth is going to be unpleasantly competitive."

Emily rolled her eyes. "You think?"

"So, if you need help putting him in his place…" Shane growled, all protective father.

Emily lifted a palm. "I can handle the situation, Dad. Just like I can figure out, on my own, how to rev up my personal life."

"So it's true?" her mom interrupted, with furrowed brow. "You do have a date with Dylan this evening?"

Talk about putting her on the spot! "In a manner of speaking…" Emily cleared her throat uncomfortably. "I know you mean well, but I really don't need any help finding a man to hang out with. So I'd rather not hear any suggestions on who I should be seeing. And I certainly don't want to be fixed up on any dates by anyone in the family!"

Finished, Emily braced herself for the emotional argument sure to come. Instead, to her utter amazement, her mother completely backed off. "You're right," Greta murmured, looking at Shane for verification, as if wanting to make sure they were on the same page.

Shane locked eyes with Greta. Something passed between them. "It would be a mistake for us to try to match-make at this point," Emily's father concluded finally.

Well, that was easy, Emily thought with relief. Astoundingly…almost suspiciously…so.

"We came in to tell you that the opening ceremony is about to start," Greta said.

"I'll be right there," Emily promised. "I just need to get a few trays of chocolate and lemon-meringue pies."

"We'll all help," her dad said.

Five minutes later, the pies were set out on the buffet tables. Shane and Greta—the charity event's hosts—were stepping up to the microphones. They spoke about the Libertyville Boys Ranch, and how much the facility helped juvenile delinquents turn their lives around.

"The institution has been so successful, they are expanding again. The problem is, they need more therapy horses for the kids to care for. So," Shane said, "I've made arrangements with the Bureau of Land Management to purchase three wild mustangs for training. Dylan Reeves—the renowned horse whisperer in the area—is going to be doing the schooling." Wild applause erupted. "When they are ready, the horses will go to the boys ranch, where they will be adopted into a very good home…."

Incredibly impressed, Emily made her way through the crowd to Dylan's side. In shock, she murmured, "I had no idea you were a philanthropist."

Was it possible the two of them had more in common than they knew?

Not surprisingly, Dylan looked irritated by her compliment. "Don't view me as some sort of saint. I'm not," he muttered gruffly, and then for good measure, added, "I'm being paid."

"Just not your normal rate," Emily guessed.

Dylan scowled. "It's a challenge," he said flatly. "I like working with mustangs. I like the fact the horses will find a good, loving home at the boys ranch." He regarded her, all tough lonesome cowboy. "Don't make more of it than that."

Hours later, Emily turned to Simone, as the after-event cleanup commenced. Emily followed Simone's gaze to where her son, Andrew, stood talking with that same group of boys.

"You're worried, aren't you?" The kids were from a neighboring town and looked like bad news.

Simone stacked serving platters onto a wheeled cart.

"I have a feeling he's going to ask me if he can go out past his curfew tonight."

"If it's not a good idea," Emily counseled, "you have every right to say no."

"I know that," Simone sighed. "It just seems like that's all I say these days."

The group of kids were edging toward a late-model pickup truck with extra lights mounted across the top. They seemed to be encouraging Andrew to ditch the cleanup, forgo getting permission and just take off.

Emily touched Simone's arm. "Why don't you go on?"

Simone's posture relaxed with relief. "Thanks. I'll make it up to you."

"No problem."

Emily cast a glance at Dylan, who was busy helping a group of ranchers disassemble the bandstand. Her brothers were off with her dad, in another direction, taking down the strings of banners and colored lights.

Pleased the event had turned out so well, she finished loading up her cart and wheeled it in the direction of the café.

No sooner had she gotten inside than a light rap sounded on the door. Xavier Shillingsworth stepped in, all young bravura. "I was thinking…the two of us should go out on a date."

Emily did not like hurting anyone's feelings. Still, this was ludicrous and she had to make her would-be suitor realize it. "How old are you?" she asked gently.

"Nineteen." Xavier slicked back his hair with his free hand. "But that shouldn't matter."

She arched a brow. Was he talking down to her?

"You can't be *that* old."

"I'm twenty-eight," Emily said drily. "That's nine years older than you. It's a big difference."

Xavier shrugged. "Doesn't matter to me. I've always wanted to go out with a cougar. And you're hot!"

Was he serious? Apparently so.

Emily went back to loading dishes in the machine. "I'm curious. You are obviously a smart guy with a lot going for him. Why aren't you in college?"

Xavier seemed flattered by the attention. "I didn't want to go. So my dad bought me a franchise restaurant to run instead."

Of course. Can't solve a problem so throw money at it instead. And while you're at it, get the problem kid out of the picture, too.

Emily smiled with encouragement. "You both may want to rethink that. College can be a fun, exciting time… with lots of girls your own age who are dying to go out on dates."

"I don't want a girl. I want you!"

Emily sighed and walked toward the exit. "Well, it's not going to happen."

"See?" Xavier caught up with her as she reached the dining room. He clamped his arms around her and crowded her all the more. "That's what I like about you. You're a real spitfire."

Not about to let him so much as try to kiss her, Emily stomped on his toe with all her might. "And you're a real horse's rear end," she spat out.

"Ouch!" Xavier hopped up and down in pain.

The door to the café opened and Dylan strode in. It took him all of two seconds to size up the situation. "Allow me." He grabbed Xavier by the back of his Cowtown Diner T-shirt and escorted him to the door.

Dylan let him go just inside the portal. "If you ever touch her again, you're going to have to deal with me."

"On what grounds?" Xavier straightened his shirt. He regarded Dylan pugnaciously, clearly spoiling for a fistfight.

She was afraid there just might be one if the kid didn't cut it out.

"I don't see an engagement ring!"

Eager to be rid of the callow youth, Emily swung open the door to the café and glared at the teenager. "I don't need a ring to be his. Now go."

"You heard the lady." When Xavier didn't immediately comply, Dylan shoved him out the door and shut it firmly in his face.

Emily turned to Dylan. She knew it was unnecessary and politically incorrect of her, but she really liked the idea of Dylan jumping to her defense. Unfortunately, it wasn't an action she could let stand as precedent.

She rolled her eyes comically. "Obviously, I was exaggerating…about being your woman."

The way Dylan was looking at her—as if he didn't know whether to kiss her or chide her—forced Emily to remember exactly how good it had felt to be held in his embrace.

"I am aware of that," he retorted.

"And for the record," Emily continued stiffly, telling herself she and Dylan would not end up kissing again, no matter what, "I don't need you to come to my rescue."

The corners of Dylan's lips twitched. "It would appear you did."

Was it possible he had enjoyed defending her honor as much as she had? Emily pushed the bothersome thought away.

"No," she corrected forcing herself to stay on track. She needed to keep her emotions under wraps. "I didn't."

"Uh-huh." Dylan came closer, all sexy, determined male. "If you change your mind..."

Emily's pulse jumped. "Why would I do that?"

"Because guys like that don't like to be told no," Dylan said in a low, cautioning tone.

Emily had been successfully fighting her own battles for as long as she could recall. "Well, in this case the kid is going to have to get used to it, because I am not interested in being his cougar."

One corner of Dylan's mouth curved upward at the notion. "He actually said that?"

So, she wasn't the only one who found the teen's proposal to her completely ludicrous!

"It was part of his come-on," she explained. "I think in Xavier's teenage fantasy I was just supposed to melt in his arms or something."

Dylan grunted in response, his disapproval evident.

"Anyway," Emily rushed on, anxious to put the embarrassing situation behind her, "I'm sure that after what just happened he'll leave me alone now."

Dylan's expression was suddenly as inscrutable as his posture. Deliberately, he inclined his head. "If he doesn't...you're welcome to be 'my woman'...anytime."

Chapter Three

"Dylan Reeves really called you *his woman?*" Simone echoed in the café kitchen early the following day.

Doing her best to keep her focus on getting ready for the morning rush, Emily shrugged nonchalantly. "He was mocking me because of what I said to that boy in the heat of the moment." The fact that Emily warmed from head to toe, every time she recalled it, was her own foolishness. "Obviously, Dylan didn't mean it because it's not true." She brought an extra large pan of golden-brown cinnamon rolls from the oven, and slid in a pan of buttermilk biscuits.

Simone manned the sausage and bacon on the griddle. She winked. "He could be—if you wanted it. Seriously… he's got the hots for you."

Emily guffawed. "You only wish my life were that exciting. Dylan is the kind of guy who roots for the underdog in every situation and he thought I was disadvantaged in that moment."

"Were you?"

Emily gave the hash-brown potatoes a stir. "I had just stomped on Xavier's toes and planned to escort him to the door. But…Dylan beat me to it."

"Wow…" Simone comically fanned her chest. "Two men fighting over you."

Emily blushed despite herself. "I wouldn't call Xavier a man," she said.

"I know." Sympathetic, Simone furrowed her brow. "What's up with that? How old is he?"

"Nineteen."

"That is way too young to be running a restaurant," Simone said.

"No kidding. But I imagine he's going to find that out the hard way."

The bell on the service door sounded, as Billy Ray and Bobbie Sue Everett came in. The married couple waited tables at the café during the day and attended community-college classes at night. Normally very down-to-earth and unflappable, they were giddy with excitement. "You-all have got to see this. We've never seen anything like this!"

All four of them rushed to the front windows. Dawn was barely streaking across the sky, but there it was—on the opposite side of the Laramie town square—a big burnished-bronze trailer-style restaurant, with an old-style saloon front, sitting on top of an enormous tractor-trailer bed. Next to it was the enormous crane that would move the Cowtown Diner onto the lot where a gas station had once stood.

Emily's heart sank. It really was happening.

"Can you believe it's actually going to be open for business by the end of the week?" Billy Ray said.

Aware the customers would soon be lining up outside the door to be let in when the café opened at six o'clock, Emily went back to the kitchen and brought out the platters of homemade cinnamon rolls and sticky buns that would be on display.

"It's only possible," Emily said, "because the building

is delivered ready to go and everything they serve in the restaurant is prepackaged and pre-made."

"It's still amazing," Bobbie Sue murmured, while quickly helping her husband set up the tables.

Emily had a sinking feeling her customers were going to think so, too.

THE LUNCH CROWDS WERE finally thinning when Dylan walked into the café at one-thirty, so he was able to get a table right away. To his surprise, Emily came out of the kitchen personally to bring him a menu. After the events of the previous day, he had suspected she might try to avoid him. He couldn't blame her; he had done as much this very morning, choosing to eat breakfast on the ranch instead of coming to the café, as usual.

But then he'd thought about it and decided that was pure foolishness. He was blowing this all out of proportion and really wanted to get back on solid ground with her.

"I don't need to see that," Dylan said, determined to keep the exchange as casual as possible. "I memorized the offerings on your menu the first week you opened."

And like most ranchers in the area, he had been eating her "cowboy cuisine" frequently ever since.

"You sure? I've put a few new things on the menu, just today."

He was sure. But since it seemed to mean so much to her, he opened the laminated menu anyway. A hand-lettered inset offered two new sandwiches and a fried jalapeño-cheese popper appetizer that was a customer favorite at the Cowtown Diner chain. "Competing already?" he drawled.

He'd figured the sight of the rival establishment would have upped Emily's competitive spirit.

Curious to know just how far she would go, he leaned back in the red vinyl booth and prodded, "Or just stealing another restaurant's signature dish?"

She ran her hand lightly over the red-and-white-checked oilcloth. "Ha-ha."

"You're better than that. Your food is better than that."

Her feisty gaze met his once again. "Says the man with the bottomless pit for a stomach."

Well, at least she still had her temper. Enjoying the exchange more than he had a right to, he angled a thumb at his chest. "Hey—you make a lot of money off me."

Emily folded her arms in front of her. "Not today, since I assume you are here to collect on my promise of free food for however long you want it."

Was it possible that the feisty, inimitable Emily McCabe was actually depressed? Dylan didn't want to think so, but there was something different about her eyes.

"I'll have the chicken-fried steak meal with all the vegetables you got, biscuits, a strong pot of coffee and two glasses of water, to start. We'll see about dessert later."

Their fingers brushed briefly as Emily took the menu and insert back. Dylan wondered if she'd thought about their kisses as much as he had last night and today. Not that it mattered, he told himself, since it wasn't going to happen again.

"And be sure you bill me for every last morsel," he added sternly.

Emily arched a delicate eyebrow.

He looked her square in the eye. "No lady pays my way."

Emily laughed out loud, ready to challenge him on that and a few other things. "So now you're calling me a lady?" Her bow-shaped lips curling in an appreciative smirk, she pocketed the order pad in her apron.

That was a lot less dangerous than calling her "his woman." Dylan figured they both had to know that.

He worked to get their conversation back on its usual smart-aleck track. "And a hothead. Not to mention a damn fine cook."

Abruptly, moisture gleamed in Emily's eyes.

Before he could question her about it, she ducked her head and turned to leave. "Coming right up," she said hoarsely over her shoulder.

Five minutes later, Bobby Sue was there with his dinner. It was as hot and fresh and delicious as always.

Dylan downed it all with relish.

He was considering whether or not he had time to order dessert before the café closed at two, when Emily's father walked in.

Dessert was going to have to wait, because he had business to conduct.

Dylan stood to greet the elder McCabe, as previously arranged. "Everything going okay so far?" he asked.

Shane nodded. "The horse trailers are due to arrive any minute."

Emily walked out of the kitchen. Obviously surprised to see Dylan standing there with her dad, she looked from one to the other. "What's going on?"

Shane greeted his daughter with a hug.

"The mustangs are coming in. We decided to meet up here because I thought you might like to take a peek at them before they're taken to Dylan's ranch."

That swiftly, the light was back in Emily's eyes. She smiled, her love of horses as apparent as ever. "I would. Thanks, Dad." She hugged her father, then turned to Dylan awkwardly. She started forward, as if to hug him, too, then reconsidered and made do with a shy nod. "Dylan. This was nice of you."

He cleared his throat. "No problem."

Emily turned back to her dad. "Tell me about the horses," she said eagerly.

"Two of them are less than twelve months old. They're traveling two to a trailer, as per bureau of land management rules. The three-year-old mare is in a stock trailer by herself. She's not yet fence- or halter-broken and may be a problem when it comes to unloading her."

Dylan figured that was an understatement. "Any of them got names?" he asked Shane.

The older gentleman shook his head. "Just registration numbers. So feel free to name them whatever you see fit while you're training them."

Simone's son, Andrew, walked in on the tail end of the conversation. A backpack slung over his shoulder, he appeared ready to assume his duties as part-time dishwasher and kitchen help. He looked at his mom, who'd come out of the restaurant kitchen. "Can I go see the horses? Maybe help the guys unload them?"

Simone shook her head. "It's too dangerous, honey."

Andrew's expression fell. "But…"

"And you have homework to do, don't you?" Simone insisted.

"Well, yeah," the fifteen-year-old admitted with a reluctant shrug, "but…"

"You'll have a chance to see the mustangs later," Simone promised. "When they're tamed."

Andrew sulked. "That'll be forever."

"Knowing Dylan and the magic he works, probably not as long as you think." Simone put her hand on her son's shoulder. "Right now you and I need to help Bobbie Sue and Billy Ray get the kitchen closed for the day. See you later, everyone." The two of them went back into the café kitchen.

Emily glanced out the window at the commotion outside. "Looks like they're here," she said, and smiled.

Shane turned back to Emily. "Do you have plans for this evening? Because if you don't, your mother and I would like you to come over to the dance hall and have dinner with us. Maybe do a little brainstorming about how you're going to weather this new competition?"

Emily bucked at the fatherly interference, even as she started for the door. "Thanks, Dad," she said over one slender shoulder, "but I've got it covered."

Shane persisted. "Just dinner, then?"

Emily pressed her lips together firmly. "I can't." Her glance shifted to Dylan's face. She gave him the look that beseeched him to play along with her. "I'm going out to Dylan's ranch, to help him get the mustangs settled."

Dylan felt for Emily. It couldn't be fun to be on the end of such constant meddling. But that didn't mean he wanted to sacrifice his own professional standing with her father—one of the most respected horse-ranchers in the state—just so she did not have to do her parents' bidding.

He tamped down his own irritation. "That's okay, Emily," Dylan said just as firmly, holding her glance deliberately. "I think I've got it."

"Oh, I know you *could* do it without me." Emily slipped out onto the street and strode toward the horse trailers, as excited and energetic as the animals whinnying in the confines. "But I really don't want to miss this!"

"AT WHAT POINT are you going to stop using me to dodge your familial difficulties?" Dylan asked Emily, after the papers transferring financial responsibility to Shane and care of the mustangs to Dylan were signed and they were headed out to their vehicles.

"Never?" Emily paused at the door of her car.

Dylan peered down at her. "Think again."

She hit the unlock button on the automatic keypad. "Look, I owe you for last night, and thus far you've refused to let me pay you back with free food, so I'm left to come up with another way to pay off my debt. This is it."

Dylan curved a hand over the top of her open door as she climbed in behind the wheel. He leaned down so they were face to face. "I repeat. You do not have to do this."

"Sure I do. For the very same reason you don't ever let a lady pay your way."

He should have known she would use his words against him.

She smiled, unperturbed. "So I'll help you with the mustangs."

Damn, if she wasn't used to getting her own way, even if it meant upsetting the hard-earned tranquility of his life.

"Just understand," Dylan said, "when you're out there, playtime is over. I'm putting you to work."

Turning the key in the ignition, she shot him a sassy look. "Bring it on!"

EMILY COULDN'T WAIT to get a good look at the horses. She bounded out of her car the moment she arrived at Dylan's ranch. She set her hat on her head and strode toward him. "What do you want me to do?"

Dylan turned, all business and all cowboy. "Honestly? Stay out of the way," he said, grimacing.

Emily blew out a disappointed breath. Before she could figure out how to persuade him otherwise, he took a step closer and growled, "I mean it, Emily. I don't want you getting trampled."

Emily followed him over to a big round corral with

high metal-bar sides. "I've been around horses all my life."

Dylan opened the gate wide and motioned for the truck carrying the two yearlings. He directed the driver to back slowly toward the opening. "These mustangs are completely different from the domesticated cutting horses your father breeds and trains. These horses are wild, down to the core."

Hand to her shoulder, Dylan guided her to the outside of the pen, then walked back around to the rear of the enclosed vehicle.

Emily's heartbeat picked up as he opened the trailer and let the first horse out.

It was a filly, about six months old, with a speckled white coat and an ivory mane, her beauty marred only by the identifying freeze marks on her neck. She whinnied as she came barreling out of confinement and raced to the other end of the pen. Emily could see she was frightened—she was standing with her tail puckered tight against her hindquarters and the back of her legs.

Dylan stood quietly, as did Emily, as the filly trembled and kept her head up.

Dylan let the second horse out—a jet-black gelding about a year old. His head was up, too—his tail wringing in anger. Obviously, he had not appreciated the long ride. Or maybe the procedure that had put the freeze marks on his neck, Emily thought. He galloped across the pen, his ebony mane flying, and took a protective position next to the smaller white filly.

They were already forming a herd, Emily thought.

Moving purposefully and calmly, Dylan stepped out and shut the gate. The first truck drove off.

The next trailer backed toward the pen.

When it was in position, Dylan opened the gate and released the third horse.

Emily caught her breath as the mare kicked and bucked her way out of the trailer. The color of ginger, she had darker-colored legs, a dark ginger mane and a striking white blaze down her forehead. Her tail was stiff and pointed up as she kicked and reared her way across the pen. Once near the other horses, she raised up on her hind legs again, her ears pinned back, whinnying furiously at the humans she blamed for her captivity.

Turning her rear to the other two horses, she backed up and pawed the ground.

Dylan smiled.

So did Emily.

"No doubt who is in charge of the herd," she said, nodding at the ginger mare.

The question was, who was going to be in charge of her and Dylan—if she spent any time alone with him? She'd only been around him a short while and she was already thinking about how thrilling it would be to kiss him again.

"So what next?" Willfully, Emily turned her attention back to the mustangs.

"I let them settle in for a few days to recover from the trip, get used to their surroundings and begin to trust this is a place they are going to like."

Made sense. "When it's time, I'd like to help you with their training," Emily offered.

Dylan glanced at her skeptically. For reasons she did not understand, his doubt hurt. "Don't think I can do it?"

Dylan shook his head and sauntered toward the barn. "Let's just say I don't think your family would approve."

Emily followed. "It wouldn't be the first time."

For some reason, Emily thought, that struck a chord—one he didn't like.

He let his glance trail over her, lazily inspecting every curve, before returning to her face. "You have a major challenge facing your business." He picked up a bale of hay and carried it back over to the corral. "Why don't you concentrate on that?"

Emily watched him cut the twine, holding it together. She scoffed and folded her arms across her chest. "I can do both."

"Really?" Methodically, Dylan broke up the square of crisp sweet hay. He tossed it over the fence. "Then you must be a superwoman."

Emily watched the mustangs. The herd was still on the other side of the pen but contemplating every move Dylan made. "I am an excellent horsewoman."

Dylan threw out the last of the feed and exhaled in frustration. He slowly straightened and poked up the brim of his hat. "Why don't you do us both a favor, Emily, and stick to cooking?"

Emily didn't know whether to slug him or kiss him. Truth was, she wanted to do both. "Why won't you let me help?"

Her pique increased his own irritation. "Because you don't work for me." He walked over to turn on the spigot and fill the trough with water. "I don't have enough liability insurance. I don't have time to train them and you, too. Pick a reason."

The mustangs made their way stealthily toward the feed. "Can I at least come by and watch from time to time?"

He rubbed the underside of his jaw, testing the stubble of afternoon beard. Their glances met and held. "If I say no, will you stay away?"

Emily offered a careless shrug. "Maybe." The silence between them drew out, prompting her to eventually admit, with a reluctantly candid sigh, "Maybe not."

His expression hardened. "That's what I thought."

She didn't know why she wanted his respect so badly in this regard, she just knew that she did, and she wished he would give her a chance to earn it. "Dylan—"

He turned off the spigot with a harsh twist.

His eyes narrowed as he regarded her intently. "Do us both a favor, Emily. Go back to your family. Work out whatever needs to be worked out." He lifted a gloved hand before she could interrupt. "And leave me—and these horses—out of it."

LATE THE FOLLOWING AFTERNOON, Dylan answered another summons from Shane McCabe. He met with Emily's father in the study of the Circle M Ranch house, where they discussed the condition of the mustangs and Dylan's plan for training them.

It was a cordial, productive meeting and, despite himself, Dylan found himself warming to the elder rancher.

Usually, he did not care for men of such power and wealth, although he never minded doing business with them. Money was money, and they easily paid the fees Dylan commanded.

At the conclusion of their discussion, Shane handed Dylan a check, as previously agreed upon. "This should cover your time and the expenses of caring for the mustangs for the first month. If you need anything else, be sure and let me know."

"Thank you."

Before Dylan could get up, Shane said, "If you've got a moment, I'd like to speak with you about the Libertyville

Boys Ranch. The director—Mike Harrigan—is a friend of mine. He mentioned your devotion to the facility."

This was headed toward territory Dylan had no wish to discuss. He lifted a hand to cut off the discussion. "It's no big deal."

Shane leaned forward earnestly. "On the contrary, it's a very big deal, Dylan. The boys ranch turns a lot of young lives around. I want to do more than just provide a few horses. So here's what I was thinking…" Shane elaborated for the next few minutes. Finally, he finished, "And given your expertise in this area, I'd really like your help in making that dream a reality."

The offer was unexpected. And amazing. Not to mention out of the question. "Thank you, sir. I'll do what I can to contribute to your efforts."

"But?" Shane sensed a catch.

"I don't think I am the right man for the setup you have in mind. I'll continue training the mustangs and then hand them over to the Libertyville Boys Ranch as promised. But that's really all I can guarantee, in terms of helping you out."

Shane had the same look on his face that Emily had on hers whenever Dylan told her no. The one that said a McCabe wasn't giving up on what they wanted, no matter what obstacles lay in front of them.

Finally, Shane rocked back in his chair.

Dylan expected Emily's father to say something like the offer was always going to be open. Instead, he steepled his hands in front of him and inquired, "So what's going on with you and my daughter?"

Dylan swore silently to himself. For the life of him he did not know how to answer that. There was desire, certainly. And he really liked her cooking. But beyond that…

His concern for his only daughter apparent, Shane

continued, "I've never seen her run after anyone the way she's been chasing you." He paused. "Usually, it's the other way around. Guys are beating down her door."

Dylan had been around long enough to know that to be true. Not that Emily had been inclined, in the past year or so anyway, to let anyone make much of a move on her. As far as he knew, she hadn't even had a date—not counting the pretend one with him.

"So..." Shane stood and looked at Dylan, man-to-man. "If I may...a word of advice?"

Dylan took the cue and got to his feet, too. He honored the elder horseman with a look of respect.

"If you don't think you will ever be serious about Emily...then do whatever you have to do..." Shane said, firmly, "but don't let my daughter catch you."

DYLAN WALKED OUT the front door of the Circle M Ranch house, still contemplating the counsel from Shane McCabe.

As much as he hated having others meddle in his business, Emily's father was right.

Emily might think she was a free spirit, but she was also vulnerable and traditional to the core.

A wild affair would never make her happy. Nor would deceiving her loved ones.

Not in the long term.

And for some reason he couldn't figure, Dylan wanted to see the pretty brunette happy.

Which made what came next all the more unpalatable.

Striding toward Dylan, his arms full of Cowtown Diner goodies, was Xavier Shillingsworth. The teen flashed a pretentious smile his way. "Going the wrong way there, aren't you, fella?"

There was no denying the snide undertone in his

words. Or the resentment in Xavier's gaze. Dylan paused on the wide front steps of the rustic fieldstone and cedar ranch house. He did not bother to smile back. "Excuse me?"

"Hired help comes and goes from the back, right?" Xavier sneered. "So…you should have gone in and out the *back* entrance."

Dylan had suffered the taunts of the snotty rich from boyhood on. He knew he should let it go, straighten the brim of his hat, ignore the little twerp and keep moving. Yet something about the guy, and the situation, had him returning equally, "Ranchers go in the front."

"And here I thought you were just another cowboy," Xavier said, as Emily and her mother drove up in their respective vehicles.

Looking gorgeous and ready for a night out on the town, Emily was first to emerge.

Xavier shifted the stack of Cowtown Diner memorabilia in his arms and turned to face Emily. "Going to be joining us for dinner this evening?"

"Uh, no," Emily murmured, appearing not the least bit disappointed about that.

Bypassing the teen completely, Emily walked up to Dylan and looked him straight in the eye. "May I have a word with you?"

Figuring he'd find out sooner than later why the feisty heiress was so piqued, Dylan shrugged. "Sure." He ambled down the steps alongside Emily, as Greta McCabe emerged from her Mercedes.

"Nice to see you, Dylan," Greta said pleasantly.

He briefly removed his hat in a gesture of respect. "Nice to see you, Mrs. McCabe."

"Perhaps you'd like to join us for dinner this evening, Dylan?" Greta continued pleasantly. "Emily? You, too?"

Emily perked up.

Xavier looked totally ticked off.

Which in Dylan's view, made it all worth it. "Don't mind if I do," he told Greta. It wouldn't be the first time he had dined with the Laramie, Texas elite, but it would definitely be the most satisfying.

Chapter Four

"Mind telling me what's going on around here?" Emily asked, the moment her mother and Xavier Shillingsworth had disappeared inside the house, and shut the door behind them.

Dylan was getting a little tired of being a bit player in the McCabe family drama. He lounged against the rail edging the porch steps and folded his arms in front of him. "You're going to have to be more specific if you want me to answer that."

Emily wrapped her hand around his biceps and led him down the steps, across the yard, into the shade. "Fine. You want to cut to the chase, we'll cut right to the chase." She glared at him. "I heard you had a meeting with my father."

Man, she had a temper! Dylan couldn't help but grin. "Spies everywhere, hmm?" he teased.

Emily regarded him with greatly exaggerated patience. "My mother mentioned it in passing."

Dylan clapped a hand over his heart, mimicking her damsel-on-high-alert attitude. "Then it was top secret!"

"I'm serious." Emily stomped closer, the delicate daffodil scent of her freshly washed hair and skin teasing his senses. She'd changed out of her casual work clothes and slipped into a sexy lavender dress that clung nicely to her curves.

His eyes drifted to her feet. Instead of the usual boots, she had on a pair of open-toed sandals, perfect for the warm spring weather.

"What did he say to you?"

Lifting his gaze, Dylan resisted the urge to touch the silky dark strands spilling loosely over her slender shoulders. Instead, he concentrated on the determined pout of her soft, sensual lips before returning his attention to her eyes. "And this is your business because...?"

She tilted her head in a discerning manner. "I know it was about me."

"Or..." He sidestepped the direct inquiry by producing the check from his shirt pocket. He waved it in front of her, like a matador taunting a bull. "Perhaps it was about...this?"

Emily exhaled loudly. "I know that's what it was about officially, dummy." Her pretty chin jutted out. "I also know he would not have missed an opportunity to privately tell you what he tells all the men I'm interested in."

Dylan liked being lumped in with her other discarded suitors about as much as he liked being interrogated. He blinked in feigned surprise. "*You're* interested in me?"

A flash of amusement sparkled in her eyes, then disappeared as quickly as it had appeared. "Ostensibly," Emily admitted. "Not really."

Dylan told himself that was irritation—not disappointment—he was feeling.

Emily paused and appeared to do a double take. "Are *you* interested in *me*?"

It was his turn to regard her with a droll expression. "What do you think?" he asked in a smart-alecky tone.

Her delicate dark eyebrows lifted. "That you are without a doubt the most infuriating man I have ever met."

Dylan noted she had enunciated every word with perfect clarity. He lifted his hat in salute and resettled it on his head. "Thank you."

Emily harrumphed. "It's nothing to be proud of."

"Maybe not in your opinion," Dylan murmured, aware he was enjoying matching wits and wills with her more than he had enjoyed anything in a long time.

Emily shook her head as if that would get her back on track. "So, why are you suddenly so eager to have dinner with me and my family?"

Good question. It couldn't be because he had started to feel protective of Emily, could it? He knew better than that. Rich heiresses were not allowed to fall for guys like him. And even if they bucked all propriety and followed their hearts, the misguided affair had little hope of lasting, because of family influence. In their case, they'd have to contend with Shane McCabe and all three of her overbearing brothers.

Aware she was still waiting for an explanation, Dylan said casually, "Maybe I'm in need of a good evening meal?"

"And maybe you're trying to get under my skin?"

"Always an unexpected bonus."

Silence fell between them.

Emily continued to study him beneath the fringe of dark lashes. "So you're not going to tell me what my dad said to you in private?" she said eventually.

And give her even more reason to rebel against her family? For both their sakes, Dylan checked his own desire. "No." He offered her his arm. "Now, shall we go in?"

DINNER WITH EMILY'S parents turned out to be a lot less formal, and more comfortable, than Dylan had expected.

Xavier Shillingsworth, on the other hand, was as much of a pain in the rear as ever.

The hopelessly inexperienced restaurateur commandeered the conversation from the moment the five of them sat down at the wicker-and-glass patio table, zeroing in on everything he felt was wrong with the way Emily was running the Daybreak Café.

"I don't understand why you're only open for breakfast and lunch, six days a week," Xavier told Emily. "I've seen the line of people waiting to get in. Why not serve dinner, too?"

"There are already plenty of places that serve dinner," Emily explained. "My mother's dance hall for one."

Xavier leaned across the table toward Emily. "So?"

She shrugged. "I don't want to compete with her."

Xavier frowned. "You compete with her at lunch."

Emily paused, a forkful of baby-lettuce salad halfway to her mouth. "It's not the same."

"Why not?" Xavier persisted, failing to notice the discreet looks Shane and Greta were giving each other from opposite ends of the dinner table.

Emily shifted in her chair, her knee nudging Dylan's briefly under the table. "Because the dance hall has live bands on Friday and Saturday evenings, and DJs in the evening the rest of the time."

Xavier grimaced. "So play music in your café."

"There's no room to dance," Emily said, still trying to talk sense to him.

Xavier finished his salad and pushed his plate to the side. "A lot of people don't dance anyway."

Dylan wondered if the kid thought he was going to attract Emily by criticizing her business sense. One thing was certain—he certainly wasn't scoring any points with her or her folks. And if he treated the rest of the town this way...

"The point is, there is no demand for another dinner place right now," Emily said matter-of-factly. "Laramie already has a handful of local establishments that have pretty much got the evening food covered."

"And maybe if you tried, you'd have standing-room-only business at dinner, too, and force someone else to close down."

Eyebrows raised all around at that.

Not good, dude, Dylan thought. Not good at all...

"I think the point my daughter is trying to make," Shane McCabe cut in with remarkable kindness, "is that in Laramie, it's not just the ranchers who help each other out. The business owners look out for one another, too."

As Dylan expected, that notion didn't go down well with their teenage guest.

Greta collected the empty salad plates and replaced them with servings of Southwestern-style meat loaf, mashed potatoes and peas. "We want all the restaurants to be successful, and of course that would include yours," she told Xavier graciously.

Xavier sat up straighter, looking affronted. "I hope you're not asking me to cut back on the hours the Cowtown Diner is open."

Shane McCabe lifted a hand. "No one's going to tell you what to do. It's your business to run, after all. We're just suggesting that you might want to join the chamber of commerce and any of the other service organizations in town that interest you. It's a good way to get to know everyone and become a real part of the community."

Xavier rejected the notion with a shake of his head.

"I'm not interested in charity work. The only thing on *my* mind is turning as much of a profit as soon as possible."

The kid just wasn't getting it, Dylan thought. The Mc-Cabes were offering him a hand up. And he was too clueless and arrogant to take it.

"When is the grand opening?" Dylan asked, attempting to draw some fire himself.

Xavier dismissed Dylan with a glance that revealed Xavier still considered him "hired help." "Friday."

Emily studied the teen, suddenly on edge again. "You're really going to be up and running three days from now?"

Nodding proudly, Xavier grinned at Emily. "I'll bet you can't wait."

"CAN YOU WAIT?" Dylan asked Emily an hour later, after they had thanked her parents for dinner and said their goodbyes.

"Very funny, cowboy."

Relieved that Xavier had finally rushed off to continue work on his restaurant, Emily ambled down the front steps to her car. Dylan was right beside her, a surprisingly steady presence.

"But as long as we're recapping..." Emily paused to search through her bag for her keys. She looked at Dylan, wondering what his take on the situation was. His attitude throughout the meal had been so maddeningly inscrutable that she had no clue. "What was Xavier's deal? He really went overboard with that intense interrogation."

Dylan leaned against the side of her car, one foot crossed over the other, arms folded in front of him. Dusk had given way to night, and the sky overhead was filled with a full moon and a sprinkling of stars.

He gave her a bemused look. "I think that was Xavier taking self-absorbed to new heights."

"Not to mention immaturity." Emily fished the keys out. "Can you believe his father bought him a restaurant?" She closed the clasp on her handbag. "Never mind plunked it down in Laramie, Texas, of all places?"

He moved closer, smelling like soap and man. "I'm sure they both figured there would be less competition here, and hence, it would be easier for a greenhorn like Xavier to succeed."

Emily bit her lip. Unable to take her eyes off his broad shoulders and nicely muscled chest, she said, "I suppose you're right about that. If the kid were in Dallas or Houston, it would be a much tougher road for him to travel."

"Although small towns come with challenges, too." Dylan looked over at her, seemingly in no hurry to move on. "It was nice of your parents to invite him over, though."

That was the way her folks were—generous and welcoming, to the bone. "They're just trying to bring Xavier into the 'fold' of Laramie business people. Obviously, my mother did not anticipate the way he was going to go after me with the third degree, hinting that I didn't know what I was doing, running my business." Emily sighed, still feeling a little embarrassed about that.

Dylan met her eyes. "And yet you were incredibly nice and patient with the kid, too," he observed kindly.

It hadn't been easy, given how obnoxious Xavier had been. But Emily had nevertheless tried to give the clueless teenager the benefit of the doubt. "I figure he probably doesn't know any other way to interact with people, given how he was likely raised."

Dylan lifted a brow and guessed. "With too much money and too little guidance?"

Emily nodded, aware she and Dylan were now close enough to feel each other's body heat. She swallowed and stepped back slightly. "Think about it. Rather than help Xavier deal with whatever issues he has that are keeping him from wanting to go to college with his peers, his father bought him a franchise and sent him off to the boondocks alone to run it." She frowned. "That doesn't exactly foretell a lot of tender loving care."

DYLAN KNEW WHAT it was like to be on the receiving end of a family with too much money and too little heart. A family that just wanted you out of the way... To his surprise, he suddenly felt a little sorry for the kid. "You're right," he said quietly. "I hadn't thought about it that way."

Empathy radiated in Emily's blue eyes. "Unfortunately, Xavier won't survive in this town for long if he continues the way he has been."

"Also true," Dylan said. Kindness and concern for one's neighbor was the norm in Laramie County, not cutthroat aggression.

Emily shrugged. "So...I figured...since my parents had taken the initiative and tried to help him acclimate more successfully, I would be as compassionate as possible, too."

That would have been fine had it not been for her personal history. Dylan lifted a brow. "Another of your makeover projects?"

Just that quickly the flash of temper appeared on her face. Emily propped her hands on her hips. "That would imply Xavier and I are romantically involved," she retorted, resentment simmering in her low tone. "You know very well we're not, and are never going to be."

Dylan smiled—she had just given him the answer he

was looking for. "So you admit you try and make over the guys you date?" he pressed.

Did her father also get in the act—behind the scenes, of course? Was that what had really prompted Shane's offer to him earlier?

Dylan hated to think so. He wanted to think the proposal put to him was merit-based. On the other hand, he also knew Shane and Greta McCabe adored their only daughter and would do whatever they had to do to see she was well matched.

Even by giving her current "love interest" a hand up...?

Oblivious to the downward spiral to his thoughts, Emily continued, "Isn't that what love is supposed to be about? Changing for the better because you're involved with your ideal mate?"

Her lips looked so soft and inviting, he wondered what it would feel like to silence her with a kiss. But he told himself to stay focused. "I thought relationships were supposed to be about *not* having to change. Being adored for who and what you *already* were. What's that saying?" He attempted to lighten the mood. "'I love you just the way you are.'"

Emily scoffed. "It's a song lyric, not a saying. And for the record—" she softened her tone wistfully "—I kind of like that you-complete-me thing."

He should have figured she would be a Jerry Maguire fan. Knowing this had to be said if they were going to be friends, he pointed out sagely, "If the man and the woman 'complete' each other, then that would imply they can't live without the other person."

"So?"

Lazily, Dylan tracked the way the breeze was ruffling her hair. He reached over to tuck an errant strand behind her ear, then let his hand drop. "What kind of life would that be?" he asked unhappily. "If everything hinged on a person who might or might not live up to your expectations?"

IT WOULD NOT be the kind of life Dylan apparently wanted, Emily thought.

She sighed, her emotions abruptly as turbulent as his.

"Anyway," Dylan continued, dropping his hand back to his side. He studied her expression. "I'm guessing your parents don't know that Xavier hit on you."

Thrilling from his brief, casual touch, Emily turned so her back was to the car. She lounged against the driver door, wishing Dylan wasn't such a hard man to get to know. But he was extremely independent—and as emotionally elusive as the wild mustangs he was going to tame....

So she needed to forget about making him her next "diamond in the rough."

After all, there was no point in pretending he would be willing to transform himself into what she wanted—any more than she would be willing to convert into what he wanted.

"I've been trying to forget that incident with Xavier." Emily forced herself to get their conversation back on track. "And for the record, Dylan," she warned, locking gazes with him, "I would prefer my family never know about all that cougar silliness."

Suddenly, the humor was back in the situation. "Why not?" he said as his lips formed a most devil-may-care smile.

Emily's exasperation returned anew. "Because Xavier's pass was ludicrous enough without adding another layer of ridiculousness to it by having my father call him to his study and sit him down for The Talk."

Abruptly, Dylan went very still, a fact which only confirmed Emily's worst suspicions. Seeing her chance to do a little more sleuthing, she added cheekily, "You know, kind of like the one I suspect my father had with *you* today, about me?"

The kind that generally sent weaker men running for the hills...

Just like that, a wall went up. "It's not going to work, Emily." Dylan was the picture of lazy male self-assurance.

She stared at him.

He stared right back. "I'm still not telling you what was said."

Emily sighed—she could have predicted that. Pushing away from the car, she suddenly felt reinvigorated. "Then how about doing something to cheer me up instead?"

Dylan pushed away from her car, too. "And what would that be?" he inquired with mock seriousness.

"Allow me to come and visit the mustangs again," Emily said, this time stepping forward to invade his space.

Dylan stayed where he was even as respect glimmered in his eyes. "Are you going to have time?"

Emily ignored the tingle of excitement that started within her whenever they were within kissing distance. "I will if we go tonight."

For a minute, Emily thought Dylan was going to turn her down. "Isn't it a little past your bedtime?" he teased in a tone sexy enough to make her want to melt right then and there.

Stubbornly, Emily held her ground, knowing she

wasn't ready for her time with Dylan to end. "It's only nine-thirty."

He continued to look down at her, considering. "And you have to go to work at four tomorrow morning."

"I can get by on very little sleep, when I want," Emily murmured in her most cajoling voice. "Please, Dylan. I've been thinking about the mustangs all day. Wondering how they're adjusting. If you've given them names yet."

Seeming to realize her interest and concern were genuine, his expression softened. "They're settling in. And no, I haven't given them names."

"Maybe I could help with that."

"Thirty minutes," he warned. "Tops. Then you have to be on your way."

"Great." Emily felt a completely uncalled-for fluttering in her middle. "You won't regret it."

THE TRUTH WAS, Dylan already regretted it. Emily McCabe might be all wrong for him, but she was also the kind of woman he could fall hard for. And the last thing either of them needed was any more complications in their already overburdened lives.

So on the drive over, he figured out how to get what needed to be done accomplished in the shortest time possible so he could send her on her way.

He led the way in his pickup truck. She followed in her car. The first problem appeared as soon as they had parked and she got out of her sporty little sedan. He looked at her shoes. No question, her sandals were not appropriate for the pen.

Emily caught his gaze and lifted a hand. "Not to worry, cowboy. I've got that covered."

And to prove it, she sashayed back to the trunk and

opened it up. Inside were enough clothes, shoes and purses to fill a closet. Deliberately, Emily fished out a pair of cowgirl boots.

"Come prepared, do you?" Dylan quipped, wondering if there was a toothbrush and nightie in there somewhere, too.

Emily shot him an arch look over her shoulder. "I'm a Texan, after all," she declared with a warm, winning smile.

She was so darn charming he couldn't help but smile back. "So naturally it follows…?"

She winked mischievously. "That I can't go anywhere without at least one pair of boots."

Dylan stood by while she bent to slip off her sandals. She donned a pair of socks and her cowgirl boots, the hem of her dress riding up her thighs as she did so.

Dylan ignored the immediate response of his body and headed for the barn. There, he switched on both interior and exterior lights, the yellow glow a beacon of reassurance in the moonlit, starry Texas night.

He came back with two bunches of alfalfa leaves.

As always, Emily was raring to go. "You always feed them this late?"

"They require up to fifteen-pound rations of hay per horse per day. Because of their small stomachs, it's better to feed and let them forage all day."

"Makes sense." Emily fell into step beside Dylan.

"And it's a way to rapidly increase their trust of me and now you."

The three horses were in a high wood-rail-sided paddock, linked by a fenced aisleway to the two round training pens—one with a roof, one without—on either end. From where the horses stood, they could see everything that was going on. Another schooling plus. By the time it got to be their turn, the mustangs knew what to expect. Which again, made it easier for all of them.

With the ease of someone who had grown up around horses, and loved them dearly, Emily followed Dylan into the paddock. "How invested are you in actually doing the naming?" she asked curiously.

"Not at all." Focused on the feeding, Dylan tore off leaves of alfalfa and put them just ahead of the trio of horses. Emily followed suit.

And so they went—dropping, moving on, dropping another two leaves, moving on—until finally the horses were following them.

Emily kept her voice low and calm. "Does that mean you'll let me do it?"

Dylan shrugged and replied before he could think, "If it makes you happy."

Emily chuckled in delight. "Oh…so you want me happy now…."

Dylan rolled his eyes. "Don't let it go to your head." Clearing his throat, he nodded toward their equine companions. "So back to the stars of the show…."

Emily regarded them carefully. "The three-year-old should be Ginger. The yearlings, Salt and Pepper."

Made sense. Dylan nodded. "I'll let the interested parties know." Finished, they stepped out of the paddock. As they strode toward the barn, Emily asked, "Do you have a horse of your own?"

Dylan slanted her a glance. "What do you think?"

"Can I meet him, too?"

Women didn't usually ask him that. But then, Dylan thought, the women he saw usually weren't interested in horses. "Sure," he said.

EMILY EXPECTED A stallion, from a thoroughbred bloodline. Instead, she found a brown-and-white quarter horse–thoroughbred mix that would likely have ended up who-knows-where had someone not stepped in and seen the potential. The gelding came closer to Emily. He stuck his head over the stall door, lowered his head and sniffed her hair, and then her face. Emily reached up to stroke his face as his warm breath ghosted over her. His eyes were alert but gentle, and she found his presence calming and reassuring. Emily took the apple Dylan handed her and presented it to his horse. "What's his name?"

"Hercules."

Able to feel the strength emanating from the horse's sleekly muscled build, Emily smiled. "It suits him." And the horse, who was anything but blue-blooded, suited Dylan.

Dylan offered Hercules a carrot. Hercules took it and luxuriated in a nose rub from Dylan, too.

Emily's heart warmed at the overwhelming affection between man and horse. She turned to Dylan. "How long have you been riding?"

"Since I was fifteen."

Unable to resist, she prodded a little more. "Did you grow up on a ranch?"

Once again, she thought, in the silence that followed her question, it was like trying to get information out of a spy sworn to secrecy. Finally, Dylan said, "No. I spent time on one later, and that's when I learned to ride."

"And realized your calling was horses."

"More or less." He looked at his watch.

"Yeah, yeah, I know," Emily grumbled good-naturedly. "Time's up. But not before I say goodbye to everyone."

She headed for the paddock situated between the round pens and stood looking at the three mustangs. They were gathered together on the opposite side of the corral, ears moving, nostrils flexing, clearly relaxed.

Scattered among other paddocks and turnout sheds in the distance were other horses Dylan was working with. They all looked pleasantly settled and were enjoying the warm spring night, too. Thinking how much she loved the peace and the tranquility of this ranch, Emily turned back to Dylan and let her enthusiasm be her guide. "When are you going to start training the mustangs?"

He lifted one large hand in an indolent manner. "I'm going to work with Salt and Pepper tomorrow morning."

As he spoke, Salt and Pepper approached them, one coming up on either side of them. First, they nosed the wooden rails and then eventually came over to Emily to investigate her. After several long moments, they put their heads on Emily's shoulders for a nuzzle.

These young ones weren't going to be that difficult to train, Emily thought, as she rubbed their faces and touched their manes. Already, they seemed used to people.

The three-year-old mare, on the other hand, was going to require more intensive schooling. Emily wanted to see how it was done. She turned to Dylan, watching as the two yearlings went over to greet him, too. "When will you work with Ginger?"

Dylan accepted their nuzzling with a grin. "Late afternoon, tomorrow."

Emily eyed the beautiful mare, who had moved closer but not close enough to touch. "Mind if I come and observe and maybe help a little?"

Dylan lifted a brow. "Sure you got time for that?"

It wasn't an invitation exactly, but it wasn't an edict to stay away, either. Emily smiled. "There's always time for something you want to do." And she really, really wanted to do this.

Chapter Five

"Looking at the Cowtown Diner is not going to make it disappear."

Guiltily, Emily moved away from the front window. Five more minutes, and the Daybreak Café would officially be closed. But with the exception of the tall, handsome cowboy standing next to her, it had been a ghost town for the past hour.

"There hasn't been a lull in the activity over there all day." Utility trucks had come and gone for gas, electricity, water and sewer. Safety inspections had been done, a neon light on the front of the diner turned on and tested.

Emily wanted to protest the burnished bronze exterior of the diner didn't fit in with the historic buildings on their side of the green, any more than proprietor Xavier Shillingsworth fit in Laramie. But the truth was the snazzy exterior and old-style-saloon design of the building added the kind of pizzazz that would have passing tourists stopping in droves.

Emily scowled. "There's a lot to do if they're going to open in two days."

Dylan laid a soothing hand on her shoulder. He leaned down to murmur in her ear, "You keep saying *if.*"

Emily blew out a gusty breath. "Wishful thinking, I guess."

Dylan said matter-of-factly, "People are going to go there, to try it out and see what they think."

Their glances meshed. "You think I don't know that?" She turned away from the window and headed back to the booth Dylan had just vacated. She picked up his empty coffee cup and dessert plate and carried both to the kitchen.

Dylan ambled after her. "Once the newness wears off, they'll be back."

The point was, Emily didn't want to lose any customers in the first place. And really, how selfish was that?

Dylan was about to say something else, when the front door opened and slammed shut. Andrew walked in, book bag slung over his shoulder. "Mom!" he yelled.

Simone came out of the back.

Andrew thrust a paper at her. "I just got a job at the Cowtown Diner!"

Emily blinked in surprise.

"You already have a part-time job here," Simone reminded him.

Andrew shot her a look. "No offense, Miss Emily, but the diner is a much more awesome place to work. All my friends at school are getting jobs there. Everyone who works there has to be either in high school or college."

Or roughly Xavier's age, Emily thought, not sure whether that was a good or bad idea.

"So…can I?" Andrew asked his mom.

Emily looked at Simone. She did not want to put her friend on the spot. "Look, it's okay…"

"No," Simone said firmly, "it's not. Andrew, you have a part-time job here and you are going to honor that commitment."

A mother-son stare-down commenced.

Simone won.

"Fine!" Andrew slammed out the back.

An awkward silence followed.

"Sorry," Simone finally said, clearly upset.

"If you need to go ahead and leave for the day," Emily murmured sympathetically.

"Thanks...I think I will," Simone sighed, rushing out the back door.

Then things went from bad to worse.

The front door opened and Xavier Shillingsworth sauntered in.

HOW MUCH MORE was Emily supposed to have to take? Dylan wondered.

"Hi, Emily. Dylan—" Xavier paused dramatically. Furrowing his brow, he asked snidely, "—don't you ever work?"

Dylan refused to pick up the gauntlet. "You're not worth the effort, kid."

Disappointed, but no less smug, Xavier turned back to Emily. "Andrew's under sixteen so he's going to need a work permit. His mother will have to fill the papers out and get them approved by the Texas Workforce Commission, before he can start."

Emily continued wiping down tables. "They've already left for the day."

Shillingsworth followed her, further invading her space. "Maybe you could give the papers to them for me, then?"

Whatever pity he'd felt for the kid the previous evening vanished. Dylan stepped forward. "You know Andrew was working here?"

Shillingsworth lifted an autocratic brow. "Yes. He told me that."

Dylan studied him. "And you've got no compunction about trying to hire him away from Emily?"

"It's business. I'll hire anyone I want who wants a job. Even, say—" Xavier gestured lazily "—Emily…"

Oh, Dylan thought. *Them's fightin' words.*

Emily, on the other hand, stepped forward, fire in her gaze. "Well, kind as that is of you, Xavier," she drawled, "I really can't see that happening. Because I actually like to *cook* the food—from scratch—not just take off the plastic wrap and heat it in the microwave."

Dylan threw back his head and laughed. Having had more than enough, he slapped Xavier on the shoulder and steered him in the direction of the exit. He seemed to be doing that a lot. "Looks like you're outmatched and outclassed, kid. So you best be on your way."

Xavier stepped sideways instead. "First of all, you'd be surprised how good our stuff is." He squared off, indignant. "And second, Emily has not asked me to leave. So…"

Emily set her chin. "I'm asking you to leave."

Xavier looked at Emily, ready to continue to push the issue. Emily remained unmoved and Dylan lifted a warning brow.

The restaurateur suddenly changed his mind and headed slowly for the exit. "My offer of a date is good anytime, Emily. 'Cause I still want a cougar for my trophy case." The kid turned around and winked. "If you know what I mean."

Emily's glance narrowed. "Goodbye, Xavier."

Reluctantly, he sauntered out, slamming the door after him.

Emily turned to Dylan. Instead of complimenting him on the great restraint he had shown, in not booting the kid out by the seat of the pants practically the second the interloper walked in, Emily glared at him. "You do not have to run interference between the two of us. I am perfectly capable of looking after myself."

Dylan was willing to be amenable, but only to a point. "Suppose I want to defend you. Me being your pretend boyfriend and all. What then?"

He had no idea what Emily was going to say. He didn't want to know, either. All he wanted, at that moment, was to stake his claim in a way neither of them would ever forget.

He wound an arm around her waist and used the leverage to pull her intimately against him. He heard her soft gasp of surprise—and delight—as he threaded his hand through her hair and tilted her face up to his.

The first contact was soft and tender. Their lips fused together. And yet there was no surrender.

It didn't matter.

Dylan had met with resistance before.

He knew gentleness and patience worked wonders.

As did a full-on kiss filled with passion and need.

He utilized both, grazing the shell of her ear, touching his mouth to her throat, the underside of her chin, her cheek, the tip of her nose, before moving once again to her lips.

And this time, when he fit his lips to hers in a soft, sure kiss, she was ready for him. Drawing him closer, she tangled her tongue with his....

The lines were blurring, Emily thought, as Dylan flattened a hand down her spine, pressing her body into his. Confusing her as to what was real and what wasn't... what was possible and what was not...

It didn't matter how hot and hard he was...or that she was the reason for it. It didn't matter that his embrace was magic, or that this fleeting embrace had her experiencing more pleasure than she ever had in her life.

What mattered was that they weren't in love.

Couldn't be.

Wouldn't be.

So even if it felt like something more, Emily told herself it wasn't.

Shaken, she broke off the kiss and pushed away. "This can't continue," she managed, drawing a jerky breath.

Not without some sort of promise that their relationship would one day be as real and true as the physical passion they felt.

Sadly, no matter how much he lusted after her, she couldn't see Dylan agreeing to that.

"I wasn't sure you'd show up," Dylan remarked when Emily got out of the car several hours later.

She had known he had figured no affair meant no working together, but she hadn't bothered to correct his misimpression at the time. "Then you must know even less about me than you think," Emily replied.

Dylan laughed and favored her with his sexy, oh-so-male presence and what-I'd-really-like-to-do-to-you golden-brown eyes.

She drew a conciliatory breath. "When I want to do something, I do it."

Dylan prodded devilishly. "And right now…?"

Emily settled her hat on her head. "I want to see you start Ginger's training."

Seeming pleased at that, Dylan dipped his head in a gallant bow and showed her the way. "Then let's get to it."

The horses Dylan was working with were housed in a maze of corrals and pastures, all feeding into a central alley. Salt and Pepper were in an adjacent paddock, grazing sedately. Ginger was by herself in another.

Dylan lifted the latch. Ginger took the opening he gave her and bolted down the aisleway. She took the first available exit and landed in a high-walled round pen. Dylan stepped in after her, closing the gate. Emily climbed onto the riser, above the pen, to watch.

"Easy, girl," Dylan said, as the beautiful mustang pranced back and forth, eyeing Dylan nervously all the while. He unfurled a long cloth line and gently threw it in the mare's direction. Ginger pranced away from it. Dylan pursued, calmly extending the line, forcing Ginger to go away from him again and again.

First in clockwise motion.

Then counterclockwise.

Across the center of the round pen.

Around the sides.

Again and again, they went.

"How long are you going to do this?" Emily asked.

Dylan cast her a look over his shoulder. He raised his hand—Ginger went faster. He dropped his hand to the side, she slowed. "Average time is about six minutes."

And then what? Emily wondered.

Six minutes later, she found out.

Dylan stopped throwing out the cloth line and simply stood quietly in the center of the pen. Slowly, he turned, so his shoulder was toward the mustang. Head bowed, he waited.

Ginger stood, trembling with nervousness.

Emily wondered what was up now.

Still, Dylan stood, his body quiet, posture relaxed, head down.

Ginger edged closer. Closer still, until her elegant thousand-pound body was right beside him.

Ever so slowly, Dylan turned toward her. Keeping his head down, his gaze on the ground, he murmured, "That's it, sweetheart. See? I'm not going to hurt you. I'm your friend."

With exquisite gentleness, he rubbed Ginger's face, then moved around to stroke the sides of her neck, her back, the vulnerable skin of her stomach, and back around to her hips and flanks. Emily watched, mesmerized, as the once-wild horse leaned into his touch, completely accepting, trusting absolutely.

"That was amazing," Emily said an hour later, when Dylan led the mustang back to the paddock where Salt and Pepper were pastured. So this was what horse whisperers did. "Do you use the same method every time?"

Dylan nodded, matter-of-fact in his expertise. "The horse has to go away from me before he or she can come back to me."

"So you drove her away repeatedly," Emily marveled. "And yet you knew she would come back to you in the end."

Dylan inclined his head. "It's basic horse—or herd—psychology."

To want what you can't have? To go where you're not supposed to be? "Or psychology in general." Emily paused. Suddenly suspicious as her next thought hit, she narrowed her eyes at Dylan. "So I have to ask—is that what you've been doing to me?"

DYLAN STARED AT Emily, hoping the conversation wasn't headed where it appeared to be. "What are you talking about?" he demanded.

Emily gave Dylan a deliberately provoking look and smiled with all the steely resolve of a Texas belle, born and bred. "You pique my interest," she observed sweetly.

Then she looked at him in a way that made him want to haul her into his arms and kiss her senseless. *Which maybe, given the heat between them, was not such a bad idea....*

Emily stepped closer yet and continued with a cantankerous toss of her head. "You only let me—or any other woman for that matter—come so close."

That was true of other women, he thought. Not Emily.

Her soft lips pursed in dismay. "Then you drive her away, again and again."

Once more, she seemed to be watching and weighing everything he said and did.

"Waiting patiently," Emily continued. "*Knowing* that she'll come back and join up with you in the end, just the way Ginger did."

If Dylan didn't know better, he would think it was Emily's heart that was hurting, instead of her pride. When the truth was, this was about something much more fundamental. He folded his arms and leaned against the fence. "You're making it too complicated," he said mildly.

She brushed past him, a censuring light in her eyes, a downward slant to her lips. "I don't think so."

He caught her by the arm and swung them both around so fast she stumbled into his chest. His own body humming with the crazy feeling of need running riot inside him, he steadied her, then planted his hands on either side of her and leaned over her, so she was pinned between his body and the smooth rails of the wooden fence.

He let his eyes slide over the inviting curves of her breasts, flat abdomen and sexy, jean-clad legs, before returning to her tousled hair, soft lips and wide blue eyes. "There's nothing complicated about me wanting you, or what I need," he told her frankly, not afraid to be bold if boldness was what was called for.

She released a breath. "Which is what exactly?"

Ignoring the flash of indignation on her pretty face, Dylan leaned even closer. He'd lost the battle to be a gentleman, but if nothing else, he would be honest. "To take you in my arms," he said very, very softly, "and make love to you."

Before Emily could do more than gasp, Dylan caught her beneath the knees, swung her up into his arms and strode toward the house. Resenting having his integrity and his actions questioned now—especially by Emily, who had spent enough time with him to know better—Dylan continued acting with the total freedom he'd enjoyed his entire adult life.

"What's complicated," he told her, as he mounted the steps and carried her on into the house, "is the notion of us being together."

His point made, that if they so chose, the two of them could do anything they damn well wanted, he set her down inside the foyer.

Not sure when he had ever been so thoroughly exasperated by a woman, he gazed at her. "'Cause there is no way you're ever going to want what I want—a no-strings affair that lasts as long as we want it to and still allows us to walk away, completely unscathed."

And that was one heck of a shame....

Sparks gleamed in Emily's blue eyes. "Want to bet?" she challenged.

DYLAN THOUGHT SHE was a chicken. That she'd never be wild and reckless and yes—*courageous*—enough to act on the needs of her body. He was wrong. And she was going to show him.

Giving him no chance to resist, Emily bounded up and leaped into his arms. She landed with her arms wrapped around his neck and shoulders, her legs locked around his waist.

Caught completely by surprise, Dylan stumbled backward, his weight falling against the wall. And then all was lost in the first thrilling rush of freedom and the impact of her lips planted squarely on his. Emily knew he didn't mean to kiss her back. Any more than she could help kissing him. And somehow that made the culmination of their mutual desire all the hotter.

This wasn't supposed to happen.

Yet it was.

She wasn't supposed to be this reckless.

Yet she was.

"Emily. Emily…" Dylan groaned.

The rush of emotion overwhelmed her. In the feminine heart of her, the tingling started. "Don't stop." She caught his face in her hands, looked deep into his eyes and whispered, "Don't stop." She celebrated the victory of being together, of leaving constraints behind. Of daring intimacy…and sex…and the possibility that every fantasy she had about him just might come true…

And he seemed enthralled, too. He deepened the kiss, exploring her mouth with his tongue, leaving not a millimeter untouched. Sensation swept through her like a tsunami, followed by a tidal wave of need. It had been so long since she had been held and kissed with anywhere near this conviction. Never mind the pure physical need.

When his hand slipped beneath her blouse and cupped her breast through the lace of her bra, Emily arched her back and trembled with pleasure. She was drowning in the incredible sensations sweeping through her. Wanting more, Emily threaded her hands through his hair and held his head. "Let's go to bed, Dylan," she whispered, her breath coming raggedly. "Right now."

Dylan paused, breathing hard. Clearly he wanted to take their lovemaking to the limit and beyond. He searched her face. "You're sure?"

"Very."

His glance dropped to the nipples protruding visibly through her blouse. He flashed her a debilitating sexy grin. His grip tightening possessively, he regarded her with a mock gallantry that kindled her senses. "Well, then, whatever the lady wants..."

He shifted her closer to his chest and carried her, still straddling his waist, through the hall and up the steps. He strode down the hall and lowered her, with surprising gentleness, onto the rumpled covers of his bed. Pausing only long enough to kick off his boots and take off hers, he stretched out next to her.

She flushed hotly as he unbuttoned her blouse, dropping kisses along the curve of her cheek, the slope of her neck, the décolletage of her bra. He looked at her lovingly as he traced the bow shape of her lips with his fingertip.

Then that, too, dropped to her breast.

He found the curve, the tip, the valley in between. Emily shuddered in response. She had never felt more beautiful than she did at that moment, seeing herself reflected in his gaze. "I knew we'd end up together," he whispered, kissing her again, desire exploding through them in liquid, melting heat.

Then he was on top of her, his weight as welcoming as a blanket on a cold winter's night, his mouth on hers in a kiss that was shattering in its seductive sensuality. He kissed her as if he were in love with her, and would be for all time. He kissed her as if he had always known they had something special and were meant to be together like this.

Emily had never before felt such deep-seated longing surge through her, driving her toward wild abandon. And these intoxicating emotions proved to be the ultimate aphrodisiac.

Feeling sexier, more adventurous than she had in her entire life, she gave herself over to the experience. Moaning softly as Dylan unclasped her bra and explored the tenderness of her skin. She arched in ecstasy with each caress of hand and lips and tongue. Then she unbuttoned his shirt and discovered the hard masculine contours of his chest. Lower still, she unzipped his jeans, releasing the burgeoning proof of his desire.

He was hot and hard all over. All warm satin skin and coarse wheat-blond hair. Determined to prove to him that she was as exciting and fiercely independent as he was, she held his eyes with the promise of the hot, languid lovemaking to come....

DYLAN HADN'T MEANT for any of this to happen.

He *had* expected to spend time with her. Maybe put on a little show of public ardor once or twice, do whatever it was she felt "couples" did together, until the facade ended.

But that was before he had watched her dare damn near everything and luxuriated in the soft, silky feel of her. Or looked into the turbulent sea-blue of her eyes and kissed her hard and soft and every way in between.

"You've got to promise me something," he whispered, as he took her to the very edge of the bed. The need to make her his was stronger than ever. "No heartache. No regrets..."

"Just pleasure," she whispered back, "in the here and now."

And those vows were all it took, Dylan noted, to get her on the same track as he. She moaned against him, kissing him ardently. Even as she surrendered, she took. Even as he gave, he found.

Determined to set the pace, he parted her legs and slipped between her thighs. Holding her close, he pushed inside her, timing his movements as she wrapped her limbs around him and lifted her body to his.

His hands caught her hips as she pulled him deeper still. Their eyes locked and a mixture of tenderness and primal possessiveness filled his soul. He knew it was just friendship and sex, but it felt like more. Although he knew it would end, it felt like it never would. And then there was no more prolonging the inevitable. Trembling, they succumbed to the swirling, enviable pleasure.

EMILY LAY CUDDLED in Dylan's strong arms for long moments afterward, still hardly able to believe what had happened. It was just sex. They'd both been very clear about that. Yet…the magic of his tender, amazing lovemaking left her feeling that Dylan intuitively understood what she wanted and needed in a way no one else ever had, or would. And that left her feeling oddly weak and susceptible.

Odds were, *vulnerable* was not what Dylan wanted to see from her. Hence, this was her chance to prove how detached she could be, too. Adopting a studied, casual look, she extricated herself from his warm embrace, rose and began to dress.

As always, Dylan saw way more than she would have preferred. He lay where he was, arms folded behind his head, seeming to intuit her emotions were in turmoil, even though his expression was inscrutable, too. "What are you thinking?" he asked finally, his voice as casual as her demeanor.

Searching for a decidedly flip remark, Emily

shrugged. "The obvious." She flashed a flirtatious grin. "That you're not just a horse whisperer. You're a woman whisperer, too."

His eyes crinkled at the corners, her backhanded compliment only partially satisfying him. He regarded her with rueful contemplation, something hot and sensual shimmering in his eyes. "This is going to be a problem, isn't it?"

His husky voice sent shivers down her spine.

Emily glanced down and realized she had buttoned her shirt incorrectly. Dismayed by the evidence of her disquiet, she opened the fastenings and started all over again. "I don't know what you mean." Her fingers trembled as much as her voice.

He threw back the covers and walked toward her in all his naked glory. "You're not the kind of woman who can get involved with someone or have an affair without asking them to commit to something for a lot longer term—and to change into what you need them to be."

Emily sent him the kind of offhand glance meant to presage a quick and uncomplicated exit. She moved away. "That's not true."

"I think it is." He sauntered closer, studying the turbulent emotion in her eyes. "I think you're waiting for some guy to come in and let you change him as much as you want, without demanding anything of you in return. And the two of you will marry and live happily ever after."

Emily kept her eyes above the waist. "I don't think that way!"

He shook his head. "The look on your face just now says otherwise."

More attracted to him than ever, Emily wiggled into her jeans. "I admit, I've never had an out-and-out fling before."

Dylan pulled on his clothes and boots. He gave her the same look her parents gave her when they thought she needed to delve deeper into the workings of her heart. "How many boyfriends have you had?"

Emily picked up his brush and ran it through her hair. "Casual?" *Meaning the kind she left with a kiss, at the door?* "Tons."

He frowned. "Serious."

Emily sighed. "Two. One in college. One about four years ago."

Dylan took her hand and led her toward the hall. "What happened?"

Emily followed him down the stairs. "The first one felt it was his duty as my significant other to try and control me."

Dylan let go of her hand as they wandered into the kitchen. "I bet that went over well."

"You can only imagine," Emily admitted drily.

He looked in the fridge. "And the second?"

Emily lounged against the counter, observing the enticing play of muscles in his chest and shoulders beneath his shirt. Within her, desire started all over again.

Forcing herself to keep her mind on the conversation, she replied, "He couldn't get along with my family."

He set a smoked chicken from Sonny's Barbeque on the counter. Added flour tortillas and a hunk of Colby-Jack. "Why not?"

Curious—because she had assumed Dylan couldn't cook—Emily moved back to give him room to work. "Ridge liked his family better. He thought they were superior to mine, and he wanted us to spend all our time— every holiday and a lot of other weekends, as well—with them."

Dylan added olive oil to a cast-iron skillet. "Doesn't sound fair."

"It wasn't." Emily paced while Dylan chopped up an onion and green pepper and added those to the skillet, too. "I tried to get Ridge to be reasonable about the situation—to at least divide the extended-family time fifty-fifty, but he wouldn't budge, so that ended that." The kitchen quickly filled with a delicious aroma.

"And since then..."

"There's been no one serious." Emily hadn't wanted to get hurt. "I haven't wanted to put myself out there, emotionally, unless I knew everything else was falling into line, that we were going to be compatible in all the ways that mattered, even if that meant one...or both of us...had to change."

Dylan wrapped the tortillas in foil and set them in the oven to heat. "And you were willing to do that," he murmured, as he grated the cheese.

Emily nodded. "Sometimes the guys were, too. But ultimately, that didn't work, either, because if you have to make yourself over to be with someone...you sort of start questioning if it's worth it."

Dylan brought out some premade guacamole, pico de gallo and sour cream. "I can understand that."

"Anyway, I got frustrated with working so hard on a personal life and failing, so two years ago I decided to start pouring all my energy into my career."

Dylan added smoked chicken to the sizzling vegetables. "And that's when you started the café."

Emily nodded, edging closer to the stove. She watched as he gave the ingredients a stir. "And then, it became my baby," she said softly. "So to speak."

Dylan brought out two bottles of cold dark beer. Emily set the table. Minutes later, they sat down to eat their smoked-chicken tacos. Emily was pleased to find the pulled-together feast was every bit as delicious as it looked.

Deciding to satisfy her curiosity as well as her appetite, Emily murmured eventually, "Okay, enough of a confessional from me. What is your romantic history like? Have you ever been head over heels in love?"

Dylan paused. "I thought I was at the time. Looking back, I'm not so sure."

"What happened?"

"I was working on a horse ranch in Wyoming, and I fell hard for the boss's daughter. Mariah was in college at the time. I only had my GED. She knew her parents wouldn't approve, so we had to see each other on the sly."

This did not sound good.

"She kept telling me that it would be all right once she finished her undergrad and got into vet school—that her parents would know she wasn't going to give up on her dream to be with me."

"But it wasn't," Emily guessed.

Dylan shook his head. "In her parents' view, a line had been crossed. There is the hired help—"

"You."

"And the rest of the cowboys and house staff. And then there is the landowner. In their view I was never going to be part of the latter."

That had to have hurt. "Did they fire you?"

Dylan nodded. "Oh, yeah, and they refused to give me a recommendation, which made it hard as hell to get another job—at least a good one—for a while."

"I see," she murmured. "Employers want to know why you left."

His face hardened. "I wasn't going to lie."

"But at the same time..."

"When you say you had to leave because of an unfortunate romantic entanglement with the boss's daughter, it doesn't look good." He exhaled sharply. "And you can forget it, if the prospective employer has a daughter of courting age."

"Which brings us back to that talk you had with my father..." she prompted gently.

Guilt flashed across Dylan's handsome face.

Emily leaned toward him. "He wanted to know what your intentions were, didn't he?"

Dylan's expression grew cagey. "He didn't put it like that."

"But he said something in the vicinity."

Dylan lifted an infuriatingly autocratic hand. "You don't need to worry about it."

"But I—" Emily stopped abruptly at the sound of high-pitched whinnying. "Dylan, did you hear that?" she asked in alarm.

"Yes." Dylan rose. "I sure as heck did."

Chapter Six

Emily and Dylan rushed out to find Andrew letting himself into the paddock with the three wild mustangs.

"Let 'em all out!" the rowdy boys shouted.

"Andrew, no!" Emily screamed.

Realizing they were busted, the three teenage boys on the outside of the corral left Andrew high and dry and bolted for the pickup truck in the driveway. Dylan and Emily made no move to stop them as they peeled out—their concern was for the trapped, shaking boy, and the three horses who sensed danger.

"Easy, now, Ginger." Dylan entered the enclosure. Head bowed, Dylan turned his shoulder toward the mare and tried to draw her in. She was having none of it. Her eyes were on the quaking boy behind him. Emily opened the gate, moving slowly and quickly, and slid inside, too.

While Dylan talked to the mustangs, urging Salt and Pepper to stay calm, Emily grabbed a hold of Andrew's arm. She guided him outside the corral and shut the gate behind them.

Dylan continued soothing the three mustangs. When all were calm, he eased out of the gate and strode toward Emily and Andrew.

"Keep him here," Dylan ordered before striding into the house.

Embarrassed and surly, Andrew yelled, "Go ahead—call my mom. I don't care."

What had happened to the once-sweet boy, Emily wondered. Who was this angry, defiant stranger?

Andrew wheeled on her. "Maybe you'll fire me from the café now, too."

"Is that what you want?" Emily asked, shocked.

"I want to do what I want, when I want."

"Andrew, you're only fifteen. You don't want to start doing things that will earn you a criminal record."

Andrew shrugged. "Maybe it's in my blood. Maybe I'm just like my dad," he asserted, as Dylan returned. "Maybe I belong in jail, too."

Was that what this was about? Emily shot a troubled look at Dylan.

Andrew glared at Dylan. "I don't know what the big deal is," he said angrily. "I didn't really do anything."

"You were trespassing, and you could have been killed," Dylan reprimanded sternly. "That's plenty."

Andrew fumed. "What did my mom say? Is she coming to get me?"

"I didn't speak with her." Dylan looked at Andrew without apology. "I spoke with the sheriff's department. They have a patrol car in the area. Deputy Rio Vasquez will be here momentarily to take you into custody."

Custody! "Was that really necessary?" Emily asked Dylan, after Andrew had been cuffed, read his rights and taken to the station.

"What would you have had me do?" Dylan stalked back into the ranch house, as impatient with her as she was with him.

"You should have called Simone!"

"The sheriff's department can do that." Dylan shoved

his wallet in the back pocket of his jeans and picked up his keys.

Emily followed him out to the pickup truck.

"This could have been handled privately."

Dylan disagreed. "If we don't hold him accountable, all this will be is a close call and an incentive to do more the next time."

Dylan caught her by the shoulders and continued before she could interrupt, "And make no mistake about it, Emily, there will be a next time—unless something happens to shake some sense into Andrew and get him off this path."

Her emotions in turmoil, Emily glared at Dylan. "What makes you so sure of that? Maybe what happened tonight is the wake-up call Andrew needs, to straighten up."

Dylan let go of her, and stepped back. "I'm not changing my mind, Emily."

She thought of all the devastation Simone had been through the past couple of years, first with the shock of her husband being arrested for masterminding a burglary ring and sent to jail, the resultant divorce, and now Andrew's incessant "attitude" and rebellion. Surely, Simone didn't deserve to relive the nightmare of her husband's tangles with the law, with her only son. "Not even if I beg you to reconsider, for the sake of my friends?" Emily asked plaintively.

Dylan shook his head. "Not even then."

"I'VE NEVER SEEN IT so deserted in here," Hank remarked, when he came into the café the next morning, accompanied by a debonair gentleman she didn't recognize.

Emily looked at her older brother. Since he'd gotten married, the ex-Marine had become as hopelessly romantic as their parents. Like Greta and Shane, Hank wanted to see everyone he loved happily paired up. Unfortunately, Emily thought, thinking back to her own love life—or sudden lack thereof—such a fate was not in the cards for everyone. Especially not her and Dylan Reeves, the spectacular sex they'd had notwithstanding…

"The Cowtown Diner is having its grand opening this morning," Emily explained.

"Yeah," Hank commiserated. "The line was around the block when the doors opened at six this morning."

Emily bristled, the betrayal she felt as unexpected as it was intense. "Did you and Ally eat there?" she asked her older brother.

Hank frowned. "Of course not. But I probably will at some point. Got to support all the businesses in town, you know. And speaking of business…I'd like you to meet Aaron Markham. He's a tax attorney and CPA from Dallas."

Emily welcomed the nice-looking man in the gray suit. "Nice to meet you."

"Since you're not busy, maybe you could sit down for a few minutes and chat with us," Hank suggested.

"How about I bring you-all some coffee and a few menus first?" Emily suggested.

She gave them their choice of tables and hurried off.

Aaron Markham seemed like a pleasant and personable man. Her brother meant well. She could not have been less interested.

Until the door to the café opened and closed and Dylan Reeves walked in, that was.

Their eyes locked.

Emily felt a thrill go through her, followed swiftly by anger.

She carried the coffeepot over to the table. Hank

tracked the direction of her gaze. "Yeah..." he murmured. "I heard what happened at Dylan's ranch last night."

"Then you also know how wrong he was!" Not waiting for her brother's take on the situation, Emily stalked over to Dylan's table. "A word with you, please?"

Dylan gestured to the other side of the booth. "Have a seat."

He only wished she were that malleable! Emily gritted her teeth. "I'd prefer to take this outside."

Dylan rose with exaggerated chivalry. "After you."

Emily ushered the incorrigible rancher through the back door, into the alley. She didn't know why she was still so angry with Dylan. She had disagreed with others plenty of times, on a variety of subjects, and never been this emotional, but somehow this felt intensely personal. As if she should have been able to talk to him and effect some change. Instead, he'd been as immovable as a two-ton boulder and, from the looks of it, still was.

"Simone had to post bail last night to get Andrew out of jail," Emily reported.

"It might have been better had she let him stay the night in a cell."

She should have known Dylan would say that, Emily thought, with quickly mounting aggravation. And when had he gotten to be such a hard case?

Emily huffed and went on, "The arraignment was held this morning. Thanks to your statement and the recommendation of the sheriff's department, the district attorney charged Andrew—and his three accomplices—with trespassing and third-degree burglary. His friends all had previous records and have been sent to juvenile detention. Only Andrew, thus far, has been released to parental custody. And rather than be relieved, he was resentful about that, too." Emily paused, shook her head. "I've never seen Simone so upset." She had told her to take a few days off—with pay—until she could get things straightened out.

Dylan listened quietly. "How's Andrew taking it?" he asked finally.

"He's angry and ashamed."

"Remorseful?" he pressed.

"I wouldn't say that."

Dylan nodded, not at all surprised.

Where was his compassion? Emily wondered in frustration. She knew he had it—he showed it to the horses he trained. He'd also bestowed it on her on more than one occasion.

"And don't say I told you so," Emily grumbled, actually as shocked as Simone that the trauma of being arrested hadn't been enough to shake some sense into the fifteen-year-old boy.

Something inscrutable flickered in Dylan's expression as he folded his arms across his chest. "I wasn't planning on it."

Emily studied Dylan, not about to let him off the hook for his part in this mess.

For a moment she thought he was going to put up the usual barrier to his private thoughts. Instead, something in his gaze shifted, became more intimate which, in turn, prompted her to admit, "I'm afraid this is going to backfire on everyone." Emily sighed. "That all it will do is make a bad situation worse."

"That's up to Andrew."

Emily wasn't used to feeling this helpless. She wrung her hands. "I feel I should do something."

Dylan placed a steadying hand on her elbow. "The best thing you can do is stand back and let it play out.

This is Andrew's life. These are his choices to make, his consequences to deal with."

Emily forced herself to remain calm. "He hasn't made the right choices thus far," she warned.

"Let's hope that changes," Dylan said. "And soon."

EMILY WAS NOT CONTENT to leave everything up to fate—or the impulsive emotions of a teenage boy in crisis. As soon as the café closed for the day, she drove over to the sheriff's department, to see what she could do.

Luck was with her. Deputy Rio Vasquez, the officer who'd arrested Andrew the night before, was just coming on duty. Her cousin, Kyle McCabe, was also on shift.

The two deputies shared the same outlook. "Dylan was right to call us and take a hard line," Rio said.

Kyle nodded. "I know it seems like it isn't that big a deal. But it is. Pranks like this are gateway crimes. The kids don't see it that way, of course. They think they're just messing around and accepting dares and having fun." He sighed heavily. "But things have a way of getting out of control—fast—with kids this age and before you know it, someone is badly hurt. Or there's a fatal car accident. And then lives are really turned upside down."

"Dylan knows this better than anyone," Rio added.

Emily did a double take. "What do you mean?" she asked.

Rio and Kyle exchanged wary looks.

Whatever they knew, Emily realized in disappointment, they weren't going to share.

"The point is," Rio continued, sidestepping her question completely, "Dylan takes the situation very seriously. And that's good. The worst thing any of you could have done is used your influence with the district attorney to try to have the whole matter dropped, before any real consequences were felt."

Dylan had said as much, but somehow it helped hearing the same thing from two such experienced lawmen.

Emily thanked them both, and Kyle walked her outside. Because he was her cousin, and they'd grown up together, he knew her pretty well. "So does this mean it's over with you and Dylan Reeves?" he asked curiously.

Emily could confide in Kyle the way she couldn't confide in her brothers. "I don't know. I'm not sure I could date anyone who is as intractable as he is, for very long." Maybe it would be best to cut her losses while the potential damage to her heart was still small.

"So it's not like the two of you are in love or anything?" Kyle teased.

Emily blushed. "Heavens, no!"

"You were just kissing him on the green, the other night...."

"You saw that?"

"Emily, everyone saw that. It looked pretty hot."

It had been hot. Their tumble into bed the evening before, hotter still. But sex wasn't everything. Even between friends. Emily bit her lip. "I'm just not sure we're compatible in the ways that count."

Kyle chuckled. "You mean he's not makeover material."

"I haven't tried to make him over." Not like she had in the past. She hadn't gone clothes shopping with him, helped decorate his place or suggested a way to further his career aspirations—like she had with the previous guys she had dated....

Clearly not seeing the difference in her approach to this male-female relationship, Kyle lifted a skeptical brow. "Well, that's good. Because unlike your previous boyfriends—who, by the way, were all way too malleable for their own good—Dylan is a man who operates on the strength of his convictions. And I don't see that changing. Not for you. Not for anyone."

EMILY HAD PROMISED herself she would not get enmeshed in any more dead-end romances. Which left her with only one choice.

"I think we should be friends," she told Dylan, when she showed up at his ranch that afternoon.

"I thought we already were. Or at least were on the way to becoming good friends."

"What I mean is," Emily explained, aware her voice sounded a little rusty, and her emotions felt all out of whack, too, "I don't think we should have sex again."

Their glances locked and they shared another moment of tingling awareness. Finally, Dylan said, "It was that bad, hmm?"

Emily told herself not to read anything into the concern in his eyes. "You know it wasn't," she murmured, blushing. The truth was she had climaxed like crazy under his masterful touch. "But sex complicates things. I don't need additional complications right now. My life is chaotic enough."

Dylan rocked back on his heels. He tore off his leather work gloves and braced his hands on his hips. "Okay."

Emily tore her gaze from his rock-solid chest and abs. She looked into his eyes, a little surprised he hadn't argued with her. She cleared her throat. "You're fine with this?"

The tension between Dylan's shoulder blades eased. "You just told me no. I respect that, and I will honor that." His gaze gentling all the more, he flashed her a crooked smile meant to conciliate. He stepped closer and lifted a hand to her cheek, briefly touching the side of her face. "That doesn't mean I still don't want to have sex with you. So," he said, and slanted her a telling look, "if you change your mind and decide you would like to have sex with me again, it's up to you to let me know."

Emily wasn't used to guys being this reasonable. Aware her face was still tingling from his brief, sensual touch, she drew a deep breath. "Okay, then."

"Okay." Another pause. He scanned her Western-wear-clad form. "Did you want to help with the mustangs?" he asked finally, as cheerful as ever when it came to his work.

Emily smiled, glad her efforts to redirect their relationship had worked out so well. "I would love to."

Dylan turned and headed for the training area. "Salt and Pepper have already been put through their paces today."

Falling into step beside him, Emily teased, "Saving the best for last?"

Dylan winked. "I figured you would show up, and since Ginger clearly is your favorite..." He walked into the round pen, motioning for Emily to join him.

This time, when he shut the gate, Ginger came right over to him. Everywhere Dylan went, the mustang followed. He petted her nose, her mane, her neck. Ran a hand under her abdomen, across her flanks and down her legs. The beautiful mare seemed to not just tolerate his handling of her, but welcome it.

A phenomenon Emily understood all too well...

"I noticed you're not disagreeing with my assessment that you've been playing favorites with the herd," Dylan said.

Flushing with guilt, Emily shrugged. "What can I say? Ginger's complicated and challenging. I'm trying to understand her."

Dylan nodded his agreement, looking as if that was a conundrum *he* understood all too well. "The question is, will she *allow* us to tame her?"

"What do you mean?" Emily watched rancher and horse interact with teamlike proficiency. "It's been less than a week and Ginger is already following you around the pen, going wherever you go...."

"You're right, she is watching my every move. Unfortunately, her curiosity is more than a demonstration of interest—it's an expression of fear." He met her eyes. "A horse doesn't bother to investigate something that it is not afraid of. A horse isn't curious unless it harbors some uncertainty. And that underlying fear can make a horse unpredictable."

Emily watched Dylan pick up one hoof. Ginger bucked slightly and wrested her leg from his light, testing grasp.

Dylan went back to stroking Ginger all over. When she was calm, he tried again, picking up her foot. Again, she resisted but he didn't back down.

And on and on it went, until at last Ginger gave in and let Dylan touch and rub and inspect all four feet without complaint.

"Now you try," Dylan said, while holding on to the lightweight training halter on Ginger's head.

Emily—whose only experience had been with the tame-from-birth quarter horses her father bred and trained—moved away from the wall.

Ginger eyed Emily warily while Dylan murmured soothingly and stroked her face. She pricked her ears and lifted her head slightly, inspecting Emily with her dark, soulful eyes. She seemed to be waiting to see if she could trust Emily as much as Dylan.

Emily took her time, just as Dylan had. Murmuring softly, she explained every step she took, every move she made. Ginger reacted in kind, calmly allowing Emily to pet her all over. Then finally, tenderly nosing Emily's hands, before gently nuzzling her face.

"I think she's in love," Dylan said softly.

I think I could be in love, Emily thought. *With both of you. If I were foolish, that is. Good thing I'm not.*

The mustang wasn't hers to keep, and neither was Dylan. Ginger had a home to go to—when she was trained. Dylan already had a home of his own; he'd made it clear for years now that he didn't want to share it with anyone.

Nothing about that seemed to have changed.

Emily shrugged off the compliment. "She knows kindness when she sees it."

Dylan slipped outside the gate and came back with two apples. He tossed them to Emily. "Reward her."

She did.

Dylan returned Ginger to the paddock with Salt and Pepper, then strode back, praise in his eyes. "Now it's time for me to reward you," he said, flashing her a sexy grin.

Emily knew what quickly sprang to *her* mind, despite their new just-friends status. Afraid she would get herself in just as deep as she had the night before if she didn't watch it, she warned herself to slow down. She put up a staying hand. "You really don't have to do that, Dylan. Just being able to spend time with Ginger is thanks enough."

"You don't want to owe anyone anything? I don't want to be beholden to anyone, either." He looked at her, his mind clearly made up. "So I'm taking you to dinner as payment. It's up to you to say when and where."

Chapter Seven

Dylan waited while Emily stood, tapping her foot and considering her options. "Tonight. The Cowtown Diner."

Where she was likely to run into Xavier Shillingsworth again? "You're joking," Dylan said mildly.

Her expression innocent, Emily swept off her hat and ran her fingers through her silky locks. "I figure we should be neighborly. And since you're paying…"

Dylan knew trouble brewing when he saw it. "I think it's a dumb idea," he said bluntly.

"Really." She plopped her hat back on her head and shot him a sassy look, determined to do what she wanted no matter what he thought. "How so?"

"Tonight is the grand opening for the dinner rush."

"So?" Her lower lip slid out in a sexy pout.

"So we're likely to have to wait for a table," he said.

Emily shrugged. "I'm okay with that. The only thing is, I want to go home and shower first."

Dylan was the first to admit he needed to do the same. "You want me to pick you up?"

She nodded. "Seven-thirty okay with you?"

"Fine with me."

It was the rest of the evening he wondered about.

DYLAN WASN'T SURE what he had expected Emily's apartment to look like inside. The glimpse he'd had of the adjacent bath and bedroom revealed a pink and frilly décor. This surprised him, because he'd never seen her wear anything pink or frilly, since he'd been in town.

The living area where he sat was a lot more predictable. She had a large overstuffed ivory sofa and a pair of mismatched wing chairs. Blinds, but no drapes. There were a lot of throw pillows in different fabrics and sizes. A couple of throws—one in burgundy velour, the other a soft sage-green knit. Nice lamps. And one wall that was all bookshelves, filled with fiction, cookbooks and horse stories.

An antique leather-and-brass steamer trunk served as her coffee table. Cooking magazines, especially ones that featured Southwestern-style cooking, were piled high. A small round table and two chairs and a kitchenette that could only be described as woefully inadequate. It didn't even have a stove or microwave, just a hot plate, sink and dorm-size fridge.

Emily swept back out, shutting the bedroom door behind her. But not before he'd caught sight of the wardrobe crisis that had just ensued. There were clothes scattered everywhere.

He liked the ones she had on, though.

Emily strode toward the kitchen counter and snatched up her purse and keys. She spun around in a drift of floral perfume. "Ready to go?"

Ready for something…that's for sure, Dylan thought, feeling an uncomfortable pressure at the front of his jeans.

To distract himself, he let his glance sift over her pretty turquoise dress and surprisingly high heels. Damn, but she had a nice body. Nice legs, too.

"You look good," he said gruffly. "Too good to be eating in an unscrupulous competitor's restaurant."

Her soft lips curved in a parody of a smile. "Thanks. I think."

Resisting the urge to pull her close and kiss her again, he said, "You know Shillingsworth is probably going to conclude you dressed up just for him."

Emily's brow arched. "Then he would be wrong— you're my date. Not that I dressed up for you," she amended quickly. "I dressed up for me. Because I like to look nice when I go out."

He studied the rosy color in her cheeks, the emotion shimmering in her eyes. "Well, you look gussied-up, all right."

Her gaze swept over his cleaned-up form, making him glad he had taken the time to iron his shirt and polish his boots, instead of just showering, shaving and finding a clean change of clothes. "So do you," she said softly.

Basking in the compliment, Dylan followed her down the stairs and into the alley behind the row of historic buildings downtown. On the other side of it was a row of slanted parking. Emily's car was there, beside his pickup truck.

Instead of going toward the passenger side of the truck, she hesitated and looked up at him. The last of the day's sunshine glimmered in her molasses-colored hair. He had to fight the urge to reach out and touch the soft, silky strands. "Want to walk or drive?"

"It's a nice evening." She caught his gaze. "It's only a couple of blocks. How about we hoof it?"

Anything to ease the pressure in the front of his jeans. "Sounds good."

She fell into step beside him.

He observed the pulse throbbing in her throat. "I've got a question."

"Fire away."

"This evening, are we still pretending we're dating? Or are we now publicly owning up to being 'just friends'?"

Her lips compressed. "Good question, since only one of my brothers has produced a potential love interest for me thus far, and my parents have ceased and desisted their matchmaking efforts entirely since we allegedly became a pair."

"Want my advice?" Dylan asked.

She cocked her head to one side and waited.

"Unless some gal has come in and swept Shillingsworth off his feet in the past twenty-four hours or so, I very much doubt the little twerp has given up on making you his cougar."

She elbowed him gently. "Careful, cowboy, you're sounding a mite jealous."

"Not jealous," Dylan corrected. "Matter-of-fact. And I'll lay odds Shillingsworth makes another pass at you tonight, whether he thinks I'm your date or not."

Emily chuckled. "Enough to wager?"

"Depends on what the stakes are."

"One home-cooked meal. Cleanup, included."

Which meant another night alone together, wise or not. Dylan extended his hand. "Okay," he said agreeably. "You're on...."

THE PLACE WAS HOPPING, when Emily and Dylan reached the newest dining establishment in town. Throngs of people stood in a line that filled the old-fashioned, saloon-style porch and extended halfway down the block, and more were arriving even as Dylan and Emily joined the line. And the patrons weren't just residents of Laramie.

Emily garnered from the bits of conversation floating around, they were flocking in from all around the county.

And why not? The Cowtown Diner oozed excitement.

Exterior speakers played popular country and western music. A waitstaff of college- and high-school-age kids kept tabs on the activity with wireless headsets, while less experienced staff circulated among the waiting area with platters of free appetizers and tumblers of lemonade, water and iced tea.

Despite herself, Emily was impressed.

Maybe Xavier Shillingsworth knew a lot more than she thought he did.

Maybe age wasn't the defining factor so much as vision. And, Emily had to reluctantly admit, Xavier had taken the ordinary visage of a franchise-restaurant into a definite step above.

"Jalapeño poppers?" asked a pretty young girl, in a short burnt-orange cowgirl uniform and boots.

Emily and Dylan thanked her and helped themselves. He leaned down to whisper in her ear, "Not as good as yours."

It wasn't. "But darn close," Emily whispered back.

If not for the faint aftertaste of frozen batter on her rival's hors d'oeuvre, it would have been a tie.

"Hey, Emily!" Without warning, Xavier zipped down to join them on the sidewalk. He nodded at her date. "Hey, there, Devon."

"It's Dylan," Emily corrected.

Dylan locked eyes with Xavier. "Nice job on all this," he said politely.

Xavier seemed taken aback by the sincerity of Dylan's compliment. "Uh, thanks. Why don't you two come with me?"

He headed off, pushing his way past the line, leaving Emily to follow. Dylan was right behind her.

She expected Xavier to show them the restaurant kitchen. She wasn't expecting their host to cut through the line and place them at the next available table, an oversize booth that clearly could have sat six. "Whatever you want, it's on the house," he told them, while the people they had bypassed grumbled unhappily.

"Not cool," Emily sighed.

Dylan nodded, but said nothing.

A waiter appeared with a menu that was twice as extensive as the one the Daybreak Café offered. Emily counted sixteen pages of choices, all accompanied by glossy color photos.

Dylan ordered the whiskey-glazed steak, baked potato and salad.

Emily ordered the grilled chicken, shrimp and steak trifecta, with spinach salad.

Both dinners were out within ten minutes. Both were absolutely delicious in the way that brand-spanking-new franchise food always was.

Xavier—who had been keeping a careful eye on them throughout—noted when they were done and promptly presented them with the dessert menu.

The Daybreak Café's sweets were all fresh and homemade. The selection here was clearly from the freezer section of a restaurant-supply store. The obligatory ice-cream sundae, New York style cheesecake and chocolate cake.

Emily breathed a small sigh of relief.

Until Xavier said, "Not on the menu are pecan pie, peach cobbler and hummingbird cake." He rested his forearm on the table and hunkered down, close enough to ask Emily impertinently, "So what do you say, Em? Ready to go out with me yet?"

EMILY RELEASED AN exasperated sigh the moment she and Dylan left the restaurant and headed off down the sidewalk. "Okay, cowboy. You win."

He slung a companionable arm over her shoulders and leaned down to whisper in her ear, "I've never see you blush like that."

Emily let her head fall back to rest against the curve of his biceps. "That's because you and I weren't the only ones who heard what Xavier said." She tilted her head to one side and looked him in the eye. "Did you see the looks on the faces of those older folks behind us?"

Laughter rumbled from Dylan's chest. "Not to mention the high-school kids to our left."

Emily sighed. "His pass at me is going to be the talk of the town."

Dylan dropped his arm and took her hand instead. "Make that all of Laramie County. Although I have to say, you turned him down very gracefully."

They paused at the corner and waited for the streetlight to change. "I tried my best. Still, he did not look happy."

Dylan shrugged. "The kid's clearly not used to anyone telling him no. To anything."

A fact that could bode ill for the immediate future, Emily thought uneasily. Because guys like that, who were all ego to begin with, were usually a continuing source of trouble when scorned.

Dylan seemed to be thinking the same thing.

The light changed. They crossed the street, their fingers still loosely entwined. "Maybe we should pretend to be dating each other a little longer," Emily murmured.

Dylan guessed where this was going. "Give him time to find someone his own age?"

Emily relaxed in relief. "Right."

The matter settled, Dylan teased, "So back to our bet."

Emily heaved a sigh. "I guess I owe you a homecooked meal now, don't I?"

A comfortable silence filled the air as they walked across the park in the center of the green, past the covered picnic area, the community grills and the flower beds.

Furrowing his brow, Dylan finally said, "The only question is...where are you going to whip up that meal? My ranch or that apartment of yours with its nonexistent kitchen?"

Good question. Since both places had lots of privacy and close proximity to a bed.

Oblivious to the licentious direction of her thoughts, Dylan paused. "What exactly can you cook there?"

"Very little. And only in emergencies," Emily admitted candidly. "Say if I'm sick and I want to heat up a can of soup. Otherwise, I go down to the café and rustle up whatever I want there."

Dylan slowed his pace as they reached her building. Emily did, too. She was enjoying the stroll so much she did not want it to end.

"What do your dates think of that?" he asked curiously.

Emily made a face. "I don't cook for my dates."

Dylan lifted an eyebrow in surprise. "Then why did you offer to cook for me?"

Because that's what women do for the men they are interested in.... But not about to tell him how intrigued she was by him, Emily wrinkled her nose and pretended a detachment she couldn't begin to really feel. "Because it was a gamble, pure and simple," she explained, deadpan.

Dylan took her in his arms, bent her backward from the waist. "Like this?"

Emily knew he was daring her to protest. Aware anyone could see them standing on the street in front of her building, she grasped his shoulders for balance, and murmured, "Just like this."

Dylan lowered his head as if to deliver another slow, sultry kiss.

Emily's heart pounded—the suspense was killing her.

Rather than touch his lips to hers, Dylan looked deep into her eyes and murmured tenderly, "I thought we weren't going to do this."

Emily released a pent-up sigh. "We shouldn't..." she said wistfully. She turned her head ever so slightly in the direction from which they'd come. "Particularly with Xavier looking on."

Dylan blinked. "You're kidding me."

"Nope. He's standing outside the diner, staring in our direction, as we speak."

"Then just to make sure he gets the message, we'd better put on a real show."

Dylan half expected Emily to protest, given how she had only recently put on the brakes. Instead, she clutched him fiercely, gave her whole body over to the sexy embrace and kissed him with the vigor she had displayed from the very first.

And even though Dylan had sworn to stay emotionally detached, it suddenly dawned on him that she made him *want* to be involved. Not just physically and peripherally—as was his habit—but totally, with mind, body and soul. And no one knew better than him what a colossal mistake that would be, given their very different backgrounds.

Emily knew, from the moment Dylan set her back upright, that their tumultuous, just-for-show kiss was about to end. The only problem was, she didn't want it to end. Didn't want to stop feeling the coaxing sureness of his lips or the warmth of his body against hers. Didn't want to stop feeling that they really might have something special here, given half a chance. And she would have kept kissing him had the sheriff's car not pulled up right beside them and Deputy Rio Vasquez gotten out.

Rio took one look at them and shook his head. "I should have known." He grinned. "We got a call from the diner that a woman might be in trouble."

In unison, Dylan and Emily both pivoted. There, standing on the diner porch, in plain view was Xavier Shillingsworth. His attention still directed their way, he didn't bother disguising the wide smirk on his face.

"Obviously," Rio continued, shaking his head, "it was a prank...."

Dylan rolled his eyes. "Those crazy teens..."

Rio turned back to Dylan. "But as long as we have you here..." He paused, his expression serious. "The sheriff's department got word late today that your request to put your ranch on the community-service list was approved."

What? Emily thought in shock.

Rio shook Dylan's hand in congratulations, then finished cheerfully, "The district attorney's office notified us that your first juvenile will be coming Monday after school. It's Andrew Saunders, Simone Saunders's son."

Chapter Eight

Emily looked at Dylan, unable to contain her hurt. Maybe it was growing up "McCabe," but in her world friends and family shared the things that were important…and this definitely fell into that category.

"Why didn't you tell me?" she asked quietly.

Dylan's lips thinned. "I had a proposal," he told her curtly. "That didn't mean it would be approved by the court."

And clearly Dylan was not a man who counted on anything before it actually materialized.

Realizing once again how little information she knew about the lonesome cowboy, and how much she wanted to know, Emily touched his arm. She lifted her face to his and drew a breath. "It's a good thing—what you're doing."

He curled his lips derisively. "And that's a surprise because…?"

Open mouth, remove foot… When would she learn to speak with her head and not her heart, where Dylan was concerned?

"Obviously, you're a good guy," Emily sputtered on with as much reassurance as she could muster. "Anyone who works with damaged horses or mustangs has a good heart. No question."

Her attempts at damage control had only minimal success.

Dylan lifted a provoking eyebrow and waited a long moment. "I hear a 'but' in there...."

Okay, so he wasn't going to sugarcoat this or make it easy. Maybe she shouldn't, either. The heat of her rising temper warming her face, Emily shoved her hands in her pockets and rocked back on her heels. "You're not usually one to get involved in other people's problems."

He shrugged his broad shoulders. "That one landed on my ranch."

"So?" Emily reacted in kind, determined to confront him whether or not he wanted her to. "It doesn't mean it has to keep on being your problem, does it?"

Dylan looked her over in a manner meant to annoy her. "Andrew is curious about horses," he explained, as if addressing a particularly slow-witted student. "Ten to one, his mom can't afford for him to take riding lessons. Jobs on ranches usually go to those with some sort of experience."

Stepping closer, Emily let his condescending enunciation pass. "You're going to teach him to ride?"

Dylan shook his head. "I'm going to teach him that horses are to be respected and cared for, not terrorized and set free by a group of possibly well-meaning but ultimately destructive teenagers. He's got to *think* about the consequences of his actions before he acts."

Emily hesitated. "And you're going to teach him that?"

Dylan nodded. "Starting next week after school, when he shows up for his first work session."

"I DON'T KNOW about this," Simone admitted Monday afternoon, near closing. "I mean, I'm glad that Dylan presented the option to the district attorney and the sheriff's department, and that his ranch was quickly approved as a community-service site, but I'd almost rather Andrew be picking up trash on the side of the road. It seems a lot less dangerous than working with mustangs."

Emily measured yogurt, flour, water and malted milk into a mixing bowl. "First of all, Dylan is not going to put a greenhorn like Andrew in with Ginger, Salt and Pepper."

Simone watched Emily add the new sourdough to the original starter. "Maybe not deliberately, but what if Andrew doesn't listen well or follow directions and does something stupid and gets hurt anyway?"

Chances of that were slim, Emily knew, but for someone like Simone—who had no experience on a ranch—the danger of livestock combined with the great outdoors loomed large.

Emily paused to combine both doughs and cover them with plastic wrap. "Would you feel better if I were out there, at least during his first session with Dylan?"

Simone relaxed. "Would you mind?"

"Not at all," Emily said.

It was a beautiful spring day. Business at the café had once again been woefully slow—while the Cowtown Diner still had throngs of people standing in line to get in. Emily was hoping as soon as the newness of the establishment wore off, business for the Daybreak Café would pick up once again, but there was no guarantee of that.

It would be good to get away. And…she had promised to cook dinner for Dylan this evening as a payoff to the bet they had made. So the sooner she got out there, the better.

"Thanks, Emily." Simone hugged her in relief. "You're a real friend."

Andrew was less thrilled to have Emily give him a ride out to the ranch.

"Did Dylan tell you that you were going to need a long-sleeve shirt, jeans and work boots?" she asked. The teen was still dressed in the T-shirt, khakis and loafers he had worn to school that day.

"Yeah. They're in my backpack."

A lot of good they were doing there, Emily thought. She smiled. "Why don't you put them on now? It would be better to arrive at the ranch, dressed and ready to work."

"Whatever." Andrew grabbed his gear and headed, slow as molasses, for the men's room.

Emily glanced at her watch. Because Andrew had taken his sweet time getting over to the café from the high school, they had less than fifteen minutes to get out to the Last Chance Ranch.

"Are you going to be late?" Simone asked, worrying anew.

Emily looked at her friend. This was where being one of four kids who had given her parents their share of grief came in handy. She knew what her folks had done to regain control in any given situation. "Don't worry about it." She patted Simone on the shoulder. "Andrew's accountability starts now."

And, as Emily expected, Dylan held Andrew responsible from the get-go. "You're late," Dylan said.

"If Emily had driven faster…"

Not about to take the blame, Emily lifted a hand. "I was going the speed limit."

Dylan frowned. "I'm going to have to report that to the officer in charge of your community service, Andrew." He paused to let his words sink in. "He may extend it, as a consequence."

Andrew sulked. "By how much?"

Dylan shrugged, unsympathetic. "That will depend on the rest of the report I give. How cooperative you were, what the quality of your work is, how much you talk back to me and so on."

Andrew glared at Dylan but said nothing more.

Smart kid, Emily thought. Now if Andrew would just turn his whole attitude around....

Dylan handed Andrew a pair of work gloves and a shovel. "Grab that wheelbarrow and follow me." The two headed off to the stable. Emily stayed where she was, just outside the stable. As she expected, it didn't take long for the fireworks to start. The exchange that followed could be heard, clear as day. "That's horse manure!" Andrew bellowed in rage. "You expect me to shovel horse manure?"

Dylan's boots sounded on the concrete aisleway as he strode toward the door. "Once you muck out the stalls, you're going to clean them with a disinfectant solution and put down fresh hay."

More indignation followed from his young charge. "There are twenty stalls!"

"Then you better get busy." Dylan paused in the open doorway, his expression stern. "I'll be back in a few minutes to check your work."

And so it went, over the course of the next three hours. By the time Simone arrived at the ranch at six o'clock to pick Andrew up, her son was filthy, exhausted and even surlier than when he started.

"I'll see you Wednesday," Dylan said.

"I can't believe I have to do this for twelve more weeks!" Andrew muttered, stalking off.

Simone thanked Dylan and left with her son.

Emily turned to Dylan. She had spent the previous

three hours gentling the two younger mustangs and was pleased that the same method they'd used on Ginger had worked on Salt and Pepper. "So what next?" she asked.

WHAT DYLAN WANTED to do was forget everything they'd previously agreed upon, take Emily upstairs into the shower with him and then to bed....

That plan was nixed by the vintage Corvette racing up his drive. Emily stared in the same direction as he. She looked shocked and displeased. "What's he doing here?"

Dylan grimaced and stared at the arrogant teen who was fast becoming a thorn in both their sides. "I'll find out."

Emily tensed. "You sure?"

"It's my property. I'll handle it." *And protect you from any more hassling in the process.* "In the meantime," Dylan said, handing her the soft cloth rope, "do you feel comfortable starting Ginger's training session by yourself?"

Emily looked longingly at the mustang. The idea of working with the horse obviously trumped whatever curiosity she had about Shillingsworth's presence.

"Absolutely. How do you want me to start?"

Briefly, Dylan explained.

Cloth lead coiled in her hand, Emily slipped into the round training pen with Ginger.

Dylan stayed just long enough to make sure the workout started off well, then turned and headed toward the adjacent parking area.

Xavier got out of his car.

Dylan strode toward him. "What can I do for you?"

"I want my shot at Emily, and I'm asking you to step aside."

If the nineteen-year-old wasn't so deadly serious in

the request, Dylan would have burst into laughter. But it was clear as the seconds drew out that this was no laughing matter. This kid was used to getting everything he wanted, no matter what the cost. He obviously could not handle the fact Emily was not interested in him.

"I want her," Xavier repeated.

And that was the deciding factor?

"A cougar is the ultimate accessory for a nineteen-year-old mogul…is that it?"

Shillingsworth's ears reddened. "You laugh now, just like my dad, but I'm going to be rich and famous, and the success of the Cowtown Diner is just the beginning. By the time I'm thirty, I'll own hundreds of restaurants, all over the country, from all the different major chains."

Well, at least they knew the kid had a working ego—and then some. "Diversifying?" Dylan asked dryly.

Shillingsworth adopted a belligerent stance. "It's smart business strategy. And before you tell me I'm too young to succeed, consider the fact that many of the major companies today were helmed by college dropouts like Michael Dell, Bill Gates and Steve Jobs."

"I hardly think you're in their league, given the fact that your restaurant has only been open four days now."

Xavier smirked. "I'm glad to see you are counting. 'Cause I am serious about doing whatever I have to do to go out with Emily McCabe."

"Do yourself a favor and accept the fact that she's already taken, kid," Dylan said, realizing the words were truer than he wished.

Xavier chuckled. "Women like Emily never stay with guys like you. Sure, she'll dally with you for a while. You've got the whole mustang thing going for you, after all, and she clearly loves horses as much as she loves her café, but at the end of the day, she wants someone from a good family." Xavier snapped his fingers. "Oh, wait. You are from a good family. Or you *were*—until you got disowned. At birth, wasn't it?"

Shock rendered Dylan momentarily silent. "Who told you that?" he asked coolly.

Xavier regarded Dylan smugly. "My lawyer has a P.I. on retainer. It was not hard to uncover. The question is, does Emily know?"

No one in Laramie knew this, Dylan thought. Which was the way he wanted it. He stepped closer, telling Xavier with a look, if he pushed this harassment any further, Dylan would take the gloves off and give as good as he got. "What's your point?"

Xavier's glance turned to the round pen, where Emily could be seen working the mustang with long, gentle strokes of the cloth lead. "I'm sure Emily wants a man with a rich, powerful family, just like her own. She won't be happy, long term, without it."

Dylan's gut tightened at the possible truth to the words. "Get off my property."

"I'm richer…and more socially acceptable…than you will ever be," Xavier boasted. "So do us both a favor, cowboy, and give the lady to me."

GIVE THE LADY TO ME. What the hell was wrong with him, treating a woman like a piece of property that could be moved around at will? Dylan fumed, as Xavier got back in his vintage sports car and drove away much faster than necessary, leaving a cloud of dust in his wake.

Scowling, Dylan wheeled around and headed toward the round training pen. Emily had finished running Ginger and was now directing her in a counterclockwise motion.

He shut the gate behind him. Emily moved gradually

toward him, still working Ginger until the two of them were close enough to talk quietly. "What was that about?"

Dylan shook off the query. "Nothing you need to be concerned about."

Indignation flared. "If it was about me, it's my concern."

Leave it to Emily to chide him because he was trying to protect her. "I thought that was my role in this scenario—as your man. To shield you from unpleasantness."

He watched as Emily turned her body to a forty-five-degree angle to the mustang. She relaxed her shoulders and dropped her gaze to the ground.

Ginger shifted toward Emily.

Emily moved away from the horse.

Ginger followed.

When Ginger nosed her shoulder and hair, Emily turned quietly. Smiling tenderly, she reached up to hold Ginger's bridle and stroked the white blaze down the center of the mare's face. The mustang luxuriated in the gentle affection as if she had been accustomed to it all her life, instead of just a few days.

Emily moved her hands over the horse's body, letting Ginger know she could trust her as much as Ginger already trusted Dylan. "So Xavier still hasn't given up on me?"

Dylan motioned Emily to return to the horse's face. He went to the wall and picked up a small featherlight training blanket. While Emily held Ginger steady, he placed the cloth on her back. "What do you think?"

Ginger bucked a little, trying to shake the blanket off.

Dylan calmed the mustang with a touch and a gentle word. He returned to get a light-weight training saddle, and brought it back. He set it atop the blanket and watched Ginger buck a little once more.

As Dylan expertly steadied the mustang, Emily said, "I think I'm going to have to speak to him."

He reached around and fastened the girths, so the saddle and blanket would stay on. Finished, he stepped back. He motioned for Emily to let go of the bridle. He took the cloth lead and began the process of driving the mustang around the pen, once again diverting her attention from the unfamiliar weight on her back.

Watching everything that was going on Emily kept pace with Dylan.

"I don't think that's a good idea," Dylan said as Ginger kept trying to buck the blanket and saddle off.

"Why not?" Being careful to stay clear of the powerful hind legs of the horse, Emily shot a glance at Dylan.

"That will only encourage him. He wants your attention—he doesn't care how he gets it."

"Then what do you suggest I do to discourage him?" Emily asked, exasperated. "He's seen us together on what at least looked like a date. He saw us kissing. He found me here, with you. Judging from what just happened, none of that matters. He still thinks he has a chance."

Dylan shrugged and stopped driving the mustang away, "We could get engaged." The reckless words were out before he could think.

Shocked, Emily turned toward him. "Be serious," she murmured clearly irritated that Dylan could suggest something so ludicrous. "We're not in love...not anywhere near it!"

Dylan stepped closer. "So marrying me is out?" he drawled, wondering if maybe Xavier Shillingsworth was right, if—in Emily's estimation—he wasn't in the McCabes' league for anything long-lasting.

"Definitely out," Emily said firmly.

DYLAN WAS JOKING, wasn't he? Emily thought. He hadn't really meant he wanted them to get engaged. Yes, they'd slept together, enjoyed each other's company and shared a love for horses, but beyond that they barely knew each other! So his suggestion couldn't have been for real. Perhaps it was some sort of test....

The question was why he'd want to appraise her that way.

Obviously, something had happened in his discussion with Xavier Shillingsworth. Something that he didn't want to talk to her about...

"You know my reputation with relationships...?" Dylan asked flatly.

Emily nodded. "That you're never going to be tamed by any woman...so no one would buy us becoming engaged." She forced herself to be logical. "Least of all my family. And trust me, we really don't want them stepping in at this point and getting involved."

Dylan studied her with a brooding expression. "Because they'd disapprove?"

"Probably," Emily was forced to admit. "Unless they thought we were right for each other."

Because we were in love.

She fell silent. "Not that I'm interested in giving up my freedom to get married, either," she said. "Besides, I doubt even that would discourage Xavier. He has such an overinflated image of himself." She paused. "I guess it's just going to take time and repeated rejection. Surely, he won't want to wait around for that long. I mean he strikes me as kind of an immediate-gratification type of guy."

He gave her a long look. "That's what worries me."

Emily waited.

"Sooner or later, Shillingsworth is going to figure out he's not going to get what he wants from you. When that happens, he's going to want you to pay for the rejection and he's going to lash out and try to hurt you in whatever way he can. And the place where you are the most vulnerable…"

With a start, Emily realized where Dylan was going with this. "…is the Daybreak Café," she finished for him.

Dylan nodded grimly.

Emily realized his assertion was true to a point. Her restaurant did matter to her immensely. But there was a place in her heart that was even more vulnerable—the place where her feelings for Dylan resided.

Chapter Nine

"About dinner," Dylan said, an hour later when the training was completed and all three mustangs were quartered in their paddock for the evening.

Emily tensed at the mention of their nondate. Her pretty forehead furrowing, she walked with him toward the house. "You still want me to cook for you this evening, don't you? As the loser for our bet?"

Dylan grinned enthusiastically. Maybe the two of them weren't meant to be lovers, but that didn't mean he didn't relish every second he spent with her.

Enjoying the disheveled state of her silky molasses hair, as well as how pretty she looked in her shirt and jeans, he asked, "Okay with you if I leave my truck parked right in front of your building all evening, instead of the alley behind?"

A pink flush flooded her sculpted cheeks as she stopped just short of his front porch. "You want everyone to see your pickup and figure out you're at my place," Emily deduced, not quite happily. "Including Xavier."

Especially Xavier, Dylan thought.

He sat down on the top step. Taking her hand, he tugged her down next to him. "Do you want to discourage him, or not?"

Emily heaved a disgruntled sigh and stretched her

long shapely legs out in front of her. She wiggled her toes and examined the flower pattern on her red cowgirl boots. "I do."

Dylan planted a hand on either side of him and leaned back to stretch the kinks out of his body, too. Tilting his head toward Emily, he continued, "Then you have to make the kid understand in every way possible there is no chance for him to edge his way in."

Emily twisted her lips and studied Dylan with narrowed eyes. "This is a competition, isn't it?"

Actually, it was a hell of a lot more than that. Although how to explain…

Finally, Dylan shrugged. "For him it is, maybe."

"And for you?" she asked, nudging his thigh playfully with her knee.

Dylan ignored the heat the brief touch generated. With effort, he concentrated on the facts they could discuss. "As your pretend boyfriend, it's my job to protect you, Ms. McCabe."

She wrinkled her nose at the unexpected formality. "And that's all there is?" she pressed, searching his face. "There's no ego involved?"

Leave it to Emily to ask the really hard questions, Dylan thought moodily. "Of course there's ego involved." He felt compelled to be honest. "I'm a man, and you're allegedly with me. How would it look if I let that little know-it-all continue to make your life a lot harder than it has to be right now?"

Something shifted in Emily's eyes. Her teeth raked her lower lip even as her voice betrayed little emotion, "So this is all about your manhood."

It's all about protecting you, Dylan thought, but he wasn't sure how she would take that. "I don't want to see you hurt. I imagine none of your other friends or family do, either."

Again, something shifted. It was almost as if a force field went up.

"Okay." Emily rose abruptly and favored him with a brisk, efficient smile. "I'll see you at the café kitchen at eight o'clock."

"SOMETHING SURE SMELLS GOOD," Dylan said an hour later, when Emily met him at the front door of the café.

Emily sure looked good, too—although he had to wonder at her choice of a Daybreak Café T-shirt and a very worn pair of jeans. In contrast, he was dressed in his best shirt and pants.

Emily accepted the bottle of wine he'd brought with a smile, took his hand and guided him inside. "I'm glad you think so," she said in that excessively cheerful voice she used when welcoming patrons to her café.

She set the bottle on the counter and led him into the kitchen. There, already laid out on the stainless-steel prep table was a flatiron steak with jalapeño butter and a cheese enchilada on the side.

"I'm thinking of adding this to the lunch menu. What do you think?" Emily turned to face him, her attitude surprisingly professional.

The notion that this evening might turn out to be special swiftly faded.

Dylan chided himself for hoping otherwise. Of course a multitasking woman like Emily would put the task of cooking dinner for him to good use and use the experience to further enhance her business.

She gestured for him to sit down on the lone stool and then waited for him to taste.

Figuring he may as well, Dylan lifted a fork. In this,

he was not disappointed. "It's delicious," he told her sincerely. "I think it would be a hit."

Emily set another plate in front of him. "What about the enchiladas?" She picked up her notebook and pen and began to scribble notes. "Were they hot enough? Too hot? Would you prefer a different kind of cheese in them, say Monterey Jack or jalapeño-Jack instead? Longhorn or mild cheddar cheese and onion filling is traditional, but queso blanco also adds something special." She sighed, thinking, then pushed several more plates at him for tasting. "But I don't know...I'm trying to appeal to the masses. And what about jicama slaw, instead of the traditional Southern?" Emily asked him rhetorically. "I tried that for a while, and to tell you the truth, it didn't go over all that great. The jicama has a taste that doesn't appeal to everyone."

"I think what you need here to advise you," Dylan said finally, when he could get a word in edgewise, "is a restaurant critic." He was only half joking. He knew what he liked. But everyone else...?

"Actually," Emily said, lighting up like a sparkler on the Fourth of July, "that idea's not half-bad, Dylan! Thanks!" She got up abruptly and went to the phone. While he watched, half in wonder, half in irritation, she made a call.

"Hi, Holden. You know that guy you were trying to get me to meet?" Emily motioned to Dylan to keep eating, then turned her back to him and began to pace. "Yeah, Fred Collier. Right. Do you think you could bring him by here tomorrow? Lunch is fine. And tell him, if possible, I'd like him to hang around for a short while after closing, so I can talk to him."

WELL, EMILY THOUGHT, after Dylan left a short time later, that was one way to end an evening on an unromantic note.

Make a "date" with someone else while your current guest is still on premises.

So what if it had been about business?

The point was she was honoring her debt to Dylan—by making him dinner—and honoring herself by keeping her options open.

And not letting this mano a mano stuff between Dylan and Xavier influence her one way or another.

So what if she got all warm and gooey inside when Dylan got protective of her in that distinctly man-woman way?

He'd said it himself. It was ego as much as friendship pushing him to become her white knight.

When Xavier backed off, as the teenager eventually would, and the business with her matchmaking family and the café finally settled down, she would no longer be a damsel in distress in Dylan Reeves's eyes.

She'd be a great gal he had once slept with, and that was that.

Much as she wanted to pretend it would turn into something more…the practical side of her knew the odds were against it.

So she had to protect her heart—and concentrate on the real problems in front of her.

Like saving her restaurant from going into a decline it might not recover from.

Because she knew better than anyone, once a café was considered second tier, for whatever reason, it often ended up faltering. Because it was just too hard to do the work if appreciative patrons did not show up in droves.

Hence, when Dylan came in for an early breakfast, she was too busy to come out of the kitchen to say hello. Ditto when Xavier showed up, a bunch of red roses in hand.

When the *Texas Traveler* magazine food reporter came

in with Holden, however, she made sure the boyishly handsome "foodie" had everything he wanted. At the end of the lunch rush, she ushered him into the kitchen to see her work space and sample even more of the food.

"It's all wonderful," Fred Collier said, his kind green eyes shining with an admiration Emily found particularly gratifying.

Then he grimaced. "But I have to wonder where the crowds are. We've been here two hours, and the place has never been more than one-third full. While across the square, at the Cowtown Diner, the throngs have not abated in the least."

Emily's shoulders sagged. She had been hoping the restaurant critic wouldn't notice.

With typical gallantry, Holden explained, "It's the full-page ads and two-for-the-price-of-one meal coupons the franchise owner put out over the weekend in all the county newspapers."

Holden paused and looked at Emily.

Surprised by her shock, he shrugged inanely. "I thought you knew. I thought that was why you called. Shillingsworth is planning to extend the offer indefinitely. The coupons are reusable."

Emily's heart sank. "The diner will never turn a profit that way," she said, rubbing at the headache starting in her temples.

"Unless it's by sheer volume of customers." Fred Collier turned to glance out the window.

Sure enough, at two o'clock in the afternoon—usually a dead time for most restaurants—the Cowtown Diner was still busy as ever.

"Can you help her?" Holden asked his friend.

Fred smiled apologetically. "I'd love to, if and when your business picks up again. I only write about places that are standing room only, and right now, the Daybreak Café no longer qualifies."

"Thanks for coming by." Emily packed up some dessert for him and walked him out.

"Sorry about that," Holden said, when she returned.

Emily stared out the window at the competition that was swiftly becoming a real thorn in her side. "Don't be," she told her big brother. "I needed a wake-up call. And this was definitely it."

"YOU'RE GETTING NEW outdoor chairs and umbrella tables now?" Dylan asked, later that same day.

The sound of Dylan's low, gravelly voice gave Emily a pleasurable jolt. Her heart had skipped several beats when he'd sauntered in for lunch half an hour ago but she'd been trying to ignore how ruggedly, casually handsome he'd looked in his soft faded denim shirt and jeans. It was bad enough she knew firsthand how his strong virile body felt pressed up against the naked length of hers without yearning to experience his hot, reckless brand of lovemaking again.

And now he was standing next to her once more, looking over her shoulder, studying what she had been studying.

"Yes. I am," Emily replied, and damned herself for sounding breathless.

She put the receipt aside and looked up the weather forecast on her computer. The rest of the day appeared warm and clear, but there was a fifty-percent chance of rain every day for the rest of the week. Which could sabotage her plans.

On the other hand, to do nothing was to automatically lose.

She turned back to Dylan. As long as they were still

"friends" who helped each other out… "I have a favor to ask. Are you available tonight to help me drive to San Angelo to pick them up?" There were others she could ask to help her, but for reasons she chose not to examine too closely, she wanted him to go with her.

Speculation glimmered in Dylan's golden-brown eyes. "Sure," he said kindly. "Do you have a big enough vehicle?"

Trying not to feel too grateful he was in her life— for that might mean starting to depend on him past the temporary time frame they'd agreed upon—Emily nodded. "I reserved a moving truck that will handle it all."

They set up an early departure time, and in half an hour, Dylan was at her door, ready to go. They took his pickup to the truck rental place and arranged to leave it in the lot there while they went to San Angelo.

Naturally, Dylan wanted to drive. A little overwhelmed by the sheer size of the truck, Emily had been hoping he would volunteer. She was independent, but not foolish enough to take on more than she could handle.

"So how did the lunch date with the food critic go?" Dylan asked casually, as soon as they were on the road to San Angelo.

"Fred Collier was a nice guy."

Dylan slanted her a glance she couldn't quite read. Too confident to be seriously threatened, he teased, "Good-looking?"

"Yes." Emily volleyed back, just as playfully. "Although I was more interested in what Fred might be able to do for my business."

Dylan sobered at the magnitude of the problems she was facing. "And…?"

Tension stiffened Emily's spine. "He's not going to

write about the Daybreak Café, at least not right now."
Briefly, she explained.

Dylan listened quietly, then shook his head in commiseration. "I'm sorry."

So am I. Emily settled more comfortably in her seat, shifting slightly to the left. Finding comfort in the intimacy swiftly springing up between them, she shrugged and forced herself to be as matter-of-fact as the situation required. "Holden's friend has a point. As did you, in a roundabout way." She studied Dylan's ruggedly handsome profile. His hair was rumpled and dark stubble rimmed the lower half of his face. He looked sexy and impatient. As impatient as she. "I have to be ready to compete a little more aggressively if I want the café to remain a viable business. And that means answering customer complaints a lot more responsively."

Hands competently circling the wheel, Dylan glanced at her curiously. The open collar on his shirt exposed the strong column of his throat. He had rolled up the sleeves of his shirt to just below the elbow.

Emily forced her gaze away from the sinewy strength in his arms, and told herself she was grateful for the seat between them.

She turned her attention back to business. "People have complained about the lines to get in since shortly after I opened two years ago. I don't have room for any more tables inside and to be honest, I liked the idea of having a sought-after commodity in such a small town." She laced her fingers together. "I thought the demand gave my place a sort of cachet not necessarily shared by some of the other larger restaurants in town."

Dylan murmured, "It was a small local haunt that anyone who was anyone knew about."

"And that alone made it special." Emily sighed. "But in retrospect I see that was a mistake."

Dylan listened, understanding that, too.

"And while I can't just put an addition on a historic building to increase seating in the café, I am permitted by the city to use the sidewalks surrounding the building. So I can put up tables that line the front and wrap around the corner immediately. And that's what I plan to do," she announced proudly, satisfied that she was back on the path to success. "Starting tomorrow morning, patrons will be able to dine alfresco."

Dylan knew that was what Emily hoped would happen. He couldn't help but wonder if she was just setting herself up for more disappointment.

It was nearly ten-thirty that night by the time they returned to Laramie, precious cargo in tow. Eleven-thirty, by the time they unloaded the truck and set up the five umbrella tables and twenty chairs. And though Dylan had handled the trip well, he noted Emily was looking pretty tired as midnight neared. Which wasn't surprising, given she had been up since four that the morning. Whereas he, as usual, had slept in until six...

Her expression supremely content, Emily stepped back, looking at their handiwork beneath the glow of the street lights. "That's really nice, isn't it?" she asked Dylan.

He nodded in agreement. There was no doubt about it—the outdoor seating added a lot of charm to the storefront of her building. He wasn't sure, however, that a four-thousand-dollar expenditure was good for Emily *financially* at the moment. But since he had no idea what the café's bottom line was, he couldn't comment.

Instead, he focused on the positive. "The outdoor seating should help a lot, when the usual crowds return." He reached out to playfully tug the end of her ponytail. "I know I'll appreciate a shorter wait time for a table."

The corners of her soft lips turned up. "When," she repeated, her blue eyes sparkling. "I like the sound of that." She sighed, then added less certainly, "I only hope the prediction comes true as soon as possible."

Dylan consoled her with a hug. Forcing himself to keep it friendly, he gave her an extra squeeze and let her go. Stepping back from her, he held her gaze and reminded, "You're an amazing chef, Emily. Sooner or later, people are going to remember that and return in droves."

Emily's slender body tensed. She lifted her hands to her head and removed the clasp holding her ponytail in place. "I hope so."

Dylan watched the spill of silky hair fall over her shoulders. Recalling their agreement, he tamped down his desire. "Want me to take the truck back to the lot?"

The tension left her shoulders. She slanted him a grateful glance, her weariness beginning to show. "If you wouldn't mind, that would be great," she told him softly. She looked around for the scissors she'd brought out of the café. "I'll stay and cut the tags off everything." She inclined her head slightly, added casually, "If you want to return, maybe we can have some pie à la mode or…something…"

Dylan didn't know what he was looking forward to more—eating one of the desserts she'd made or simply spending more time with her. "Sounds great," he said. Eager to get back, Dylan took off.

EMILY WAS NEARLY DONE cutting off the tags, when footsteps sounded. She looked up to see Xavier coming down the sidewalk, toward her.

Great. Just what she did not need!

Looking like a teenager who'd just had his car keys taken away, he started right in on her, demanding pugnaciously, "Why didn't you come out of the kitchen today when I brought you flowers?"

Emily wondered if the spoiled teen's bullying had ever worked on any woman. It sure did nothing for her. "I was busy."

His jaw thrust forward in what looked like a permanent pout. "You're making a mistake. You should date me, not Dylan Reeves," he told her scornfully.

Emily drew a bolstering breath and tried to be kind. "Xavier, I am sure there is a cougar somewhere right now who is calling your name. Some woman who would be delighted by the ardent attentions of a much younger man. It is just not me."

He blinked as if he couldn't believe the rejection. "I'm a great guy."

"Who is trying to run me out of business," Emily couldn't resist pointing out.

"A great guy who wants to succeed," Xavier insisted.

Emily moved to the next table and continued cutting off tags. "Then I wish you all the best. Now, if you don't mind, I have my own problems to deal with."

Once again, the kid refused to take the hint and, instead, followed her from place to place. "Dylan Reeves acts like a hero, but he's not." Xavier positioned himself so she had no choice but to look at him. "Dylan Reeves is a *criminal*, Emily."

Xavier's words carried an implicit threat that chilled Emily to the bone. She paused long enough to look him in the eye.

"What are you talking about?" she demanded evenly, all the while telling herself this could not be true.

He smiled smugly. "Dylan is a former juvenile delinquent, with a very long record. He spent time at the Libertyville Boys Ranch as a kid."

If that was correct, Emily thought, privately reeling at the news, it certainly explained a lot. Why Dylan had insisted on taking such a hard line with Andrew from the get-go. Why he was so involved with philanthropic work for the boys ranch. Maybe even why he was incredibly committed to his profession.

Determined to keep her feelings to herself, she regarded Xavier evenly. "Dylan Reeves is also my friend. And I don't let anyone talk trash about my friends."

Xavier glared at her. "You're a McCabe, a member of the most powerful, respected family in the state."

Was that why he had chosen Laramie as a site for his franchise diner? So he could hook up with her? The idea seemed bizarre and yet it made sense. The kid was definitely a social-climbing, billionaire wannabe who was looking for a shortcut to success. Perhaps he'd set his sights on the Laramie, Texas McCabes, because they had powerful ties to ranching, oil and technology—as well as a host of other potentially lucrative professions, like commercial real estate development, moviemaking and the designer clothing industry....

"There are plenty of other respected, powerful clans with single daughters. Girls," Emily emphasized bluntly, "more your age."

"None on par with the McCabes," Xavier argued back. "Or you."

Emily didn't really know what to say to that. It was true—her family was enormously successful. Enough to attract all kinds of people just looking for a quick ride to success. That didn't, however, make it right. She wished she knew a way to explain that entry into her world was not an immediate guarantee to personal happiness. But she knew that would fall on deaf ears to an obviously emotionally neglected kid like Xavier, who'd likely used money as the method to solve every problem. Deep down she sensed what the kid *really* needed was what she'd had—lots of familial love and attention....

Sometimes, too much attention.

"You'd really choose a small-time horse trainer over me?" he asked finally, aghast as the reality of the situation finally began to sink in.

"Horse whisperer," Emily corrected, "and I already have." She looked at Xavier with the little bit of patience and compassion she had left. "So I would appreciate it if you and I never had this discussion again, because it's clearly uncomfortable for both of us."

Hurt and astonishment gave way to boiling anger. "This is really the way it's going to be?"

"It really is," Emily stated firmly.

He balled his fists at his sides. "Then you're going to be sorry. You *both* will. *No one* disrespects me and gets away with it."

DYLAN ARRIVED, JUST as Shillingsworth stormed away. He parked his truck at the curb, in front of the restaurant, and came toward her. "What was that all about?" he demanded.

Emily's pulse picked up. "Let's take this inside, okay?"

Dylan searched her eyes, recognizing right away that something was wrong. "Did he hurt you? Because if he did..."

"He didn't touch me—it was just a verbal exchange."

She led the way inside the café and shut the door after them.

Dylan waited, his brow furrowed in concern.

Emily swallowed hard and then drew a breath. "Xavier told me you had a criminal record."

Dylan's shoulders slumped. "It's true."

Hurt warred with confusion. "Why didn't you tell me any of this before—when it sort of came up because of Andrew?" she asked, feeling her cheeks heat.

He folded his arms. "It wasn't relevant to us."

She bore her eyes into his. "I thought we were friends."

His expression remained impassive. "We are."

Doubt reared. "Good friends tell each other stuff."

Silence fell as the moment of reckoning came. Emily expected Dylan to shut her out again, but he became unexpectedly gentle, let his guard down. "What do you want to know?"

Figuring if they did this right, it would take a while, Emily walked into the kitchen. "Everything. How and why you landed in juve—"

Dylan sat down on a stool. "I stole a car."

Emily set a chocolate-chip-pecan pie and a carton of vanilla ice cream on the prep table. "There has to be more to it than that."

His lips thinned. "There always is. There's no excuse for what I did."

Emily waited, but nothing else was immediately forthcoming. "What did your parents think?" she asked quietly.

"My father left before I was born. And my mom died during routine surgery when I was fourteen. This happened after."

"Did family take you in?"

"They were asked. But they didn't want me any more

than they wanted my mom or me when she got pregnant at sixteen. So I was sent to foster care."

Emily's heart went out to him. "You must have been hurt."

Dylan inclined his head. "And angry enough to act out, the same way Andrew is acting out now. I fell in with a bad crowd. And did something really stupid, trying to prove I was tough." He paused, reflecting stoically, "Who knows what would have happened to me if I hadn't been sent to the Libertyville Boys Ranch? The people there turned my life around."

Emily cut two pieces of pie and topped them with ice cream. "Is that where you became interested in horses?"

Dylan accepted the plate and fork with a nod of thanks. "Learning to care for and about animals is a great lesson for kids, because animals are like us. They just want to be loved and understood."

He said that so easily. It was the first hint of real sentimentality she had seen in him. Emily yearned for more.

"*Do* you want to be loved?" Emily murmured curiously before she could stop herself. "Because sometimes, Dylan, I am not so sure."

Suddenly he grinned, as at ease with his sexuality as she was with being part of a family. He stood and walked around the table to take her in his arms. "In my way, yes, Emily, I want to be loved," he murmured softly.

An erotic thrill whispered through her, as hot and exciting as the feel of his body next to hers.

Emily tried to contain her disappointment that he wasn't more romantic in his view, that he still didn't want what she wanted—a love that would last forever. "You mean physically," she guessed, her pulse pounding.

Dylan shrugged, as matter-of-fact as ever. "It's a lot less complicated."

The question was, could she ever be satisfied with just that? *Was this a risk she was willing to take?*

Chapter Ten

Dylan didn't know what Emily was going to do. He knew what she was *tempted* to do. The slight hitch in her breath, the quickening of the pulse in her throat, the way she leaned slightly toward him, all told him that she was as ready to make love with him again as he was with her. At least, physically.

Emotionally was another matter. There, she still had her reservations, he decided. He couldn't blame her.

The two of them weren't well suited.

And never would be. Unless one of them changed significantly, and that was about as likely to happen as a snowfall in the Texas spring...

Her mood suddenly seeming as ambivalent as his, Emily edged away. "Well, I better go in. I have to get up at four, to get breakfast started in the café."

The gentlemanly thing to do would be to wish her well and let her go. But the desire flaring between them was almost impossible to resist. So Dylan found himself saying, "Are you planning on helping out with the mustangs tomorrow afternoon?"

Emily smiled. "Tell Ginger, Salt and Pepper I'll see them then."

Happy he had a reason to keep seeing Emily on a regular basis, Dylan promised he would.

Bypassing the temptation of a good-night kiss, for fear of starting something that would be tough to step away from, Dylan headed home.

He spent the night dreaming about Emily, and woke, wanting her more than ever.

Storm clouds obscured the dawn.

By the time he had finished caring for the herd, rain was pouring down. Just in time to ruin Emily's breakfast rush. What was left of it, anyway.

Dylan drove by the café. Because of the weather, the exterior was deserted. Inside, the Daybreak Café looked just as sparsely attended.

While down the street, the Cowtown Diner had a respectable crowd inside, from the looks of it, and no line at all outside.

Knowing the hungry cowpokes had to be somewhere, Dylan headed for the feed store.

Inside, as he predicted, were three dozen cowboys and ranchers, using the inclement weather as reason enough to get their supplies in. Among them were all three of Emily's brothers.

Holden McCabe was the first to approach Dylan. He extended his hand. "I want to thank you for doing your part to help scare off Shillingsworth."

Not sure he should be accepting congratulations for having had a fling with Emily, Dylan returned the handshake, anyway. "I guess you heard—"

"About that arrogant kid setting his sights on Emily?" Hank McCabe prompted, joining them. "Everyone knows about it. Shillingsworth has been running all over town for a week now, embarrassing himself by telling people that Emily is going to be his cougar."

"Which in itself is no surprise," Jeb chuckled. "Given that our baby sis is such a bum magnet." He shook his head in mock consternation, then turned back to Dylan. "Fortunately, whatever she is pretending to have going on with you has caused the kid to change his mind. As of last night, Shillingsworth is saying he's no longer interested in Emily."

"Which of course is good news to us," Holden said.

Maybe not, Dylan thought, if the kid made good on his promise to seek revenge on their sister, and him.

Jeb ran a hand across his jaw, ruminating, "The mystery is that Shillingsworth ever thought he had a shot with her in the first place."

"Clearly, he doesn't understand what it takes to be a McCabe, or fraternize with one," another cowboy said, joining the group. "The sense of integrity and community..."

"Unfortunately," Holden said, "it doesn't matter how many suitable guys are attracted to her, or who we introduce her to, she always ends up with the completely unmarriageable types."

The feed-store owner walked up to join the group. "So maybe that means you have a shot," he ribbed Dylan with a grin. "Since you've vowed not only to never get married, but never be tamed by any woman."

Not about to publicly confess he was beginning to wonder if he should reconsider that declaration, Dylan shrugged.

Figuring Emily would not want anyone getting the idea that the two of them had once been intimate, Dylan kept up the expected ruse. "And for good reason, since freedom is the most important attribute a man can possess," he boasted with the expected machismo. "And the only thing that will ever guarantee happiness."

Everyone fell silent in an abrupt, uncomfortable way that let Dylan know he had missed something important.

He turned slowly. Emily was standing in the open doorway of the feed store. The distressed look on her face said she had heard just about everything.

EMILY KNEW some guys acted as if matrimony was a prison sentence when they were standing around, shooting the breeze. It was one thing to be aware of that; another to witness it when she was the person supposedly carrying the potential ball and chain guaranteed to bring a lifetime of misery to whomever she one day married.

If she ever married.

That prospect seemed less likely every day.

In the meantime, she had a job to do. An awkward silence to end… "Hey, fellas," she grinned, sauntering nonchalantly forward, as if all her romantic hopes had not just been crushed to smithereens. She pulled the sheaf of coupons from the plastic protector in her hand and slapped them down on the feed-store counter.

"I hope you-all are hungry," she informed them in her sweet-as-pie Texas belle voice. "Because we've got quite the special going over at the café this morning. Buy one of our bottomless cups of coffee, and you'll get a free breakfast entrée. But the special is only good for today."

Hoots and hollers echoed throughout the warehouse-style feed store. There was a near stampede for the coupons and then the exit. Giving Dylan and her brothers no chance to say anything to her, she followed the hungry cowboys out the door.

As Emily had expected, the next few hours were incredibly busy. Although the tables outside were empty due to the downpour, the inside was hopping, just the way it used to be.

They served one hundred customers between seven

and ten, and because she extended the special through lunchtime, another seventy-five after that.

Finally, it was time for closing.

And that was when Dylan Reeves walked in, his expression inscrutable. "I want to talk," he said.

"I can handle things down here," Simone said.

Bobbie Sue and Billy Ray concurred. "We'll clean up and close up," they said.

Figuring what she had to say to Dylan was best accomplished without an audience, Emily thanked them and led the way to her apartment over the restaurant.

Dylan shrugged out of his rain slicker.

He continued to look at her in his very sexy, very determined way. "About what you heard this morning at the feed store…"

"I think I got the gist of it."

He adopted a no-nonsense stance, legs braced apart, hands bracketing his waist. It would have been very intimidating had she allowed it to affect her. She didn't.

"The guys were just…"

Emily lifted her chin, daring him to try and spin it. "Having a chuckle at my expense? I know. Not to worry… I'm not serious about you, either, Dylan. I know better than that." And if she hadn't before, she did now.

"If I were interested in being tied down…" he said.

"Or tied up," Emily said, trying to lighten the mood with her flip comment. "I'm sure you'd just rush to the phone and call me."

Dylan ignored her comment and kept his eyes on hers. "You're an amazing woman," he told her quietly. "Everyone knows that."

How had this turned into the preliminary to a break-up speech? Emily wondered. And why did it hurt so much to think that was what it might be?

None of this had been real. She knew that. Didn't she…?

Years of being the kid sister, and hence the recipient of her older brothers' incessant teasing and interference, enabled her to regain her footing and pretend she was okay with all this.

Emily cleared her throat with exaggerated enthusiasm. "And you're an amazing man," she recapped for him, cheerfully. "And neither of us are interested in marrying each other. So it's okay." She flashed a reassuring smile she could not even begin to feel. "Really."

The narrowed eyes indicated he disagreed with the attempt to just write off the mishap and move on.

Fearing that he would say something that would make her want to forget all about this and forgive him, she leaned closer still. "I get that we are just helping each other out in the short term." Emily took a bolstering breath and forced herself to hold his eyes in the same deliberate way he was holding hers. "I understand that you are a distraction for me from all my problems in the same way I am a source of free meals and an occasional horse wrangler for you."

Finally, he saw where this was going.

Dylan's lips thinned into a grim line. "You really think that's all we are to each other?" He studied her incredulously. "Aides-de-camp?"

She had to be logical, *stop* trying to turn guys into all they could be, *start* accepting them for who and what they were. And no matter how much it hurt, leave it at that.

Resolved that no matter what happened she would not cry, Emily faced Dylan. "That's a fancy term, cowboy, but given how all this started, with me asking you to be my pretend boyfriend? Glorified assistants slash occasional companions are all we can be to each other." She set her jaw and finished flatly, "All we should be."

That said, she showed him the door. The look on her face warned him not to expect anything to change any time soon.

FOUR DAYS LATER, Dylan was in the Last Chance stable, commending Andrew on a job well done, when he heard the sound of Emily's car. He finished giving Andrew instructions on the making of the bran mash the horses would be getting for dinner, then walked out to the edge of the stable.

Emily was already heading toward the paddock where the three mustangs were waiting.

The younger two had already received their two training sessions for the day. Ginger was still waiting for her second schooling.

All looked glad to see the pretty dark-haired woman striding happily toward them.

Despite the way they had parted, Dylan was glad to see her, too.

"Why does being out on a ranch always make me feel better?" Emily asked the horses as she approached the pasture fence. The three mustangs, which had been standing together against the fence, moseyed over to greet her.

Emily stepped up on the second rail, the action making her tall enough to reach them. She smiled and ran her hands over the faces of the white filly and the black gelding, offering both a carrot for their trouble, and then turned to the leader of the mustangs, three-year-old Ginger.

The mare stuck her head over the fence, too, wanting her treat. Emily gave it to her first, then waited to see what Ginger would do.

Just as she'd done during the past three days of training Ginger pushed her head toward Emily, wanting to be petted.

Dylan knew how that felt, too.

Although they had seen each other numerous times over the past week, Emily had managed not to touch him once.

Or look him in the eye, either.

He'd given her the space she seemed to require, but that didn't mean he didn't miss her.

And that was a surprise.

Dylan had never missed any woman who had come in and gone out of his life. He'd never *allowed* himself to do so.

With Emily, it wasn't a choice.

He felt the way he felt.

Just as she felt the way she apparently felt.

"How is it," Emily continued in a soft voice Dylan would not have been able to make out, had he not been coming up behind her, "that horses in general and you in particular always lift my spirits no matter what else is going on?" she asked Ginger rhetorically.

Dylan wanted to know the answer to that, too.

Had he been a fool to think—even after the downward turn of their relationship—that Emily had rushed out to see him, as well as the mustangs? That she enjoyed his company as much as he enjoyed hers, even when she was still obviously angry with him? Or was he the one believing in fairy tales now? Indulging in wishful thinking… hoping someone would change even when they showed no real disposition to do so…?

As if sensing the conflicted nature of his thoughts, Ginger nickered softly in response and swung her head toward Dylan, dipping her nose.

As Dylan reached up to pet the mustang, Emily turned slightly and caught sight of him. He inhaled the familiar scent of her hair and skin. "You look tired." The words were out before he could stop himself.

She lifted an eyebrow at the unusual display of over-protectiveness.

Dylan had to admit he was a little stunned himself. He didn't usually comment on the shadows beneath anyone else's eyes. Even eyes as pretty as Emily's.

The intimacy in her expression faded as quickly as it had appeared. "It's been crazy busy at the café all week, from open to close," Emily said with a shrug. "Even with the tables outside, we are jam-packed."

Dylan was glad she was getting her clientele back.

It was easy to see why.

Thus far this week, the specials had changed every day. After the success of her free entrée with a cup of coffee, she had gone on to offer a half-price breakfast special—which had been a fruit plate, biscuits and breakfast casserole. The third day it had been all the blueberry pancakes you could eat, for a dollar. This morning, there had been huge fifty-cent cinnamon rolls and coffee. Dylan had eaten there all four days.

The lunch specials the café was showcasing were just as amazing.

"I guess the additional promotions and the specials are really working out for you?"

Emily beamed. "I've got all my regular clientele back and then some."

"Good to hear." He liked to see her so blissfully happy and content.

Emily released a stress-filled breath. "Which is why I need to be out here today. Breathing in the fresh air and spending some time with the horses really helps me unwind."

"You could do that at your folks' ranch."

Emily moaned and playfully clapped both hands over her ears. "Yes, but at a price. My parents would want to talk about the financial details of my café."

Dylan had wondered about that himself—even though he knew it was none of his concern.

But as long as they were on the subject… "They might have a point."

Emily lifted her hand. "I know I'm losing money, Dylan. I had no choice. Xavier was driving me out of business with his coupon deals."

Dylan's muscles tensed. "How is Shillingsworth?"

"I don't know—I haven't seen him. He put some college kid in charge of the Cowtown Diner and went back to the city a few days ago."

This was news.

Dylan searched her face. "You think he's given up?"

Emily bit her lip. "I wish. But…probably not. He's probably just figuring out some other way to exact revenge on me."

"Let's hope not."

Whatever the situation was, Emily did not want to discuss it. "Enough chitchat. What are we going to do with Ginger today? Put the riding dummy back on her back and lead her around the ring?"

With Emily's help, Dylan had gotten the smart, adventurous horse used to the blanket and saddle. Then he'd progressed to the noisy plastic bags tied to the saddle horn. They flapped against her sides, where an actual rider's legs would go. And finally, a riding dummy that weighed fifteen pounds, strapped to the saddle. Now, she was ready for more. As was the woman beside her.

"Actually, I had something more exciting in mind. That is if you're up for it," Dylan said.

THIS WOULD BE a whole lot easier if she weren't still so attracted to the lonesome cowboy, Emily thought as Dylan stepped into the paddock.

Throat dry, she watched him attach a lead to Ginger's halter and lead the mustang back through the fenced aisleway to the round training pen.

As they walked together, he explained, "It's time for Ginger to get used to the weight of a rider. She likes and trusts you, so I'd like that rider to be you."

Excitement bubbled up inside her, along with pride at having been chosen to do this. "I won't get thrown?"

Dylan favored her with a sexy half smile. He took the blanket and saddle and put them on the big mustang. "Not if we do it my way," he said reassuringly.

While Emily gently stroked Ginger's forehead, Dylan bent to attach the girths around the mare's middle.

"And how is that?" Emily asked, gazing into the horse's dark eyes. Ginger stared back at Emily, her ears fixed forward, in a sign of happy curiosity and trust.

"I'll show you." Dylan secured the stirrups and walked around to take the mare by the bridle. He stood close to Ginger's head, on the left. Then gestured for Emily to come around, on his right.

"I want you to put your left foot in my right hand, instead of the stirrup. Take hold of the saddle horn and lift yourself up, so you are leaning against the middle of the saddle. Stay as erect as you can, to give her a chance to get used to your weight. But you can still jump off and back, away from her, if need be."

Ready for action, Emily nodded her understanding.

Dylan gave her waist a reassuring squeeze. "I'm going to hold on to your left leg with my right hand, to keep you steady at the same time I'm holding on to her with my left hand. Okay?"

Emily had seen Dylan do the same thing with the riding dummy, so this was merely a reenactment of what they had done the previous day. Only now she would be the rider.

She looked at Ginger, doing her best to imbue the mustang with confidence and courage, then turned to Dylan. "Let's do it."

The first time she hoisted herself, Ginger promptly moved in a way that shifted Emily right back off.

Dylan caught Emily in one arm, holding on to the now-prancing Ginger with the strength and gentleness of his other.

"It'll happen," he told them both softly. "You just have to trust that it will."

Emily nodded. Took a breath. And tried again.

And again she was shaken back off.

And so it went.

For the next dozen or so times, Dylan was right there to catch and steady them both.

Eventually, it became a game.

Ginger chewed her bit and pushed them both away with her nose, dancing back and forth all the while.

Emily knew then that Ginger never would be a docile, mutely accepting pet. After all, this was a mustang who was meant to state her opinion often. As if on cue, Ginger turned her head from side to side and whinnied softly, her voice carrying throughout the training pen.

"We're going to get through this," Emily told her, already imagining the day she'd be able to take Ginger on a wild canter through the surrounding plains and meadows. Horse and rider as one.... And then, almost as suddenly, as if she were imagining it, too, Ginger allowed Emily to grab the saddle horn, step up and hold on.

THE TWO FEMALES WERE a beautiful sight, Dylan thought in satisfaction as he let go of horse and half rider and used the long cloth lead to urge them both to circle the training pen.

By now, Emily had one foot in the stirrup. Her body was resting against the saddle, her middle draped across.

Ginger was moving forward, not quite trotting, not quite walking.

Testing, it seemed.

Liking what she felt.

Of being one with the equally feisty and daring spirit that was Emily.

And just that suddenly, Emily did what they had *not* agreed upon, Dylan noted furiously. She shifted and brought herself all the way down into the saddle.

Caught as much by surprise as he, Ginger reared up on her hind legs.

Emily slid backward.

Momentarily lost her balance.

And somehow managed to hang on before all hell broke loose.

Fear roiled through Dylan as he watched Emily being catapulted off, falling into the wooden-railed side and finally landing with a hard thud on the dirt floor of the round training pen.

Chapter Eleven

Dylan didn't know whether to read Emily the riot act or kiss her. The truth was he wanted to do a little of both. Ginger was equally on edge; the mare had backed up against the wall of the round pen and was standing still, head hanging down slightly, ears up and motionless.

Dylan swiftly closed the distance between them and dropped down beside Emily, who was now up on her elbows, looking more peeved than in pain.

He watched her sit up farther and test her limbs, apparently finding nothing broken. His relief morphed into anger. "You could have been seriously hurt."

Emily accepted his hand and struggled to her feet. She dusted off the seat of her pants and tilted her head. "But I wasn't."

Dylan kept one eye on Ginger, who was still standing against the wall, watching them both. Figuring the best thing to do was put the horse to pasture, he went back to Ginger and took her by the lead. "If I'd had to tell your parents you'd been injured…"

Emily came toward them both. "No point in worrying about something that never happened." She boldly met his eyes. "I'd like to keep going."

Wishing he didn't want to pull Emily into his arms

so badly, Dylan said, "You really want to get back up on that horse?"

Emily removed the elastic band from her hair. "Halfway. No more," she declared smoothing the dark strands away from her face, putting her hair back into a ponytail. "Just to let Ginger know nothing's changed, that this is still going to be expected of her."

Dylan studied the flush in her pretty cheeks and the furrow of determination formed along the bridge of her nose. "You promise you'll do what I ask *and no more* this time?"

Emily took a step closer and said softly, "I promise."

So up she went.

This time, maybe because she felt she had made her point in tossing Emily to the ground, Ginger accepted the rider's weight against her side.

And this time, Dylan did not let go of either of them.

Half an hour later, they finished the training session on good terms. Emily praised Ginger warmly as she turned her out into the paddock and then faced him.

In that instant, Dylan noted the stain on the back of Emily's burgundy cotton shirt. It was right across her shoulders, beneath the caked-on paddock dirt, and he knew exactly what had caused it.

"Now you are really overreacting," Emily said, minutes later, after he had said goodbye to Andrew and escorted Emily into the ranch house.

Dylan did not think so. He tapped her in the vicinity of the spot. "Unless I miss my guess, that's dried blood."

Emily didn't look all that surprised.

Which meant that she knew she'd been scraped up at the time. She just hadn't wanted to stop what she was doing to tend to the skin injury.

His exasperation with her grew.

Emily shrugged. "So I'll go home and take care of it."

Feeling the pressure building at the front of his jeans, Dylan decided to dial it back a notch. He had to stop wondering if she missed touching him as much as he missed touching her. He had to stop thinking about kissing her again. Concentrate on the here and now, and the first aid obviously required.

He eyed her injury, knowing it bore further inspection. Sooner rather than later. Enough time had elapsed already, given the bacteria-laden setting. "How?" he countered. "There's no way you can reach that on your own."

Emily looked up at him. "You're offering to bandage me up?"

"Yes." Figuring enough time had been wasted, Dylan motioned for her to turn around.

Emily made a face but obliged.

Dylan plucked the collar of her shirt away from the nape of her neck and peered down. Best he could tell, the scrape was four-by-six inches or so. Smack-dab between the shoulder blades. "I'll take care of it for you," he offered dutifully, "but it's going to have to be thoroughly cleaned first, and the best way to do that is to hop in the shower."

Wincing, Emily adjusted her shirt. "You really are a pain."

He regarded her with barely masked impatience. "I could always call your family, let one of them take care of it." Then he wouldn't have to go through the torture of touching her without making love to her.

Emily continued to scowl at Dylan. "Don't you dare." She sighed loudly and gave him a vaguely accusing look. "And don't you dare tell them I got thrown, either. My parents would have a fit."

And maybe with good reason, Dylan thought, given the poor judgment Emily had shown earlier today.

Hand beneath her elbow, Dylan steered Emily toward the stairs. "I'll need the duffel bag in the trunk of my car...."

He remembered the extension of her closet. No one could ever say Emily did not come prepared. "Give me your keys and I'll get it for you."

Emily dug in her pocket for her keys. "Thanks."

Dylan tore his gaze from the enticing flatness of her abdomen. He did not need to be thinking about the snug fit of her jeans any more than he needed to be thinking about the clinging cotton of her shirt. "Towels are in the linen closet. Bathroom's—"

"I remember where it is, cowboy." Emily slapped the key in the palm of his hand, her fingers warm and silky against his skin.

Because, Dylan thought, she had been there before. Not just upstairs, but in the same place he'd like to have her now—*in his bed.*

He searched for some nonexistent gallantry and shot her a glance. "I'll get you some clean clothes." And while I'm at it, he promised vehemently, I'll do my best to obliterate these reckless thoughts before they land us both in hot water.

DYLAN WAS AS GOOD as his word, Emily noted. By the time she had washed the dirt off her face, he was back, her duffel bag in hand.

Unfortunately, the only things in there were another pair of jeans and two pairs of socks.

He lounged on the other side of the open bathroom door. "Problem?"

Yes, Emily thought in frustration, there were no extra

undies. But Dylan didn't need to know that, she told herself sternly. Pleasantly, she explained the portion of her predicament she wanted him to know about. "Apparently, all the extra riding I've been doing, coupled with my lack of time to get any laundry done, has left me without a clean shirt."

"Want to borrow one of mine?"

Emily tried not to think what it would feel like to be wrapped in his clothing. And not want to make love with him again. "If it's okay."

He nodded, as overtly casual as she. "No problem."

By the time Emily got out of the shower, a clean navy blue shirt was hanging on the inside of the bathroom door. He had managed to put the shirt there without opening the door more than an inch or actually coming in. Truth be told, Emily was a little disappointed about that.

She'd wanted to think she was so irresistible that a rogue like Dylan couldn't help but make a pass at her.

Instead, he was nowhere to be found.

Sighing her disappointment, while simultaneously applauding his good sense, Emily finished toweling off. Despite the warm soak, the scrape on her back was still raw and stinging. She debated over putting on the bra and panties she had just taken off, but they were as sweaty as the rest of her discarded clothing, and she couldn't bring herself to put them on again when she felt so nice and clean.

Frowning, she slipped on Dylan's shirt, rolled up the sleeves and buttoned all but the top closure. The soft navy cotton fabric voluminously cloaked her middle and floated down past her hips. Grimacing, she tugged her jeans on over her bare skin. Luckily, they were one of her oldest, softest pairs.

Telling herself that her lack of undies didn't matter—it

wasn't as if he hadn't seen her naked before, anyway—she put on her socks, bundled her filthy clothing together and headed down the stairs.

Dylan was in the kitchen, standing next to the counter, as he went through the items in the Last Chance Ranch first-aid kit. He turned, devilry gleaming in his eyes. "It's not too late," he drawled.

Yes, Emily thought wistfully, as her heart skipped a beat, it was.

It was way too late.

He winked as the corners of his lips turned up into a warm, teasing smile. "If you want to call a real medic…"

Emily rolled her eyes and set her bundled clothing on the floor. Working to still her racing pulse, she stepped toward him. He was right. Taking a light, carefree attitude was best. "Don't be silly. You can do this."

The look on his face said he knew that—he just didn't know if he should. Emily understood his hesitation. After the feed-store debacle, they'd agreed not to make love again, yet already the tension between them was sky-high. And she hadn't even partially disrobed yet.

Telling herself she could handle this, just the same way she handled him, Emily turned. Her back to him, she unbuttoned the second, third, fourth closures. Easing the fabric open, she simultaneously clutched it to her breasts and pushed it back and down so the shirt fell across her shoulders and lowered over her spine.

She winced as cool air assaulted the raw scrape that traversed the skin between her shoulder blades.

"You're lucky you didn't break anything." Dylan picked up a spray mix of antiseptic and anesthetic lotion.

Emily closed her eyes in anticipation of more pain, muttering, "I'm too stubborn to break anything."

"I hear that's what your father used to say when he was rodeoing," Dylan murmured.

She exhaled. "I guess a little recklessness runs in the family," she agreed.

"No doubt." His warm breath brushed over her skin.

Emily hitched in a breath as the liquid hit her scrape, stinging at first, then promptly cooling into blissful numbness.

Relieved, she let out another slow breath.

Looking into his eyes at that moment would have been dangerous, but she could feel Dylan's smile. It was as warm and soothing as his touch.

"Now for the antibiotic cream," he said.

Emily tensed despite herself. "That's got to hurt less, right?"

"You shouldn't feel much at all," Dylan predicted.

He was right. She felt no pain with the application of the thick white cream, but there was no way *not* to feel the gentle strokes of his fingers across her back. No way not to be aware of the pearling of her nipples beneath the shirt he'd lent her, and the curl of desire sweeping through her insides.

By the time he had finished, it was all she could do not to tremble, she wanted him so much.

Sounding a lot more unaffected than she felt, he closed the cap on the tube. "We could bandage this, if you want."

"I think it's probably better to leave it open to air, don't you think?"

Emily tried to adjust her shirt with her free hand, but found that to be an impossible task.

Again, Dylan stepped in to help, lifting the fabric away, easing it up and over her shoulders with gentlemanly care.

Embarrassed by her unprecedented vulnerability,

glad for the modest coverage, Emily pushed the buttons through the holes. Only when she was sufficiently cloaked did she turn back to face him once again.

Aware her whole body was still aching with the need to be touched and loved, Emily forced herself to put aside her yearning and look Dylan square in the eye. "Thank you," she managed.

Dylan rested a companionable hand on her shoulder. "You're welcome." He paused, smiling. "Thank *you* for helping out with Ginger."

"But not for taking too much upon ourselves, too fast?" Emily teased, wishing he would throw caution to the wind, forget their earlier promises and kiss her.

Dylan shook his head, in deadpan censure, then he dropped his hand to his side. "Had you not done that, you never would have been thrown," he reminded mildly.

Emily sighed. She guessed it wasn't going to happen. He wasn't going to make a move on her after all. And really, she schooled herself firmly, it was for the best.

She stepped back. "I'm aware of that." Unable to bear the intimacy in his eyes, coupled with the need welling inside her, Emily looked down at her clothing. "Unfortunately, I can't go back into town dressed like this." She screwed up her face comically. "Not without causing a lot of talk anyway."

He tapped her playfully on the nose. "And we certainly don't want that."

Emily wanted Dylan to pull her against him and kiss her, taking the decision out of her hands.

"You can use the washer and dryer, if you want." He stepped back. "I'll make myself scarce and give you your privacy."

Here it was, Emily thought, the opportunity to put the fierce yearning aside and keep to their agreement. And maybe she would have had he not seemed tempted, too. The daredevil inside her was back, stronger than ever.

She curled her hands over his biceps. "That's not what I want."

Dylan swallowed. "If I stay, you know what is likely to happen."

"And you think that'd be wrong for me?"

His eyes gleamed. He came closer, all lazy, swaggering male. "You're a McCabe. You're meant to be married to someone from a family just like yours."

And marriage, Emily knew, was not what Dylan wanted. He might have, of course, if he'd believed in happily-ever-afters. But he didn't.

And that meant she had a choice to make too that would require her to take a giant leap of faith.

She splayed her hands across Dylan's chest, her determination to succeed stronger than ever. "I know what everyone thinks. That I have to have what my family wants for me. That I can't be with any man without trying to change him, but that's just not true," she whispered, her growing feelings for him giving her courage. "I can be with you—without asking you to change—just like you won't ask me to change." She wound her arms about his neck and rose on tiptoe. "Let me prove it to you."

Dylan's jaw set. "I'm not the kind of guy you need, Emily. I never will be."

Emily ignored his quelling expression and instead focused on the pulse racing in his throat. "What I need is my freedom, Dylan," she stated stubbornly. "Just like you need yours."

Dylan's eyes shuttered to half-mast. Already, he was giving in. "Emily…"

Luxuriating in his surrender, she pressed a finger to his lips. "No promises, Dylan. No thinking about what tomorrow will bring. Just…this." She kissed him, sweetly, tenderly.

"You say that now," he protested against her mouth on a rough exhalation of breath.

Emily took both his hands in hers. "And I mean it." She stared deep into his eyes, promising, "We'll be together as long as it feels right, as long as I need a boyfriend to stave off Xavier and run interference between me and my family, and you need help with the mustangs." Her heart pounding, she drew a bolstering breath. "After that, we'll go back to each doing our own thing and go our separate ways. With no complications and no regrets. Just a few memories to keep us warm on cold winter nights."

Dylan studied her, still gripping her hands. "You're talking friends with benefits?"

Emily shrugged, unwilling to put even that much of a restriction on what it was they were agreeing to. Aware he was hard and male and strong in all the ways she had ever wanted, she whispered back, "Friends with *temporary* benefits, Dylan."

Looking as if she were everything he had ever wanted, too, Dylan smiled. He threaded his hands through her hair and brought her face up to his. Slowly, he lowered his lips, tilted his head to better accommodate the kiss. His eyes closed. "You drive a hard bargain, cowgirl. But one I feel compelled to accept." He kissed one corner of her lips, then the other.

"What can I say?" she whispered fiercely, pausing to deepen the kiss. "I want what I want…and what I want, Dylan, is you."

So much…

"Well, then," he answered in a deep, sexy voice that kindled her senses all the more, "let's make it happen."

He reached for the zipper on her jeans. As he drew it down, cool air assaulted her skin. The warmth of his palm followed, then his touch. She surged and writhed, surrendering her body, and then he was pressing her back against the counter, pushing her pants all the way off.

"Dylan," she moaned, her legs opening even wider. His hand slid between them, stroking the tender insides from knee to pelvis and back again. She was teetering on the edge…bursting with heat and sensation. "Dylan," she cried out, even more urgently.

His eyes dark with passion, he slid downward. Smiling at what he found, he teased her gently, "I like you without panties." And then before she could do so much as take a breath, his mouth was there, his fingers parting the delicate skin and sliding inside. Driving her crazy. Making her shake as more moisture flowed, until she quivered in ecstasy and nearly collapsed with the pleasure of it. Swells of almost unbearable sensation sweeping through her, she opened her eyes. "I wanted to wait for you."

"You will," he promised hoarsely. Rising, he opened her shirt, claimed the softness of her breasts. Admiration shimmering in his eyes, he stroked her nipples. Then he captured her skin in a kiss so hot and sweet and tender it had her shuddering all over even as she demanded more.

Not to be undone, she unbuttoned his shirt and pressed forward so her nipples rubbed against the work-honed muscles of his chest. The delicious friction made her groan. That, along with her subsequent kisses, made him hard. Really hard. So hard he did not protest when she finally tore her lips from his, eased down the zipper of his jeans and dispensed with his clothes from the waist down.

She was determined to make this as good for him as he had for her. She tempted…discovered…adored, until his legs were taut and his breath was rasping in his chest. He brought her upward, to sit up on the counter. He stepped between her legs with a resolve that had her surrendering all over again.

Together, as erotic moments passed, they looked their fill.

"I don't know how we got so lucky," Dylan rasped out, "but for once I'm not going to question it." And then he was kissing her again, shifting his strong hard body until it became part of hers, and she was lifting her hips and wrapping her legs around his waist, bringing him closer still.

Caught up in something too powerful and primal to fight, Emily took him into the warmth of her body, and then discovered their bodies were made for each other after all. Awash in sensation, she let sheer abandon overtake her. Their ragged breaths meshed as soulfully and completely as their hot, passionate kisses. And then it happened, just as he'd promised it would. He pressed into her as deeply as he could go and they were soaring, flying free. Boundaries dissolved in a wild, wanton pleasure unlike anything she had ever known.

Afterward, they clung together, breathing hard. And Emily told herself it was a very good thing she was *not* in love with Dylan or he with her. Because if that had been the case, they'd *both* be in a heap of trouble.

MORNING CAME FAR too soon, and with it a whole new host of problems. "Xavier Shillingsworth is back," Bobbie Sue Everett reported, shortly after the café opened.

Telling herself that nothing was going to alleviate the glow she felt, Emily continued whisking eggs. "How do you know that?"

Bobbie Sue frowned. "Because he just took the corner

booth and ordered one of everything on the menu, to be brought to him one dish at a time."

Emily sighed. "Or in other words, he intends to be here awhile."

"All morning, from the way he was talking."

Dylan—who'd been occupying a seat at the counter— ambled into the kitchen. Seeing him reminded Emily of the hot, passionate lovemaking of the night before and the fact that she could not ever recall being this happy or feeling this adored.

Dylan took up a proprietary post next to Emily, all lazy, swaggering male. "Want me to get rid of Shillingsworth?" he asked.

Emily shook her head. "He has as much right to be here as any other customer, and if he wants to pay me several hundred dollars for the privilege, so be it."

Dylan came closer and gently touched her cheek. "You know he just wants to make trouble."

Emily's heart warmed, still she cautioned, "You don't need to protect me."

Dylan grinned. "As you pointed out to me in the past, needing and wanting something are two different things. And since I am your, uh…"

"Pretend boyfriend?" Simone put in, from the other end of the griddle.

Emily blinked at the unexpected sarcasm.

"Hey." Simone held up a hand in her own defense. "I know I owe you a debt of gratitude for everything you've done for my son, Dylan. Since Andrew started doing community service at Last Chance Ranch, he really is turning around, attitudewise. But that doesn't mean I want to see Emily hurt. And games that get this complicated usually end up hurting someone."

"Well, it's not going to be either of us," Emily told her friend firmly, exasperated to find yet another person trying to watch out for her. She looked the tall handsome cowboy in the eye. "Dylan and I know where we stand."

The question was...would friends with temporary benefits be enough to make either of them happy, even for the short haul?

Fortunately, Emily had little time to think about it, as the café began to fill with cowboys looking for the day's bargain. Dylan went back to sit at the counter and keep an eye out for Shillingsworth. Emily and Simone manned the griddle and ovens, while Bobby Sue and Billy Ray Everett waited tables.

All would have gone smoothly, had it not been for the astonished scream, which reverberated through the Daybreak Café, a short time later.

Emily dropped what she was doing and rushed into the dining room. A female diner Emily had never seen before was standing, still screeching, and pointing at her plate. Aware that every head had turned toward the female diner, Emily raced forward. "What is it?"

"A cockroach!" the woman shrieked even louder. She pointed at her plate. "Right there!"

Sure enough, Emily noted in disgust, there was a dead three-inch cockroach, peeking out from beneath a half-eaten Western omelet that Emily had prepared herself. Horrified, she grabbed the plate. "I am so sorry."

"How could this have happened?" The woman threw down her napkin and bolted for the door, as if the hounds of hell were after her.

And so it went.

At seven-thirty, another patron Emily had never seen

before found a shard of broken glass in his bowl of oatmeal.

At eight-fifteen, a young man in a college T-shirt discovered what looked like a mouse tail inside a breakfast tortilla.

Through it all, Xavier sat in his booth, a fake look of concern on his face.

By then, Emily's brothers had all come in to the café. They were standing with Dylan, near the cash register.

"Normally, I'm against physical solutions to problems...." Holden said.

Jeb squared his hat on his head. "But some pranks just aren't funny."

Hank nodded grimly. "And a person needs to be shown the door."

"I agree." Dylan looked all three of Emily's brothers in the eye.

When had Dylan lost his outsider status and become one of them? Emily wondered in shock.

"Well, I don't." She forced herself to keep a low profile. "I object to the kid garnering even that much attention." She cast a look over her shoulder at the smugly observing teen. "Don't you guys get it? He wants to be the center of attention. He wants to be able to lodge a complaint that I refused to serve him."

"You have every right to do so," Jeb said.

"And if I do, he'll make a fuss and try to figure out a way to get it in the news. This isn't the kind of publicity that I want. Trust me, guys. Just ignore him and he'll eventually give up, pay his bill and leave."

All four men disagreed.

But for some reason Emily couldn't decipher, her three brothers looked to Dylan to decide. "It's whatever Emily wants," Dylan said finally.

Emily had very little time to regret her decision.

Because just then, the door opened, and an inspector from the health department walked in.

"ARE YOU OKAY?"

Emily looked at Dylan, glad he had remained with her during the day's upheaval, yet uncertain how to answer that. She shut the blinds and put the Closed sign on the door. Turning back to Dylan, she ran a hand through her hair. "Considering the Daybreak Café just got an eighty-three out of a possible one hundred points?" Renewed horror ran through her. "Dylan, I've never gotten less than a ninety-eight!"

Dylan followed her into the kitchen. "The inspector knows those incidents this morning were bogus."

It hadn't made a difference, though, Emily thought glumly. "He still had to come out and do his job. And give me demerits for the customer complaints, even though he couldn't find a single thing that would have substantiated the validity of the infractions." Feeling weary to her soul, Emily sat down on a stainless-steel kitchen prep stool. She buried her face in her hands.

Dylan rested a compassionate hand on her shoulder. "If it's any consolation, your brothers and I still want to take Shillingsworth out behind the barn."

Emily rolled her eyes. "McCabes don't do violence on others and you know it. It doesn't matter what the situation is, there is always a civil way to resolve it."

His expression serious, Dylan pulled up a stool and faced her. "And a not so civil way," he said bluntly.

Emily smiled. "You certainly inspired uncivil notions in me last night," she murmured, the feel of his knee pressed against hers, reminding her of the unbridled pleasure they had discovered.

His eyes crinkled at the corners. "Same here...but we digress."

Emily had never had a boyfriend so willing to take on her problems. "So we do."

"It seems to me I heard tales of your dad dueling in the streets with that movie star Beauregard Chamberlain over your mother."

"That was years ago, and he just did that to get my mother's attention. It's why she married my dad. Or so the legend goes."

Their eyes locked, held. A feeling of peace stole over her.

"I could challenge him...."

Emily caught the humor in his glance. "I don't think so."

"So what next?" Dylan asked eventually.

Emily traced the shape of his hand. "What do I want to happen? Or what do I think will happen?"

He caught her palm in his. "The latter."

Emily relaxed into the comforting warmth of his grip. "I imagine my parents—" she winced as the sound of voices could be heard outside the back door "—will have gotten the news and be stopping by."

Seconds later, Shane and Greta walked into the café kitchen, just as Emily had figured. Behind them was an entire contingent of McCabes. Brothers, sisters-in-laws, aunts, uncles, cousins. Everyone, it seemed, who had been in the vicinity and was remotely available had joined the force.

Emily's aunt Claire, a noted lawyer, stepped forward. "You may not be able to sue yet, but you can certainly send a formal cease-and-desist letter...."

Kevin McCabe, from the sheriff's department, advised, "I say we start an investigation."

And that, Emily found, was just the beginning of the free-flowing support from her family and friends. Everyone had an idea. Everyone was willing to help.

Everyone except, it turned out, the person she most wanted at her side.

Chapter Twelve

Several hours later, Emily found Dylan right where she expected him to be—on his ranch. For once though, he was laboring indoors. "Why did you leave?" she asked quietly, her emotions in turmoil as he ushered her inside his ranch office.

Looking handsome as could be in a blue chambray work shirt and jeans, he sat behind his oversize oak desk and squinted at the computer screen. "It was a McCabe family caucus. I'm not a McCabe."

Emily edged closer, her heartbeat accelerating as she took in the familiar fragrance of sandalwood and spice. "You were welcome to stay."

"I thought it was better, under the circumstances, if I didn't."

Emily knew her family in its entirety could be overwhelming. They seemed that way to her sometimes. However, she still wanted Dylan to be a part of her life. And her extended relatives were a huge part of that.

He pushed Print and, rocking back in his chair, watched the invoices appear in the tray. "What did you come up with?"

Emily leaned against the corner of his desk. She liked the intimacy of being here with him like this. "My uncle is starting an investigation into who the customers actually were…where they came from. Apparently, after they made the calls to the health department—which were from disposable cell phones—the accusers vanished into thin air."

Dylan reached past her for a stack of preaddressed envelopes bearing the Last Chance Ranch logo. "Which makes you think they were part of the scam?"

Emily studied the movements of his large, capable hands, wondering how he could be so strong and yet so tender, too. "Beau thinks they may have been professional actors. He's using his connections to check with the talent agencies and theater troupes around the state." She watched Dylan match the invoices to envelopes. "Hopefully, they'll find something soon. Unfortunately, Xavier has already tried to get it in the local news."

He shifted his gaze to her face. "Any takers?"

"Not so far." Emily twisted her lips in consternation. "Everyone smells a setup."

Dylan added stamps. "As do I," he said with a frown.

Restless, she stood and shoved her hands in the back pockets of her jeans. "All my regular customers are pretty enraged. The phone has been ringing off the hook."

Dylan dropped the envelopes in the out basket. He switched off his computer and stood. "Is that why you came out here? To get away?"

And be with you.

But not sure how that revelation would go over, Emily swallowed.

"And help train the mustangs," she said, wary of driving Dylan away with her sudden neediness. Because that was new, too. This wanting to be with a man more than anything else in the world.

She pushed on, "I know my family can be overwhelming at times…especially when they're all together…."

His expression became inscrutable. "I told you before, I don't do family drama," he said.

Emily remembered but that explanation gave her only partial relief. Maybe because she was starting to want so much more.

But that hadn't been their agreement she reminded herself. Their agreement had been to be together as long as it was good, without trying to change each other. To live and let live…the way each had become accustomed to doing.

"Right. Anyway…" Emily moved closer. "We now know what Xavier meant when he said he was going to make me pay. The question is…" She paused to give her words weight. "What is he going to try and do to you?"

Dylan shrugged. "Nothing much he can do. Financially, I'm in good shape. And I doubt anything he would have to say about my horse-whispering abilities would hold up under scrutiny."

Emily relaxed. "True. All potential customers would have to do is look at the mustangs, and how far they have come in just ten days, to know how talented you are."

Dylan reached past her to turn off the desk lamp. "I also have a lot of current and former clients who will vouch for me."

The near contact sent a thrill shimmering through her. Emily dropped her hands and stepped back. "I still think he's going to try and hurt you, the way he hurt me today."

"And I think we shouldn't worry about it. Not tonight, anyway." Dylan slid a hand beneath her elbow and steered her out the door, toward the paddock where the mustangs were quartered. He grinned. "Not when your three pals are waiting to see you."

To Emily's delight, they spent the next few hours working with all three horses. Dylan still would not let

Emily get all the way up in the saddle with Ginger—he wanted the horse to get used to Emily's presence at her side first. So they worked out, this time in complete accordance with Dylan's wishes. Then they fed and watered the mustangs, before heading to the ranch house.

"You staying for dinner?" Dylan asked Emily casually as they crossed the threshold.

Her heartbeat accelerated. "You inviting me?" She worked to keep her voice casual.

Dylan nodded, matter-of-fact. "We could go out. My treat this time."

Emily groaned at the thought. "Please don't make me go back to town, not tonight. I don't want to run into anyone who wants to talk about the sabotage, and I sure as heck don't want to look at the Cowtown Diner from my apartment."

"Then here on the ranch, it is. Got anything to change into?"

Emily had made sure to replenish the "wardrobe" in the trunk of her car. Glad things had returned to normal between them, she winked and picked up the pace. "Several things, as a matter of fact."

An hour later, both of them had showered and changed into fresh clothes. Dylan stood at the stove, searing, in a cast-iron skillet, two rib eye steaks he'd pulled from the freezer.

Realizing this was how "friends with benefits" operated, Emily found a package of mixed veggies to steam in the microwave, and a crusty loaf of bread. Cold bottles of beer and hunks of white cheddar completed the menu.

"That looks delicious," she said, as the two of them set their meal on his kitchen table.

Dylan got out the steak sauce. "I'm good at everything I do. Or hadn't you noticed?"

Emily added napkins. "Modest, too."

"Hey." He made no effort to stifle a cheeky grin. "It ain't braggin' if you've done it."

Emily gave him an amused once-over. "Spoken like a true Texan," she drawled right back.

His gaze roved her V-necked T and jeans, before returning to her face and hair. "You look good in here." His gaze lingered on her lips.

Emily tingled in every place his eyes had touched, and some places they hadn't. "Right at home, hmm?"

He held out her chair. "Like you belong." He paused, hand on the top rung, then added, more specifically, "On a ranch—not in an apartment in town."

Emily's hopes lifted and fell in short order. Again, she shook it off. So Dylan hadn't said what she'd initially thought he had meant. So what? He was still paying her a compliment.

She patted his arm amiably in return. "Those steaks look good." She turned away. "Let's eat."

Dylan caught her by the waist and brought her back against him. While her pulse raced, he gently nipped her ear, lifted the veil of her hair and kissed her throat. "And after that," he whispered sexily, "I've got plans for us, too...."

DYLAN WAS AS GOOD as his word.

Unfortunately, the bedside alarm went off at three-thirty.

Emily groaned as it continued to blare in her ears. Normally, she didn't mind getting up and going to the café. Cooking in the early morning to an appreciative crowd was one of her very favorite things.

But then, she thought, stretching languidly, most days she hadn't been up most of the night making love. Most nights she hadn't fallen asleep wrapped in Dylan's warm, strong arms.

He reached over and shut off the sound of country radio. With a moan that echoed her own reluctance, he nuzzled her hair affectionately. "Tell me you heard that."

Emily groaned again. "I heard it." Her voice was muffled against the satiny skin of his shoulder.

He chuckled, kissing her again. "Tell me you're getting up."

Emily opened her eyes and slowly sat up. "Against my will...I am." She reached over to take his hand. "Thanks for a great night," she said softly, knowing she had never felt so appreciated and well loved.

He kissed her knuckles tenderly. "Ditto."

They looked at each other in companionable silence.

Emily had no idea what was on his mind, but there were many things on hers, none of which were permissible to say under their current arrangement.

Things like...*I know what we agreed upon but I might be falling in love with you, anyway.*

Or...*I wish I never had to leave, that we never had to be apart again.*

And even...*How would you feel if we changed the rules...just a little bit?*

But Emily couldn't say any of that because she was a McCabe and she had given her word that her fling with Dylan was casual and temporary. And like it or not, she had to honor that commitment as surely as she would have honored any other that she made.

So she reached over and turned on the bedside lamp.

Through sheer force of will, she tossed back the covers—and saw Dylan's gaze drift hotly over everything that wasn't covered by eyelet lace camisole and tap pants, as well as everything that was.

Emily felt a flashpoint of desire that resonated deep within her heart. "If I don't get up now," she told him, resisting the magnetic pull between them, "we both know what will happen." The same thing that had happened last night…and the time before that…

Regret that she was leaving glimmered briefly in his eyes. Fortunately for them both, he too was a realist.

Dylan threw back his covers and got up. "You're absolutely right about that," he agreed gruffly.

For once in her life, Emily found herself wishing she weren't quite so independent and strong-willed. She headed for her clothes, tossing the casual words over her shoulder. "So…I'm out of here as soon as I'm dressed."

Dylan was right behind her. He clamped a possessive hand on her shoulder. "I'll go to town with you."

That was a surprise, since the diner wouldn't be open for several more hours. Emily turned, curious. "Assigning yourself my protector?"

Dylan shrugged. "Something like that." He paused. "Do you mind?"

Emily shook her head. "Not at all."

For Emily and Dylan, the next few days were blissfully calm and happy. The two of them worked with the mustangs every afternoon, ate dinner together each night and then made love. Dylan drove into town with Emily in the mornings and had breakfast with her before heading back to the ranch to work.

Their only worry was another onslaught from their teenage nemesis. Fortunately, the "McCabe posse" was having some success linking the incidents in the café to Emily's competitor, and they hoped to soon have enough proof to be able to simultaneously pursue legal action and clear her name with the health department authorities.

"Well, I for one, am glad to see Shillingsworth get what he had coming to him today," Simone said Thursday afternoon, when the Daybreak Café had finally closed and all that was left was the cleanup.

Bobbie Sue and Billy Ray brought in filled bins of dirty dishes and silverware and began loading them into the big commercial dishwasher. "The Cowtown Diner didn't have a single customer today, except for a few tourists who wandered in at midday," Bobbie Sue said.

Billy Ray added, "And it's been that way for the last three days."

Andrew walked in from school, backpack slung over his shoulder. "Shillingsworth has started laying off staff. Half my friends who got jobs there got let go yesterday, due to lack of business."

The past couple of weeks had been so tumultuous, in so many ways. Emily didn't want to take anything for granted. She grimaced. "It could still pick up."

Everyone else exchanged looks. "I don't think so," they all said finally, in unison.

"People have wised up," Simone declared. "It doesn't matter how young or inexperienced or even rich he is. They know who and what he is. They're not going to support his kind of tactics."

"Yeah," Andrew said, helping himself to a leftover piece of pie and a glass of milk. "There are too many good guys around here, like Dylan, for anyone to put up with someone that cutthroat and mean-spirited."

Emily breathed a sigh of relief. "I just wish it hadn't happened." The uneven business had wreaked havoc with her books.

Which was why she had finally allowed Jeb to bring his friend over to meet her.

DYLAN HAD JUST FINISHED paying the farrier when Xavier walked into the stable.

"Falling down on the job, aren't you, cowboy?" Shillingsworth began.

Not sure whether to feel sorry for him or just loathe him completely, Dylan took a firm grip on the kid's arm and propelled him away from the quartered mustangs, who had just had their feet trimmed and their first set of shoes put on.

Left to the wild, and their own devices, they would not have needed protection on their tender feet, since wild horses moved from place to place only when necessary. But now that they were becoming domesticated, the horses would be expected to cover greater distances, often on hard ground. Hence, protecting their hooves was essential.

Dylan continued pushing Shillingsworth out the door. "I'm sure you have better things to do with your time than visit me."

"You're right about that." The kid regarded him with derision. "But I didn't want to let the opportunity go by to clue you in on your lady friend."

"This isn't high school," Dylan announced flatly.

"Meaning what?" Xavier taunted. "Because you and Emily are over twenty, you both have an open relationship? Because if that's the case it would certainly explain why she's sitting in the café, getting cozy with that guy her brother took over to meet her a little while ago."

Another fix-up engineered by Emily's brothers? Dylan knew there were supposed to have been three. Only two had happened thus far. Still, he would have expected Emily to refuse the opportunity, now that he and she were so involved.

"Thanks for your concern," Dylan told Shillingsworth

drily, calmly escorting him all the way to his Corvette. "But Emily and I have an understanding."

The restaurateur's snide expression remained unaltered. "That covers her cheating on you?"

Dylan opened the door with his free hand and shoved the spoiled teen behind the wheel.

It wasn't cheating… It probably wasn't anything. There was no reason for him to feel this jealous and threatened. "Goodbye, Xavier."

He sneered. "I'm still going to get even with you, you know."

Dylan knew the kid would *try*. In reality, there was very little he could do. He leaned over and offered parting advice with as much kindness as he could muster. "One day soon you're going to figure out this is not the way to win friends and influence people in Laramie, Texas."

"And one of these days, you're going to have to leave this all behind and go back where you came from, too!" Shillingsworth scoffed.

He started the engine and spun the car around. Deliberately driving over the lawn around the ranch house, he roared off in a plume of dust.

Telling himself he had nothing to worry about, Dylan went back to work. He expected Emily to show up the same time Andrew did, around three-thirty. Instead, Simone dropped her son off.

As had been the case all this week, Andrew showed up dressed in rugged Western clothing, ready to work. "What do you want me to do first, boss?" He squared his hat on his head. Anticipating the usual answer, he looked around for the wheelbarrow and shovel.

Dylan lifted a staying hand. "I've already mucked out the stalls."

Andrew raised his brow in surprise. And for good reason, Dylan noted, since that was usually his first job of the day. "It's time you learned how to lead and saddle a horse," he explained.

Excitement shone in Andrew's eyes. "Ginger?"

Not quite. "You can learn on my horse, Hercules. For now, Emily is the only one besides me who can help with Ginger."

Andrew grinned and followed Dylan into the stable with all the excited swagger of a kid heading to his first rodeo. "Miss Emily is really good with the mustangs, isn't she?"

Dylan nodded. Funny, how much he enjoyed working with this kid. He had never figured he would be a mentor. But there was no doubt about it—he was making strides with the once-recalcitrant kid. "You're right about that." He smiled. "Emily's got the McCabe gift with horses."

"Speaking of Miss Emily... She tried to get you on the phone but you didn't answer, so she asked me to tell you she would be pretty late getting here today. She's talking with this friend of her brother's."

So what Shillingsworth had said was true. Dylan handed Andrew the bridle and bit, and asked casually, "At the café?"

"They started there," Andrew confirmed, "but then went up to her apartment 'cause they needed privacy. Anyway, she'll be here later. When she's done with whatever she and the other guy are doing."

"Thanks for the info." Dylan picked up the blanket and saddle. He continued down to Hercules's berth, sure the meeting was innocent enough. It was the fact it was happening at all that bothered him. Had Shillingsworth been right? Did he have cause to worry?

Chapter Thirteen

Emily walked into the stable and stopped in her tracks. Dylan was standing next to the mustang, a dandy brush in hand. "You're grooming Ginger?" This was a first as far as she knew.

"About to." Dylan flashed her a look that was all business. "Want to help?"

"Sure," she said with a shrug, checking her need to greet Dylan with a long, heartstopping kiss. His body language and curt tone made it painfully clear that he was not in the mood for romance.

Her glance averted, Emily entered the stall and rubbed the mustang's face and neck. "Hello, pretty girl," she murmured softly. "Did you miss me? I missed you today."

Dylan took the left side of the horse. "I think this is happiest I've seen Ginger look all day."

Blissfully aware how content she felt whenever they were together, too, Emily plucked a rubber currycomb from the bucket of tools. "Surely you exaggerate," she said dryly. "I know Ginger adores you."

"And how do you figure that?" Dylan lifted his brow.

"Because you're good in the saddle, too." Abruptly aware of the double entendre, Emily blushed. "Er, corral. Okay…" She kept on combing and gave him a humorous glance that begged for mercy. "I'm going to stop now."

Because none of this is coming out right. And because, although I can't quite say why, I have the feeling something is a little off between us, unlike the last time we were together.

Adding to her worry, Dylan looked disconcerted, too.

Like he wasn't sure what to make of the shifts in their relationship, either. First they were strangers, then adversaries who'd joined forces to ward off her matchmaking parents—and an unwelcome suitor—and now finally temporary lovers who'd agreed they weren't destined to be anything serious.

"I get what you mean," he resumed his usual easygoing manner. "And you're correct. Horses respond to trainers who are in control of their emotions."

And Dylan was that, all right, Emily thought ruefully to herself. The only time he let go of his emotional armor at all was when they were in bed.

Once they were out of each other's arms, it was business as usual. A friendship based on a shared love of horses and ranch life and good, Texas-style food.

But even that was not guaranteed to last, she knew.

Dylan had been clear on that. And she had concurred.

Deep down, she wished she had never made the pact with Dylan to keep things casual. But she was leery of changing anything and have the lonesome cowboy end up feeling trapped.

So she would do as promised and make it easy on him when the time came… She just hoped that wasn't for a good long while. Years, even…

Using short, straight strokes, they brushed the mud from Ginger's coat. Dylan seemed as lost in thought as she.

"You're awfully quiet," Emily said eventually, wishing he would confide in her more. Instead, she felt like there was still so much she did not know. Might never know if it were left up to him.

Dylan rubbed a damp sponge over Ginger's face. "It's been a long day."

Emily stood on the other side of the horse and finished working the knots out of Ginger's mane. She moved so she could see Dylan's face. His expression was as maddeningly reserved as ever. Finally, she guessed, "Are you ticked off at me for not making the training session this afternoon?"

"No." Dylan used a massage pad over the mare's sleek neck muscles. "I understand you had other stuff to do."

Emily worked on the knots in the tail. "I did." She fell silent once again, thinking.

"Now who's exceptionally quiet?" Dylan teased. He gathered up the tools, gave Ginger a final pat and stepped out.

Realizing they had probably done enough for the first session, Emily praised Ginger softly and stepped out of the stall, too. She joined Dylan in the cement-floored aisle and fell into step beside him. "Sorry. I was thinking about my meeting with Randall Schwartz, the guy who sells prepared foods to restaurants. He's a friend of Jeb's."

Dylan led the way into the tack room. He deposited the tools on a shelf bearing Ginger's name. In a corner, there was a sink. "I thought you weren't interested in that." He gestured for her to go first.

Emily pumped soap onto her hands. "I wasn't... I'm not." The aroma of juniper and mint filled the air. She lathered, rinsed and shook off the excess moisture.

Dylan stepped in for his turn. His shoulder nudged hers slightly in the process. He turned, his face close to hers. "But?"

Emily couldn't help but note how strong and large his

hands were. She swallowed, pushing away the memory of his gentle, capable touch. "I'm beginning to think I may have to consider cutting a few corners."

They walked out of the stable.

Realizing she needed a sounding board, and she wanted it to be Dylan, Emily continued matter-of-factly, "My business is in trouble."

Dylan escorted her across the yard. "Because of the competition?"

Emily nodded and sat down on one of the rough-hewn chairs on his porch. "I went over my books this afternoon, after closing. Because of everything that has happened the last few weeks…" she sighed, recalling, "First—no customers. Add to that, the financial loss I took on all those specials I offered to draw patrons back in."

Misery engulfed her as she shook her head. "This month is so far in the red that it's wiped out my entire profit for the year to date." She swallowed, loath to admit, "I'm going to have to dip into my personal savings to make payroll and pay the suppliers next week."

To Emily's relief, Dylan did not judge her fiscal recklessness. "Which is where Randall Schwartz comes in."

She nodded. "Randall showed me how I could cut costs if I used wholesale pre-made biscuits, muffins and desserts instead of making them up fresh every day. He has a full line of precooked meats, veggies and casseroles, too."

"But…?"

"We're back to my original problem. I don't want to sacrifice quality. At all. Ever. 'Going microwave' guarantees the demise of any restaurant. Proof of that is in any of the many once-popular chains that went bellyup, or are still around but are definitely third or fourth tier now."

Dylan lounged against the porch railing, listening, his hands braced on either side of him.

In the background was a spectacular April sunset, the blue sky framed by a horizon streaked with shades of pink, red and gold. "Well, then, you don't want to do that," he said, understandingly.

"I absolutely do not want to do that." Emily vaulted to her feet again, too restless to stay in one place for long. She paced back and forth, the sound of her boot heels echoing on the wood-plank surface. Whirling around, she threw up her arms in frustration. "The whole point of coming to the café is to get hot, home-cooked food when you're too tired or busy to prepare it yourself."

Dylan settled more patiently on his perch and sent her an admiring glance. "That concept has worked well for you so far."

Emily trod closer. "The tough thing is, I'm going to have to keep offering some sort of daily special if I want to keep the customers coming in the door."

Dylan's eyes narrowed. "You've spoiled them?" he guessed.

Emily rubbed the tense muscles at the base of her neck. "You know how it is. Everybody loves a bargain...."

Dylan motioned for her to turn around and he took up the kneading for her.

She closed her eyes and let herself relax into his soothing touch. Eyes still closed luxuriantly, she let out a long breath. "And I get that it will bring people in the door." She pressed her lips together in stubborn determination. "Which is something I need to keep doing, whether the Cowtown Diner survives the recent downturn in their business or not."

Needing to look into Dylan's eyes again, Emily swung around. She placed her hands flat on his chest before pulling away once again. "The question is, how do I afford to do it?" she mused.

The subtle lift of an eyebrow. "No answers?"

Emily grimaced in frustration. "Not a one. Not tonight anyway!" Restless again, she began to pace.

After a moment, Dylan left his perch and sauntered slowly toward her. He looked as if he wanted to distract her with a kiss. "I'm sure you will work it out," he soothed.

Emily's heart began to race. "I'm sure I will, too, in time."

Not sure she could do this tonight, have a no-strings-romp in Dylan's bed without falling head over heels in love with him—and wanting a lot more than a temporary fling out of the bargain—Emily forced herself to ease away.

Ignoring the flash of disappointment on his face, Emily kept the focus on her business difficulties. "Certainly there a lot of people chomping at the bit to help me."

"Like your parents."

"And my brothers, and their friends." She hesitated. "Remember Aaron Markham, the accountant slash tax lawyer I met a couple weeks ago?"

Dylan nodded, his eyes guarded.

"Well, he's called several times, wanting to meet with me again. He's sure he can help. Even Fred Collier, the food writer has called me back, wanting to know if 'anything has changed' that would give him reason to come back to the café again, anytime soon...."

Dylan's glance narrowed. "Sounds like he wants a date."

Was Dylan jealous at the thought of her spending time with another guy—someone who had the seal of approval from her brothers and was in the market for marriage? Or was Dylan just as perceptive as ever?

Emily shrugged, her uncertainty increasing. "Maybe. I didn't really get that vibe from Fred the day we met, but sometimes, after the fact, you begin to think…hey, maybe I should have gone after that or pursued someone a little more aggressively."

Or eschewed immediate pleasure and held out for more than just a temporary fling…

But she hadn't.

And Emily couldn't really say she regretted having made love with Dylan, even if she was not going to get a forever commitment out of him…

Because to have not ever felt what she'd felt in his arms would have been a lot sadder than having to one day say goodbye.

Or that was what she kept telling herself.

She snapped out of her reverie when she realized Dylan was giving her a really odd look.

As if he had figured out at least part of what she was thinking. The part of her that wanted to throw a lasso around him and put a wedding band on his finger.

Emily struggled to contain the self-conscious warmth moving into her face. She really had to get a grip. "You know what I mean."

Dylan nodded. Determination tightened every strong, tall part of him, and he inched closer. "I know you're a fine-looking woman," he murmured, wrapping his arms around her waist.

Emily caught her breath as the softness of her body slammed into the hardness of his. She splayed her hands across his chest, felt the beat of his heart. "And you're a fine-looking man. But it takes more than looks to make a match, Dylan."

"I agree." His low voice rumbled in her ear. "It takes this." He bent his head to hers. The kiss was electric and all-enveloping. Her body responded like tinder to a flame, and she kissed him with growing passion. Knowing she was caught up in something too powerful to fight, shivers of unbearable sensation swept through her.

"And this," Emily told him. She pressed into him, her breasts lodged against the solid warmth of his chest, her tummy cradling the hardness of his sex. She kissed him back, again and again, melting against him in complete surrender. Ready to take the pleasure where and when she could, she let her own desires…for marriage, for family…go.

Maybe they didn't want the same things out of life, Emily reasoned. Maybe they never would. But they still had the here and now. And heaven knew, a love affair this passionate was not likely to occur again. Not in her lifetime.

Dylan threaded his hands through her hair. "I want to go upstairs and make love to you all night long," he whispered. Tilting her face up to his, he captured her lips in one long, sweet and tender kiss.

It was the kind of kiss that made her feel loved. That made her feel wanted. That made her feel she was already his, and vice versa.

A thrill soared through Emily.

His hands shifted down her spine, fitting her against him. His lips found the soft, sensitive spot behind her ear. He drew back to look into her eyes. "Tell me you want the same thing."

Another shiver went through her.

Emily laced both hands around his powerful shoulders. She steadied herself even as her lips, still damp from his kisses, curved upward. "That sounds like a proposition I can handle."

"It's more than a proposition." Dylan bent, laced an arm behind her knees and swung her up into his arms. Holding her tightly to his chest, he carried her inside. His eyes danced with an affectionate light. "It's a promise of all the wonderful things to come."

They made it as far as the stairs before he had to stop and kiss her again. One thing led to another, and by the time they'd finished dallying, they'd both lost their boots. And jeans. Their shirts came off midway up the stairs, and their socks were strewn in the hall.

By the time they reached his bed, they were laughing, and ready for more. "I knew I'd get these off eventually," he teased, relieving her of her bra and panties.

"I'm not the only one who is going to be naked." Emily divested Dylan of his boxer briefs.

Erotic moments passed as they each looked their fill.

"You are so beautiful," he whispered.

And aroused, she thought as she regarded him in the shadowy light of dusk. "You're pretty incredible, too," Emily said, taut and aching to be touched.

"So where do you want to start?" Dylan asked, trailing a hand down her hip. He kissed her shoulder, moved to her collarbone, then the tip of her breast.

Emily knew there was no reason to rush, no need to deny the feelings swirling around in her heart, no reason to worry about tomorrow. The last of her inhibitions melted away; she was in over her head and sinking fast. She reached for him wantonly and drew him toward the bed. "Wherever you want as long as we do everything you want and then some."

"Sounds like a plan," he rasped playfully, tumbling her down onto the sheets.

The next thing she knew they were lying on their sides. Emily closed her eyes as he kissed her lazily and worked his way up her thighs. His palms found her as her hands found him. They kissed and caressed until their whole bodies were melting against each other in boneless pleasure.

"Now," she murmured.

He shifted so she was beneath him.

Then slid lower still.

This wasn't what she meant…but it turned out to be exactly what she needed.

Emily went catapulting over the edge.

Dylan slid between her thighs and surged against her. Emily moaned in response. She wrapped her arms around him and brought her legs up so they were locked around his waist.

Dylan wanted to pretend the two of them weren't meant to be together, long-term, that this closeness would suffice. But he knew it wasn't true, that the promises they had made to each other, to let go and move on when the time was right, were vows they were not going to be able to keep.

Maybe she didn't love him, maybe she never would, but when they were together like this it felt as if they belonged together. And in this instance, Dylan knew, belonging together was enough.

It was late morning, when Emily finally awakened to see Dylan stroll into the bedroom, tray in hand. She struggled to a sitting position, unable to help but think how good it felt to be together like this.

Dylan winked as their eyes met. "Since you have the day off…"

Emily moved her eyebrows teasingly in return, murmuring, "Thank heavens for small miracles." And it did seem like a miracle to be here with Dylan, at his ranch, after a wonderfully exciting and satisfying night of love-making. *And* have him bring her breakfast in bed! How had she gotten so lucky? Emily wasn't used to getting what she wanted in the romance department.

Usually, it was anything but.

And that made her uncertain…despite telling herself that given all that had happened recently, she had no reason to be.

Dylan waited for her to adjust the pillows behind her, then set the tray across her lap. "Are you going to be able to hang out here with me today?"

Emily smiled. "I was thinking I could help you with the horses. Maybe bring my mare Maisy over, and have Hercules, you and me all go for a ride."

"Sounds good. After you ride Ginger, that is."

Emily paused. "*Really* ride her?"

"I've worked with her a little more. I think she's ready for it now. The question is, are you?"

Was he kidding? "Wait and see."

An hour later, Emily was out in the round pen. Dylan brought Ginger in on a lead.

They started the session the way they always did, using the long cloth line to drive Ginger away. Emily constantly moved into Ginger's space, pressuring her at the flanks, gently yet firmly herding her forward.

Finally, when Ginger's head was level, her body nice and relaxed, Emily turned ninety degrees, offering her shoulder. She kept her head down, her body relaxed. As always, Ginger turned and came back toward Emily. She kept walking, quietly praising Ginger all the while.

The mare came closer still.

Lowered her head, bowed to Emily in respect.

Dylan, watching from the center of the paddock, walked forward to hold her by the bridle. "I'll attach the reins. You put on the saddle."

Working like a well-practiced team, they readied the mustang. And this time, when Emily stepped up into the saddle, Ginger didn't only accept Emily's weight, she seemed to welcome it. She moved cautiously at first, then more and more boldly, until she was trotting around the pen.

From there, they went to a pasture, where a nice trot turned into a canter and then a full-fledged gallop around the perimeter.

When they had finished, Emily couldn't stop grinning.

"Congratulations on a job well done." Dylan gave her a high five. "We're well on our way to training her."

Emily beamed. "My family has got to see this!"

The minute the words were out, Emily knew she had made a mistake. Dylan didn't do family drama. Or meetings. Did that also mean he didn't do family parties? To her relief, whatever reservations he had quickly faded. "Of course your dad is going to want to see this," he said.

"My mom, too," Emily added, serious. "You can't really invite one without the other."

There was a brief hesitation, then Dylan gestured magnanimously. "Whenever you want," he said with a wide smile.

Taking this for the good sign it was, Emily said, "Tonight?"

Another hesitation, although briefer. Dylan nodded. "Call them right now."

Emily bounded off. "I will."

No sooner had Emily gotten off the phone with her parents than the phone rang again.

It was Simone. "You are not going to believe what is happening in Laramie right now!"

SHORT MINUTES LATER, Dylan and Emily stood side by side at her apartment window, watching the gas, electric and water be cut off to the site.

Xavier Shillingsworth was nowhere in sight during all this, and was still a no-show when the enormous crane moved forward to pick up the Cowtown Diner and lift it over onto the same double-wide tractor-trailer truck it had arrived on.

By late Sunday afternoon, the burnished bronze building was only a memory.

Emily turned to Dylan, "I can't believe they are moving out lock, stock and barrel, just like that."

Dylan couldn't, either. And yet, with the ongoing investigation closing in and legal action pending... "Customers here weren't going to go back. It was probably a good business decision to move the franchise restaurant to Big Springs."

Emily squinted. "I'm not sure he'll have any better luck there."

Dylan shrugged. "You never know. Shillingsworth might have learned something from all this."

Emily frowned. "One could hope."

"So about that little get-together at my ranch this evening..." Dylan interjected.

Emily's eyes lit up. "Seven o'clock okay? It shouldn't take long. All I'm going to do is give Ginger a few turns around the round pen for them."

Dylan found her enthusiasm contagious. "Take as long as you want. You deserve to show off for them."

She searched his face. "Would it be all right if I invited my brothers, too?"

Dylan knew if he was going to be part of Emily's life, he would have to get used to having her family around, too.

"The more, the merrier," he said.

Chapter Fourteen

"Looks like we're early," Shane McCabe said.

A good half hour early, Dylan noted, which wouldn't usually have been a problem. He could have easily entertained the horse rancher and his lovely wife, shown them around his property and had a good time doing it.

But that was before he'd begun sleeping with their only daughter.

Recalling his last conversation with Emily's dad, who had warned Dylan not to toy with Emily's feelings, Dylan ushered the couple inside his ranch house.

"Where should we put these?" Greta asked, indicating the four catering-size foil containers bearing her restaurant name.

Dylan relieved Greta of her burden and led the way.

What had started out as a brief horse-training demonstration for Emily's parents had turned into a potluck gathering for her entire family.

Dylan had no experience hosting a crowd. He usually went into town to socialize. He hoped he had enough plates and silverware. Or that someone had thought to bring disposable dinnerware. "I think the best place is the kitchen."

"I can put these in the oven for you, if you like," Greta offered.

There was a lot of Emily in her mom, and vice versa. Dylan smiled. "That'd be great. Thanks."

"So have you given any thought to the offer I made you?" Shane asked.

"I'm honored that you asked me to join forces with you in a nonprofit venture," he replied.

"But you're turning me down," Shane said with disappointment.

"I'd like to continue to train mustangs for you. I prefer to do it as an independent contractor."

Shane pressed, "We could do a lot of good if we founded a mustang sanctuary. We could take any wild horses that ranchers rounded up, train them and see they went to good homes."

"We can do that now without legally joining forces."

Shane studied Dylan for a long moment, and an awkward silence filled the room.

Greta moved to the window. "I think I heard another car," she said, slipping out.

"Is this because of my daughter?" Shane asked, upfront as ever.

As long as they were being candid... "Did you ask me because of your daughter? Because you were trying to somehow bring me into the fold?"

"McCabes don't just help family," Shane responded kindly. "They also help friends and neighbors."

Determined to learn the truth, Dylan said, "That's not really answering my question."

Shane folded his arms in front of him. "Are you involved with Emily, this pretend-dating business aside?"

Dylan hesitated. This was not a discussion he should be having with Emily's father until after he'd had it with Emily. "I don't know how to answer—"

"And you shouldn't have to," Emily interrupted.

Dylan and Shane turned in unison.

Dressed in jeans, boots and an embroidered turquoise shirt, she looked prettier than Dylan had ever seen her. Angrier, too.

Emily strode forward, blue eyes flashing. "I'm not a child, Dad."

Shane straightened, his need to protect his daughter unabated. "I never said you were."

Emily stabbed the air with her finger. "Every action you, Mom and my brothers take says you all think I need protecting."

"Honey, you're our only daughter," Greta cut in.

"I'm a grown woman." Emily stood next to Dylan and linked arms with him. "And I deserve one heck of a lot more respect than you are showing me right now."

Before anyone else could say anything, Jeb and Holden appeared in the doorway. "Hey, sis!" Jeb said jubilantly. "When are we going to see the amazing demonstration?"

Her cheeks still pink with indignation, Emily muttered, "As soon as everyone is here."

As if on cue, the doorbell rang. More McCabes arrived, along with Andrew and Simone and Bobbie Sue and Billy Ray. The commotion in the kitchen increased as everyone brought their dinner contributions into the house.

Happy to have the tense family drama between Emily and her parents cut short, Dylan escaped the calamity and headed off to get the mustangs ready.

When Emily came out to the barns, with her gaggle of devotees streaming out around her, her mind seemed solely on the task ahead. Dylan forced himself to do the same.

Ginger, Salt and Pepper all performed as admirably as Dylan and Emily had hoped. The two younger horses—

who were not big or strong enough to be ridden yet—went through their training exercises with ease.

Emily was clearly ecstatic. As was Dylan.

She ended the demonstration of the three-year-old mare's prowess with a solo canter around the pasture.

Dylan was as proud of Emily—and the work she had done—as he was of the horses. And he wasn't the only one. Her family whistled, clapped and shouted their approval as she came back to dismount and take her bows. For the first time, Dylan began to understand the allure of being a McCabe. The support they offered, the expression of love was unbelievable.

"So what's next?" Jeb asked.

"We test them to see if they've bonded to us—become part of our ranch family—as much as it appears they have," Dylan explained.

Further questions were cut off as another car sped up the lane and stopped short of them. Dylan swore as the male behind the wheel cut the engine and got out. This was exactly what they did not need.

EMILY KNEW IT was Dylan's ranch, but Xavier was only there because of her. She put up a hand before Dylan could intervene.

"I'll take care of this." She handed off Ginger's reins to Jeb and she walked toward the interloper. Silence fell.

Shillingsworth handed her a thick manila envelope.

"A parting gift." Xavier smirked as if he still held the high card.

Knowing forewarned was forearmed, Emily took it reluctantly and undid the clasp. Inside was a thick folder bearing the name of a private investigator. "What is this?" she snapped.

He stared at her, his expression ugly. "A complete dossier on your friend there."

Emily stiffened. "I already know all about Dylan." At least the parts that are important...

Xavier gestured expansively and said even louder, "Then you also know he is one of the Texas Reeves. The railroad tycoon."

Emily turned to Dylan. On the surface, his expression was as inscrutable as usual. In his eyes, she could see a burning anger.

"Normally, that'd be a good thing." Xavier spoke to the crowd as if lecturing a class. "If the family acknowledged him, that was. Unfortunately, they do not."

Aware the ranch yard was so silent you could hear a pin drop, Xavier rubbed his jaw and continued. "I couldn't understand it until I went to see his grandfather myself." He shook his head. "You ought to see the fabulous mansion they live in. Anyway, I told the old man all about Dylan—where he was living, what he was doing, that he was trying to work his way into the famous Mc-Cabes by romancing one of their daughters."

Emily broke in pointedly. "That sounds more like your plan."

Xavier ignored her. "The old man didn't care. He said that it didn't matter who Dylan eventually married. Dylan was always going to have his father's white-trash blood, and that to hear about his grandson only reminded the old man of the way his own daughter ruined the family name by giving birth to a bastard that was no better than the lowlife that sired him—"

Emily didn't know where it came from. She had never been violent in her life. But suddenly the file folder was dropping to the ground and her hand was flying through the air.

Her fist connected with Xavier's jaw. To her disappointment, she didn't seem to hurt the obnoxious spoilsport a bit. She did shut him up momentarily, however, as everyone stared on in shock.

It was then that Dylan stepped in, cool, calm and collected as ever.

"Emily, why don't you take everyone inside?" Dylan suggested, a dangerously civil edge to his low tone. "I'll escort this *gentleman* to his car."

Equally tense and irritable looks were exchanged all around. Evidently confident Dylan could handle it, they all complied with Dylan's request.

Only Emily remained.

Dylan looked at her. "Go inside, Emily," he repeated.

Dylan hadn't talked to her in that unwelcoming a tone since the first day she had shown up, asking him to pretend to be her date for the evening. Her lips parted in shock.

Xavier grinned triumphantly, pleased at the rancor his unexpected appearance had created.

"Right now," Dylan commanded.

Emily didn't want to leave, his tone brooked no argument. Heart pounding, spirits sinking, she turned on her heel and stomped off.

"You're not good enough for her."

Dylan picked up the papers and shoved them into Shillingsworth's hands. "So you said, several times."

Ignoring the danger he was in, Shillingsworth thrust out his jaw pugnaciously. "Her family may try to bring you into the fold, but at the end of the day, everyone knows you can't make a silk purse out of a sow's ear, and they'll cut you loose, too—the same way your biological family severed ties."

Dylan wanted to say the McCabes weren't like that. He knew different.

They loved their daughter and wanted only the best for her.

They wanted all the things he didn't know how to give her. Like the foundation—through generations of example—for a good solid marriage and a happy family.

A husband who had a background she could be as proud of as her own.

As much as it pained Dylan to admit it, that wasn't him. Never had been. Never would be.

Shillingsworth continued his last hurrah. "One of these days soon, she'll realize she's made a mistake hooking up with you at all. When that happens, she'll dump you flat, buddy."

Not if we part amicably, Dylan thought, determined to protect Emily in whatever way remained. Unimpressed, he lifted a brow. "I doubt she'll come running to you."

Shillingsworth shrugged, apparently having finally let go of that particular fantasy. "That much I figured. Which is too bad. Emily missed out on a good thing with me—I could have shown her the world. Because I am not just a trust-fund baby whose money will eventually run out. I'm going to be filthy rich one day, all on my own."

"I'm sure they'll make a movie about you," Dylan returned dryly.

"They will! And I'll have all the women I want!"

"Good luck with that," he retorted.

"Just not here in this one-horse town."

His patience exhausted, Dylan propelled the kid into the driver's seat and shut the door. "You better get started, then. Time's a-wastin'."

"Don't I know it!" Shillingsworth released an obnoxious laugh, coupled with an invective-laced adios, and sped off.

Dylan could tell Shillingsworth was finally satisfied he'd gotten his revenge on both Emily and Dylan. The residents of Laramie would never see the kid again unless legal action dragged him back.

He turned to see Emily coming up behind him.

Her cheeks were pink with indignation, her eyes full of worry. "What did he say to you just now?"

Wishing things were different, Dylan exhaled. "The same thing he's been alleging all along, that I'm not good enough for you."

Emily recoiled with hurt. "That's not true."

Wasn't it? Dylan had seen the looks on all the Mc-Cabes' faces when Shillingsworth was describing his conversation with the old man. They'd been as shocked and revolted by the coldhearted account as Dylan would have expected them to be.

There was no way they'd want their daughter to be exposed to such familial disdain and cruelty, even by marriage.

Dylan swallowed and forced himself to do the right thing. To finally be as noble as he should have been all along.

He shrugged, keeping his tone carefully matter-of-fact. "Not that it matters. We knew this was only a temporary thing anyway, right?" He paused to search her eyes, protecting Emily the best way he could.

"Well. I—" she stammered, but he cut her off.

"Emily, let's not dance around the truth, okay?" he muttered. "It was always understood that we'd eventually go our separate ways."

Emily blinked. "But what about the mustangs…the test you talked about…?"

Dylan had inadvertently put her through so much; he wouldn't rob her of that. "You're welcome to participate in that, of course," he reassured her.

Emily's lower lip trembled. "When are you going to do it?" she whispered.

Dylan pushed away the powerful feelings welling up inside him. "In ten days or so. I'll let you know when I set it up."

"Dylan…"

He cut her off with a gallant lift of his hand. "We have guests, Emily." It was all he could do not to wrap his arms around her. "Don't you think it's time you went to see about taking care of them?"

A flush started in her neck and swept into her face. Looking near tears, she asked hoarsely, "Don't you want to come inside, too?"

Dylan figured he had embarrassed her enough. "I'm going to see to the horses—get them settled for the night."

Aware they were no doubt being observed by the whole McCabe contingent, Emily struggled to regain her composure. "All right, then. I'll see you in a bit." She went back in to oversee the potluck dinner.

Dylan exited the ranch and left Emily to say good-bye to everyone on her own. He felt sick inside, but he knew he'd done the right thing. Because Shillingsworth was right—it would never work. Had he and Emily been smarter and more honest, they would have realized that from the very beginning.

Chapter Fifteen

Dylan was in the stable late the following afternoon when he heard a car motor. He walked out to see Andrew waving goodbye to his mom. "You're not scheduled to work today."

The teen walked slowly toward him, hands thrust in the pockets of his jeans. "I thought you might need some help with the mustangs. Emily not being here and all…"

As if Dylan needed reminding about that.

In the past twenty-two hours, all he'd done was think about her and wish things had been different. But they weren't…and he needed to remember that.

He motioned for Andrew to follow him. "How is Emily?"

Andrew plucked the leather work gloves from his back pocket and hurried to catch up. "She's real busy."

Dylan had tried to stay focused on other things, too. For once, concentrating on the needs of the horses in his care did nothing to stanch the overwhelming emotions welling up inside him. He stalked into the barn and picked up a fresh bale of hay, handed another off to Andrew. "I saw a Closed sign on the café when I drove into town today."

"She's taking the whole week off."

Another sign that things weren't right with her, either,

although in her case her actions could all be financially motivated. "How come?" Dylan stopped to get a pair of clippers to cut the twine.

They both carried the hay into the stable and set it down in the center aisleway. "Well, today, anyway, she's busy meeting with the three guys her brothers brought in to talk to her. And then about five others are coming in, too."

Dylan felt a surge of possessiveness that was no longer justifiable. Telling himself his interest was only cursory, that if she were selling shares in her business or looking for outside investors he might be interested, too, Dylan asked casually, "All at the same time?"

Andrew helped break the two bales into equal flakes. "No. One after the other. Emily's real serious about it. She says the meetings all have to be private."

Okay, that could mean anything....

Andrew and Dylan stuffed the hay nets with feed. "Emily says she has to concentrate on her future now more than ever—and she wants to get things taken care of as soon as possible. That's all I know."

Dylan weighed the nets on a spring balance, to ensure the proper level of feed for each horse. Then he and Andrew brought them to the individual stalls and secured them at eye level on the wall.

Andrew grabbed a broom to clean up any leftover bits of hay that had fallen to the floor. Dylan studied the lingering concern on the boy's face.

"Is that the only reason you came out here?" Dylan asked as they walked out of the stable. "To tell me that?"

Andrew drifted toward the pasture fence. He looked toward the far corner, where Ginger, Salt and Pepper congregated in a corner, basking in the late-afternoon sun and the gentle spring breeze.

Andrew hooked his arms over the fence rail. He kept his gaze trained forward. "Actually, I wanted to ask you about the stuff Xavier Shillingsworth said about you being from a not-so-nice family."

Dylan knew how difficult it was for the fifteen-year-old to let anyone know what was really on his mind. "I imagine a lot of people want to ask me about that," he replied with as much candor as he could muster.

Andrew gulped and turned to Dylan. "Did it make you feel bad having him say all those things?" He squinted and turned his gaze to the horizon again. His hands gripped the rail in front of him. "'Cause it always makes me feel bad when people talk about my dad being arrested and being sent to jail."

Dylan started to say the expected—that it didn't matter what others thought and therefore he refused to let it bother him. But he knew that wasn't true.

"It hurts," he said finally, deciding to go outside his comfort zone and give the troubled teen the uncensored honesty he deserved. "It makes me feel I'm being blamed for something outside my control."

Andrew shifted again and braced his body against the rail. "Does it make you mad?"

"It used to—now I just find it kind of sad and discouraging. And, of course, unfair."

Andrew clenched his jaw. "Some parents think because my dad did bad things, and I have his blood, that I'll do bad things. So they don't want me being friends with their kids or asking their daughters out on dates."

Dylan hadn't known that was happening. He was pretty sure Simone and Emily hadn't, either.

Andrew hastened to add, "Most of the kids are okay—they'd like to hang out with me but they're just not allowed to. Only the kids who have parents who don't care what their kids do—"

"Kids who are already in trouble of some sort," Dylan interjected, guessing the rest.

Andrew nodded. "Those kids are always allowed to go places with me. No problem."

Which explained, Dylan thought, Andrew's entry into a bad crowd shortly after moving to Laramie. It wasn't because he had wanted to be part of that group; he hadn't felt he had any other options. "Did you ever tell your mom this?"

Andrew hung his head. "I didn't see the point. She feels bad enough about the stuff my dad did, and the trouble it caused for us back in Houston. We had to pack up and start over someplace else. I didn't want to make it worse for her. But at the same time," Andrew continued in a rusty-sounding voice, "it can get really lonely, when you don't have any other kids to go places with who aren't going to get you in trouble again."

"Yes," Dylan said, knowing from his own experiences that was the case. "It can. But it doesn't have to stay that way, Andrew. Now that we know what the situation is, I can vouch for you with other parents." He put a reassuring hand on Andrew's shoulder. "So if you need a reference, you have them call me. I'll assure the other parents that you are a good influence for their kids."

"You'd do that for me?"

"I gave you a community-service job on the ranch, didn't I? I'm teaching you how to care for horses. Of course I'll do that for you."

Andrew grinned his relief. "I didn't think anyone would understand. But then, I guess you know all about this kind of stuff. Because your background isn't considered great, either. Since you were disowned at birth and several times since."

Dylan winced. *Gee, when you put it like that...*

Andrew's brows drew together. "Is that why you and Emily broke up?" he blurted out, perplexed. "Because she found out that you don't have the kind of family she does and now she doesn't want to go out with you anymore? Are you being discriminated against, too?"

Dylan held up a staying hand. "Emily's not like that."

She was the kind of woman who made him believe in happily-ever-after, who made him want the fairy tale for himself.

Andrew frowned, still not getting it. "Then why did you leave the party like that last night, without saying goodbye to anyone?" he demanded.

Easy, Dylan thought. *Because she's a wonderful woman who deserves to see all her dreams come true.* And those dreams included being with a man who understood how to be part of a big, happy family, a man who knew instinctively what to do and say and belong. Instead of someone who was always waiting for the other shoe to drop.

Fighting the turbulent emotions, Dylan cleared his throat. He looked at Andrew, man to man. "I didn't come back to the ranch house last night as I figured Emily had been embarrassed enough. I couldn't see doing it to her over and over again in the future. Because all of that will come up."

"My background will come up, too. But you're willing to be my friend and vouch for me."

"That's different," Dylan retorted.

"How?" the teen persisted.

"It's complicated," he said finally.

Andrew scoffed. "When adults say that it usually means they're in love or something."

"*Or something* being the operative words in this case," Dylan said.

Had he and Emily not promised to keep it casual, to never change, to part amicably before things got convoluted and messy?

"Yeah, well," Andrew grumbled, as the trio of mustangs saw them and started their way, "as long as we're talking straight to each other... I gotta say, I think you humiliated Emily more by leaving the party that way, without even saying good night to anybody or anything."

Guilt wound its way into his heart. And stayed. He'd figured he had been helping, by exiting quietly and unobtrusively, instead of staying and being the elephant in the room. "Did she say that?" he demanded, his mouth dry.

Or was this Andrew misinterpreting?

Andrew looked at Dylan as if he was an idiot. "Emily didn't have to complain about it. My mom and I could both see she was really hurt." Andrew stopped and shook his head. "You really ought to go to her and apologize. Try and do something to make it right."

EMILY HAD JUST shut off the café coffeemaker and was getting ready to clean up, when her mother walked in. Emily knew she was concerned and that she'd show up eventually to talk to her.

"Full calendar today, hmm?" Greta started sympathetically. She opened up the bag she'd brought with her. Inside were two pints of premium ice cream—Godiva chocolate for Emily, coconut-pecan for her mother.

Emily accepted the gift with a thank you and found two spoons. "I decided to finally start tackling the café's problems head-on. I actually got a lot of offers of help, some very interesting."

As comfortable in a commercial kitchen as she was in her own home, Greta pulled up a stool to the central worktable. "Are there any you are going to accept?"

Emily brought two glasses of ice water over to the table. "Yes. I've already set up time to meet with five of them again."

Greta smiled. "That's great."

Emily savored her first bite of dark-chocolate ice cream. "But that's not why you came over to talk to me."

"Your father and I are both concerned about Dylan."

Pushing aside the memory of the sexy rancher, and all he had once meant to her, Emily savored another bite. Like it or not, she had to move on in this regard, too. "I can't help you."

Greta studied her carefully. "You're no longer friends?"

No longer friends with temporary benefits, that was for sure, Emily thought miserably, wondering how something that had felt so right could go so wrong so fast.

"Our reasons for seeing each other are over." Knowing she had to unburden herself to someone, she said, "I know we put on a good show from time to time, Mom, but it was all just pretend."

A twinkle appeared in Greta's eyes. "Really."

Now was not the time for her mother to get overly romantic in her outlook. *"Really,"* she reiterated.

Greta sipped her ice water. "What about the feelings in your heart? Are those pretend, too?"

Emily flushed. "It doesn't matter. Dylan's right…he's never going to be the guy I need."

I need someone who wants me, for now, for always.

Someone who is willing to negotiate and adapt, grow old with me...

"Because he's not ethical."

Where had her mother gotten that idea? "He's ethical!"

Greta's elegant eyebrows furrowed. "Not strong-willed enough to take you on, then?"

Emily choked in exasperation. "Have you met the man?"

Greta savored another bite. "I guess, then, he's lacking a tender side."

This, Emily thought, was beginning to get annoying. "Have you forgotten he's a horse whisperer? Honestly, Mom, Dylan is the most gentle, intuitive man I have ever met in my entire life." He knew how to kiss her and touch her and hold her. When to talk, and when to just let her be...

Greta wrinkled her nose, thinking. "Then it's his background."

There was no doubt about it—most of his family life had been heartbreakingly sad. "He can't get over the cruelness of the rejection. And to have it happen again, last night, through Xavier, in front of everyone in our family." It had been a nightmare, and not for just him.

"It is a lot to have to accept," Greta remarked quietly. "Especially when he is so deserving."

Emily set down her spoon. "You know what the worst part of it was?" Her mom shook her head, listening. "The fact that I couldn't help him and be the kind of life partner he needed when it actually happened. I wanted to help him. I wanted to do or say something to make it all better for him, but in that moment, I didn't have a clue."

"You stood up for him. You made the first move to send Xavier on his way."

"That was easy, Mom. I'm a McCabe—I know how

to stand up for family. But I didn't know how to handle the rest of it or what to say to him that would have made it all okay. Instead, when put to the test, I faltered, and he…left."

"That doesn't mean the two of you have to break off your whatever it is you've been having."

What had they been having? An affair? Or something a heck of a lot more?

"Unless you're angry with him."

"I'm disappointed," Emily admitted miserably.

"Why?"

"Because I kind of feel he lumped me in with everyone else who has let him down. He didn't give me a chance to grow and learn and do better. And be what he needs. I'm not like that. Instead, it was like, 'well…obviously this isn't going to work.'" Angry tears sprang to her eyes. "Like he expected that at any minute I would turn my back on him, because of his horribly callous relatives… so he called up this agreement we had made to end it at the first sign of trouble and dumped me first!"

Greta struggled to follow the logic. "So, if you had dumped *him* first it would have been okay?"

"*No!* The point is, I wouldn't have dumped him at all!"

"Isn't that what you're doing now?"

Emily fell abruptly silent.

She struggled to explain how something that had started out so simply—as a reckless and ill-thought-out ruse to avoid some matchmaking—had evolved into something so passionate and meaningful—and ultimately devastating, as well. "We had an agreement—" Emily struggled not to cry "—that we wouldn't try to change each other. The way I always tried to change the guys I dated. Dylan didn't want to be another fixer-upper for me.

"But did that also mean we shouldn't try on our own

to change for the better?" She wondered fervently. "Because I thought that's what people in love did! I thought just being together made them better people. And that implies change, doesn't it?"

"Usually, unless the two people involved are absolutely perfect individuals to begin with," her mother replied. "And personally, I can't think of a single instance where that has happened."

"So he *is* being unreasonable!" Emily crowed, more hurt and angry than ever.

Greta released a gusty breath. "Look, Emily, I know you and your brothers are all grown. And I really do try and stay out of your love lives as much as possible."

Emily couldn't help it—she laughed out loud. *"Really?"* she echoed, reacting to the audacity. "Because, several weeks ago I heard you were trying to set me up with some mystery guy that you thought would be just perfect for me."

Greta looked chagrined they were suddenly back to that. "Your brothers told you," she murmured, actually blushing.

Emily threw up her hands in exasperation. "They're my sibs! Of course they warned me!" She aimed a censuring finger her mother's way. "The only one who didn't tell me about The Guy Who Might Be The One For Me was you. *You* backed off before ever uttering his name!"

Greta replaced the top on her ice cream. "There was a reason for that," she said, rising to her feet.

"And it was?" Emily stood, too.

The self-conscious pink in her mother's cheeks deepened. She cleared her throat as if making a grand announcement. "You were already kissing him at the time." Greta paused to let the weight of her words sink in.

"Frankly, your father and I concluded we didn't *need* to do anything else to get you to give the guy a second look."

Emily's mouth dropped open. "You really wanted me to be with Dylan?"

Her mother was firm. "We really did."

Wow. And Wow again. "And now?" Emily ventured at last.

Greta grabbed her purse. "Honey, that's up to you. We'll back you in whatever you decide." She resacked her half-finished pint and headed for the door.

A still-reeling Emily followed close behind, aware for the first time in hours her heart held a smidgen of hope. "But…"

Her mother turned before going out the door. "Nope. No more advice," she reiterated firmly, looking Emily straight in the eye. The air reverberated with maternal and familial love. "Because the wisdom you need—" Greta took Emily's hand and placed it over her daughter's heart "—is already *right in here*."

EMILY TOOK HER mother's advice and spent the next week searching her soul for the answers. Her chance to put her feelings to the test came a few days after that, when she met Dylan at a private mustang preserve 130 miles from the Last Chance Ranch.

By the time she arrived, ready to witness the wild horses' first big test, he was already there, unloading the three mustangs and his own gelding from the four-horse trailer. The youngest two were outfitted with reins and lead lines; the older two horses were saddled up.

Emily got out of the Circle M pickup truck she had borrowed from her father and walked over to join the group. In the distance, they could see the resident herd of mustangs, grazing sedately in the 100-acre preserve.

But it was the man next to her that held her heart captive.

It had only been a week and a half, yet as Emily looked into those familiar golden-brown eyes, it felt so much longer. Too long.

She swallowed, trying not to notice how handsome he looked, with his hat tugged low over his brow, a new haircut and a fresh shave. Or how good he smelled, like sandalwood and leather and soap.

"Tell me again how this is going to work," Emily said.

His eyes were alight with kindness and another emotion she couldn't identify. "We're going to lead the horses a little closer, and then dismount and let the mustangs go." He flexed his broad shoulders lazily. "See what they do, given the choice."

"Well, of course they're going to race off to be with the other mustangs," Emily said in frustration. Horses were herd animals, after all. Unlike humans, they always chose to be with their kind over being alone.

He gave her a brief, officious look. "I reckon that's so."

Emily's anxiety rose. "It doesn't bother you?"

Dylan adjusted the stirrups on Ginger's saddle. "If they've bonded, the way we think they have, and become part of the Last Chance Ranch family, they won't stay away from us for very long," he explained.

"And if they haven't?"

Dylan offered Emily a hand up into Ginger's saddle. As soon as she was situated, he climbed onto Hercules's back. "Then they'll likely never make reliable domesticated riding horses." He frowned. "They'll always be looking to run off, first chance they get, and they wouldn't be suitable for the boys ranch."

He reined in Salt and Pepper, and they headed off at an easy canter. They stopped again, atop the hill overlooking the pasture. Ginger was already prancing around in excitement. Salt and Pepper followed suit. Only Hercules, Dylan's well-trained gelding, remained calm and almost uninterested.

Dylan climbed down and tied his horse to a tree.

Emily dismounted, too. Together, they removed Ginger's saddle, all three mustangs' bridles and bits and stepped away.

The moment Ginger realized she was free, she turned back, gave them one last look, then reared around and took off. Salt and Pepper followed her, both going at top speed, too.

Emily stood, boots planted firmly in the grass, arms folded in front of her, watching. Would they stay or come back? she wondered, her heart pounding.

Within her, there was so much sadness and disappointment. She knew now it was foolish, but she wished Dylan had given her the slightest sign. She'd really thought she and Dylan were going to be the ones riding off into the sunset together, that they'd spend the rest of their lives training and caring for mustangs in need of a good home.

Instead, here they were, acting as if they'd never been anything more than the most casual of friends. Acting as if their lovemaking…the long intimate talks…the joy they'd felt when together…hadn't mattered.

Here they were, about to say a final goodbye to each other, too, as they watched the three mustangs join the herd—without a thought as to the possibilities they were leaving behind. Tears blurring her eyes, unable to stand seeing any more, she turned and began walking away.

"Emily," Dylan rasped.

Emily could hear him behind her, gaining ground.

She rushed on, feeling as if her heart was breaking. What had made her think she could handle any of this, she wondered, as she dabbed at the moisture flooding her eyes.

She wasn't strong enough to love and let go.

She didn't want to forge on alone.

Yet that was the only choice she had.

"Emily!" Dylan caught her by the shoulders and spun her around to face him.

Fifty yards away, Hercules chewed grass sedately. As if all was right with the world...

"What?" Emily snapped.

Dylan looked just as impatient. "Why are you crying?"

Emily sniffed. She'd never thought Dylan insensitive—until now. "Why aren't *you*?"

He seemed puzzled. "We don't know yet what they're going to do."

Emily cast a look at the mustangs they'd just let go—now romping with the herd of wild horses. "I think it's pretty clear." They were leaving her, just as Dylan had left her.

He frowned, nowhere near ready to give up. "They're exploring their options."

Emily harrumphed. That sounded like a line and a half!

Dylan surprised her by saying, "Kind of like you and that long line of guys you were interviewing at the café the other day?"

Was the rough note in his voice possessiveness? Emily tensed and folded her arms in front of her. "How did you know about that?"

Dylan's eyes darkened. "Andrew might have mentioned it."

The silence strung out between them.

"So I guess you're back to dating," he said deferentially.

Emily adopted his businesslike attitude. "I'm back to saving my café. I've decided to respond to customer demand and expand."

His face relaxed and he moved closer still. "The tables outside aren't enough?"

Emily basked in his nearness. "No." She pressed her lips together. "And as we've already proved, they aren't available in inclement weather, either. I've applied for permits to put in an elevator and make my apartment over the shop into a second dining area and a separate party room." She smiled in triumph. "It looks like I'm going to get it, too."

He stroked his jaw. "So the guys…"

"Were all volunteering to help me in one way or another. Construction will start right away. I'm going to pay them in meal vouchers."

"That's a great idea."

"Thanks," she said.

He sobered, every inch of him resolute male. "Where are you going to live in the meantime?"

Finally, a problem she hadn't had time to solve. Emily bit her lip. "I don't know yet. Everyone in the family has offered to put me up for the duration, until I can afford another place, but…"

"Too much interference?" he guessed.

"Too many questions I don't want to answer." *Don't know how to answer.*

He took her hand in his and squeezed it tightly. "If you're looking for a roommate—" he looked her right in the eye "—I volunteer my place."

THIS WAS WHAT she wanted, Emily thought. And yet… She put up a palm to keep him from coming any nearer. "I can't go back to that, Dylan. To thinking only about the moment we're in, never knowing what tomorrow is going to bring." She cleared her throat. "Freedom is important, but…"

He came closer anyway, wrapping an arm about her waist. When she would have drawn away, he held fast. "You want more than that." His voice was a sexy rumble in his chest.

Emily drew a stabilizing breath and forced herself to be completely honest. "I need more than that, Dylan. I need to belong with someone, not just for right now, but for the rest of our lives." Trying not to notice how warm and solid and right he felt, she splayed her hands across his chest. Her voice trembled as she admitted, "I need permanence and security and family."

"Suppose I could give you that happily-ever-after?" he propositioned huskily.

She blinked back a mist of emotion, and reminded him, "You don't do family drama, remember?"

"I didn't used to—until I hooked up with you."

Ignoring the sudden wobbliness of her knees, Emily tried to figure out where this was going. "What are you talking about?" she asked, acknowledging the sudden reckless beat of her heart.

He tightened his grip on her, and said thoughtfully, "I had a talk with your dad."

"I know. You turned down his offer to go into business together."

"Not that conversation." His lips curved into a sexy smile. "Another one," he told her softly, gazing into her eyes. "I spoke to him yesterday and asked his permission."

A shiver swept through her. Aware how close she was to breathlessly surrendering to Dylan on any terms, she drew back and regarded him sternly. "This isn't funny."

"It's not supposed to be." He continued to search her face. "It's supposed to be romantic." He let the words sink in, then flashed the impish grin she loved so much. "And by the way?" he explained. "Your dad said okay."

Her parents *had* always wanted her to be happy. "You seem surprised by that," she noted, coming closer once again.

Sorrow mingled with joy on his handsome face. "I wasn't sure your family would think I was good enough for you." He swallowed, then began to relax. "Apparently, I am."

And suddenly, Emily and Dylan were right back where they had started. With her family calling the shots—or trying to—where her love life was concerned.

Tears of exasperation blurred her vision. She knew that if she and Dylan were ever to be happy, there were a few things they had to clear up first.

She stepped back, throwing up her hands in aggravation. "What is it with me that I keep getting these half measures?"

Dylan blinked. Apparently, she thought temperamentally, *this* hadn't been in his plan.

"What's *half measure* about me asking your father for your hand in marriage?" he demanded right back.

No longer sure who was taming who, or even who *should* be taming who, she retorted, "Gee, Dylan, I don't know. Maybe the fact that I kind of like to make those types of great big life-altering decisions for myself?"

Dylan narrowed his eyes. "You want me to ask you first?"

"For heaven's sake! Yes, I want you to ask me and not anyone else!" Emily blurted out her feelings before she could stop herself.

With a grin as wide as Texas, and a sparkle in his

eyes, Dylan got down on his knees. He swept off his hat, set it against his chest and tilted his face up to hers. He was, at that moment, the epitome of masculine sexiness.

A few days ago, Emily would have happily succumbed. She would have thrust herself into his arms and kissed him wildly and let him kiss her back, and then let that lead where they both knew it would—to a hot session in bed.

Not anymore.

Not with all there was at stake.

She glared at him, waiting to see just how deep and real his commitment to her truly was. Because without that...

"Emily." His smile broadened all the more. "Will you marry me?"

She tugged on his hands and pulled him upright so they were squaring off—cowgirl to cowboy—once again.

"Why?" she demanded, aware the wrong rationale would not only break her heart, it would destroy them forever.

But this once, Dylan let down his guard and didn't disappoint. He wrapped his arms about her waist and regarded her with all the tenderness and affection she had always wished for.

"Because I love you, Emily," he said softly, looking deep into her eyes, with a tenderness that took her breath away.

"I love you the way I never thought I could love anyone. The way I'll never love anyone again." His voice caught. He forged on, the words coming from deep in his soul. "And because you're a part of my heart now, and I'll never be happy without you."

Emily's lower lip trembled. "I'll never be happy without you, either. And I love you, too, Dylan, so very much."

Relieved to finally be able to admit what was in her heart, Emily went up on tiptoe and kissed Dylan with every bit of the passion and love she felt. She kissed him until the moment became real, the romantic aura around them stunning in its power and intensity. And then she kissed him some more and let him kiss her back. Knowing what had started out as a temporary liaison wasn't temporary at all.

Finally, Dylan unlocked their lips and drew back just far enough to ask, "So…about my proposal?"

Emily cuddled close, still free-thinking and independent enough to insist, "It's yes to the roommate, no to the marriage."

He arched his eyebrow.

Practically, she explained, "I want us to live together first."

It was Dylan's turn to be wary. "That's not very traditional."

"So?"

"Your family isn't going to like that," he warned.

"It's not my family's decision—it's ours. And I want us to work things out in our own time and our own way, without anyone in my family pushing us to the altar." She met his eyes. "So what do you say? You…me…and the freedom to pursue everything and anything we've ever wanted?"

Emily felt a whisper of breath behind her. A very hot, gusty breath.

She turned, came face-to-face with a stealthily moving Ginger. Salt and Pepper were coming up right beside the mare.

Joy flowed through her as Ginger hooked her face over Emily's shoulder, in the equine version of a horse-to-human hug, then reached over and affectionately nosed Dylan's face and shoulder, too.

Emily laughed. "Well, what do you know, cowboy. I think our family's back."

Dylan chuckled, too. "And just in time," he stated, his eyes twinkling with happiness. "Because my answer to *your* proposal is yes!"

Epilogue

One year later...

"I can't believe we're doing this." Emily told Dylan as she took her place in Maisy's saddle, the voluminous folds of her white lace-and-satin wedding gown floating out about her.

Her groom-to-be grinned and climbed onto the magnificent Hercules. Resplendent in his tux, Dylan mugged at her seductively. "Yeah, you can."

Emily reached across and clasped his hand. She smiled, too. "Yeah. I can."

"It has been quite a year, though," he murmured.

Yes, Emily thought, it had.

They had secured proof linking Xavier Shillingsworth to the scandal in the cafe. An out-of-court settlement had been reached, both with her and the county health department, compensating them for their losses.

After that, her café had been remodeled in record time.

Emily'd had to scale back on the daily specials a bit in order to keep the books nicely balanced in the future, but thanks to an expanded, updated menu and additional seating, customer satisfaction was at an all-time high nevertheless.

Dylan had accepted her family into his heart as readily as they had taken him into theirs.

Andrew had plenty of friends and was now a ranch hand on the Last Chance, working at Dylan's side whenever he wasn't in school or out socializing.

The only difficulty, if there was one, was the fact they'd had to take all three of the mustangs on to the Libertyville Boys Ranch, as promised.

Saying goodbye to the three beloved mustangs had been hard—until Emily saw how much the boys there loved horses, and how much Salt, Pepper and Ginger loved them back. She'd had to admit that the once-wild mustangs would have great lives as therapy horses.

And so now, it was on with the future. *Their* future, Emily thought, as Dylan stopped, atop a ridge. In the valley below, their family and friends waited.

He turned to her. "Before I give the signal for the musicians to start, I want to talk about the wedding gift."

He reached into his pocket and withdrew an envelope. Inside were photos of two beautiful mustangs.

Emily knew immediately what he had done. Entranced by the love of her life's generosity and acknowledging the unique challenges ahead—she asked, "When are they arriving?"

"The day after we get back from our honeymoon in Wyoming," Dylan reported proudly.

Emily chuckled. "And now my gift for you." She reached down and removed the envelope she had taped to the inside of her white satin cowgirl wedding boot.

She handed them over with a comical wrinkle of her nose. Dylan studied the photos—of two more mustangs—and began to laugh.

"Four mustangs," he said in awe.

Emily grinned, thinking how exciting it was going to be to start all over again. "Apparently."

Dylan slipped out of his saddle and pulled her out of hers. He wrapped his arms around her. "Think we can handle it?"

Emily wreathed her arms about his neck, rose on tip-toe and kissed him soundly. She looked deeply into his eyes. "Cowboy, I think we can handle anything as long as we're together."

Dylan murmured his agreement. He kissed her back leisurely. "So what do you say we ride on down there and get married?"

Emily hugged him with all the love in her heart. "I think that's the best idea ever," she beamed.

* * * * *

A COWBOY TO MARRY

Chapter One

Libby Lowell had just ducked into a deserted corner of the Laramie Community Center to check her BlackBerry when a shadow loomed over her. It was Holden McCabe, as big and broad-shouldered and chivalrous as ever....

Libby frowned at the good-looking man who had been her late husband's best friend, wishing, as always, that the six-foot-three rancher did not feel so compelled to watch over her.

Ignoring the way his shirt brought out the cobalt-blue depths of his eyes, she smiled tersely. "If you're here for what I *think* you are, Holden, I have to warn you...I am *not* in the mood."

His smile full of mischief, Holden inclined his head toward the buffet tables on the other side of the crowded venue. "For pumpkin or pecan pie?"

Libby rolled her eyes and leaned in a tad closer. The truth was, she was stuffed to the gills from the delicious holiday meal. All she really wanted now was a nice long nap. "For any well-meant but totally unsolicited advice," she corrected. The kind that Holden thought Percy would have given her, and hence, intended to deliver in her late husband's stead.

Holden rubbed a hand across his chiseled jaw and

continued to play dumb. "Why would you think I want to tell you what to do?" he asked.

"Maybe because just about everyone else has at some point or other today." Libby lifted a lecturing finger before he could interrupt. "And don't pretend you don't know what I'm talking about, because I saw you talking to my employees, earlier, as well as at least a half dozen area ranchers."

He shrugged his shoulders amiably, then folded his arms in front of him. The motion drew her eyes to the solid, muscular contours of his chest.

Swallowing, she turned her attention to his ruggedly attractive face.

Libby didn't know what was wrong with her. She had known this man for years now. And yet...

Holden leaned toward her. "Of course I was chatting with everyone. It's Thanksgiving." And this year, everyone was eschewing private family gatherings to attend a holiday fund-raiser for the local children's home, an event Libby had helped organize.

Not about to have her suspicions blown off, Libby lifted an eyebrow in challenge. "Really? Because it didn't look like any of you were discussing the probable outcome of the upcoming University of Texas and A and M football game." Which was what all the men would normally be talking about. She paused again and looked straight into his mesmerizing eyes. "Admit it, Holden. Everyone is coming to you. Trying to enlist your help."

Keeping his gaze locked with hers, the handsome meddler flashed a dimpled smile. "People are concerned."

"Well, they shouldn't be," she snapped.

Holden leaned in even closer and murmured, "The fear is you are acting rashly...."

"And unwisely?" she couldn't help but add.

Frown lines bracketed his sensual lips. "Because of the holidays."

Thanksgiving, Christmas and New Year's had been hard in the two years since Percy had died. Made even worse by the fact she had no other family left, on either side.

It was just her and the ranch-equipment dealership she had inherited from the Lowells. Stuck in a place that reminded her of all she had lost and would never have again. At least if she stayed in the small but thriving West Texas town of Laramie.

Which was why she had finally come to her senses and decided to stop delaying the inevitable and move on with her life, once and for all. No matter how hard it was going to be initially, she had to do it.

Ignoring the softness of Holden's gaze, Libby scrolled through the text messages on her BlackBerry until she found the one she wanted. It was from Jeff Johnston and said, Tomorrow evening at seven-thirty all right?

Libby typed in: Perfect. Meet me at the dealership. We'll go to dinner from there.

Aware of Holden reading over her shoulder, she flashed him another insincere smile, turned off her phone and slipped it back into the pocket of her black cashmere blazer.

"You're really going to pursue this?" His low, sexy voice rang with disbelief.

Was she? When just agreeing to meet with Jeff Johnston made her feel extremely disloyal? Libby pretended a cool she couldn't begin to really feel. "This is my decision, Holden."

It didn't matter what Percy or his family would have wanted, she reminded herself purposefully. None of them were here any longer....

Holden clamped a gentle hand around her elbow, the action sending ribbons of sensation flowing beneath her skin. "No one is saying otherwise."

Libby stepped back, pushing aside the sudden on-slaught of sexual feeling. For years, she had been devoid of physical yearning. Only to have it all come rushing back now, with the aching desire to be touched, held... loved.

Which was something else that could not happen in this small town, where everyone still saw her as the late Percy Lowell's wife.

Fighting off her increasing feelings of disloyalty, she said, "They just want me to keep everything status quo."

"They want you to be happy," Holden corrected, look-ing as if he and he alone had the solution to that, too. "We all do."

Libby looked at him stubbornly, aware of the rest-lessness inside her. She was thirty-two now, and over-whelmed with the sense that life was passing her by. How would she feel at thirty-four, thirty-five, if she didn't act...?

"Then forget how you and everyone else feels. And give me room to pursue a possible agreement with Jeff Johnston in my own time and in my own way."

"I KNOW WHAT YOU'RE thinking, Holden, but Libby is not your responsibility."

He turned to Libby's best friend, Paige. The pediatric surgeon, and wife of his cousin Kurt, had made her way to Holden's side the minute Libby stormed off in a huff.

Not wanting their conversation to be overheard, he ducked into the empty storeroom where the banquet ta-bles were usually stored. "I promised Percy I'd look after her and make sure no one took advantage of her," he reminded Paige.

"And you have—for over two years now. But Libby is a grown woman, fully capable of making her own decisions."

"In certain regards," he conceded. In others, she was still way too giving—and unconsciously sexy—for her own good.

Paige lifted a brow in quiet dissent.

Which prodded Holden to argue, "I don't have to remind you how emotional and overwrought she was after Percy's death." So deliriously "happy" she was practically walking on air one moment then completely devastated the next….

The look on Paige's face told him she recalled the same tumultuous swings in Libby's moods. "That was grief and hormones."

And guilt on his part. Terrible, haunting guilt.

"Beyond all that…" Paige paused. "She made a mistake—an understandable one."

One, Holden acknowledged painfully, that he and Libby had recklessly gone on to make even worse, and were both still trying to get over.

But Paige didn't know about that. And hopefully never would.

He scowled. "The point is, none of it would have happened had Percy been alive."

Libby wouldn't have trusted him with her secrets and thrown herself joyously into his arms…or called him just hours later, sobbing hysterically, begging him to take her to the emergency room. Only to find out that the terrible malady she'd thought she was experiencing didn't exist after all.

It had been a horrible, embarrassing mess. One they still hadn't figured out how to handle.

Oblivious to the complicated nature of his thoughts, Paige sighed. "You're right. If Percy had been here, she probably wouldn't have gone off the deep end like that."

And, Holden thought, he would not have been the one to take a distraught Libby home from the hospital in the wee hours of the morning, or been pressed into staying until dawn until Paige was finally off duty and could be with her....

Paige continued with the matter-of-factness of a physician. "The point is, that time has passed. Libby's pulled herself together and made a success of the family business she inherited from the Lowells."

"To the point," Kurt McCabe stated as he strolled up to them, "that a rival businessman wants to purchase it."

Not surprisingly, the gravity of the situation had the rest of Holden's family joining them, too.

"And that," his brother Hank interjected with the expertise of a cattle rancher, "could spell trouble for all of us."

"Or not," Holden's other brother, Jeb, concluded, with the ease of a man used to taking life as it came. "From what I understand, there's nothing thus far to indicate Jeff Johnston is a shyster."

"And nothing that tells us he is not," their dad, Shane McCabe, warned in a brisk, businesslike tone. "The only thing we do know for certain is that we all need heavy farm equipment to run our ranches. And if anything happens to the tractor dealership here, we'll have to go a hundred miles to get sales or service."

"That would definitely be a pain," Holden's brother-in-law, Dylan Reeves, said, "but I think we can all agree it's not the main worry for any of us."

Holden's mother nodded emphatically. "Our main concern is Libby," Greta said with feeling. "None of us want to see her hurt. And, sad to say, the sale of the Lowell family business could be a lot more devastating to her than she thinks."

AT THE BEHEST OF HIS FAMILY, Holden decided to give it one more try. Unfortunately, by the time he emerged from the storeroom, Libby had already left for home. Holden stopped by the dessert table, picked up some sweets to go and drove to the Lowell residence on the edge of town.

The magnificent two-story stone-and-cedar farmhouse was located just across the road from the tractor dealership. Surrounded by a white picket fence and a beautifully landscaped yard, it had been in the Lowell family for three generations. Libby's Range Rover was parked in front of the detached garage. Holden parked his pickup beside it.

He was just getting out, foil-covered plate in hand, when a third vehicle drove up. The compact sedan contained two women—Miss Mim, the retired town librarian, and the twentysomething college grad, Rosa Moncrief, who had taken over from her.

So much for spending time with Libby and getting to the heart of whatever was bothering her, Holden thought.

"I am so glad you're here!" The older woman hurried forward to give Holden a hug, while the younger one shyly said hello. "We need all the help we can get."

Help for what? Holden wondered, as Libby stepped out onto the porch, looking more exquisitely beautiful than ever. She had already changed out of her party clothes into boot-cut jeans, suede moccasins and a fitted flannel shirt that made the most of her slender five-foot-five frame. Her silky, honey-blond hair had been swept up into a ponytail. She had a pair of sexy reading glasses on her face, a thick novel in her hand. As always when he was near her like this, Holden found it difficult to turn his gaze away or stifle the protective feelings welling up inside him.

Part of it was because he had made a promise to protect her. The other part wasn't quite so gallant....

Oblivious to the depth of his interest in her, Libby looked curiously from one to the other. "What's going on?"

"A bit of a conundrum." Her colorful earrings jangling, Miss Mim rushed forward to hug Libby, too. "I hope you don't mind—we asked Holden to join us."

Libby flashed him a look that said she did not exactly share the elder woman's sentiment, but smiled and beckoned everyone inside.

Holden set the plate of desserts on the hall console while Libby took their jackets. "Now, tell me what's gotten you so upset," she urged, as she led them into the sweeping living room, with its mix of comfortable modern furniture and priceless antiques.

Miss Rosa gulped. "You know we've had problems with the water lines in the library all year. Well, yesterday morning we had another leak, and Rowdy Whitcombe had to come out and start pulling up the floor. This time, he wasn't able to fix it, and he left with everything still torn up." She sighed. "Naturally, I called the county to find out what in the world was going on. All they would tell me was that a few others were coming to assess the problem and that I should get everyone out and keep the facility closed until further notice."

"That sounds...ominous," Libby murmured, trading concerned glances with Holden.

Wishing he was sitting close enough to give her hand a squeeze, he nodded back.

"Which is why I got involved," Miss Mim confided with an unhappy sigh. "But by then the government offices had closed for the Thanksgiving holiday."

Clasping his hands between his knees, Holden leaned forward. "Did you try talking to Rowdy?"

Miss Mim nodded. "He wasn't at liberty to reveal much at this juncture, but said that if the situation was what he suspected, the library might be closed for a good long while."

"Which would be a problem," Libby said worriedly. "So many residents depend on it."

Holden knew she spent a lot of time there, too. Books had always been of great comfort to her. Even more so after Percy died....

"Plus—" Miss Rosa's low voice quavered "—we have all those Christmas events planned for the children, starting Monday. All the book clubs in the area have signed up to use the space for their holiday parties. Not to mention all the free literacy tutoring that goes on there." She wrung her hands in distress. "I'd arranged for a tree and everything!"

"And we all know," Holden murmured, "how bureaucracy can slow things down."

"No kidding!" Miss Mim turned back to Libby, her gaze intent. "We're going to need a real crusader. Which is, of course, why we came to you!"

Libby smiled. "I'll do everything I can to help."

"Me, too," Holden promised.

Beaming, Miss Mim and Miss Rosa stood. "With a Lowell and a McCabe on the job, how can we go wrong?" the older lady joked.

Holden went with Libby to show them out. "Actually,

you'll have a lot of McCabes," he promised, "as soon as I let the family know what's going on."

Briefly, Libby's expression looked pinched. "As far as the Lowells go, it's just me. But I promise you I'll give the situation my all."

Thanks were given. More hugs ensued. And then the two librarians slipped out the door.

"Well." Libby squared her slender shoulders and drew an innervating breath. "There's never a dull moment around here."

"The people of this community have come to rely on you," he said.

Unhappiness glimmered in Libby's green eyes as she regarded him. "That's not what I need to hear."

He had hurt her. Again. Without meaning to do so. He injected as much gentle levity into his tone as he dared. "What *do* you need to hear, then?"

She snorted indignantly. "Oh, something along the lines of you understand that although I have done everything I could to live up to the wishes of Percy and his parents in maintaining the Lowell family tradition and legacy in Laramie...you also know I'm leading a life I never intended to lead."

"I thought you liked running the dealership." She was certainly good at it.

She peered at him through narrowed lashes. "I like managing things, keeping things running and solving problems. I have no passion for farm and ranch equipment, per se."

He flashed her a cryptic smile. "You don't dream about combines and harvesters?"

Contrary as ever around him, she replied, "I have the occasional *nightmare* about a delivery not arriving in time for a rancher to harvest the crop that's going to feed his cattle all winter."

Holden cleared his throat, regarding her steadily. "You're serious."

She wandered back into the living room and plopped down on the sofa with her book. "Oh, yes."

He watched her slide her reading glasses back on her nose. "You never said anything."

She winced again. "That would have been ungrateful, wouldn't it?" Libby paused in the act of opening her novel. "Here I am, having inherited a beautiful home, a thriving business and the mantle of the esteemed Lowell name."

Holden sat opposite her and studied the elegant contours of her face.

"When all I really want, if I'm to be perfectly honest…" Libby raked her teeth across the velvety pink softness of her lower lip.

He gripped the arms of the chair and rocked forward slightly, guessing, "All you really want is your husband back."

A pained silence fell between them. When she spoke again, her defenses were up. "We both wish that were possible."

"I'm sorry, Libby."

"Please." She lifted a delicate palm. "Don't apologize. Not again…"

How could he not? Holden thought with a fresh flood of guilt. "If Percy and I hadn't gone on that white-water rafting trip in South America right after my marriage busted up…"

The light faded from her eyes. "He knew you were devastated when you lost the baby and Heidi, all at once."

The reminder of his loss had a wealth of undercurrents. "I never should have married her."

Libby sighed, perceptive as ever. "That's true, since shotgun weddings have a very low success rate. But," she continued with laudable understanding, "you're a noble guy...and you were head over heels in love with her."

Holden folded his arms over his chest. "Even if it turns out Heidi didn't feel the same way." To his ex-wife, he had been her rebound guy from another relationship.

"You did what you thought was the right thing, in marrying her," Libby soothed.

"And failed, anyway."

She nodded, recalling compassionately, "And Percy wanted to cheer you up."

Wearily, Holden shoved his fingers through his hair. "I should have said no."

"Then Percy would have gone alone."

Holden looked at her in disbelief.

Leaning forward, Libby took off her glasses and confided, "You weren't the only one unhappy at the time, Holden. Percy was feeling hemmed in. He was tired of running the dealership in the wake of his parents' death, tired of living the 'expected, ordinary' life. He needed that little burst of pure freedom."

Holden grimaced in regret. "But he had responsibilities. We both knew the Rio Suarez could be dangerous." Many of the rapids were a grade four plus...!

Libby shrugged, clearly not as inclined to rewrite history as Holden was. "If your raft hadn't started to take on water and collapse the exact moment you hit the rapids," she said with a resignation that came straight from her soul. "If Percy hadn't jumped to save you..."

"And succeeded," Holden stated hoarsely.

"He never would have slammed into those boulders

himself, or broken his leg and nearly drowned, until you and guides saved him. He wouldn't have needed to go to the hospital in San Gil, which was miles away, over rough terrain. His wounds wouldn't have become infected, and he wouldn't have started running a fever."

"And begged me to watch over you."

Abruptly, Libby looked as numb as she had at the funeral. "Had none of that happened, Percy would have lived." She stood and gazed deep into Holden's eyes. "But he didn't." Restlessly, she paced the length of the room. "And now you and I are here. Dealing with the aftermath of my late husband's reckless nature, each and every day."

Holden caught up with her. "You have to know," he croaked, gripping her hands,"if I could take it all back…" *Make your life better. Make you happy again…*

"I know, Holden. You would." Libby squeezed his palms, then let go. Sadness glimmered in her green eyes as she confessed, "And I would, too. But we can't. Instead, we have to deal with the fact that around here, I will always be Percy's 'tragic' widow. The keeper of the Lowell legacy, and the go-to person for all community problems needing solving. Around here, I'll never be just me. The Libby who grew up in Austin, and who wants a different kind of life.

He sighed heavily, watching her pained expression as she continued speaking her mind.

"Just as you will always be remembered as the guy who got quickly and unceremoniously dumped after Heidi lost your baby. The difference is, you've always lived here. You have tons of family in the area. And a ranch that you've built that will be your legacy from here on out." She met his eyes. "Divorced or no, this is the life you are *supposed* to be leading. Mine was here only as long as Percy was alive."

She had thought this through, Holden realized in shock. "You're serious about moving on, then."

"After more than two years?" Libby put her glasses back on her nose. "Yes. Very."

"So if this Jeff Johnston comes in with a good offer..."

"Or even a decent one," she affirmed.

"You'll take it."

Libby nodded, keeping the wall around her heart intact. "And I'll sell the house, move on...and never look back."

Chapter Two

"You're sure this is going to be okay?" Rosa asked Libby nervously on Friday morning.

Libby nodded and waved the library employee toward the dealership showroom. "You can set up a return desk over there in the corner. The books on hold—and the checkout and information counter—can go next to that."

Miss Mim came to join them. She'd brought with her a small army of library volunteers carrying armloads of supplies, boxes of books, even a computer. "Hopefully, we won't need to be here more than a couple of days."

Libby smiled at both librarians. "I'm sure we'll get this straightened out by then. In the meantime, library patrons will have a place to go for the essentials and information."

The dealership business was carrying on as usual. Two ranchers were in the offices, signing papers on new tractors and equipment. Another three were lined up to arrange service on their machines. And Lucia Gordon, the receptionist, was headed straight for Libby, a handsome thirtysomething man in a tweed sport coat and jeans by her side.

The tall stranger smiled as he reached her and held out his hand. "Libby Lowell, I presume?"

She grinned back. "The one and only."

He shook her hand. "Jeff Johnston."

Libby's jaw dropped in surprise. "I thought we weren't meeting until this evening."

"I wanted to let you know I had arrived and checked in at the Laramie Inn." Jeff looked around. "Plus I thought it would be good to see the place through the eyes of a regular customer." His brow furrowed as he noticed the temporary library being set up. "What's going on over there?"

Libby noted he didn't look pleased. Briefly, she explained the problem, as well as her solution, adding, "That's the way things work in a small town. We all go the extra mile to help each other out."

Jeff rubbed a hand across his jaw, considering that. "None of the customers seem to mind."

But, Libby noted, the next man coming into the dealership seemed wary. Not of what was going on in the corner, but of the man she was standing with.

Holden reached her and nodded at Jeff. "Johnston."

"McCabe."

Libby fought off a second wave of surprise. She squared her slender shoulders. "You two know each other?"

An inscrutable glint appeared in Holden's eyes as he informed her casually, "We met a little while ago at the Daybreak Café."

Which wasn't surprising, Libby guessed, since the restaurant owned by Holden's sister, Emily, was *the* place in town to have breakfast.

"I was chatting up the locals, asking around, to see how people felt about the dealership," Jeff explained.

Libby tensed, not sure how she felt about that. Shouldn't any questions have been directed at her first?

"Anyway, we're still on for dinner this evening, right?" Jeff asked.

She nodded.

"Great. I've got a lot of questions and things I'd like to discuss." He inclined his head and strolled off.

Holden gave Libby a steady look that sent heat spiraling through her. "Tell me you're taking someone with you. Like a lawyer."

Clearly, Holden didn't trust Jeff Johnston. For reasons that had more to do with his loyalty to her late husband—and to her—than to Johnston's overarching ambition, she suspected.

Libby folded her arms and moved closer to him. "I'm not paying a lawyer to sit through polite get-to-know-each-other chitchat."

Holden looked at her soberly. "Obviously, Johnston wants it to be more than that. He appears anxious to get you to sign on the dotted line, here and now."

She stepped back. "Then Mr. Johnston will be disappointed," she said firmly, uncomfortably aware that she'd had the same impression of the businessman. "But if it will make you feel better...you can tag along," she offered reluctantly.

Holden grinned as happily as if she had invited him into her bedroom. "Seriously?"

Doing her best to quell her conflicting emotions, Libby nodded. She did not want to depend on Holden, emotionally or otherwise. She had allowed herself to do that once, right after her husband's passing, and the result had been disastrous for both of them. To the point that guilt and discomfort from that time were still with both of them.

But she was smart enough to know that the easiest way to keep one man from becoming too aggressive with her was to put another equally driven and protective man into the mix. So for now, for tonight, she would allow her late husband's best friend to appease his conscience by employing his innate gallantry on her behalf, once more.

Having decided that, she sighed.

Glancing up at Holden, she couldn't help but note how good he looked in that green corduroy shirt and jeans. His short dark hair was thick and rumpled, and his face had the shadow of beard that came from going twenty-four hours without a razor. But it was the cobalt-blue of his eyes, the compassionate set of his sensual lips, that really drew her in.

"Thanks for inviting me," he said.

Libby gave him a glance that warned him not to get too carried away. "It makes more sense to have you at the table with us than to have you hovering somewhere in the background, trying to watch over me from a distance." Which, she knew, he was likely to do, given the depth of his concern about the potential pitfalls of the situation she was in.

And if she was completely honest, Libby admitted, she wouldn't mind having Holden at the first official meeting.

The handsome rancher was bound to be a lot less emotional about the proposed transaction than she, and would give her perspective on everything said.

In certain situations, two were better than one.

This, Libby figured, was one of those times.

"I DIDN'T REALIZE THE TWO of you were dating," Jeff Johnston said to Holden and Libby after they had ordered their meals.

Taking comfort in the laid-back ease of the Wagon Wheel Restaurant, she sipped her iced tea. "Holden is here as a friend."

Jeff quirked a brow. "Do you always take friends to business meetings?"

Aware that her throat still felt parched, and that she was far too conscious of Holden and his sexy masculine presence, Libby took another drink. "No."

Jeff glanced at her curiously. "Then...?"

She searched for an explanation for herself, as well. Ignoring Holden's equally probing look, she told Jeff, "You wanted to know how the ranchers in the area feel about the dealership. Holden can tell you that."

The other man turned to him. "How is the level of service?"

"Excellent," Holden stated promptly. "First and foremost, prices are fair."

"Almost too much so," Jeff countered. "Since the profit the company is taking on sales is slightly below the industry standard."

"It's a competitive market," Libby interjected. "We aim to please."

"And they do," Holden said candidly. "From the time you walk in the door, Lowell Ranch Equipment employees are there to help you decide what heavy machinery you need, and how to obtain financing. And they are just as dedicated when it comes to providing any service or parts required. Because of that, they have a very loyal customer base."

"You're not just saying that because Libby is your 'friend'?" Jeff chided.

"Libby doesn't need me to exaggerate on her behalf," Holden said, beginning to sound a little irked at the remark. "Lowell Ranch Equipment has been in business for three generations, and has served a hundred-mile rural area for the last seventy years. The commitment of the sales and service staff has never wavered."

Jeff nodded, as if his research had garnered the same data. "I notice a lot of the employees are older, though. Fifty plus…"

For the thirtysomething Jeff, that was a problem, Libby noted unhappily. "Ten of our employees are in that age demographic—they have worked at the business their whole adult lives. Three others are in their twenties, but equally as committed to careers with us."

He frowned. "Meaning you would be opposed to me letting at least some members of your staff go, and bringing in my own people?"

She stiffened her spine, the tough businesswoman inside her coming to the fore. "I won't sell to you unless there is a guarantee you'll continue to employ every person currently working there for as long as they want to stay, at their current salary and benefits."

"You realize that could sour the deal," Jeff warned.

Libby turned her hands palm up. "Then it does."

He sat back in his chair as their dinners were put in front of them, and considered her position. "Well, that explains why everyone is so loyal."

Libby picked up her knife and fork. "We've had virtually no turnover, because it is such a good place to work. The fact the customers know who they are going to be dealing with is a comfort to them. Everyone feels like family."

Jeff cut into his steak. "In my experience, business and personal affairs don't mix."

She took a bite of her grilled redfish. "That may be true in Houston. It's not the case in Laramie." She paused long enough to meet Holden's encouraging glance, then asked Jeff, "Why do you want LRE so badly?" He had been calling her every few months since Percy died, asking if she wanted to sell.

He added butter to his baked potato. "I specialize in acquiring businesses with no internet presence and taking them online. LRE would be my biggest acquisition yet. I see great potential for growth. In fact, you could stay on if you want, Libby, because I'm not going to be there more than once a week—if that—and I'll need someone to manage it."

"Thank you for the offer, but—no. I'm selling because I want out."

"You're planning to leave the area, then?"

Out of the corner of her eye, Libby saw Holden tense. "Yes."

Jeff leaned toward her. "What about the house? Are you interested in including it in the sale? 'Cause I'm going to need someplace nice to stay when I'm in town."

Libby hesitated. How did she feel about that? "We could negotiate," she said cautiously. "If the price is right, of course."

"Can I see it tonight?" Jeff asked eagerly, while Holden tensed even more.

Ignoring his obvious disapproval, Libby shrugged. "I suppose a brief tour would be okay."

Victorious, Jeff smiled. "Then let's do it!"

They talked more as they ate. No one wanted dessert, so as soon as the check was paid, they went out to their vehicles. Libby took the lead in her Range Rover, with Jeff following in his Maserati and Holden trailing behind in his pickup truck.

Her self-appointed protector looked even grimmer when they arrived at the house.

The first thing that caught Jeff's eye was the Lowell photo gallery that lined much of the foyer and both walls of the grand front staircase. "Wow." He stopped at the framed pictures of three generations of Lowells, then he studied Percy and Libby's wedding photo.

"You were awfully young when you got married."

She had been. "Twenty-two. Right out of college."

"And you were married how long?"

Libby noticed Holden studying the photos, too, with the familiar mixture of grief, guilt and sadness. "Almost eight years."

Jeff turned back to her. "I can see why you want to sell," he told her empathetically. "Residing here must feel like living in a mausoleum."

Aptly put, Libby thought.

"The tour?" Holden said, looking irritated again.

Libby inhaled and braced herself for another slew of questions from the ambitious businessman. "Let's get started," she said. *So I can put this evening—and the onslaught of confusing emotions—behind me.*

HOLDEN KNEW LIBBY WAS ticked off at him. And maybe he was overstepping his bounds. But when Jeff Johnston asked to see the second floor…

"Not a good idea." Holden moved to block the way to the stairs.

Jeff turned to Libby with a goading smile. "I thought the two of you weren't involved."

"We're not," she said, a hint of color coming into her cheeks.

Maybe not in the traditional way, Holden thought. But they were linked through Percy's memory. And he had made a promise not to let anyone take advantage of his best friend's widow. A promise he would continue to carry out until his dying day.

"Actually, we are," he stated flatly.

Libby's jaw dropped in shock. "I can't believe you just alluded to that," she said, glaring at Holden.

It didn't matter, he thought, because Jeff clearly believed him, not Libby. And Johnston's obvious respect for another man's territory would keep him from making an untoward pass at Libby, at least for now.

"I'm going to head out," Jeff said, his demeanor slightly less personal as he backed off. "But I'll be in touch."

"I look forward to it." Libby's tone was crisp and businesslike. Spine stiff, she walked him to the door.

As soon as he'd left, she whirled back to Holden and inhaled, the action lifting the soft curves of her breasts. A pulse worked in her throat as she kept her eyes meshed with his. "You had no right to tell Jeff Johnston he couldn't go up to the second floor."

Holden found himself tracking the fall of honey-colored hair swinging against her shoulders and caressing the feminine lines of her face. Wondering if it was as silky to the touch as he recalled, he asked, "You were really going to let Jeff Johnston see the bedrooms?"

"No, of course not." Libby propped her hands on her hips and sent him a chastising look. "Not without having a chance to tidy up and get the property ready to show!" She inched closer, inundating him with a drift of cinnamon perfume. "But that's not the point, Holden."

Desire sprang up within him, as surely as irritation had. Reminding himself she was off-limits for a whole host of reasons, he returned carefully, "Then what is the point?"

Their eyes locked, providing another wave of unbidden heat between them. "You intimated to him that you and I are having a fling."

"No." Holden savored her nearness, and the pleasure

that came from being alone with her, in a way they hadn't been for months now.

He turned and wandered toward the cozy family room in the back of the house. "I said we are involved," he corrected, as he passed another row of photos, of Percy and Libby together, involved in all the outdoor activities Percy loved.

Reminded that Libby was once his best friend's wife, Holden shoved his hands in the pockets of his wool trousers and drawled, "I just didn't say *how* we are involved."

She stepped out of her heels and stood holding the sexy shoes, as if she wanted to lob them at his head. "Same difference," she snapped.

Holden let his glance drift down her spectacular pantyhose-clad legs to her toes. "Really?" His gaze returned slowly and deliberately to her face, pausing on her lips, before moving to her long-lashed green eyes. Ignoring the threat of the stilettos, he leaned closer still and dropped his tone to a husky whisper. "'Cause I don't remember anything sexual or romantic happening between us."

Libby sniffed and sent him a quelling look. "Only because you came to your senses and put a stop to it."

Wanting something wasn't the same as *taking* it. Particularly when they both had been lost and hurting, searching for any way to end the pain.

As it turned out, Holden recalled soberly, neither of them could have lived with that.

Curtailing his rising emotions, he shrugged. "You said it was for the best."

Libby kept her distance, eventually drifting over toward the fireplace, where she pivoted, her back to the mantel. Raking her teeth across her lower lip, she admitted quietly, "And that was true. I wasn't myself that night."

For a long time, Holden had let himself believe that.

Now, cognizant of the tension that charged the air between them, he studied the mixture of regret and longing in her eyes. Found himself theorizing before he could stop himself, "And maybe you were yourself, Libby. Maybe your instincts *were* right."

Another shadow crossed her eyes. "What are you saying?"

Holden looked at the gold broken-heart pendant shimmering against the delicate ivory of her skin. Lower still, he could see the hint of cleavage in the V neckline of her black cashmere sweater dress. "That if I hadn't been such a gentleman... If I had allowed us to follow through on our urges..."

Maybe she wouldn't have held him at arm's length all this time. Maybe they could have shrugged off that flare of desire and gone back to being friends. Kissed and found out there was no chemistry between them, after all. Or argued and cleared the tension that way.

Instead, they had been adult about it. Distant. Careful. Unerringly polite. And tense as could be.

Libby studied him with a brooding look. "I know you're trying to be gallant here, Holden. But we have to face facts. I was the one who wanted to kiss you that night. Not the other way around."

Noting the raw vulnerability in her expression, Holden felt his heart go out to her all over again.

He realized it was his turn to be honest. No matter how much it complicated their lives. "You're wrong about that, Libby," he told her hoarsely.

His gaze lingered on her, as he paused to let his words sink in. "I would have given everything I had that night to see where that burst of physical attraction would lead."

She shook her head. "But we couldn't because I was a wreck. In some ways I still am a wreck."

Not sure what she meant, Holden stared at her.

Libby lifted her hands. "It's this house, Holden. The dealership. I can't be either place without feeling like Percy's wife." Her voice caught and her lower lip trembled. "That's the real reason I can't stay here in Laramie. If I do, I'll never be able to move on."

As Holden looked around, he saw what she meant.

The home was brimming with signs of Percy and his folks, and the generations who had lived here before that.

It was clearly a Lowell domain.

Holden recalled that Libby had suggested a few small changes after they had taken over the residence, when Percy was still alive. All had been gently but firmly refused. Libby, in her usual genial way, had stopped bringing up the subject. And although she could have redecorated since Percy died, she hadn't. Probably because it would have felt disloyal, an insult to his memory, or disrespectful to his wishes.

No wonder she felt trapped, Holden mused sympathetically. He edged closer. "You want to get married again?"

Determination stiffened her slender frame. "Of course. I want to fall in love. I want to have kids. I want to feel like everything good is still ahead of me."

Everything she would have had, Holden thought, on a fresh wave of guilt, had her husband still been alive.

"Then you're going to have to do a lot more than just sell the dealership and the house," he told her sternly. "You're going to have to start dating again."

Libby eyed him mockingly. "Thank you, Dr. Phil."

"I'm serious."

"I know you are." Her hips swaying provocatively, she strode past him toward the kitchen.

Like every other room in the house, it had been decorated long before Libby arrived on the scene. And although the color scheme was okay—if you liked bleached oak cabinets and beige walls—the once top-of-the-line appliances were definitely showing their age. As were some of the wall hangings and wooden blinds.

"The only problem is, no one will ask me out."

She hit the switch, flooding the room with light, then headed for the fridge.

Holden followed her lazily. Glad she had decided to do something to distract them from the new tension between them, he watched her rummage through the contents until she emerged with a chocolate-and-peppermint Yule log from the local bakery.

His mouth watering for more than the sweet, he settled against the counter.

"That's because you're still putting out the I'm-a-widow-and-therefore-off-limits-to-anyone-with-any-sensitivity vibe."

Libby stood on tiptoe to reach the dessert plates. "I am not."

He came forward to help her, steadying her with a hand to her waist. "Yeah...you are." He finished getting the dishes down for her. "But we can fix that."

Her lips pursed stubbornly. "How?" she asked, cutting two slices and handing him one, complete with a fork.

Holden settled opposite her at the table. Their knees touched momentarily. Regretting the contact—and the sizzle of warmth it engendered—he pulled back and continued to focus on solving her problem. "By finding you a rebound guy."

Libby frowned. "I get that you're trying to help me, but why would you want any other guy to sign up for that—after what you went through with your ex?" She scowled protectively, like the close friend she had once been before their ill-fated kiss-that-never-quite-happened. "Heidi broke your heart! To the point that you've never dated seriously since."

"I haven't dated seriously because I haven't found the right woman," Holden corrected bluntly. "But I should put myself out there if I want to move on, too. And I do."

Libby went very still. "What are you suggesting?"

Holden's spirits rose as the idea took on momentum. "That we both shake off the rust. Get back in the game."

Libby licked the frosting off the back of her fork. "By that you mean…?"

"Go out to dinner. Attend holiday parties. Really celebrate the season. Who knows? If you and I get back in the habit of dating again, it might give us both a whole new outlook on life."

Libby's soft lips took on an enticing curve. "Meaning what?" she murmured cynically. "I might be so content I won't want to sell the dealership and move out of town?"

He grinned at her sarcasm and lifted a palm. "I'm just saying…"

Silence fell as the notion stuck. They studied each other.

Libby took the last bite of her dark chocolate cake, savoring the sweet decadence. "So, cowboy with all the answers, how do you propose I find my rebound man?"

Chapter Three

"You're looking at him."

Libby stared at Holden, sure she hadn't heard right. "Why in the world would you do that, after the way you were hurt the last time?"

"Unwittingly being someone else's rebound person is what makes me right for the task. I know you still love Percy and always will. It's not going to be easy for you to move on."

Guilt threatened to overwhelm Libby. She and Percy *hadn't* been in love at the end. But no one knew that.... "Don't put me up for sainthood," she said quietly. She had enough of that from the community every single day. "Because I'm not the perfect woman and I was never the perfect wife."

"Percy sure thought otherwise."

More guilt flooded her heart.

"He'd never met a woman who was more accommodating."

Libby pushed back her chair and carried her plate to the dishwasher. "Which is one reason I'm so unhappy," she remarked lightly. "I've spent too much of my life trying to please everyone else."

Holden put his dish and fork in the machine, too. Then

he leaned against the counter, watching her. "Your aunt Ida?"

Libby could feel him sizing her up, trying to figure out how to convince her to stay where he could keep an eye on her, and hence, continue to fulfill his deathbed promise to her late husband.

Wishing she weren't so aware of Holden's presence, Libby retreated into scrupulous politeness. "I was only seven when my parents died. Even though my aunt was in her fifties at the time, she took on the responsibility of raising me." She sighed. "I loved her dearly and will always be grateful to her for taking me in. But…because I was her only remaining family and she mine…she was paranoid about potential dangers and kept me on a very tight leash."

"I remember you had to live at home with her while you were attending UT."

Promising herself she was not going to fall prey to the attraction between them, Libby nodded. "Part of it was that she needed someone to take care of her by then, but the other part was that she didn't want me doing anything the least bit reckless."

"Which is where Percy came in," Holden guessed.

Libby made a face. In retrospect she could hardly believe her recklessness. "After Aunt Ida passed, that was all I wanted to do. Percy took me skydiving and hiking and taught me how to water-ski." More than anything, the diversion had helped her survive her mourning.

Holden moved closer, holding her gaze in an increasingly intimate way. "You don't do any of that stuff anymore."

Hanging on to her composure by a thread, she rubbed a nick on the counter with her fingertip. "I guess I had more of my aunt in me than I realized because I never really liked it."

Any more than I like selling tractors and ranch equipment now.

"But…at the same time—" Libby lifted her chin, drew a deep breath "—I had something to prove. Once that was accomplished, my total freedom to finally do as I pleased verified that I actually wanted a more sedate lifestyle." She flashed him a rueful smile, aware that what had comforted her had eventually ended up nearly doing him in. "Which was where you entered the picture.…"

"I went back to doing those things with Percy when you stopped."

"And—contrary to what you might have thought—I really was appreciative."

"That I took your place?"

"I knew Percy wasn't going to stop indulging in physically challenging activities. He was too much of a daredevil for that. I was glad he had someone trustworthy and levelheaded to go with him."

Holden's expression radiated guilt, and silence fell between them.

Compassion for his plight forced her to go on. "So you see, Holden," Libby continued gently, "you have already done more than enough for both Percy and for me. You really don't have to squire me around, the way you did tonight."

"Suppose I want to," Holden said. "What then?"

She blinked. "Why would you want to do that?" she demanded.

Merriment turned up the corners of his lips. "Because it occurs to me now that I need a rebound woman as much as you need a rebound man."

Her heartbeat kicking up a notch, Libby studied him. "You're serious."

Holden lounged against the counter opposite her, his arms folded against his chest. He stared at her with a steely resolve that matched her own. "Think about it. I'll always view you as Percy's wife."

Trying not to think what his steady appraisal and deep voice did to her, Libby appraised him right back. "And I'll always regard you as his best friend."

Cynicism twisted a corner of his mouth. "So there's no chance either of us will take a dating arrangement to heart."

Libby began to see where he was going with this. His proposal could be the solution to both their problems, as well as a bridge to the future. "It'll just be part of the process we both need to go through to get back out there."

"Right," he said casually. "Kind of like riding a bike…"

Stubbornly, she kept her eyes locked with his, even as her heart raced like a wild thing in her chest. "We're going to need ground rules," she warned.

He accepted her condition with a matter-of-fact nod. "The more specific, the better."

"How long should we do this?"

He shrugged, considering. "Through New Year's?"

Libby drummed her fingers on the countertop. "That would get us all the way through the holidays."

His big body began to relax. "It's always good not to be alone this time of year."

She nodded and took a deep breath. "Invites too much pity. Which—" she leaned in close "—is something I think we can agree neither of us needs."

A companionable silence fell between them. Searching for other pitfalls, Libby said, "What about our friends and your family?"

Holden grimaced, suddenly looking like a knight charged with protecting his queen. "I don't see any need to make a big announcement. They'll figure it out. Eventually."

She appreciated his desire to shield her from hurt. And while she didn't need his chivalry, in this one instance she supposed it wouldn't hurt to accept it. "That would lessen the pressure."

"And perhaps the scrutiny, as well."

He was right in that respect. There was nothing worse than having everyone tracking the progress of a new romance, and then broadcasting the "latest developments" to everyone they knew.

"What about sex?" Libby pressed, perfectly willing to keep their process of renewal private. "Because if you're expecting to go to bed with me as part of our bargain..."

Holden winced, as if he found the whole idea painful and awkward. "I don't think we need to make it a condition of the relationship," he interjected swiftly.

Libby breathed a sigh of relief.

"On the other hand..." he continued with a wicked smile. He was ready for whatever came.

Was she?

Hit with a sudden case of nerves, Libby cleared her throat. "I'm not sure I..." She stopped, unable to go on. There were shortcomings she did not wish to discuss. Her ability to hold a man's attention in the bedroom topped the list.

Holden frowned, all protective male again. "Then don't worry about it," he said, his gaze sincere. "We're only going to be together for six weeks. Then we'll be moving on. Frankly, it might be better for our friendship if we didn't consummate the dating thing."

Libby relaxed again. "Thank you."

Not that she was surprised. Holden McCabe was always a true gentleman.

"IS IT TRUE?" Several LRE employees confronted Libby the next morning the minute she walked in the front door. "Are you really planning to sell Lowell Ranch Equipment?"

Lucia Gordon, the dealership receptionist, wrung her hands. "We figured you were just talking to Jeff Johnston to price him out of the market and get him to stop calling you."

"Today, I've already had requests from him to fax all the financials over to him at the Laramie Inn, ASAP," Vince Hunt reported.

Libby directed the group into her private office, where everyone stood shoulder to shoulder. She put down her purse and coffee mug. "He should not have asked you that. He should have come through me for any further information he needed."

"Percy left the dealership to you because you're the last of the Lowells and he expected you to take care of it," Manny Pierce reminded her. "Not end three generations of Lowell family tradition and cash in." The senior mechanic frowned. "We're really disappointed in you, Libby."

"As well as worried about our jobs," Swifty Mortimer added.

Libby worked her coat off and slung it over the back of her desk chair. "No one is going to lose their employment over this. That I can promise you."

Skeptical glances abounded. Clearly disgruntled, everyone filtered out.

The rest of the workday went just as badly.

Near 4:00 p.m., Libby walked over to the warehouse to do the end of November inventory.

She had just climbed into the cab of a deluxe combine harvester to compare the serial number and price with the information they had in their computer system when Holden McCabe walked into the building.

How was it, she wondered, that he knew intuitively just when to show up to save the day or lighten her mood? Despite her decision not to rely on him emotionally in any way, her heart gave a little leap.

Oblivious to the hopelessly dependent nature of her thoughts, Holden lifted one brawny arm in acknowledgment. He strode confidently toward her.

Her heart took another little leap of anticipation as he neared.

Appearing concerned, he climbed into the enclosed cab beside her and shut the door.

His shoulder and hip brushed hers as he settled onto the bench seat. "What's going on?" he asked her as he shot her another concerned look.

Trying not to notice how much space his tall, muscular frame took up, Libby swallowed. She hadn't wanted to cry on his shoulder this much since the night he had brought her home from the emergency room.

She drew another breath as her pulse picked up a notch and a guilty flush heated her face. "Pretty much what you'd expect, under the circumstances. All the employees are mad at me. They think I'll be betraying the Lowells if I sell."

He studied her empathetically. "Sometimes you have to forget pleasing everyone else and make yourself happy." He shrugged and briefly squeezed her forearm. "I'm thinking this is one of those times."

Libby released a tremulous breath and raked a hand through her hair. "You really do understand." And she needed that. Even though she was convinced she was doing the right thing, this situation left her feeling more vulnerable than she had expected.

With a cajoling smile, and another pat on her arm, Holden predicted, "And everyone else will understand, too, given a little time. In the meantime—" he released her and sat back "—I've got some more bad news—if you think you can handle it."

Aware how her arm was tingling from that brief, comforting touch, Libby turned her attention to the rotary thresher attached to the front of the machine. She took a second to brace herself for the second onslaught of the day. "Go ahead," she instructed wearily.

He rested a powerful forearm on the hydraulic steering wheel. "The library has been closed indefinitely. Apparently, what Rowdy found beneath the subflooring was asbestos that had been used for electrical insulation and soundproofing."

Libby winced. "That sounds dangerous."

He nodded. "It can be a real health hazard if it starts to deteriorate, and this stuff looked pretty old." Cheering slightly, he added, "The good news is all the AC filters and surfaces in the library building tested clean of any microscopic fibers that could be inhaled, so no one's been in danger thus far. But it's going to have to come out."

She sighed wearily as she waited for him to continue.

He met her level gaze. "And it's going to be a very expensive proposition. The initial estimate from the hazardous-material experts is a quarter of a million, and the county doesn't have it in the budget."

Libby's heart sank as she contemplated the loss. "So what are they going to do?"

"Try and find the money somewhere, but the earliest that will happen is January."

She clapped a hand over her heart. "And in the meantime?"

"The county is arranging for Laramie residents to have privileges in neighboring county library systems."

"But those are thirty-five miles away, minimum!" Libby declared in dismay.

Holden exhaled, looking disappointed, as well. "It's the best the county can do."

She turned toward him urgently, her knee bumping his thigh in the process. "There has to be a better solution!" she protested hotly.

The corners of his lips curved upward. "Miss Mim and Miss Rosa are collecting suggestions as we speak." His glance sifted slowly over Libby's face, lingering on the flush in the cheeks and her lush bare lips, before returning to her eyes. "In the meantime, I was thinking. It is Saturday...so how about tonight for our first official date?"

HOLDEN WAS SURPRISED but pleased that Libby assented right away. "The distraction might be just what I need...."

He'd half feared she would get cold feet about the whole arrangement and try to beg off, but she hadn't, so they agreed to meet at her house at seven-thirty.

Leaving her to finish the inventory, Holden went home to the Bar M ranch to take care of his horses, shower and change. Figuring there would be less pressure on them if they had dinner and saw a movie, he printed out the listings for the theater in town and the multiplex in San Angelo, then headed back to Libby's place.

He stared at the vehicles lining her driveway and clogging the parking lot of the now-closed dealership across the road.

Her home, he soon found out, was just as congested.

Twenty-five or so women were crowded into the spacious living room. Miss Mim and Miss Rosa were holding court.

The topic? The library, of course.

"The problem is," Rosa was saying as Holden took off his coat and joined the group, "there's no available building in Laramie where three floors of books could be housed temporarily."

"I have an idea," Libby said. "It's a little unusual, but…"

All eyes turned to her.

"What if we divided the books up into sections, much the way they are now, and looked for host homes in town to function as mini-libraries? We could put the information online and still have a help desk in the LRE showroom. Hours could be limited. Say two hours, three times a week, max, for each farmed-out section of the library. That way, the books would still be available to local residents, and they wouldn't have to travel to a neighboring county."

"What an amazing idea!" Miss Mim said.

Holden thought so, too.

The room erupted in applause.

More excited talk ensued.

Holden's sister, Emily, appeared at his side. "Libby is quite the heroine, isn't she?"

"Yes," he murmured, "she is."

Not that this was a surprise. It didn't matter what the problem was. Whether it be a personal or civic matter, Libby was always first in line to help. The first to start or lead a crusade. Everyone in Laramie knew that, which was why the library volunteers and personnel had convened here tonight. Because they had known that when presented with a particularly thorny problem, Libby Lowell would know just what to do.

Holden couldn't help but admire Libby as she confidently held court. She wasn't just gorgeous as all get-out. She was smart and kind, and could think outside the box.

In fact, he had never met a more fascinating woman in his life. And if she hadn't started out as his best friend's girl, he might have pursued her himself.

His sister broke through his reverie. "And if I didn't know better—" Emily smiled and playfully punched Holden's arm "—I'd think *you* had a thing for her."

"WHAT WERE YOU AND EMILY talking about?" Libby asked, after everyone had left.

She thinks I am falling for you. Which is ridiculous, since at the end of the day I'll still see you as the woman who was once married to my best friend.

Pretty sure Libby was not ready to hear any of that, Holden shrugged indolently and cut to the chase. "Like everyone else I know, my sister wants me to get out there and start dating again."

Libby kept her eyes on his a disconcertingly long time, then lifted her chin and regarded him suspiciously. "Did you tell her about us?"

Holden tried not to notice how much trouble she had gone to for their "first date." She had put on a ruffled Western blouse, formfitting brown cords and lace-up tan boots. Her hair had been swept up into a loose, sexy knot on the back of her head, her lips softly glossed. She smelled of her trademark cinnamon-and-spice perfume.

He forced himself to sound as casual as they'd agreed they would be.

"I figured we would actually go out first." *See how it went.* "Speaking of which…"

"I know." The enticing curves of her breasts pushed against the fabric of her blouse as she inhaled. "I'm sorry." Her tiny reindeer earrings jangled as she tilted her head slightly to one side. "I didn't mean for that to happen, but when Miss Mim and Rosa called, wanting to brainstorm and bring along a few others, I couldn't say no."

Holden's glance fell to the delicate hollow of Libby's throat before returning to her eyes. "I understand."

She raked her teeth over her luscious lower lip. "I didn't expect it to go on so long."

Aware he was beginning to get aroused—also not part of their bargain—he glanced at his watch. "It's only nine-thirty. We could still do something." Anything to kill the desire building within him.

"Like what?" Libby moved around the room, picking up a few stray glasses and plates. "The late movies have already started."

She hurried past him, her long, sexy strides adding fuel to the fire already burning deep inside him.

"And most of the restaurants are already closing down. Not that I'm hungry—" Libby chattered on, setting the items in the sink "—since everyone who came over brought some sort of food."

Holden caught up with her and put the things he had gathered down, too.

Aware she looked increasingly tense and worried—as if afraid to be alone with him—he put his hands on her shoulders. "Relax."

She tensed even more at his touch. "Sorry." Swallowing, she forced a nervous smile, stepped back.

This would not do.

Holden shook his head in mute rebuke. Using humor to ease the sudden stress, he winked. "You're as skittish as a cat who just had her tail caught beneath a rocking chair."

The comparison worked to quell her nerves. "Funny." Libby returned his droll look with one of her own.

"Seriously." Holden stepped back and suggested smoothly, "We could go out and get a beer. Listen to music at the dance hall."

Libby lifted an elegant brow. "And no doubt run into your mom—because she owns the place?"

He rubbed his hand across the back of his neck. "You're right," he admitted. "That would be a little claustrophobic for a first date. Even a very casual one."

Libby sighed and held up a hand in surrender. "Maybe we should just call it a night," she said apologetically. "Try again—I don't know—sometime next week."

Holden knew a woman about to back out on him when he saw one. He caught up with her in the hall and kept pace. "What's wrong with tomorrow?"

Libby frowned at the sight of a dirty glass she had missed. She picked it up and held it in front of her like a shield. "I'm going to be at the library to help remove the uncontaminated books that are coming to my home. After that, I'll be busy setting up temporary stacks in my living room."

"I can help with that," Holden volunteered.

She shook her head. "You don't have to."

He studied her, knowing they could not leave it like this and expect things to get any better between them. "I want to," he insisted quietly.

Libby seemed completely at a loss as to what to say or

do next. Which in turn made Holden take a step closer, and ask, "Are you trying to get rid of me?" He scanned her head to toe, his eyes narrowed suspiciously. "Because you suddenly seem *very* nervous." And he wanted to know why…so it wouldn't happen again.

"I'm just wired," she said evasively, setting the lone glass on the foyer console rather than carry it all the way back to the kitchen. She jammed her hands on her hips. "It's been a long day. A lot has happened."

"Mmm-hmm." Holden studied her some more. "Sure it's not something else?" he prodded.

She widened her pretty eyes, all innocence. "Like what?" she asked with Texas belle sweetness.

And if there was one thing Libby was not, it was a coquette.

Holden stepped even closer. "Like the kiss…that *almost* happened. That is still on both our minds every time we are alone."

Color swept into Libby's cheeks. "So what if it is?" she taunted defiantly. "I'm sure we'll get rid of the notion sooner rather than later."

Holden grinned, the man in him rising to the womanly challenge in her. "I prefer sooner," he murmured.

Libby scoffed and tossed her head. "Well, so would I! But…there's no way to do that."

"Sure there is," Holden told her confidently. "I'll show you."

Chapter Four

Holden threaded his fingers through her hair, then bent and kissed first her temple and then her cheek.

"Trust me," he whispered, as his mouth drifted slowly, inevitably toward hers. "This is the only solution…if we're ever to have any peace…."

Much as she was loath to admit it, Libby knew he was right. Giving in to the curiosity that had been plaguing her for years now, she went up on tiptoe. Holden groaned, pulling her flush against him. Her heart racing, Libby parted her lips to the investigating pressure of his. He responded by kissing her even more deeply. Her entire body going soft with pleasure at the unhurried coaxing of his lips and the seductive stroking of his tongue, she wrapped her arms around his neck and tilted her hips to his.

For the first time in her life, she began to see what she'd been missing. This was the kind of kiss she had always dreamed about and never received. Evocative. Inundating. Tender. The kind that made her feel all woman to his man. The kind that made her feel that being close to someone again might not be such a crazy idea, after all….

HOLDEN HADN'T COME HERE tonight intending to kiss Libby. In fact, his plan had been to delay the physical indefinitely.

But that had been before he'd seen the veil come over her eyes yet again, in a way that made him wonder why intimacy of any kind with him was such a threat to her.

And suddenly he knew.

He broke off the kiss, dropped his arms to his sides and stepped back. "All this time I thought the reason you were so ill at ease with me was because we almost kissed." He paused, looking deep into her eyes. "But that isn't it at all. Is it?"

OF ALL THE THINGS she did not want to discuss, her foolish behavior had to be at the top of the list. "I was an idiot that night, long before I hurled myself at you." One giant mess of hormones and pent-up emotion.

He gave her an understanding glance. "You thought you were pregnant."

Misery engulfed her. "And I wasn't."

Holden caught her hand when she would have turned away. "But you didn't know that when you called me and asked me to drive you to the hospital." He squeezed her palm compassionately. "You thought you were losing your baby."

Libby leaned into his touch despite herself. "Had I been with child, that baby would have been three months along. Instead, all that was happening inside me was a lot of cramping and the beginning of the worst menstrual period ever! I've never felt so ridiculous or been so humiliated in my entire life."

Holden studied her. "And Paige and I witnessed it."

Libby struggled to get a grip. "The difference being that Paige is a physician and a woman." Her best friend had been able to view the situation with the clinical detachment that Libby had needed. Holden had reacted much more emotionally. Which had made her feel even worse about dragging him into the situation, and dumping all her problems on him.

"I never thought less of you." He wrapped his arms around her shoulders and pulled her close. "My heart went out to you that night," he murmured against the top of her head. "You'd just lost Percy a couple of months before, and when you thought you were having his baby, you had such joy." His warm breath touched her ear.

In an effort to shield her eyes from his probing gaze, she let her head rest against his chest. "And guilt, and a million other things," she whispered as a flood of tears pressed hotly behind her eyes.

He brought her closer yet, one hand moving down her back in long, soothing strokes. "Why guilt?"

Maybe it was time she began to unburden herself. And who better to tell than Holden, who had his own regrets?

Fighting the overwhelming sadness she felt whenever she thought of all that preceded and followed Percy's tragic death, she looked him in the eye and took another halting breath. Finally, she asked what she had never dared voice before. "You don't know the real reason Percy insisted on taking that trip to South America, do you?"

"He said it was to cheer me up after my divorce was final," Holden replied in a low, gravelly voice.

Libby dabbed at the moisture beneath her eyes. "Well, that was part of it," she said finally, drawing back.

He brought her back into the curve of his strong arms. His touch was more brotherly than anything else, despite their earlier flirtation with passion. "And the other...?" he murmured.

Libby struggled to get her emotions under control. "Percy and I had been arguing about starting a family. I really wanted a baby."

Holden nodded, his grip tightening protectively.

"But Percy didn't." The tears she had been doing everything to block flowed anyway.

Holden frowned.

Libby pressed on the bridge of her nose to keep more tears from falling. "He already felt tied down." She gulped and forced herself to go on, get it all out. "He felt he had gotten a raw deal. Inheriting the responsibility for the family business years before he was ready to assume it. Having the woman he married turn out not to be so adventurous and wild at heart, after all. The last thing Percy wanted was the responsibility of a child. Not then, he said, maybe not ever." She shook her head, remembering that last awful fight. "I was devastated."

Holden exhaled. "And angry, I'm guessing."

She forced a watery smile, then she dabbed at her eyes again. "Very. The presumption that we would have children, if for no other reason than to carry on the Lowell name and bloodlines, had always been there."

She looked up at Holden, wanting him to understand. "Suddenly...with the death of his parents—and the absence of that familial pressure to produce grandkids— there was no reason in Percy's mind to go forward with a family at all. So he scheduled the trip with you to Colombia, and that was that. There was not going to be any more discussion about it when he came back.

"I was so angry and disappointed I didn't even kiss him goodbye before he left."

And then he had died....

Leaving her with even more to grapple with.

Holden shook his head. Swore softly. "Libby. I had no idea—"

She held up a hand. "I know—no one did." Feeling calmer now, she pulled away. "Anyway, that's why I had such a crazy mix of emotions when I suspected I might be pregnant after Percy died. I was happy about the baby, but knew he wouldn't have been. It felt like a miracle and a lifelong burden of guilt, all in one."

"Stress can do funny things to a person's body."

Libby nodded, appreciating Holden's attentiveness, even as she warned herself not to get too used to it.

Still, she needed to talk to him tonight. Needed the brand of comfort only he could give. "The doctors said my devastation over Percy's death and the acrimonious way we parted, combined with my longing for a child, made my hormones a mess. I was barely eating or sleeping. I was dizzy and nauseated, more often than not. And I went three months without a period before I realized it."

Holden reached over and tucked a strand of her hair behind her ear. "It's only natural you concluded what you did."

Silence fell between them as she looked deep into his eyes, noticing yet again what a ruggedly handsome man he was. It was more than just the symmetry of his features or the strong line of his jaw. It was his kindness and compassion. His easygoing attitude and humor. The way he could always make a person feel better with an offhand comment or smile.

"You really think that?"

"Yes. I do." He hugged her briefly.

She drew back again, feeling as if a weight had been lifted off her heart. "I'm glad we talked about this."

"So am I." He looked as if he, too, had felt a wall come tumbling down.

"But now we really have to call it a night." *Before I start making this into something more romantic and meaningful than it really is.*

His expression radiated a distinct male satisfaction as he prodded, "So, our first official rebound date…?"

"...will have to wait until we help Miss Rosa and Miss Mim temporarily relocate the Laramie Public Library," Libby finished firmly.

He squinted as if doing some mental calculations, then said, "Just so I know you're not backing out on our agreement."

"I'm not," she promised.

She just needed to make sure that when it did happen, she was composed enough to acknowledge the date for what it was.

Otherwise, it could mean trouble for both of them.

THE IMPROMPTU MEETING at Libby's home the evening before had involved mostly women. The gathering Sunday afternoon at the library was mostly of men. And for good reason, Libby thought, as she searched the sea of helpers for the person she most wanted to say hello to, since the task involved moving literally thousands of books to their temporary new homes.

"Looking for someone?" Paige teased, coming up to stand beside her.

Libby continued scanning the crowd. "Holden."

Her friend handed her a roll of tape, a marker and two collapsed cardboard boxes. "Not here yet. He should be soon, though." She guided Libby to the toddler section, where work was already under way. "What's going on with the two of you, anyway?"

Libby ducked her head and focused on putting the box together. "What do you mean?"

Paige pulled up a kid's chair and sank into it. "Why was he at your house last night, looking like he was ready to go out? And why were you so dressed up?"

Libby flushed. Leave it to her best friend...

"And speak of the devil," Paige murmured with a cheeky grin.

Libby turned to see Holden coming to join them. He had on an old UT sweatshirt and a pair of threadbare jeans, and he hadn't shaved. His dark hair had that rumpled, just-out-of-bed, can't-be-bothered-with-a-comb look, and he was carrying a tool belt in one hand, a pair of leather work gloves in the other. Her pulse raced at the sight of him. "Hi," she said, unable to help recalling the kiss they had shared.

He looked as if he was doing the same. Even though she had panicked and kicked him out early.

"Hi," he said, in a softer, sexier tone than usual.

Paige scoffed. "You can't tell me something *isn't* going on!"

Holden announced, deadpan, "We're going to date. We just haven't decided when."

"What?" She turned back to Libby. "Is he pulling my leg?"

Holden looked at Libby, daring her to deny it.

It was now or never, she thought. Time to jump in all the way.

Or let this chance to start moving on pass her by. She inhaled deeply, stepped closer to Holden and dived in. "We're talking about being each other's rebound date."

"That's the craziest thing I've ever heard!" Paige declared as her husband joined them.

"Crazy like a fox, maybe," Kurt declared in amusement.

Holden put on his tool belt. "All we're looking for is a short-term thing to get us over the hump."

Genuinely worried, Paige said, "Hearts get broken this way."

"Ours won't," Libby retorted, as Holden wrapped a companionable arm around her shoulders and gave her a reassuring squeeze.

NEVERTHELESS, AN INTERESTING question had been raised. And it stuck with Libby the rest of the afternoon.

"Do you think Paige was right?" she asked Holden much later, when they were working at her home.

Volunteers had moved the living-room furniture to the garage for safekeeping. The large space was now filled with the partially disassembled child-size tables and chairs, and the waist-high bookshelves that comprised the newborn to age three section of the library.

Holden opened a box labeled A-C and set it next to the appropriate shelf for her, then returned to his task of putting legs back on tables. "Paige wants us both to be happy. She's just not sure this is the way." He paused to drive in a screw with a battery-powered tool. Finished, he set the table right side up and turned to Libby with a smile. "I, on the other hand, think we've come up with a great plan to get ourselves back in the saddle."

His confidence was catching.

"You're right," she said, bolstering her courage. She knew Holden would never hurt her. She was foolish to worry.

AN HOUR LATER, the work was done and Libby and Holden stood back, admiring the newly assembled toddler section. It was just as it had been, Holden noted with satisfaction, right down to the wooden train table and the colorful charts and posters on display.

Looking flushed and disheveled, Libby turned to him. Her high ponytail bounced from side to side and she had dirt smudged across her casual cotton sweater and jeans.

She had never looked prettier. "Did you eat anything at the library?

Holden shook his head. "I was too busy."

Admiring you...

"Then you must be starving. Because I am!"

Holden saw the opening and took it. He removed his tool belt and set it aside. "Want to go out?"

Libby looked down at herself and then him. He was just as grubby as she was. "Would you mind eating here?"

Was she kidding? She was a fantastic cook.

"Not at all." In fact, he was happy to see her feeling comfortable enough with him to invite him to stay. It reminded him of all the dinners he'd had there with her and Percy, before the accident. Some with Heidi, some without. It hadn't mattered. He'd always had a good time in Libby's kitchen. Maybe because she was like the women in his family, able to put people at ease....

She led the way back to the kitchen, where she turned on the oven and put a pan on the stove. Then waggled her eyebrows at him facetiously. "Have your culinary skills improved any?"

Was it Holden's imagination or was it already getting hot in here? He lounged against the counter, trying to stay out of her path. "I can boil water," he joked.

"Want to try and help me, anyway?"

This was something, Holden knew, that Percy had never been willing to do. "Sure," he said. If this was a test regarding his dating ability—as it suddenly seemed to be—he was determined to pass it.

"Okay, then." Libby got an armful of ingredients out of the fridge, another from the pantry. She paused to pull her V-neck sweater over her head and set it aside, then pushed the sleeves of her white long-sleeved T-shirt to her elbows. "I make soup every Sunday evening."

Holden tried not to notice how the cotton fabric clung to the curves of her breasts. "When did this start?"

"After Percy died. I couldn't seem to manage anything that required even a moderate amount of concentration. But soup was foolproof."

Holden chuckled. "Then it sounds like the perfect dish for me."

"Not to worry. I know it doesn't sound very filling, but I'll whip up some quesadillas for you, too. In the meantime—" she got out a bag of chips and a jar of salsa and arranged them on a serving dish "—you can munch on these, since our main course is going to take about an hour to prepare."

"Thanks."

"No problem." Looking increasingly at ease, she handed him a cutting board and knife. Then a green pepper, a red pepper, several ripe tomatoes and an onion. "Think you can chop these up into little pieces?"

It was his turn to smile. "Oh ye of little faith…"

Libby mugged comically as she started mixing chili powder, cumin and garlic powder, and the aroma of Southwestern spices filled the kitchen.

Enjoying the camaraderie that had sprung up between them, Holden cut the seeds and stem out of the peppers. He was more awkward than she was, but could still get the job done. "I'm guessing we're making tortilla soup?" he asked eventually.

Purposefully, Libby lined up boneless chicken breasts on a rimmed baking sheet, drizzled on olive oil, sprinkled on spice and put that into the oven to bake. "You guessed right."

"Now what?" he said when he'd finished dicing.

She poured a little more olive oil in the bottom of the stockpot. The heat of the stove had her sculpted cheeks glowing pink. "Pour the veggies in here and then stir them around."

He tried not to think how much he had enjoying kissing her, or how sweet and feminine her body had felt pressed against his. Even now, he fought the urge to hold her in his arms again.

"You mean sauté them?"

Merriment danced in her green eyes. "You really aren't as unschooled as you look."

Holden laughed and started stirring as directed.

Shaking her head in amusement, Emily opened containers of chicken broth, tomatoes with jalapeño peppers and black beans. All were added to the sizzling veggies. The quarters were close, and Holden's shoulder nudged hers as they worked. "It's starting to look like soup." He could smell the chicken roasting, too.

"As soon as we put the meat in…" Libby paused.

His brow furrowed, Holden fixed his attention on the window above the kitchen sink.

She came closer, in a drift of soap and shampoo, and studied his face. "What are you looking at?"

Clearly, she didn't think there was much to notice in the backyard. Especially at dusk on a cold winter's day. Holden frowned. "Was there snow in the forecast?"

Libby's shoulders brushed his. "There was a ten-percent chance of rain, but—"

He pointed toward the glass. "Does that look like rain to you?"

She stood on tiptoe to get a better view. "I don't know…it's so gloomy. How can you tell?"

"One way to find out." He headed for the back door.

As he had hoped, Libby was right behind him.

Laramie was far enough north that it snowed at least

once a year, usually only a couple inches at a time. And it melted the next day. So this wouldn't be unprecedented.

Holden stepped off the porch and into the yard. He held his palms out, as did she. Sure enough, he realized with a smile, it was snow! Tiny white flakes that swirled in the wind and dotted their faces and hands.

Libby laughed in delight, her voice soft and musical, and maybe the best thing he'd heard in a long time. "Wow," she exclaimed, even as she shivered in the cold winter air. "It never snows this early in December."

Holden wished he had a jacket to put over her. The best he could do was wrap his arm around her shoulder and draw her in close. "It's doing it now," he said, laughing in turn.

She leaned against him as they stared up in wonder, watching it snow.

"It's not going to stick, but…" Libby turned toward him, as captivated by the magic of the moment as he was. "I still can't believe it," she murmured, looking deep into his eyes.

Holden brushed snowflakes from her hair. "Believe it," he said. And then he did what he'd wanted to do all day. He pulled her against him and kissed her again.

Her lips softened, yet were not quite pliant. She wreathed her arms about his neck and pressed close, as if savoring his warmth and his strength, but not sure if she should let it go any further, or open up the floodgates.

Even so, it was all the encouragement he needed. He cupped her face in his hands and deepened the kiss, wondering all the while what it would take to make her feel as giddy with longing and crazy with desire as he felt at this instant. Wondering what it would take to make her surrender…

LIBBY HAD THOUGHT if she kept it casual, kept them busy, this wouldn't happen. He wouldn't look at her in that certain way that made her feel all-woman. He wouldn't pursue her.

They wouldn't end up falling victim to the sizzling physical attraction between them.

But they had.

And now?

All she knew for certain was that when she was with Holden like this, her problems seemed a lot more manageable, her life more exciting.

He made her want to relax and move forward and play. But she wasn't a carefree girl anymore, Libby scolded herself, as the feel of his muscular frame pressed against hers sent sensations flooding through her body.

She might be *feeling* a little love-struck at the moment—probably because she had been alone so long—but it didn't make a reckless liaison any less dangerous to her heart.

She could still be hurt. Terribly.

So could he.

And that, as much as anything, was why they had to stop.

Before they did something they would both regret.

Breathlessly, she tore her mouth from his and pushed him away. "Holden. We can't."

"Sure we can." His lips closed on hers again before she could murmur another word. He kissed her long and hard, until she finally relented and kissed him back just as passionately. Again and again, until the future beckoned and her icy-cold heart began to thaw. And Libby knew this rebound romance of theirs was going to be trouble.

Big trouble.

Chapter Five

Libby was setting up the art center the library provided for the little ones when the doorbell rang the next evening. It was Holden, who, freshly showered and shaved, smelled every bit as good as he looked.

She smiled. "Hey, I didn't expect to see you tonight."

He strolled in, took off his leather bomber jacket and hung it on the coat tree next to the door. "Miss Mim assigned me as your volunteer helper for the library hours at your home."

Tingles rippled through Libby as she gazed up at him. He towered over her and made her feel petite. "Did she do that on her own or...?"

Holden's eyes twinkled at the corners. "I might have had something to do with it."

Libby's breath stalled halfway up her windpipe, reminding her just how long she had been without a man in her life.

"What did she say?"

Holden wrapped his arms around her and brought her flush against him. "She clapped me on the arm and said, 'Good luck and Godspeed.'"

Libby couldn't help it—she laughed.

A little levity was what she needed after the day she'd had.

"How are things going at the dealership?" Holden asked, brushing a brief, platonic kiss on her hairline and releasing her.

She went back to prepping for their little guests and parents, setting out coffee, cartons of juice and milk on ice, and cookies. "It was a weird day."

"How so?" Holden arranged the crayons and paper, and several sets of blocks.

Finished, Libby straightened. "Jeff Johnston was supposed to call me to get more information so his guy could do one evaluation of the property. See if it came up the same as ours. He didn't."

Holden kept his eyes on her face. "Hmm."

"Apparently, he's still running around, talking to the local ranchers, one-on-one. Trying to get a feel for the customer."

Holden closed in on her slowly. "That may not be all bad, if Johnston turns out to be a responsive business owner. People might feel a lot better about the sale. Which in turn means less pressure on you, if that is the road you're deciding to take."

If. Libby ruminated over Holden's choice of words. "Does that mean you still hope I won't sell?"

"I hope you won't leave Laramie. Not the same thing."

Did any of that have to do with them kissing on two separate occasions? Libby wondered, as a thrill ran through her.

Or the way the evening ended the night before, with the snow flurries stopping as abruptly as they had started, and them both being a little on edge…?

Not sure whether to feel guilty about any latent disloyalty to Percy, or happy that they both now knew they were capable of moving on.

Physically, anyway…

Holden cleared his throat. "What about the rest of your day?"

"Even stranger. There's a lot of tension at the dealership. Despite my reassurances that I am looking out for them, people are worried about their jobs."

"Guess that's to be expected," he rationalized.

Libby sighed and shook her head. "We were supposed to get the showroom decorated for Christmas between customers, but with staff suddenly taking a disproportionate amount of 'personal time' and the number of local ranchers coming in to chat and see if the rumors about a possible transfer of ownership are true, that didn't happen, either."

Holden perched on an arm of the sofa. "I could help you with that."

She strolled closer, studying him all the while. "Aren't you pretty busy, too?"

"During the day." He lifted his broad shoulders in a lazy shrug. "My evenings are free. And since the mini-library is only going to be open from five to seven on Monday, Wednesday and Friday evenings, that leaves tomorrow and Thursday free."

"You're sure you wouldn't mind?" Libby asked appreciatively.

His smile was slow and sexy. "Ply me with more of that delicious soup and I'll be there promptly at closing."

Libby flushed at the memory of his lips on hers. "I'll do better than that, since you're really going to have to work."

His eyes twinkled once again. "I think I'll be up to the task."

Libby was, too. That was the problem—it was difficult to be around Holden and not fantasize about all the possibilities.

"I KNOW CINDY IS ONLY six weeks old," the proud young mother told Holden seriously, shortly after the mini-library opened. "But now that she's looking around, I really think I should start reading to her."

He smiled. "It's never too soon to engender a love of reading. Let me show you where the board books are housed."

While he was busy, another half dozen mothers came in, all doing their best to guide their excited children through the process of choosing new reading material.

"Honestly," one particularly harried young mom said, as Libby was checking out the books by hand, "sometimes I don't know what I was thinking!"

Libby knew the woman was joking about the challenge of having three rambunctious boys, roughly a year apart in age. Still...

"Was that as hard on you as it was on me?" she asked Holden after they had closed down for the night.

He gathered up the stray crayons. "I love kids."

Libby hunkered down to straighten the stacks. "You know what I mean."

"Yeah. I do," he admitted. "And being around newborn babies is particularly hard for me." His jaw tightened. "It makes me think of the baby Heidi and I lost, when she miscarried." He turned to Libby, his eyes bleak. "It was a boy, you know."

She felt his pain like a blow to the solar plexus, and she swallowed. "I didn't. Oh, Holden." She went to him and hugged him close. "I'm so sorry."

Libby had never really comforted Holden at the time. She hadn't known what to say. Now, having been through her own loss, she did. She swallowed again and drew back. "It's always going to hurt."

Grimly, Holden went back to gathering up the stray

crayons. Finally, he straightened. "A lot of people tell me it will stop. Maybe not now, but—" he turned his brooding glance to hers "—when I actually do have a child."

Libby took his hand and gave it a reassuring squeeze. "I think you'll be happier when you have a child to replace the one you lost. I don't think you'll ever stop grieving. I suspect there will always be a place deep inside you that holds the sadness." She met his gaze. "A part of you that will wonder what if Heidi *hadn't* miscarried at five months along, if the baby's heart defect had been detected…and they would have had more of a chance to do something about it."

Jaw clenched, Holden nodded.

Libby gave his fingers another squeeze and let go. "Most of the time I don't think about it. I don't let myself. But tonight…" She lifted a hand and sighed. "With all those babies and toddlers…"

"I know." Holden's gaze turned compassionate. "It was hard on you, too."

Restless, she began to pace. "It reminds me that I'm thirty-two. Time is passing. I've got to get a move on if I want to have a baby of my own. And I do."

"So do I."

They looked at each other. She had an inkling what his bright idea might be. Libby flashed a weary smile. "That might be a last resort, Holden. But we're not anywhere near a last resort."

He smiled again, with the trademark McCabe mischief. "Just checking…"

Libby pushed aside the desire roaring through her, and forced herself to think rationally. "In the meantime, if you want to opt out of the volunteer assignment here, and help one of the other mini-libraries instead…?"

Holden shook his head. "My family has been after me

for months now, pushing me to forge ahead, and they're right," he said with his customary determination. "I need to deal with this, Libby. Let it strengthen my resolve to have a family, instead of scaring me away."

She grinned and clapped him playfully on the shoulder. "Now you're talking."

"So…" He stepped back, all easy charm once again. "About that first date."

Persistence of this type usually annoyed Libby. But not here, and not now. Unable to help herself, she sent Holden a flirtatious glance. "We keep putting it off, don't we?"

Those blue eyes twinkled. "No time like the present."

Libby looked at her watch. They both needed a diversion. And a movie theater was a safe enough venue. "Want to see a nine-o'clock show?" she asked cheerfully.

Holden reached for his coat. "You read my mind."

THEY STOPPED BY the Dairy Barn and grabbed burgers, fries and peppermint shakes. The place was full of teenagers, so they took their meal over to the park and sat at a picnic table in the shelter. It was hard to believe they'd seen snow flurries the evening before, although none of the precipitation had stuck. But that was Texas in December—thirty-two degrees one day, sixty the next.

He ripped open a packet of ketchup. "I noticed you don't have a Christmas tree yet. Are you planning on getting one?"

Libby ignored the romantic aura of their impromptu picnic and rummaged through the bag, looking for salt. "I've got one being delivered to the dealership for the showroom tomorrow afternoon." She frowned. "I haven't decided what to do about my house."

"What do you usually do?"

Libby's recent memories were glum. "Last year I passed. It seemed like too much effort to put one up just for me."

Holden sent her a stern look. "That's totally unacceptable."

"Uh-huh." She regarded him through narrowed lashes. "Do you have one up at your ranch house?"

He wrinkled his nose in chagrin. "Uh…"

"I thought not." She looked down her nose at him.

"Hey." He pressed a palm to his chest. "I was going to go and cut one down next weekend." He favored her with a speculative glance. "You're welcome to come with me if you want."

Libby blinked. "To a Christmas tree farm?"

"To my property. I have pine trees on the Bar M."

She dabbed her mouth with a paper napkin. "That sounds…"

His eyes lit up. "Festive?"

Libby grinned. "Like a lot of work."

His lips curled in mock exasperation. "I take it, then, you've never done it."

"Wielded an ax on a poor unsuspecting tree?" she responded, deadpan. Enjoying their banter, she sat up straight. "No, I have not."

"If it will make you feel better, I'll be sure to do all the chopping and heavy lifting, and I'll replace any trees we take with seedlings in the spring."

Libby liked the idea of that, as much as she liked hanging out with him. "You'd do that for me?"

Holden toasted her with his peppermint milk shake. "In exchange for some home-baked Christmas cookies? I sure would."

"WELL, I DIDN'T FORESEE that ending," Holden murmured later as he walked her to her front door. "A romantic comedy where the guy *doesn't* get the girl?"

Libby lingered beneath her porch light. She knew it was silly, but she'd had such a good time she didn't want the evening to end. She thrust her hands in the pockets of her red down jacket. "Kind of defeats the purpose of the movie, doesn't it? In my fantasies, I want everything to work out perfectly."

Holden's lips took on a rueful curve. He thrust his hands in his pockets, too. "I know what you mean. There's comfort in thinking that at least somewhere, some couple is deliriously happy."

Libby's mood turned wistful. "Even if they're only a fictional couple?"

"Hey." He lifted his hands amiably. "Got to take what we can get, in this life."

"How well I know that," she murmured.

They continued staring at each other.

Libby ignored what she knew was prudent and took reckless action instead. She angled her chin. "Want to come in?"

His wide shoulders relaxed. "Maybe for a minute."

She unlocked the door and decided to make this an actual practice run, thereby giving it parameters and a purpose. "I feel as awkward as I would on a first date."

"Same here."

Silence fell. Their smiles widened and the butterflies inside her grew. Tingling with anticipation, Libby drew breath.

Holden's jaw tautened. He took her hand, suddenly reserved. "Maybe we should just say good-night," he suggested quietly.

Giving her no chance to protest, he drew her into his arms.

Libby knew he meant the kiss to be sweet—and short. She could tell by the first, closemouthed press of his lips to hers.

She also knew that wasn't going to be enough. She wanted to feel connected to him. It didn't matter that she was too caught up in the moment to think rationally. Or that taking their relationship to another level would be incredibly risky. He was so big and strong and undeniably male. It had been a long time since she had felt so beautiful and so wanted. And the kiss that had started so innocently quickly turned passionate.

Ever the gentleman, Holden started to put on the brakes and break it off.

Frustrated, Libby drew him back. "Don't go."

His hands settled on her shoulders and gripped hard. His expression was shadowed with a mixture of self-discipline and regret. "You'll hate me in the morning if I stay," he murmured grimly. "Maybe even sooner."

Libby shook her head, scarcely able to believe that what had happened before was happening again. "No, Holden. I won't," she said desperately.

Briefly, emotion flashed in his eyes, but it was gone before Libby could decipher it. "If I could believe that…" he said, all traces of the ardent suitor disappearing as swiftly as they had appeared.

"For once, I just want to do what I want," Libby confessed, wanting—needing—him to see where she was coming from. "And what I want right now, Holden, is to make love with you."

Chapter Six

It was impossible, Holden thought, to be around Libby and not want to take her in his arms and move heaven and earth to protect her. And if this was what she needed to get through the holidays…

Tightening his grip on her, he hauled her against him and angled his head over hers. And then they were kissing in a way that felt incredibly right, in a way that demonstrated they had a lot more love and life in them than either of them had previously thought. He knew they'd be fools to throw chemistry like this away if it provided the catalyst they both needed to jump-start their personal lives.

And yet Holden knew he couldn't let things get too far out of control. He would kiss her and hold her for a few minutes and then that would be it.

But the more their mouths meshed, the more his gentlemanly intentions went by the wayside. His hands seemed to have a life of their own, and she didn't mind one bit as he found her soft curves.

Had they not lost their balance as she tried to lead him, still kissing, toward the stairs, who knew what would have happened?

But they did stumble, bumping into one of the framed photographs.

Libby managed to catch it before it crashed to the floor.

As she stood holding it in her hands, they both looked down and saw Percy's image staring up at them.

Libby drew in a sharp breath. Guilt and uncertainty flashed in her eyes, and Holden felt a sharp stab of disloyalty, too.

Her shoulder slumped. "I guess I'm not as ready to move on as I thought," she admitted with a sigh.

Was he? Holden wondered.

Especially if it meant betraying his late best friend?

Seeming to read his mind, Libby carefully put the photo on the foyer table. Her chin held high, she turned and took Holden's hand.

She wore the same look she had on her face whenever she spoke about selling the dealership and moving on with her life.

"But I'm also not willing to call a halt entirely." She paused and looked deep into his eyes. "I want to see you again." She squared her slender shoulders. "Tomorrow night okay?"

She really had changed, Holden realized in surprise. Gone were the traces of the ultra-accommodating woman his best friend had failed to appreciate.

Mesmerized by the strength of character he saw in her eyes, he curtailed his own fast-threatening-to-get-out-of-control desire, and murmured teasingly, "You sure you want to see me again so soon?" What they were feeling was already pretty intense.

"We entered into this so we can practice being part of a couple again. The point is…" Libby paused and drew a bolstering breath. "Dating after such a long drought is not going to be easy, Holden. We both knew that going into this. There are going to be glitches and missteps.

Plus horrible feelings of guilt, probably. And kissing is bound to be awkward, too. So…who better to share it with than each other?"

Was she really thinking they could limit this to kisses? He was still aroused.

Quirking his lips, he retorted, "Gosh, Libby, when you put it that way…"

Completely recovered, she leaned toward him, the only clue that she'd been at all affected by their embrace being the faint imprint of her nipples against her sweater. "I'm serious, Holden. I really do want to try this again. We had a lot of fun up to now."

She had a point, he realized.

He smiled, thinking how good it had felt to share a picnic with her in the park and sit side by side in the movie theater, sharing a bucket of popcorn and some Junior Mints candy. "We did at that."

Libby perked up. "So we'll see each other again tomorrow night?"

Her enthusiasm was contagious. "I'll pick you up at seven-thirty."

She tilted her head, curious. "Where are we going to go?"

Nowhere, Holden thought sagely, anywhere near a bed.

HOLDEN ENTERED THE Bar M stable just as Kurt finished examining the gestating Lady. Holden nodded at the beautiful silver mare with white feet and a dark gray mane, then turned to his cousin. "How is she doing?"

Kurt stepped out of the foaling box, vet bag in hand. "Great. Although we got the results of the blood tests back, and the results are just as you suspected they'd be. The antibodies are up significantly."

Which meant they were facing hemolytic disease in the foal, Holden thought.

Kurt continued casually, "You know what to do, so there shouldn't be any problem, but if you run into difficulty, just call me."

He nodded. "Sure thing."

His cousin joined him in the aisle. "You still want me to look at the foal that was born this morning?"

Holden nodded and he led the way. "Mind if I ask you a question?"

"Go ahead." Kurt carried his veterinary bag into the stall. Exhausted from the rigors of giving birth, the big bay mare was lying on her side in the straw. Her colt was cuddled up next to her tummy.

"You're happily married," Holden remarked, as he stepped in to gently help the wobbly-legged colt to his feet.

"I certainly am, and I don't mind saying, it's great." Kurt checked the foal's limbs and evaluated the flexor and extensor tendons. "Had I known just *how* great, I would have—"

He stopped abruptly, the way blissfully married folks always did when they realized they'd put their foot in it.

"It's okay," Holden remarked, looking forward to the day he wasn't known as a divorced rancher who'd had his heart broken. "I know I failed big-time at the marriage business, first time around." Because if he hadn't, he and Heidi would have stayed together after the loss of their baby.

"Still—" Kurt paused to listen to the colt's heart and lungs "—I didn't have to rub it in."

"It's fact. I'm dealing with it. Moving on."

Kurt looked up in surprise, as Holden plunged on.

"Which brings me back to my question. How would you feel if something happened to you…?"

Kurt peered at the foal's gums. "Meaning I go to the big tent in the sky?"

He nodded. "And another guy came along and put a move on Paige?"

His cousin removed a thermometer from his bag. "I don't think I would feel anything in that scenario, because I'd be dead."

Holden brushed off the joke. "I'm serious."

"That's what worries me." Kurt stripped off the first pair of gloves, donned another and drew blood for the lab work. Then he studied Holden. "This is about Libby Lowell, isn't it?"

"I promised Percy I would look after Libby if anything ever happened to him."

"And you have." Kurt gave the antibiotic and tetanus injections. "We all know that."

"I asked to be her rebound guy. And she offered to be my rebound woman."

Kurt examined the colt's navel stump. "Did you agree?"

Hell, yes. Out loud, Holden said rhetorically, "What do you think?"

"Only now you're having second thoughts," Kurt guessed, leading the infant colt to its mama to suckle.

"It sounded easy enough at the outset," Holden confided as the foal began to nurse. "Libby and I planned to date each other through the holidays—to sort of get our sea legs back. And then that would be it. We would go our separate ways, move on to real relationships."

The other man nodded approvingly at the foal's vigor, before turning back. "So what's the problem?"

"We're just a couple days into our grand plan," he

confessed, as they stepped out of the stall. "And I'm not sure we can keep our emotions in check."

Kurt removed the stethoscope from around his neck. "What are we talking here…physical attraction?"

"And guilt—that this is not what Percy had in mind when he asked me to take care of Libby."

Kurt packed up his vet bag. "He wanted Libby to be happy. He wanted her to be safe."

"Yeah?" Holden started out of the barn.

His cousin fished in his pocket for his keys. "He probably also wanted her to be loved."

Holden's mood remained skeptical. "By his best friend?"

Kurt lingered next to his pickup truck and thought a moment. "I don't think jealousy exists in heaven. I think all those negative emotions are filtered out. They'd have to be, for anyone to have eternal peace."

"You've got a point there," Holden said quietly at last.

Kurt tossed his gear in the cab. "You and Libby, on the other hand, are still here on earth. So you're going to have the whole gamut of emotions to deal with, whether this works out the way you two envisioned or not."

Holden turned his face into the wind, eyeing up the gray clouds overhead. Christmas and New Year's would be here sooner than they thought. And with that, the end of his arrangement with Libby. "So what are you saying? It's only going to get worse?"

"No clue. The only thing I do know—" Kurt slapped him companionably on the back and flashed an encouraging grin "—is that you, my friend, are in deep."

"LIBBY?" VINCE HUNT ASKED shortly after the dealership closed for the day. "Got a minute? We all have something we'd like to say to you."

Her nerves jangling, Libby walked out into the showroom, where all her employees were gathered. She was pleased to see the staff had gotten together and decorated the showroom for Christmas, as tradition required, making Holden's help that evening unnecessary.

The head of financial services continued, "We're sorry about the way we confronted you the other day. Since then, we've all had the opportunity to sit down with Jeff Johnston individually."

So that was what had been going on....

Speaking for the service department, Manny Pierce chimed in, "He let us know that he really takes care of his employees, and he is planning to run the business on the same model Southwest Airlines uses."

This was news. "You'd each own a small part of the company through profit sharing?" Libby asked in surprise.

Heads bobbed happily.

Lucia Gordon smiled. "He's really focused on building each business he owns into a cohesive team. Plus he said he would give us all written contracts and guaranteed salaries and bonuses for the next five years."

"After meeting with him one-on-one, we realize he's a decent guy," Swifty Mortimer said. "So we're all okay with it now."

"Not that we want to see you go," Manny Pierce hastened to add. "But...we understand."

Libby was so shocked she didn't know what to say. Finally, she managed to thank everyone for their support.

"And one more thing," the receptionist said, handing Libby a slip of paper. "This call came in while you were with that last customer."

Holden's name was scrawled across the top. The message beneath read: "Sorry about tonight. Rain check?"

Not sure what that meant, Libby worked to keep her expression inscrutable. "That's it?"

Lucia shrugged. "He sounded like he was in a hurry."

"Okay, thanks."

Libby went into her office and tried to reach Holden, both on his cell phone and on the ranch line.

There was no answer either place.

Which meant what? she wondered, beginning to feel a little upset. Had he learned the dealership had already been decorated and changed his mind about spending time with her tonight? Or was it more than that?

Realizing there was only one way to find out, Libby got in her car and drove out to the Bar M ranch. She hadn't been out there in almost two years, and she was surprised to see how much had changed.

There were now countless pastures and four large stables, a barn and the original fieldstone ranch house with the steeply pitched roof.

Holden's pickup was parked in the drive. Light spilled from one of the buildings, and she headed that way. Holden was inside, kneeling next to a newborn foal, slipping a muzzle over its head.

He looked up as Libby slipped into the stall.

"Hi," she said softly, amazed as always at the fragility and wonder of new life.

She knelt down beside the foal, which was the spitting image of its mama—silver body, dark gray mane, white feet.

Holden flashed her a sexy smile. "I guess you got my message."

"Yeah." He was really in his element.

Wishing she'd thought to change into jeans and boots, or at least brought some with her, Libby hunkered down beside him, being careful not to get the goo from the birth on any of her nice work clothes. "What are you doing?"

Holden went to the cooler in the corner and brought out a bottle of what looked like formula. "Prenatal tests determined this foal has hemolytic disease. In other words, there was a blood group incompatibility between the dam and the sire. Antibodies are produced during pregnancy that, if ingested by the foal, would destroy her red blood cells."

Admiring Holden's competence, Libby asked, "Sort of like Rh disease in humans?"

"Right." He shook the bottle, making sure its contents were mixed. "Although in babies, it's a little more complicated. With horses, all we have to do to keep the foal from harm is substitute compatible colostrum for the first thirty-six hours, and make sure Willow here doesn't nurse and ingest any of Lady's."

"Hence the muzzle," Libby guessed.

"I'll milk the mother six times a day and discard her colostrum, to prevent any from being transferred to the foal, and feed Willow by hand. Then she'll nurse at her mother's side, as per usual."

"Wow. You really know your stuff."

He grinned. "Breeding and training quarter horses is my profession."

And, Libby thought admiringly, he did it very well.

"Want to help with the first feeding?"

Was he kidding? "Love to," Libby said.

Holden produced the bottle for the newborn and a wooden bench for Libby to sit on. With gentle hands, he undid the muzzle and helped them get situated, with Willow braced and supported by Libby's knees.

Looking content but exhausted, the mama horse lay on her side, watching.

As the sleek little foal began to suck on the bottle, Libby was filled with tenderness. She slanted Holden an appreciative glance. "No wonder you couldn't make our date."

"Sorry I couldn't leave a more detailed message. I just figured I would call you later. I didn't expect you to drive all the way out here." Holden paused to study her, his expression maddeningly inscrutable. "Why *did* you drive all the way out here?"

Libby flushed and struggled to keep her guard up. Before her heart went from foolishly wishing for more than a rebound-dating experience with Holden, to being completely vulnerable.

She forced herself to glance away from him. "I tried calling—there was no answer."

He braced his hands on his hips, his eyes guarded now. "Did you think I'd changed my mind about helping you and I was standing you up?"

Libby drew a breath, reassuring herself that even after the hot intensity of their kisses, they were in no real danger of actually hooking up. They were both much too sensible for that. She gestured with her free hand. "First of all, the decorating has been done today by LRE staff. And, after last night…"

Holden's jaw set with McCabe resolve. "We were smart to stop when we did. Continuing after the picture fell…well, that would have been really awkward."

It certainly had broken the mood.

Libby gave a sigh of relief. "So it's not just me."

"It's not just you." An indecipherable emotion crossed his face.

As they headed for the exit half an hour later, when the foal had been fed, Holden put a hand on the small of Libby's back and surveyed her closely. "Since you're here and things are calm in the barn for now…want to come inside with me?"

She ignored the heat radiating from his palm. "Sure."

Together, they crossed the yard and walked into the two-story fieldstone ranch house.

Unlike her home, where photos of Percy and his family abounded, Holden's house had been wiped clean of any memory of Heidi and their marriage. But then that was to be expected, since they were divorced. As she looked around, Libby couldn't help but wonder if that was a healthier way to live, in the wake of loss.…

Casually, Holden advised, "Make yourself at home. I'm going to shower. After that, maybe we can rustle up some dinner."

Left alone, Libby wandered into the kitchen, switched on the lights and got her second surprise of the evening.

Chapter Seven

"What's all this?"

The icy note in Libby's voice stopped Holden in his tracks.

He ran a hand through his freshly shampooed hair and followed her gaze to the stacks of paperwork on his kitchen table. Too late, he realized he probably should have told her about this when she first arrived at the ranch.

He'd certainly meant to mention it.

Had she not showed up so unexpectedly and looked so damn gorgeous in tailored black slacks and an evergreen wool blazer, he probably would have told her. Instead, all he'd been able to focus on was how soft and silky her hair looked, falling about her shoulders.

Holden edged closer, taking in the agitated color in her sculpted cheeks and the stormy set of her luscious lips. Calmly, he brought her up to speed. "Jeff Johnston stopped by earlier today. He gave me the full sales pitch. Told me how good this would be for you."

She raised her chin. "Bottom line?"

Okay, so she was ticked off at him. Holden matched her contentious tone. "He wanted me to use my influence with you to try and get you to sell to him."

She released a short, bitter laugh. "And you said?"

"That you're a very intelligent woman who likes to make up her own mind. I also warned him that tactics like this were not likely to put him in your good graces."

Libby watched him get the coffeemaker out. "You can say that again."

Holden poured coffee grounds into the paper filter. "I'm not the only rancher he's visited. He's been making the rounds of all your customers."

"And my employees." Frowning, Libby told Holden about the meeting she'd had with her staff before she had come over to see him.

Holden added water and switched on the machine. "How do you feel about that?"

"Honestly?" She leaned against the counter and rubbed the toe of her suede pump across the wide-plank oak floor. "I don't know what to think." She bit her lip. "He seems to have convinced everyone that he would do one heck of a lot better job running the dealership than I have."

"And that hurts," Holden guessed, wrapping a consoling arm about her shoulders.

Libby settled into the curve of his arm in a drift of cinnamon perfume. "I thought I had done a good job." She shook her head. "Sales are on par with what Percy—and his parents—managed. I've given everyone bonuses and cost-of-living raises."

"I know they all appreciate that."

"Yeah." Libby fell silent.

"I thought this was what you wanted."

"So did I," she admitted.

Sensing there was more, he waited.

She ran her hands through her hair, then turned to look up at him. "I didn't expect to get what I wished for so quickly." She stepped back slightly so they were no longer touching.

Holden pushed aside the need to pull her into his arms and kiss her again. "Has Johnston come in with a number yet?" he asked.

"No." Libby sighed. "But given how determined he is to make the deal, I can't imagine he would offer anything insulting."

"You can still turn him down." *Stay here in Laramie.* "Keep the business in the family, so to speak."

Regret pinched the corners of her mouth. "Actually, Holden," she said softly, "I can't."

LIBBY COULD TELL by the way Holden was looking at her that she was acting like a flighty woman unable to make up her mind.

She couldn't help it. Her emotions were a mess. And who better to hear why than the man who had already seen her at her worst, and thought no less of her?

"I still feel bad about selling, because even though the Lowell name will be on the dealership, there'll be no one from the family actually involved in running the business."

He got two mugs from the cupboard. "And that ends three generations of tradition."

Libby frowned. "That's not what Percy or his parents would have wanted."

Holden filled the mugs with the fragrant brew. "You're right." He paused to pass her one. "As much as Percy sometimes resented being handed a career, he was proud of what his family had built."

Libby sipped the hot, delicious coffee. "I'm proud of it, too. And now I'm on the brink of ending that."

Holden took her elbow and led her to the living room.

"Have you thought about keeping the dealership yourself and just hiring someone else to run the day-to-day operations?"

She settled on the handsome leather sofa. "I'd still have to be involved on some level. And that would keep me from moving on to a life of my choosing."

"Which would be where?" he asked as he sat down beside her.

Libby turned toward him. "I don't know that, either. I was thinking Austin, because I grew up there, but most of my friends have moved away." She drew a bracing breath. Became way too aware of the soapy clean scent of his hair and skin.

Pushing aside a mental image of Holden in the shower, she forged on. "Would being there just remind me of losing Aunt Ida?"

Compassion shone in his blue eyes.

Libby swallowed. "I could certainly relocate to Dallas or Houston. There would be plenty of opportunity for whatever I might choose to do with my life."

"But no family or friends."

She traced the UT insignia on the coffee mug. "I don't have family anywhere."

Holden lifted his mug to his lips. "That will change."

She met his eyes and didn't look away. "Will it?" she countered softly, feeling a little depressed again, like the hero in *A Charlie Brown Christmas*. "I don't seem to have much luck in that department."

Holden put his coffee aside. "I know you feel unattached, Libby. Sometimes I feel that way, too."

She set her mug down in turn. "But you have all those McCabes."

He took her hand in his and turned it palm up. "And no wife or kids of my own."

Libby couldn't imagine how anyone as kind, handsome and smart as Holden would ever go through his entire life alone. "That will change."

He traced her life line with his index finger. "That's what everyone says."

And yet he remained skeptical.

"Once we start dating again, actively looking, we'll find what we want," Libby declared.

She knew what *she* wanted. Someone just like Holden.

He let go of her hand and studied her. "You really think so?"

"We have to." Restlessly, she got to her feet and paced over to the window, where she looked out at the dark night. "Because I can't go on this way, Holden." Her voice caught. "I can't live the rest of my life without family ties."

He rose and walked toward her, all empathetic male. "You could become an honorary McCabe."

Libby knew Holden wanted her to have everything she would have if her husband hadn't died, but this was getting ridiculous. "You really are taking this 'a life for a life' thing too far."

One corner of his mouth quirked. "What's wrong with having a place to go on every holiday?" he challenged, his gaze roving her face. "A group to hang out with?"

"How would your parents feel about that?" Libby retorted.

He shrugged and slid his hands into the back pockets of his jeans. "They *want* me bringing a new woman into the tribe."

"As your wife," she pointed out.

He tilted his head to one side. "You're my girlfriend. Well, practice girlfriend." Mischief glimmered in his expression. "In the loosest sense of the word."

Libby ignored the tingling sensation in her middle. "It doesn't matter how serious we are. Or aren't." She couldn't bear to experience anything that only invited more loss, as this eventually would.

Holden clearly felt otherwise.

"Girlfriends get invited to family events," he stated sagely. "Friends, too, for that matter."

Libby rolled her eyes. "Friends who have no place to go."

Holden put his hands on her shoulders. "I'm serious, Libby." He waited until she looked him in the eye. "There is no reason for you to spend this Christmas and New Year's or any other alone." His grip tightened protectively. "I want you to spend it with me and my family, and I'm not taking no for an answer."

Misery warred with the building excitement within her, but Libby forced herself to be practical. "You're going to have to," she retorted.

He dropped his hands, stepped back. "Why?"

"Because, Holden, I know what it's like to start out as one thing—a beloved niece, a girlfriend, a wife—and then turn into more of a liability than either of us could ever imagine. I don't want to be that again. Not for you. And certainly," she finished heavily, "not for your entire family."

LIBBY WAS JUST GETTING ready to leave for work the next morning when the doorbell rang.

Thinking it might be Holden—whom she'd parted with awkwardly the evening before—she went to answer the door and found Holden's mother there.

"I hope you don't mind my dropping in this way," Greta said. She had a coffee shop bag in one hand, a cardboard beverage holder in the other.

Libby ushered the elegant older woman inside. As usual, Greta's curly silver-blond hair was impeccably coiffed. She had on a trim denim shirtdress and a festive green Christmas cardigan that complemented the bright smile on her face.

"Holden said you liked vanilla lattes and cranberry scones, so that's what I brought," she said warmly.

Libby took her coat, then led her into the formal dining room. "I do. Thank you."

They chatted a moment about the weather, and the thus far fruitless efforts to get the county officials to fund repairs on the library.

"But I know you didn't come over here at eight-thirty in the morning just to discuss this," Libby said. "What's on your mind?"

Greta sipped her latte. "I understand you and my son are dating."

"Very casually," she replied.

"So you don't see this leading anywhere…?"

In her wildest dreams? Libby clamped down on the fantasies their two kisses had inspired. If she was smart, she would not allow herself to go there.

"Realistically? I don't see how it could," she finally replied.

Greta nodded. "Holden told me as much, too."

Disappointment spiraled through Libby. That was the problem with even casual dating, she thought. It could still leave you hurt and wanting—needing—more. Especially at this time of year…

"Holden said he invited you to spend the holidays with us."

And not just one Christmas and New Year's, but all the holidays from here on out.

Libby worked to contain her lingering sadness. "That's right. He did."

"And?" Curiosity filled his mother's eyes.

Libby reminded herself that leaving Laramie was the only way she would ever be able to build a life for herself, and get everything she wanted, like a husband and children. "I know Holden's heart was in the right place, that he feels for me because I have no family of my own left. But…"

When she couldn't go on, Holden's mom filled in the rest. "You think assuaging guilt and making good on a deathbed promise to your late husband aren't reason enough to bring anyone into the family, even unofficially."

Leave it to her to cut straight to the chase.

Libby sighed, relieved to be able to be forthright, too. "It sounds like a good solution now. And it probably would make me feel less alone during the holiday season."

"But…" the older woman prompted.

Libby grimaced. "But what happens when the rebound relationship Holden and I have embarked on ends, and he's with someone else?" She shrugged and pushed the unpleasant thought away. "I can't see his next girlfriend being comfortable having his old girlfriend—even a decidedly platonic one—at family gatherings. Can you?"

Greta relaxed. "To be honest, I don't see that as a problem. Our family has grown so much and our get-togethers have gotten so large…. Plus, by the time that happens, you might very well have your own special someone to bring with you, too. Or you might be at your new love's family gathering instead of ours."

Oddly enough, Libby did not see that as a comfort, either. Although it should be….

Greta continued gently, "What I do see as a continuing difficulty is the confusion Holden feels about *how* he is supposed to look after you in Percy's absence. Right now, the responsibility is all on his shoulders. Clearly, the obligation is weighing on him."

Libby began to see where this was going. "But that might change if he felt others were looking after me, too." In the loving, caring, all-inclusive way that the McCabes were famous for...

His mom nodded. "If you became part of the McCabe tribe, you'd have any number of people you could call on, at any time, to help and support you in any way you needed."

The burden would be lifted from Holden's heart.

Finally seeing a way out of the morass they'd found themselves in for two long years, Libby concluded, "Reassured, Holden would be able to move on with his life. He would be able to be happy again."

Greta smiled. "You both would."

"I THOUGHT LIBBY WAS coming with you tonight," Shane McCabe said when Holden arrived at the Annie's Homemade food-testing facility.

Because the family had a lot to accomplish that evening, and dozens of McCabes to do it, the gathering was being held in his aunt Annie's place of business. The large space was outfitted with dozens of picnic tables and still had plenty of open floor. Outside, where most of the men were at the moment, trucks were being unloaded, Christmas trees trimmed, spare greenery carried inside.

Trying not to be disappointed that another of their "dates" had taken a detour, Holden pulled on his leather work gloves and told his dad, "Scheduling conflict. I've got a foal that still needs hand-feeding. Libby had library hours at her home. So she's meeting me here."

A fact that had deprived him of picking her up and driving her in his truck, like a real date, Holden mused in disappointment.

Shane set a Christmas tree upside down. "How is the sale of her business going?"

Wade and Travis joined them and began trimming trees, too.

Holden picked up a small handsaw, appropriate for the job. "As far as I know, she's getting everything she is asking for from Jeff Johnston."

Holden's dad and two brothers stopped what they were doing and exchanged surprised looks.

Holden exhaled, glad to have the three accomplished businessmen to use as a sounding board. "Yeah, I know. Generally, when something seems too good to be true, it is. And whether she wants to come right out and admit it or not, Libby intuits that, too."

Silence fell. The tree trimming and bundling resumed.

Holden wrapped a net around a spruce ready for transport to the Kiwanis Club's holiday lot. "I've done some research, checked into Johnston's other acquisitions. He seems to have the golden touch when it comes to expanding a business and taking it onto the internet. Neither Libby nor I have been able to find any formal complaints lodged against him that would indicate he's done anything even borderline unethical or illegal."

"And yet—" Shane added another trimmed tree to the pile "—something about this situation just doesn't sit right, does it?"

"I don't like the way he's gone behind Libby's back, talking to all her employees, promising them the moon so they'll get on board with the sale," Holden admitted.

Travis sawed the lower limbs off a tree. "Not to mention chatting up all the ranchers in the area, to make them believe he would do a much better job of meeting our needs than Libby ever could."

"Intense competition in the business world is expected," Wade pointed out as he piled the shorn strips of greenery onto a wheeled cart. He shook his head in mute disapproval. "Stabbing rivals in the back is not."

Which in a way, Holden thought, was exactly what Johnston was currently doing. *If* his intentions were of the nasty, competitive ilk...

Holden struggled to be objective, but it wasn't easy when Libby's well-being was at stake. "I'm trying to be fair. To consider whether Johnston is simply being proactive—and attempting to reassure everyone, in advance, that his intentions are as honorable as he professes. Or—" he grimaced, considering the alternative "—is Johnston's behavior an indication that he is a hell of a lot more cutthroat than we know, and Libby really needs to beware?"

Another concerned silence fell.

"What do you want us to do?" Shane asked.

Wade was a multimillionaire investor, his uncle Travis and his dad prominent members of all the ranching associations in the state. Among the three of them, Holden knew they had a powerful, knowledgeable network of acquaintances. "Use your connections. Ask around. See if there's anything you can find out about Johnston that might be a red flag."

His dad guessed the rest. "And while we're at it, don't mention to Libby what we're doing."

Holden ignored the faint hint of disapproval coming from all three older men. Determined to keep his promise and watch over Libby, whether she liked it or not, he said drily, "You may have heard she doesn't like being protected."

"We'll do what you ask, son," Shane promised with the understanding of a man who had been happily married for over thirty-five years. "But don't be surprised if Libby doesn't thank you for it."

Chapter Eight

"If I didn't know better, I would think I just walked into Santa's Workshop," Libby teased, when she finally met up with Holden and he escorted her inside the Annie's Homemade testing facility.

The McCabes gathering was a beehive of activity that included every conceivable yuletide activity. Wreaths were being made for the Kiwanis Club. Gift baskets assembled for the Blue Santa organization. Stockings sewed for the Community Chapel bazaar.

Everywhere Libby and Holden looked, there were children playing, adults laughing. Christmas carols resonated in the background, adding to the festive mood, and the sweet smell of sugar cookies scented the air.

Recognizing them immediately, Paige and Kurt's two-year-old triplets rushed over to greet them. They looked adorable in red velvet dresses, white tights and cute black boots with knit uppers. Arms outstretched, the little girls shouted, "Holden! Libby!"

Grinning, Holden scooped up Lori and Lucille. Libby picked up Lindsay. Dark curls bouncing, cherubic faces grinning blissfully, the toddlers chatted away, talking in two- or three-word sentences.

"So Santa is coming?" Libby asked, a wave of maternal contentment flowing through her as she cradled the little one in her arms.

All three girls nodded enthusiastically.

Looking as happy as she felt, Holden asked, "Are you going to bake cookies for him?"

There were more nods, along with shouts of "cookies!"

The notion planted, the girls wiggled out of their arms and raced over to the buffet tables, where their mom was helping Annie McCabe replenish the plates of refreshments for the volunteers.

Paige and Annie waved at them before turning to give the triplets the cookies they were asking for.

Holden's mother welcomed Libby and him with warm hugs. "Thanks for coming," she said with a beleaguered sigh, running a hand through her curls. "As you can see, we need all the help we can get. Do you want to eat or work first?"

"Work," Holden and Libby decided in unison.

Greta gave them a considering glance. "Okay, then. I'll put you right to work. We have a lot of toys that were donated for the children's home in San Angelo that need to be wrapped, so I'll put you on that, Libby. Holden, we have some saddles that are going to the boys ranch in Libertyville, that need to be cleaned and reconditioned...so I'll leave that to you."

"Why so much all at once?" he asked.

It was usually a little crazy this time of year, but not *this* chaotic... And why were things being done in such a way that would keep the men and woman largely separated this evening? he wondered in frustration. Why couldn't his mother have set things up so he could be by Libby's side throughout the evening?

Not that Libby looked all that distressed about being left on her own…

Oblivious to the disgruntled nature of his thoughts, Greta answered, "Everyone in the family wants to get together. We all want to help the community. And like every year, it seems all the civic and charitable organizations want everything done at once."

"I know what you mean," Libby sympathized. "Every weekend in December you have to choose where you're going to go, who you're going to help. And with the library in flux this year, too…"

"A lot of events are held simultaneously," Holden noted.

Her mind already searching for a solution to the problem, Libby murmured, "It'd be nice if they could coordinate it so more people could participate in all the events."

"Wouldn't it?" Greta agreed wistfully, looking hopeful that Libby's idea would eventually see the light of day. "In the meantime, Holden, the saddles are out in one of the barns. Your dad can direct you. And, Libby… right this way…"

Three hours later, the tasks were completed, gifts stored or dispersed, sleepy children carried out.

Disappointed that they hadn't spent more time together—hadn't even been able to grab a bite at the same time—Holden walked Libby out to her car. He knew it was late. Nearly eleven. But he still wanted to spend time with her. The kind they would have if they'd been on an actual date.

"Want to come by my ranch and see the foal? It's been thirty-six hours since she was born, so I can remove the muzzle and let Willow have her first feeding with her mama."

An event that for Holden was always a thrill, no matter how many horses he had bred and ushered into the world.

Luckily for him, Libby did not even hesitate. "I'll meet you there."

"I CAN'T BELIEVE HOW MUCH stronger she seems," Libby murmured as Holden removed the muzzle.

They watched the foal and mare nuzzle each other in the warm and cozy straw-lined stall before getting down to the business of nursing.

Holden tenderly stroked the mother and her newborn, then paused to adjust the Velcro straps on the foal's warming blanket. Satisfied that all was as it should be, he stepped back.

Admiring how gentle he was with the horses, and how much they seemed to love him, Libby murmured, "Willow is certainly happy to be able to nurse at her mama's side." You could practically feel the bliss radiating from them both.

Holden moved closer to Libby and folded his arms. "One of the best things about being in the horse-breeding business is the constant reminder of the wonder and the fragility of life."

She turned toward him, her shoulder brushing his in the process. From this angle, his profile was even more rugged, his expression poignantly tender. She couldn't help but think what a good father he would be.

"Although," Holden added, "as in most professions, there are certainly days I don't enjoy."

Inhaling the scents of saddle soap and leather clinging to his skin, she said, "It must be really hard on you when things go wrong."

A pained expression crossed his face. "It is," he admitted ruefully.

Libby thought about the child he had lost to miscarriage, and the child she had wanted and never been blessed with.

The intimacy of the moment, coupled with the understanding in his eyes, prompted her to confess, "Tonight was hard, too."

Holden swung around to face her. "Being around so much of my family?" he asked. "'Cause I know we McCabes can be overwhelming, especially en masse...."

Libby held up a hand. "No. Joining the gathering tonight was the easy part. Everyone made me feel so welcome, especially your mom and dad." Being part of a family again, even unofficially, had felt good. "It was seeing all your cousins and siblings, the people our age, who are happily married and have kids." She paused to look into Holden's eyes. "They were all so happy. Enjoying the holiday season so much!"

He eased out of the stall and held the door for her.

Smiling in appreciation, Libby joined him in the cement aisleway. As they headed toward the barn exit, Holden gave her a fond glance and mused, "That makes you feel like you're missing out."

They shut the door to the heated barn and walked across the lawn, shivering in the wintry air. Impulsively, Libby slipped her hand in Holden's and eased closer to his body heat. It was late. Almost midnight. But she had no wish to go home.

Bypassing her car, she asked curiously, "Doesn't it do the same to you?"

Looking pleased she had decided to stay awhile longer, he led the way into the house. "Of course. Especially at Christmas, but I try not to dwell on it." He switched on lights in the foyer, living room and kitchen.

"The fact is," he continued pragmatically, "there are

a lot of happy people our age who are way ahead of us when it comes to establishing their own families. But there's really not much either of us can do to catch up."

Unable to help herself, Libby teased, "Besides start dating again?" Which they were doing, albeit not very well, thus far.

Holden shook his head. "To create the chemistry necessary for the foundation of any enduring relationship. Bottom line, the spark between a man and a woman is either there—or it's not."

And it was there with the two of them. How well she knew that. So the question was…what were they waiting for?

HOLDEN KNEW THE INSTANT the mood changed. Her lips parted ever so slightly. Her irises darkened. Her whole body leaned toward him.

Yet even as desire surged within him, the memory of their last tryst returned. He took her face in his hands. "If you don't want me to kiss you again…" he warned hoarsely.

Libby's hands moved from his chest to his shoulders, before clasping behind his neck. She rose on tiptoe, her breasts brushing against his pecs. "That's just it, Holden," she whispered back. "I do."

Blood thundered through his veins as he threaded his fingers through her hair, then lowered his mouth to hers. "Then heaven help us both," he growled. "Because that's what I want, too."

It didn't matter that their "dating" was supposed to be nothing more than a means to an end, a way to get them back into the habit of going out with others. Something happened when they were together. And it was more than hormones. More than grief or guilt or the need to give her a reason to live her life fully again.

What they had together was no longer obligation, Holden thought. It was…magic. It fulfilled a need that was deeper and more powerful than anything he had ever known.

And he sensed, from the hot, passionate way she was clinging to him and returning his kisses, that she felt the fierce pull of their attraction, too.

LIBBY HAD KNOWN it was dangerous to go back to Holden's ranch tonight. More risky still to step inside the house with him, this late, with nothing on her mind except quelling the deep-seated loneliness she had been feeling.

She told herself to go with the physical part of the experience and keep her emotions safely in check.

Yet as his hard body pressed against hers, and his fingers brushed along her jaw, her skin heated and her pulse fluttered wildly. He tasted so good, so incredibly male. She moaned as his lips dominated hers and he invaded her mouth with his tongue. He kissed her so thoroughly he took her breath away, until she whimpered softly and clung to him, every inch of her tingling with need.

And he wanted her, too—she could feel it in the hardness of his body. And that left her aching and vulnerable, wanting desperately to see where lovemaking with him would lead. Despite her decision to remain unaffected, yearnings she had pushed aside came rushing to the fore. It had been so long since she had felt so feminine or desired.

Never had she been kissed and touched so gently and so masterfully.

Filled with abandon, she whispered, "Let's go upstairs."

"I'm all for that." Tucking an arm beneath her knees, Holden carried her to the second floor and down the hall to the master bedroom.

Her heart raced as he set her down.

Afraid she might do something really foolish—like fall head over heels in love with him—if she didn't set some parameters, Libby cautioned, "Just so we're straight. We're merely…"

Once again, he read her mind. "Practicing here?"

"Yes."

What a relief he understood that because of their previous connections, this could never go anywhere beyond the here and now.

Holden unbuttoned her blouse and kissed her collarbone. "I am a little rusty."

Relaxing, Libby unbuttoned his shirt, too. Tugged it from the waistband of his jeans. Damn, but he had a nice chest. Solid, warm, with satin skin and flat male nipples buried in the mat of crisp dark hair. Broad, muscular shoulders, too. She caressed it all with her fingertips. "Then that makes two of us."

He bared her to her waist and let his glance drift over her, taking in her soft curves and jutting nipples. Exploring her breasts with his mouth, he murmured, "I'm thinking it will all come back to us."

And come back to them it did.

They undressed each other at leisure, exploring as they went, then stretched out next to each other on the bed. Murmuring in pleasure, he kissed his way down her body. When she arched her spine, moving against him, he shuddered, too.

"I want you now," Libby breathed, drawing him upward once again.

Together, they sheathed him. Trembling, impatient,

she opened herself to his possession. Holden caught her by the hips, lifted her, and then they were one. Overcome with sensation, shuddering with pleasure…

"You feel so good," he whispered.

So right, Libby thought, rising up to meet him. Her body closed around him, their coupling as honest and exciting as she had hoped it would be.

"So do you…"

Reveling in the freedom to go after exactly what she wanted—when she wanted it—she wrapped her arms and legs around him, drawing him as deep inside her as he could go. Making him aware of every soft inch of her, every need. And she was just as clued in to him. As he dived deep, she sighed and gasped in surrender. Then all reason fled, and they were lost in the passion—lost in each other—and the sweet, searing satisfaction.

"WE NEED MORE ground rules."

Those weren't the words Holden expected to hear after making hot, wild, incredible love. He sat up in bed, watching Libby rise and begin to dress.

He had always known she had a good body. However, he had never expected her to be this beautiful, naked. Her peachy skin was silky and smooth, her feminine curves gorgeous.

He eyed the mussed strands of honey-blond hair framing her face and falling across her slender shoulders as she buttoned up her blouse.

"Rules for this?" Holden asked, admiring the view from where he sat.

Libby tugged on her jeans. "Absolutely!"

Holden slanted her a cajoling grin. "Some things are better left spontaneous."

She wrinkled her nose at him and circled the bed. Snatching her socks off the floor, she sat down next to him to tug them on.

Her feet, Holden noted, were as stunningly attractive as the rest of her. His eyes roved over her slim ankles, nicely formed arches and heels, and those dainty toes gleaming with hot-pink nail polish.

"In normal cases, I would agree." Libby leaned forward to snag her boots. Soft blue denim molded her derriere and thighs.

Grabbing hold of a boot with both hands, she tugged it on, then changed legs and donned the other. Finished, she rose to her feet and whirled to face him. "But this isn't the usual situation...."

Figuring this argument could go on for a while, Holden decided to get comfortable. He reclined on one side, his head propped up on his hand. "I agree," he said lazily, a little irked to find Libby pretending the two of them hadn't just enjoyed really outstanding lovemaking—the best of *his* life, anyway!

Locking eyes with her, he stated firmly, "It's better."

Color flooded her cheeks. "Because there are no strings?"

"No expectations," he qualified, determined to hold on to what they had, whether she cooperated or not.

Her brow furrowed quizzically.

"You keep saying you don't want to be anyone else's ball and chain," he pointed out with as much patience—and common sense—as he could summon.

Libby ran both hands over her hair, restoring order to the sensually mussed strands as best she could. "Never mind your responsibility—out of grief and guilt."

Holden surveyed her head to toe before returning with

laser accuracy to her green eyes. "So isn't it better if we forget trying to plan ahead and just let what's bound to occur happen all on its own?"

Chapter Nine

It was a good question, Libby thought, and one she would have preferred not to have to answer.

"Look, Holden, I enjoyed making love with you."

He pulled back the sheet and stood. "And I really enjoyed making love with *you*."

Libby swallowed at the sight of all that masculinity. She tried not to think about the sizzling sexual promise of his body joining with hers. Forgetting for a moment how good it had felt to be clasped in his arms, she continued sternly, "But sex wasn't part of our rebound-romance agreement."

He grinned, striding toward her in all that naked glory. Stopping just short of her, he reached down and snagged his boxer briefs. Slid in one leg, then the other. "I agree." He brought the gray jersey up his rock-hard thighs to his waist, a move that did nothing to disguise his eagerness to make love with her again. "It's a totally separate clause in the implied contract between us."

Libby propped her hands on her hips and locked eyes with him once again. "One we haven't negotiated," she pointed out.

"Until now."

Was she ready for this?

She inhaled a jerky breath. Put up a staying palm. "Holden…"

Disappointment flared in his eyes. "I'm guessing you need time to think about it."

Libby stiffened. "We both do."

He gave her a look that indicated this was not the case for him. "You're pulling away," he said, his eyes darkening.

"It might be good for both of us to take a day or two to clear our heads," she volunteered softly.

"I disagree." Frown lines bracketed his sensual lips. "I see nothing to be gained by losing momentum. Unless—" he came a step closer, his assessing glance roving over her upturned face "—that's what you're counting on?" He caught her wrist and lifted it to his lips. "To get us both to a place where we can't just pick up again?"

Skin tingling, she pulled away. "I can't believe you just said that to me."

He didn't back down. "You'd prefer I be my usual gallant self?"

Libby struggled to maintain her composure in the face of all that masculine determination. "Well, yes," she admitted.

"Sorry." He seduced her with his deep, sexy voice. "For once I'm going to speak what's in my heart and on my mind—whether you want to hear it or not."

He threaded his fingers through her hair then cupped her cheek in his hand. "I enjoyed making love with you just now. Actually…" He paused to sit on the edge of the bed and pull her onto his lap. "Not enjoyed. Loved. You have no idea how amazing it felt to have you beneath me and me inside you as deep as I could go."

Able to feel the strength and heat of his arousal, she stared at him in disbelief. "Holden!"

Arms laced around her waist, he regarded her steadily. "And whether you want to admit it or not, you enjoyed it, too."

His honesty triggered something deep inside her, something she'd never dared face before. She tried to act with a coolness she couldn't really feel. "You want the truth?" she countered, unsure whether to kiss him again or send him away. "I loved making love with you, too."

His mesmerizing eyes met and held hers again. "So?"

Aware they were headed into dangerous territory, Libby said, "The fact that our chemistry is so good scares me."

"Why?" Holden countered calmly. "You know I'd never hurt you."

That was the problem. She looked down at her jeans and pleated the denim between her fingers. "I know you wouldn't mean to, any more than I'd mean to hurt you. But…" Her voice caught for a moment before she could go on. "Sometimes things that happen in the heat of the moment don't last."

Looking as conflicted as she felt, he ran his palms over her shoulders and down her arms, eliciting sensations everywhere he touched. "Are we talking about you and me now? Or you and Percy?"

Libby slid off his lap and sat beside him. "Percy." She sighed.

Holden took her hand gently. "I'm listening."

She grimaced. "I feel disloyal saying it."

He squeezed her hand before releasing it. Tenderly, he touched her face again, cupping her chin with his palm. "You owe yourself more than you owe him. You always have."

Her emotions in turmoil, Libby vaulted off the bed

once again. "I know that. But it doesn't make it any easier."

Holden followed her to the window, where she stared out at the bleak darkness of the night. She knew she had to unburden herself to someone if she was ever to have any peace. She wanted it to be Holden.

She looked at him and forced herself to admit the truth. "Percy married me only because his parents wanted him to get married."

Holden did a double take. "What?"

An unsettling silence fell between them. "It came out in that last fight we had, before Percy went off to South America with you."

Holden's mood shifted from concerned to perplexed. "I don't understand."

"I told you that we were arguing about having a baby. I wanted one…he wasn't ready. In the heat of the moment he finally admitted that. If it hadn't been for unrelenting pressure from his parents to produce an heir that would one day carry on the family business, he said he never would have asked me to marry him."

Holden's jaw hardened. "That's true," he confirmed, beginning to see the full picture. "Percy's folks were on his case, big-time, right before he met you. They wanted a grandchild while they were still there to enjoy one."

She nodded, beginning to feel a little better now that this was all coming out. "And Percy thought I was perfect," she recalled with weary resignation, reciting the facts that had come out in her last awful argument with her husband. "I was shy and sheltered enough to please his parents and be easily malleable, with no familial commitments of my own to mess with his. And yet eager enough for excitement and adventure to do most anything he wanted, too."

"Sounds...calculated."

"I know." Libby hitched in a breath, forcing herself to be fair. "But I don't think it was at the time. I believe Percy was just trying to please everyone while still being able to please himself. I think he thought it would work out. That our love for each other would be strong enough to withstand the dullness of everyday married life."

Holden leaned toward her. "Only it wasn't."

"Once the ring was on my finger," Libby admitted, "he lost interest in sex."

"That must have been devastating for you!"

Shrugging off the humiliation, Libby rushed on. "I told myself it was normal. That all couples went through that, and we couldn't stay in the honeymoon phase forever. And I concentrated on pleasing him in other ways."

Holden held her gaze. "But Percy didn't care about home-cooked meals or a nice apartment or your devotion to learning his family business."

"No." Libby smiled sadly. "He wanted adventure, in increasingly risky venues."

"Like rock climbing and white-water rafting and black diamond skiing."

She threw up her hands. "And I just couldn't do it. I was afraid. So—" she shrugged and moved away from the window "—I suggested he do more of those things with you, and he was happy for a time."

"Until?" Holden lounged against the wall while she paced.

"I told him I wanted a baby." Libby knitted her fingers together. "And then the sex pretty much stopped altogether."

She strode forward and forced herself to continue, despite the lump in her throat and the tears gathering behind her eyes. "I couldn't bear it if the same thing happened with you and me, now that we've gotten through the awkwardness that followed my hysterical pregnancy, and have started to become friends on our own."

"Which is why you need some space."

She warmed at the understanding in his level gaze. "Yes. I know you've been lonely, Holden. So have I. But I have to really think about this." She paused and drew an innervating breath. "Before we get into a place where we could do real damage."

"I could have told you agreeing to date Libby platonically was a bad idea," Kurt told Holden the next evening, when he went over to his cousin's house for dinner. "Setting up parameters like that boxes you in."

Paige handed Holden a cup of coffee and shooed everyone away from the dinner table. As she led the way to the family room, where the triplets were already playing, she stated her view. "Romances start all kinds of ways. Look at ours...." She flashed a grin at her husband, then turned back to Holden. "Kurt and I absolutely loathed each other—until the triplets were left on his parents' doorstep and I was drafted as their official foster mother."

"True." Kurt smiled, remembering his unconventional introduction to fatherhood. He sat down beside his wife on the sofa and kissed her temple. "Just goes to show what idiots we were."

Paige leaned over to kiss him back.

Holden held up a hand, only half teasing. "Guys! Stop with the PDAs." If he was going to work his dilemma out as quickly and efficiently as he wanted, he needed the two lovebirds' full attention. "I've got a problem here."

Paige straightened. Suddenly more love doctor than pediatric surgeon, she stated soberly, "Yes, you do. And

it's more than the jelly and barbecue sauce that the triplets got all over your shirt during dinner."

Holden looked down at the mess, abruptly wishing he
and Libby had such little domestic problems every day,
instead of the really big one confronting them.

Kurt toasted him with a coffee mug. "If you want to
pursue Libby, you have to forgot about your chances of
success and go after her with everything you've got."

Paige snuggled into the curve of her husband's arm.
"Kurt's right about that. We women respond to persistence."

That, Holden knew. It was the rest of the situation that
bothered him. "How can we be sure it's not a rebound
thing for either of us?"

Paige tightened her fingers on Kurt's forearm. "Is she
still in love with Percy?"

Holden frowned. "I don't think so."

"Do you still have unrequited feelings for Heidi?"

"Definitely not."

Paige went to her computer and looked a few things
up. Finally, she sat back in relief and said, "Then, tech-
nically, it can't be a rebound romance for either of you,
no matter what you're calling it. For that to occur, you
still have to be reeling from your breakup." She paused
and looked up from the screen. "According to the experts, once you've come to terms with what happened, it
doesn't matter how much time has or hasn't elapsed. It's
safe to go on and start dating seriously again."

One problem down. "That's good to know," Holden
murmured.

The big question was, how was he going to convince
Libby that he would never lose interest in her the way
her late husband had?

BE CAREFUL WHAT YOU WISH FOR, Aunt Ida had often cautioned. And in this situation, Libby thought Friday evening, her late aunt might just be right.

Libby had asked Holden to give her space.

And he had. For the past forty-two hours and thirteen minutes she had not heard from or seen the handsome rancher.

He hadn't even shown up for toddler library hours at her home. Miss Mim had served as her volunteer, helping patrons select and check out books. And now the two of them were headed to the Lone Star to meet Miss Rosa for dinner.

As Libby drove to the restaurant and dance hall, which was owned by Holden's mother, the retired librarian sized her up from the passenger seat. "You seem depressed, dear."

Libby was. So much so that she felt like crying. And she never cried.

"Are the holidays getting you down?"

"A little," she admitted.

The rest was Holden and the notion that she might be walking away from the best thing that had ever happened to her.

"The cure for the yuletide blues is staying busy."

Libby smiled. "I know. And I have been." She had even more activities planned for the upcoming weekend.

Sadly, none included Holden, who in just one week had become much more important to her than she could have imagined.

Miss Mim took her arm as they walked across the parking lot. "I hope you have your thinking cap on. Miss Rosa and I are going to need every bright idea you can muster up this evening."

"I'll do my best to be brilliant," she promised, tongue-in-cheek.

Miss Mim smiled.

Always happy to be helping someone, Libby smiled back.

Her spirits lifted even more as they walked into the restaurant. A beautiful tree stood in the lobby. Christmas music wafted from the stereo system. It being Friday evening, the place was crowded with families and couples on dates.

Greta McCabe met them at the hostess stand and showed them to a table by a window. "Your dinner partners should be here momentarily."

"Dinner partners?" Libby echoed in confusion. She thought they were only meeting Miss Rosa.

"I invited someone else to help us brainstorm ways to solve the library crisis," Miss Mim said, with sudden choir-girl innocence. "I hope you don't mind."

"Why should I..." Libby took in the librarian's sudden smile and followed the direction of her wave.

Holden McCabe. Of course.

Why had she not seen this coming?

And why did he have to look so devastatingly handsome in a black blazer, light blue shirt and well-fitting jeans?

"Ladies," Holden said, inundating Libby with his sexy scent as he neared. The familiar aromas of leather and soap mixed with the familiar masculine fragrance of his skin.

A shiver slid down Libby's spine as he paused to greet her with a casual hug and kiss to her brow that spoke volumes about his intentions—to everyone in the place.

Still smiling, he held out a chair for Miss Rosa, then paused to gallantly clasp Miss Mim's hand and say hello to her, too. Having worked his magic on all three women, he circled the table and sat down next to Libby, his knee nudging hers slightly as he settled his tall frame.

She looked into his blue eyes. And felt yet another whisper of desire.

"So," Holden said as soon as their drink and appetizer orders had been placed. He looked directly at Miss Mim, "I scouted around, just like you asked, and here's what I've been able to find out from the county commissioners."

"The news is bad, isn't it?" she fretted.

Holden nodded. He leaned back as tall glasses of mint-flavored iced tea were delivered, and baskets of fried onion rings and Southwestern egg rolls were put in the center of the table.

When the waitress had disappeared, he continued, "The estimate on the repairs needed to remove the asbestos and reopen the library has come in at close to a quarter of a million dollars."

Miss Rosa gasped. "That's more than our bare-bones operating budget for one year! It doesn't even include the purchase of new books or magazines."

"Let me guess," Libby said. "The county doesn't have the funds."

"And things are so tight right now there's no way to get them. So the plan they are going to present to the public, and vote on in January, is to keep the facility closed for one year, stockpile the unused operating funds and then start the repairs—which are estimated to take anywhere from three to six months—in December of next year."

"That's unacceptable!" Libby cried.

Holden gestured. "I told the commissioners the citizens weren't going to like it. They don't feel they have any choice."

"There's always a choice," Libby said, unable to contain her fury.

All eyes turned to her.

"Maybe the county doesn't have the funds, but that doesn't mean we have to sit back and take it," she fumed.

"We could try and raise the funds privately," Miss Mim offered.

Miss Rosa sighed. "But that would take a long time, too."

"And that's the other bad part," Holden said, looking at the young woman, who was just out of college. "They may have to let the entire staff of paid employees go, too."

"So I could be looking for a job." Miss Rosa burst into tears.

"Don't you worry about that," Libby said fiercely.

Holden nodded. "We'll all work together to find you something here in Laramie, with equitable pay, until the library does reopen. And the same goes for all the hourly employees. How many are there?"

"Three." Miss Rosa relaxed in relief.

Silence fell.

"Maybe we could approach some of the various charitable foundations in Texas to help us," Libby said. "We could start a letter-writing campaign, tell them what the community has already been willing to do to keep our library going. Who knows? Five thousand here, another two or ten there—if we can get enough help from all sorts of sources, we might just reach our goal."

Miss Mim smiled. "That's the spirit! I knew we could count on you. You always know what to do. There's no one better to lead a crusade."

And, Libby thought, if she sold her business as planned, she would definitely have the time to take it on.

The rest of the meal was spent brainstorming various

ways to start the fund-raising process immediately. By the time Miss Mim was ready to be driven back to her apartment in the Laramie Gardens Senior Center, they had a game plan to execute.

Libby started to rise.

Miss Rosa lifted a staying hand. "I'll drive her home."

"Yes, dear," Miss Mim ordered, with a wink aimed Holden's way. "You two stay here and enjoy your coffee."

The two librarians left.

"I think Miss Mim is matchmaking," Libby said.

The corners of Holden's lips turned up. "I think you might just be right," he drawled.

"I also think you might have something to do with it."

He chuckled. "I think you're right about that, too. Although, I did want to be here tonight for the library's sake, too. It's an important institution. It means a lot to the people of Laramie." His expression turned tender as he covered her hand with his. "The way you handled that crisis was quite impressive."

Libby blushed. She didn't know why his admiration meant so much to her. It just did. Modestly, she replied, "I haven't really done anything yet." *Except maybe fall a little harder for you....*

She swallowed emotionally. "You were great, too, by the way."

"We make a good team," he said with a gleam in his eyes.

They were certainly beginning to, Libby thought wistfully.

"Let's celebrate." He tugged her by the hand, took her onto the dance floor and spun her around.

"Holden?"

"Hmm?" His hand tightened around her waist, and he pressed his cheek against hers.

Libby sighed and tried not to feel too comfy. It was, as she might have predicted, a losing battle. Using her elbows, she wedged a bit of space between them. "The band hasn't started yet."

He glanced up at the empty stage. "Oh, yeah." With a bemused look on his face, he let her go. "Wait here."

Libby had no doubt Holden knew how to turn on the music. His mother owned the restaurant and dance hall, and he—like the rest of his siblings—had grown up working here, whenever they weren't toiling on their dad's horse ranch.

Seconds later, dance music poured from the speakers.

Libby flushed as he rejoined her and took her in his arms. "Am I supposed to be getting a message from all this?" she asked.

"I sure hope so."

Her heart skipped another beat as Lady Antebellum sang, "All I want for Christmas is you."

Chapter Ten

"That was some romantic gesture," Libby remarked several fun-filled hours later. Way past midnight, the Laramie streets were quiet. A full moon shone overhead in the black velvet sky. Christmas wreaths decorated the light posts all along Laramie's historic Main Street. Every storefront and business was decorated to the hilt, adding to the festive air. But best thing of all, Libby thought, was being here with Holden.

Just the two of them.

He smiled down at her. "I'm glad you liked dancing with me."

Libby shivered as the cold winter breeze blew against them. "You didn't have to keep spinning me around for the last four hours." They had closed the place down, which was another first for her. Leaving only when the rest of the staff bailed, too.

Holden tucked her into the curve of his body. "You know us Texans." Lazily, he guided her toward the parking lot. "Do it up big or don't do it at all."

Libby laughed and ducked her head, resting her cheek against the solid warmth of his chest. "I'm beginning to get that sense of you," she murmured.

Finally, they reached her Range Rover, with his pickup truck several rows over. Standing in the parking lot, Libby wished Holden would build on what they had started and kiss her passionately.

Instead, he stepped back, shoved his hands in the pockets of his leather bomber jacket and said, "What are your plans for tomorrow?"

Libby blinked. "Tomorrow?"

"Saturday. You know." He spoke clearly, enunciating every word. "Do you have to work?"

Brought swiftly back to reality, Libby sighed. "Unfortunately, I do. Jeff Johnston is coming by the dealership with his accountant and his lawyer to take a look at our books and get more information, so he can estimate the value of Lowell Ranch Equipment and formulate a formal offer."

Holden ran a palm beneath his jaw. "You could do that for him, you know, simply by putting a price tag on the business."

Libby rocked forward onto the toes of her suede boots. "I'd rather he take the lead."

Holden's lips quirked in amusement. "So you can counter."

She preened. "I have learned a thing or two since I started working there, many moons ago."

Holden sobered. "I guess you have."

Silence filled with longing followed. Still he didn't kiss her, didn't make a move. Doing her best to stifle her frustration, Libby continued, "And then I promised to work a booth at the Community Chapel bazaar."

Holden inclined his head. "The kissing booth?"

If only, Libby thought. She gave him a droll look. "You know they don't have kissing booths at the church. In fact, I don't think they have them anywhere anymore. Too many germs."

He nodded, deadpan. "It is flu season."

Libby smiled. She didn't know what his deal was. All she *did* know was that she couldn't get enough of him—and she sensed that this malady was only going to get worse.

"Which reminds me," Holden continued, looking down the street at the now-closed pharmacy. "I need to get my shot."

Libby winced. "So do I. I haven't had time for that, either."

Holden quirked a brow. "Want to do that together?"

Libby scoffed, not sure whether he was joking or not. "Get our flu shots?" she echoed, more intrigued with the cowboy in front of her than ever.

"We could keep each other on track. Stop the procrastination!" he teased.

"I guess we could at that," Libby drawled.

Serious now, Holden said, "They offer them at the pharmacy, you know. We could go over after the bazaar. Say around six? I'll even let the pharmacist know we're coming."

He meant it! About protecting them both from illness and spending time with her. "You'll make reservations," she repeated.

"Like I said." He shrugged easily. "It will keep us focused."

They needed that. "All right," Libby said impulsively. "You're on."

Hand to her spine, he guided her toward her car. "And after that, we'll see."

Libby rummaged for her keys and hit the unlock button on the pad.

Heart racing, she slanted Holden a sideways glance. "See what?"

"Don't know." Mischief sharpened the attractive lines

of his face. "But it's a magical time of year." He looked deep into her eyes and contented himself with a light, friendly peck on her head. "Anything can happen."

"I HEARD WHAT WENT ON at the Lone Star last night," Paige said the next day, when she met up with Libby at the community center where the bazaar was being held. She playfully elbowed her. "Dancing without music?"

Libby tied on her change apron. "I know it sounds lame. It was actually…romantic." Unable to help herself, she flushed self-consciously.

Paige moved in for a closer look. "You both have it bad, don't you?"

Libby started straightening the boxes of donated chocolate candy and fruit baskets. "What do you mean?"

Her friend shrugged and set up the cash box. "I've never known Holden to make a fool of himself over a woman. Even with Heidi he was somewhat restrained in his affections."

He hadn't been restrained at all when Libby and he had made love. On the other hand…

Figuring she could use some perspective from a friend who had the happily-ever-after thing down pat, Libby remarked, "He was restrained last night."

Paige glanced at her, curious.

"He walked me to the parking lot." Libby winced, recalling. "But not even a kiss good-night."

Paige chuckled. "Second rule of male courtship—leave 'em wanting more."

Or maybe, like Percy, he didn't want her at all….

Libby pushed the disturbing thought away.

"He's being respectful of you," Paige said.

Libby harrumphed, thinking of the beautiful night and full moon and perfect opportunity that had gone to waste. "I didn't want gallant last night," she muttered in frustration.

Paige drew her to a corner of their booth, well out of earshot of others setting up. "Is that what you said to him?" she whispered.

"Well, no," Libby admitted, wondering if she would ever be able to go after what she truly wanted.

Still studying her, Paige stated, "So in other words, Holden is sticking to the prescribed plan laid out by you."

I guess. "Speaking of which." Having figured out Holden's lack of action was her own fault, Libby pushed on with the rest of her confession. "He asked me to go with him tonight to get our flu shots."

Her friend blinked in surprise. "The couple that vaccinates together, stays together?" Her eyes twinkled. "It's good, though. He lined up the next date. That means he is serious."

Libby pushed a strand of hair behind her ear. She had hoped for romance, but now that she had it, she didn't know what to do. "I'm very confused."

"Don't be." Paige hugged her. "Just go with it. Let fate show you what will happen next."

Four hours later, the church bazaar was over and Libby headed to the pharmacy. Holden got out of his pickup just as she pulled up beside him in the parking lot.

Looking handsome as ever, with his dark hair ruffled from the winter wind, he shoved his hands in the pockets of his bomber jacket and gave her a teasing once-over as she joined him.

"You're not going to faint on me, are you?" he asked.

Libby rolled her eyes and resisted the urge to lean in close to the protective shield of his tall, strong body.

Still feeling a little peeved that he hadn't given her

a proper good-night kiss the evening before—no matter what she had said days earlier—she shoved her own hands in the pockets of her sophisticated red down jacket. "No. Of course not." Unable to resist, she slanted a mocking glance his way. "Are *you* going to faint on *me?*"

Holden rubbed his palm contemplatively along the rugged line of his jaw and peered at her in concern. "Maybe we should have some smelling salts on us, just in case."

Libby couldn't tell whether he was joking or not. She did know he had worked just as hard at the booth he and Kurt had run, as she and Paige had at theirs.

She slowed her steps as they reached the entrance, delaying the moment they actually went inside. Burning with curiosity, she asked, "Why did Kurt slap you on the back like that when we were leaving?"

Holden turned toward her and tucked an errant strand of her hair behind her ear, the backs of his fingers caressing her cheek slightly in the process. Then he shrugged. "Why do men always slap each other on the back?" he asked, all innocence.

"I don't know." Libby rocked forward on her heels and propped her fists on her hips. "Encouragement?" she guessed.

Holden nodded. "Exactly."

Libby told herself the satisfied gleam in his eyes had nothing to do with the passionate way they'd made love to each other a few nights earlier. "Why do you need encouragement?" she pressed.

Holden grinned and leaned in closer still. Almost close enough for them to kiss. "Why do you think?"

This flirting was beginning to be fun. It was also showing her a whole new side to Holden McCabe.

Maybe he wasn't so guilt-ridden and far too responsible for his own good, after all.

Maybe she had been wrong to insist on a sexual time-out....

He opened the door to the pharmacy and ushered her inside. Ten minutes later, they had both filled out their forms, paid the fee and received their injections. Band-Aids on, they were free to go. "So now what?" Libby said as he helped her with her coat and slipped his on, too.

Holden's hand moved to the small of her back as they made their way toward the exit.

Unfortunately, the aisle they had randomly chosen was filled with contraceptives and sexual aids and lotions. Appearing oblivious to the products lined up to the left of them, Holden leaned in closer and murmured in her ear, "Well, if we were still rebound dating, I know what we'd do."

So did Libby, unfortunately. If she spent any time at all alone with him, she would undoubtedly end up in his bed, enjoying herself every bit as much as she had before. Consequences be damned!

Trying not to flush, she hurried on down the aisle toward the safety of the greeting cards stacked at the other end. Then, taking his hand, she hurried Holden out the door and across the lot to their vehicles.

Only when they had were safely out of earshot of everyone did she release her grip on him.

Their eyes met, and she felt a heady sensation deep inside her. "You're trying to get me to change my mind," she accused. *About everything.*

"I'm trying to get you to take us off Hold."

Here was her chance.

She could play it safe, the way she had been.

Be loyal to everything she had known in the past.
Or take a risk.

AS THE SECONDS TICKED BY, Holden wasn't sure what Libby was going to do. He could see she was as deeply conflicted as he, that she didn't want to risk their fast-growing friendship with a more intimate relationship that might or might not work out, for even the short run.

"On one condition," Libby said finally, beginning to smile. "It has to be something fun. And holidayish."

Holden's tension eased. Playtime was something he could handle. Especially with Libby.

Given where they were standing, it didn't take long for the next idea to hit. "How about some holiday greenery for the front grilles of our vehicles?" Decorating your ride was a fine Texas tradition. One, as far as Holden knew, that she had never participated in.

"You're serious."

Having picked a winner, he raised his shoulder. "We'll make it a contest."

She slapped her thigh. "Now you're talking!"

Enjoying the lively spark in her dark green eyes, he continued the challenge. "Whoever has the best-decorated wreath wins."

Her lips curved in a delicious smile. "The winner—?"

Remembering the silky feel of her skin, wishing he could forgo convention and kiss her again, Holden decided, "The winner gets the meal of his or her choice. The loser cooks said meal."

Libby propped her hands on her hips and challenged him with a tilt of her chin. "Can you cook?"

He waggled his eyebrows. "There's one way to find out."

Laughing and teasing each other good-naturedly, they

headed for the Kiwanis lot. It was crowded with people selecting trees, garlands and wreaths.

Holden and Libby concentrated on the latter.

Soon after, the next debate began.

She shook her head disparagingly at the wreath he was looking at. "Having one that large is ridiculous."

But Holden liked it. It wasn't sissy—it was man-size. He chucked her playfully on the chin. "Haven't you heard? In Texas, everything that is bigger—is better."

Libby struggled not to laugh. "I don't think that's exactly how the saying goes." She pursed her lips thoughtfully. "That medium size would be perfect for my Range Rover."

"I don't have a problem with that, as long as I get the large one for my pickup."

"Then size can't matter in the final analysis," Libby bargained.

Holden's eyes lit up in a way that told her he had found another meaning for her words. "I'm sure it won't," he said smoothly.

Libby flushed. "You're not going to behave yourself at all this evening, are you?"

She made it damn hard not to think about making love. "Hey—" Holden angled a thumb at his chest "—I figure as long as we're spending time together, we may as well be ourselves."

HOLDEN HAD A POINT, Libby knew.

For reasons she chose not to examine too closely, she wanted to drop her guard, too. Even though she suspected where that would likely lead. "Then I'll take the Mama Bear size and you can take the Papa Bear size," she said.

Holden grinned and paid for the wreaths. From there, they drove to the arts-and-crafts store. On a Saturday evening so close to Christmas, it was crowded with shoppers eager to pick up what they needed to complete their own decorating.

Libby headed straight for the yuletide aisles. She filled her shopping basket with red velvet ribbon, pinecones, and silver and gold ornaments while Holden stood patiently by.

Finally she turned. "Aren't you going to get anything?" she asked in consternation.

He regarded her with the same indulgence doting men used for their wives. "I was waiting for you to finish."

Libby swallowed, pushing the idea of marriage away. "I've got what I need. So you better get a move on, cowboy."

Grinning, Holden headed off to the college-sports section. He picked up a University of Texas banner, miniature longhorn cattle mascots, and footballs and basketballs.

"That's not Christmassy," Libby said with a perplexed frown.

He laughed, soft and low. "It is to me." Then he leaned down to whisper in her ear, "Where's your school spirit? You're a UT grad, too."

Tingling with desire, Libby straightened. "Men!"

He regarded her with comically exaggerated exasperation. "Women!"

And they were on.

After Libby paid for their purchases—over Holden's protests—the two of them went back to his ranch and spread their purchases out on the family-room floor. Holden turned on a Chris Botti Christmas CD. As the sexy trumpet music filled the room, they began working in earnest, ribbing each other all the while.

An hour later, they took their creations out to the

driveway. Using coated wire, they attached three points of the wreaths to the front grilles of their respective vehicles, then stood back to judge their handiwork.

As Libby admired his breathtaking creation, she had to admit Holden had done a stellar job.

He had passed on a bow, and instead threaded the evergreen wreath with burnt-orange and white ribbons, the university colors. The official Texas banner was wired to the center of the wreath. Miniature longhorn mascots, footballs and basketballs served as ornaments.

Hers was equally gorgeous, though. She had tied a fancy, red velvet bow to the top of her wreath and studded the evergreen boughs with pine cones, and gold and silver ornaments.

"Much as I'm loath to admit it, I think yours is better," Holden said finally.

Libby shook her head. "Yours is definitely more original."

They exchanged grins.

He held out his hand. "A tie, then?"

She fitted her palm against his. "Agreed."

Their fingers remained entwined. "So…who makes who dinner?" he asked eventually.

Who cared about eating, when her date for the evening looked so sexy?

Telling herself all good things come to those who wait, Libby reined in her skyrocketing desire and suggested cheerfully, "Suppose we do it together?"

A sensual smile lifted the corners of his mouth. He seemed as eager to spend time with her as she was with him. "Good idea. Although I have to tell you, my fridge isn't nearly as well stocked as yours."

He wasn't kidding, Libby soon found out.

There was part of a chocolate-peppermint pie from

his sister's restaurant. A gallon of milk, another of orange juice, a six-pack of Bohemia beer. A package of hot dogs and buns, mustard, ketchup and pickles. The pantry held a bag of chips.

"Looks like we're having an indoor cookout," she sighed.

"Sounds good to me."

As Holden built a fire in the fireplace, Libby located the long-handled forks for grilling. They set up picnic-style in front of the hearth. When he smiled at her, she suddenly realized that nothing was as simple as it seemed.

MOST WOMEN WOULD HAVE turned up their nose at the meager offerings in his fridge and insisted he take them out for a proper Saturday-evening dinner. It was only eight-thirty. There were plenty of places in Laramie still open.

But Libby seemed content to rough it right along with him. He was content just sitting there in the soft light, listening to the music and watching her.

"You keep smiling," he said after a while, aware that there was magic in the air and it was all due to her.

"I was just thinking about how happy I am right now." Her lips curved in a gentle smile. "I haven't felt this much Christmas spirit in a long time."

Holden fitted a hot dog on a long-handled fork and gave it to her. "What were your holidays like as a kid?"

She shifted closer to the fire and held the meat over the burning oak. "Memories of the holidays with my parents are a little fuzzy, since they died when I was in elementary school, but I can remember them taking me to see Santa Claus at the mall, decorating a tree, having Christmas dinner in a restaurant."

There was such warm affection in her voice. "And after that—with your aunt Ida?" Holden prodded.

Libby moved over slightly, so he could cook his hot dog, too. "Aunt Ida was all about the little things," she reflected fondly. "Perfectly decorating the tree and the rest of the house, baking gifts for all the neighbors, caroling.... After she passed, the holiday season lost a lot of its joy for me. But maybe that's because I let it..."

Holden's shoulder nudged hers as they both tried to keep their hot dogs from getting too close to the flames. "I remember Christmas with Percy's family was always a little tense."

"And for good reason." She handed Holden her fork and then set about opening up two whole-wheat buns. "All his parents ever wanted was to spend time with him. And all Percy ever wanted was to head for the slopes." Libby squirted on mustard. "He loved his folks, but he still had one foot out the door all of Christmas Eve, much to their displeasure. We usually left for New Mexico or Colorado right after present opening on Christmas Day."

Holden helped transfer the deliciously charred hot dogs to the buns. "And once you were there?"

She added potato chips to both their plates. "He skied every second he could on the black diamond runs, which were way too difficult for me. So—" she sighed wearily, munching on a dill pickle "—we usually spent a lot of time apart. Although we'd usually meet up for a late dinner in a restaurant."

Holden opened a beer for her. "Did you ever try to change that?"

"You know Percy." Libby took a sip of the golden liquid. "He wanted what he wanted, when he wanted it... and that was that."

And, Holden was willing to bet, she had never complained.

He had loved his late friend, but in this respect, Percy

had been a donkey's rear end, because Libby had deserved so much better.

"What about you?" she asked as they began to eat. "What were your Christmases like as a kid?"

Holden watched the play of firelight on her honeyed hair. "Just what you would expect." He shrugged. "Fun, loving. All the traditional stuff. Lots of family." He sobered. "That changed when Heidi and I got involved."

Libby finished her hot dog and munched on a chip. "How so?"

"The first December Heidi and I were together, we were just beginning our relationship. Heidi learned she was pregnant. The crisis colored the holiday."

"She wasn't happy?"

"Not really. Not the way I was." Again, Holden's shoulder touched Libby's as they turned their attention to the flames. "Looking back now, I realize she wasn't over her ex. At the time it happened, I thought it had to do with the fact that she was expecting a baby and we weren't married." Wearily, Holden continued, "Heidi knew her family wasn't going to like that—or the fact we had been dating only a couple of months. So we went to Cabo, to elope."

"And then in March, she miscarried," Libby recalled.

Holden nodded, the memory making him grim. The six months he had been married had been the unhappiest of his life, yet he'd felt like an utter failure when it all fell apart.

He swallowed and pushed on. "In June, Heidi told me she didn't love me, was never going to love me, asked for a divorce and left town."

A compassionate silence stretched between them. Libby reached over and took his hand and Holden exhaled. "Our marriage ended in September."

She looked down at their laced fingers. "And then you and Percy went off on that last trip, and he died later that month."

Holden gave her hand a squeeze, let go. "I haven't felt a lot like celebrating the holidays since."

Another silence fell, this one not so easy to bridge. "I understand," Libby said softly at last. "I used to feel the same way."

Holden noticed her use of the past tense. "And now?" he pressed, suddenly realizing how much was hinging on her answer.

For the first time in a long while, Libby looked at peace. "I'm thinking it's time to turn the page, start over," she said emphatically. "Really enjoy the holidays for a change."

Absorbing the sight of her, so lovely and intent, Holden grinned. Together, they stood and carried their dishes into the kitchen. "That being the case, maybe we should do something about that." He took her arm and led her back toward the living room.

"Like what?" Libby asked, her eyes sparkling as they settled back on the floor before the fire.

Desire welled inside him. "Like this."

Chapter Eleven

The next thing Libby knew, Holden's arms were around her and his head was lowering to hers. She gasped as their lips forged. Waves of anticipation swept through her and then his mouth was locked on hers in a slow, sexy kiss that stole her breath. She melted against him, her breasts pressed against the hardness of his chest.

He was so warm and so strong. So unbelievably tender in his pursuit of her. She felt completely overwhelmed by the exciting masculine taste of his mouth, the tantalizing stroking of his tongue and the sweet, evocative pressure of his lips. She sighed in contentment as he deepened the kiss even more, commanding and seducing. She felt the sandpapery rub of his beard, inhaled the unique leather-and-soap fragrance that was him and sank ever deeper into his embrace.

Still kissing, they shifted. He guided her backward, so she was lying on the rug before the fire. He was beside her, his leg wedged between hers.

Libby loved how he challenged her to stop trying to please everyone else, and worry instead about pleasing herself. She loved the reckless, womanly way he made her feel.

He wasn't afraid to take desire to the limit, and for the first time, he made her want to do the same.

It didn't matter if they loved each other, although she was beginning to feel as if she might be falling for him in a major way. It didn't matter if this was meant to work out for the foreseeable future, or just the holiday season. Libby wanted Holden. She wanted to feel alive. Blessed. And joyful. She wanted this gift of time and caring and passion. The intimate emotional connection only he offered. And this one holiday, she was going for it all.

HOLDEN HADN'T MEANT to kiss Libby this evening.

Oh, he had known he would hold her in his arms again. He had known from the way she looked at him, whenever she thought he didn't see, that she felt the new yearning between them, too.

He *hadn't* planned to let his passion for her get ahead of him, or risk having her feel that this was something that translated only into physical needs.

He lifted his head. "I want to take it slow."

Libby flashed a sultry smile and kissed him again, seeming as enthralled by the free-flowing desire between them. "So do I."

Tenderness surged through him. He wanted to honor and cherish her in a way she truly deserved. And that meant taking his sweet time pursuing her. He wanted to give her all the consideration and latitude that she had so obviously been missing. "You know what I mean."

She looked up at him with misty eyes, making no move to pull away. "I know what would be wise, and I know what I want," she murmured, her heart pounding in cadence to his. "And they aren't the same things at all."

She kissed him once more, surrendering even as she was seducing.

Gathering her close again, he gave in to the feelings surging inside him. He kissed her long and hard, slow and deep, reveling in their burgeoning passion. Until he felt her trembling and drew back once again, wanting to make sure. "Libby…"

She arched against him. "Make love to me, Holden. Right now and right here. And I'll make love to you.…"

The steadiness in her voice and eyes was all the invitation he needed. He swept off her sweater, her bra, her jeans. With her help, he dispensed with his shirt. Barechested, he stroked his hand down her body, charting the dips and curves. And still they kissed, the connection getting hotter and more erotic. Libby was wild in a way he could never have imagined, free and sexy and celebrating what they felt.

She made a muted whimper of pleasure when he captured her breasts. Luxuriating in the silky texture, he palmed the softness of the feminine globes and rubbed the erect tips with his thumbs, caressed them with his lips and tongue.

Determined this night would be every bit as memorable as he could make it, he moved back to her mouth, putting everything he had into the kiss. Her lips were pliant beneath his, giving and testing, her body soft and surrendering.

Aware that nothing had ever seemed as right as this, he set about exploring the rest of her. Removed her panties. Slid a throw pillow beneath her head, and stretched out beside her on the rug, knowing that every moment they delayed, their mutual gratification would be multiplied tenfold.

Libby locked eyes with him and reached for his fly. "I want you naked, too."

Not about to let himself get ahead of her, he chuckled. "In due time."

With a mixture of tenderness and primal possessiveness filling his soul, he kissed his way from the nape of her neck, across her breasts, to her navel.

The need he wanted to see glimmered in her eyes.

Feeling a little like a conqueror who had just captured the fair maiden of his dreams, he moved lower still. She gasped as he found the silkiest, sweetest part of her, the softness of her body giving new heat to his. Loving the fierceness of her response to him, he kept right on tantalizing her, until at last she fell apart in his arms. Satisfaction rushed through him, along with raw, aching need.

He moved upward, rubbing his chest against her bare breasts, savoring the feel of her budding nipples, then took her mouth in a slow, hot mating dance.

Libby moaned and shuddered once again. "Holden…" The sound was part praise, part plea.

Her palms slid around his back, massaging the muscles on either side of his spine, then dropping to the waistband of his jeans.

"Naked," she repeated insistently.

He grinned as she rolled him onto his back, moved over him and divested him of his jeans and briefs.

He caught his breath as she straddled his hips and moved slowly, provocatively lower. Found him with her hands and lips, kissing and caressing him in all the ways he had fantasized her doing. With her hair falling across his abdomen, she enticed him further, whispered playfully, "See? This is nice, too."

"Really nice," Holden agreed.

And then there was no more waiting. For either of them.

Not about to climax without her, and needing to possess her, he pulled her upward. He shifted her onto her back and stretched out over her, taking control once again.

"We can try something else later. Right now, I want you this way."

Her head fell back in an age-old gesture of feminine surrender that heightened the excitement between them even more. "I want you this way, too." Murmuring in pleasure, she wrapped her arms and legs around him and lifted her hips to his.

"I'm glad we agree." He penetrated her slowly, sliding his palms beneath her, lifting her and filling her as she opened herself up to him even more.

And then they were one, kissing each other hotly, moving urgently, coming together again and again until there was only this moment in time. This heat. This passion. This connection that neither one of them had expected to find.

Thrills swept through them, again and again, until there was nothing but this gift as they writhed together. Until there was no more denying their ardent yearning for each other, no more delaying the inevitable. Spirits soaring, they succumbed to the swirling pleasure.

And Holden knew what he hadn't before. He no longer saw Libby as his rebound romance, but as the woman he wanted—the only woman for him.

"COME WITH ME," Holden urged early the following morning, as Libby gathered up her belongings and prepared to head back to her house.

"I already told you I was planning to attend. Your mother sent me an email invitation for the brunch." It was going to be held at Shane and Greta's ranch. The only people who were attending, aside from herself, was their immediate family.

She hadn't been slated to go as Holden's date, Libby thought as she sat down to pull on her boots. More like an "informally adopted" member of the family. This was part of her and Greta's strategy to take some of the responsibility of looking after her from Holden's shoulders.

And had Libby not followed her own swiftly building desires and made hot, passionate love with Holden, the strategy might have worked.

Regret that she hadn't exactly done everything she could to make sure Holden was relieved of his feelings of guilt and responsibility toward her filled Libby's heart.

She was being selfish again. Reaching out to him, letting him be her lifeline and a way out of her own residual grief and loneliness. When what she should have been doing was helping him extricate himself from the promise he had made to her late husband.

Holden held out his hand to assist her to her feet. "I want us to go together."

Together, they headed down the stairs to the foyer. "And make a statement," Libby guessed, not sure how she felt about that. On one hand, she was as thrilled by the possessive note in Holden's low, sexy voice as she had been by the way he'd made love to her.

On the other…she had become involved with Percy far too swiftly, and look how that had turned out in the end. Holden had done the same thing with Heidi. Again, with disastrous results.

When it came to relationships, going slow seemed to be necessary for success. What she and Holden had done the night before—passionately making love and then falling asleep wrapped in each other's arms—was anything *but* cautious.

Undeterred, Holden helped her into her coat. "I want everyone to know we're dating."

Libby adjusted her scarf around her neck. "They already know that."

He lounged against the banister as she searched for her keys. "They knew we were on...and then off."

"And now we're on again." Flushing at her presumptuousness, Libby abruptly stopped talking. The last thing she wanted to do was take too much for granted here and end up being a burden to him in much the same way she had been to Percy. Belatedly, she looked at Holden in apology and amended, "Through the holidays, anyway."

The inscrutable look was back on his face. "How about as long as this works for both of us?" he suggested amiably, after a moment. "No need to put a time limit on it."

As he sauntered closer, Libby struggled not to notice how sexy and self-assured he looked.

He took her in his arms. "And, instead, let's take it one day at a time."

Which would give him an out, should he want one, she supposed. It was sort of a guarantee she wouldn't become a burden, once the initial excitement of their sexual coupling passed, and she was more than okay with that.

Telling herself she was doing this as much for herself, as for him, Libby murmured, "Okay."

"DON'T YOU LOOK PRETTY today," Greta told Libby two hours later, when she and Holden arrived at the Circle M for brunch.

Libby hugged Holden's mother warmly. "Thank you." She felt as if she was glowing, inside and out. And not just from the lovemaking. It was the sense of family she suddenly had, too. The knowledge she no longer had to be alone.

"Holden, you look happy, too."

He winked. "I am happy, Mom."

"I can see that," Greta said thoughtfully, giving her son a meaningful look.

Seconds later, they were surrounded by the rest of the clan. Hugs and hellos followed.

Holden went off for a word with his dad, ostensibly to help him empty ice into big, stainless-steel tubs, but it was clear more was going on than that.

Emily frowned at the tense exchange, visible through the kitchen window. "What's going on between Dad and Holden?"

Jeb's wife, Cady, shrugged. "No clue."

Hank's wife, Ally, kept a poker face. "I'm not sure, either," she said eventually.

Maybe not, Libby thought, studying Greta's careful, polite expression. But Holden's mother knew something.

Even if she wasn't about to reveal what, in front of Libby.

Just that quickly, the warmth Libby had felt when she'd joined the family gathering faded.

She'd had a glimpse what it would be like to be a Mc-Cabe. But she was a far cry from ever really being part of the clan. No matter how hard Holden's mother was trying to bring her into the fold.

"What happened?" Holden asked later, after the gathering had broken up and they were driving back to her house.

Libby turned to him. "Maybe you should tell me."

HOLDEN HAD KNOWN it was a bad time to talk, but his dad hadn't wanted to put it off. Holden turned his glance away from the wheel of his pickup long enough to ask, "You saw me outside with my dad?"

Libby folded her arms in front of her. The action served to emphasize the lush curves of her breasts beneath her open coat and Christmassy sweater. "All the women did."

That didn't necessarily mean anything.

Pink color sweeping into her cheeks, Libby continued her inquisition. "Was your father warning you not to get involved with me?"

"Is that what you thought?" Holden asked in surprise.

Her lips set in a feisty pout, she tossed her head. Strands of silky hair, already tousled from the wind, swished about her shoulders. "It would make sense."

"No, it wouldn't," he told her frankly, glad they were nearly at their destination so he'd be able to stop driving and focus all his attention on her. "My dad likes you. He wants to see me married again, and so does my mom."

Arms still folded militantly, Libby settled deeper into the bench seat. "Then…?"

Struggling to contain his own emotions, Holden turned on his left signal light. "I asked him—and my uncles—to do me a favor." Obviously, not a good move on his part. Holden slowed his truck as they reached the town limits. He grimaced, bracing himself for the fireworks ahead. "I'm not sure you're going to like it."

She released an indignant breath, looking so pretty that all he could think about was kissing her again. "Tell me anyway," she demanded.

He stopped at a traffic light. "I asked them to talk to everyone they knew in the business community throughout the state and find out what they could about Jeff Johnston."

Libby shifted toward him, clearly interested, her eyes narrowed in cool speculation. "And?"

"He's clean, as far as his dealings go. Everything in his process is legal and aboveboard."

Intimacy simmered between them. "I could have told you that. I had the dealership attorney, Claire McCabe, do a background check on Johnston before I ever even entertained the idea of selling to him."

Holden knew they were headed into dangerous territory. "There can be things about a person that don't show up in a background check."

Her brow furrowed. "Such as?"

"He's known to be a very tough negotiator."

Libby tilted her head and gazed over at Holden. "That hasn't been my experience. In fact, to date he's been more than willing to work with me, even agreeing to keep the Lowell name on the business."

The change in traffic light forced Holden to move on. "Don't you think that's odd?" He waved at a friend manning the Salvation Army holiday donation bucket in the corner.

Libby waved, too, then turned to scowl at Holden. "Jeff realizes the Lowell name is synonymous with quality. He knows full well that customers are going to be wary enough about the change, without altering the name and logo, too."

Holden couldn't argue.

"And," Libby continued heatedly, "this is a way to keep the memory of Percy and his ancestors alive in the hearts and minds of all the people they served over the years."

Holden turned again and headed toward the dealership. "I can't see that sentiment meaning much to a tycoon in the making like Jeff Johnston."

"It may not, but it means something to the employees who work at Lowell Ranch Equipment, and Jeff realizes what an integral part they all play in the success of the dealership. Our customers depend on the relationships they have built with our sales and service staff members."

Holden did not deny the personal touch went a long

way. But there was also ego involved. He approached the driveway to Libby's home and turned into it, pulled up close to the house and cut the engine. "According to my dad, Johnston has put his moniker on everything he owns."

"Well, not in this case. Besides," Libby said, "with the plans Jeff has to build up the business by adding an internet component, he'll probably make much more than I do now. As will all the employees, since they're going to own five percent of the business, once the deal is set."

Holden only wished negotiating a deal of that complexity was easy. "So you're not in the least bit worried..."

"You don't have to worry," Libby declared. "I've got this handled."

Easier said than done, Holden thought, as he and Libby gazed at each other with mounting emotion. Especially given the promise he had made to Percy, and Holden's own private need to shield her from harm.

But that was a story for another day. Right now, he needed to keep them spending time together. And there was only one way to do that.

Chapter Twelve

Libby stared at Holden as if she couldn't possibly have heard him correctly. "His and her Christmas trees?" she repeated.

Holden knew he was pushing it, but if Libby really was going to leave Laramie and relocate elsewhere after the sale of her business and home, his time to woo her was limited. Too limited. He gestured expansively. "We already have his and her wreaths."

She angled her head, clearly unconvinced. A wealth of consideration came and went in her bemused expression. "I know you mentioned getting one from your ranch earlier, but given the time crunch…what's wrong with getting them from the Kiwanis lot?" she challenged softly.

He leaned closer, inhaling her seductive cinnamon perfume. She was dodging intimacy again. "Where is the fun in that?"

Without warning, the sparkle was back in her green eyes. She planted a gloved hand in the center of his chest, successfully holding him at bay. "I suppose," she said drily, "you're going to tell me?"

Holden wished he could do a lot more than that. But knowing he was going to have to be a lot more patient if he wanted to make her his, he said, "For maximum holiday enjoyment, we need to obtain our trees the old-fashioned way. Unless—" he paused and peered at her through narrowed eyes "—you're not up to the task?"

Libby glared at him. "Excuse me?"

"Well," Holden drawled, enjoying matching words and wits with her, "it could be a little arduous." He puffed out his chest and flexed his muscles, then made a show of studying her much more feminine and slender form. "Trekking through the fields to the woods." He made another show of studying her legs. "Locating the perfect trees for each of us. Chopping them down, dragging them back. Yeah." Holden let his gaze drift slowly over her midriff before returning with taunting deliberation to her face. "You're right. Such rigorous physical activity on such a beautiful winter afternoon probably is a little much to expect you to do."

"Please." Libby rolled her eyes and released her seat belt. "I am certainly up to the task. All I need is a proper pair of boots and warmer clothing."

Because she said she would be "just one sec," Holden waited in the truck while she dashed inside. Five minutes later, she came rushing back out again.

Gone were the dressy sweater and slacks she had worn to brunch. In their place were a nicely worn pair of midnight-wash jeans, cream-colored thermal underwear beneath a trendy red-and-black buffalo-plaid flannel shirt and a vest with a marled sheepskin lining. She had tucked a flat-brimmed, dark brown Stetson on her hair and put rugged, shearling-lined boots on her feet.

She looked incredibly sexy—all fine Texas woman—striding toward him. Holden felt his heart thump in his chest.

Damn, but she was beautiful.

And until now, so underappreciated.

He promised himself she would never feel like a "ball and chain" to anyone again.

LIBBY HADN'T EXPECTED TO have such fun, driving and hiking all over Holden's ranch. But as they climbed fences, navigated rocks and traversed the rugged terrain where he taught and trained his cutting horses, she found herself laughing more and more.

"I think you know where the best trees are," Libby teased, enjoying the brisk winter weather as much as the rugged rancher leading her on this merry chase. "You're just pretending you don't."

Holden flashed her a sexy grin, denying nothing, then turned his attention back to the grove of mostly mesquite and a few gnarled live oak trees. With nary an Afghan pine in sight.

Abruptly all victorious male, he reached up and grabbed a bushy growth from an oak. He snapped it off, then showed the familiar green leaves and white berries to her. "Maybe this is what I've been looking for."

Libby stroked the plant reverently. "Mistletoe!" she said in surprise, her mind automatically shifting to thoughts of kissing Holden beneath the symbolic evergreen leaves. Now, that was romantic!

"Yep." He broke the mass of greenery in half. "One for you. And one for me."

She looked at the cluster. "His and her mistletoe?" Libby held up her portion, deciding it could be cut up even more, into manageable little clumps. Maybe tied with red ribbon...

"This way we'll both have some handy whenever the need arises," Holden told her with a wicked smile.

Her pulse racing almost as much as her fantasies,

Libby threw back her head and laughed. "You are something, Holden McCabe!"

He grinned and held out a hand, to help her climb back over the fence they had just vaulted.

"Now we'll go look for the trees," he promised, wrapping a proprietary arm about her waist.

Ten minutes later, he had driven his pickup to a small grove of what looked to be cultivated pine trees along the edge of his property.

Libby braced her hands on her hips, studied the selection and shook her head. "You knew these were here all along."

Holden acknowledged it to be true, with a slight shrug and an insufferable wink. "Yeah. I just didn't know where the mistletoe was."

She rolled her eyes at his bad-boy antics. This was a side of him she didn't see enough.

He got the ax out of the truck, then stood back, admiring the small grove. "So which one do you think you want?" he asked.

Enjoying the fragrance of pine and the wintry sunshine, Libby studied a six-foot-tall tree with well-spaced branches. She walked back and forth, observing it from all angles and taking her time. Finally, she sighed. "That one, I think."

Holden's blue eyes were twinkling as he gazed down at her. "Sure you don't want a taller one?"

He was obviously going to draw this out as much as possible, insuring they spent more time together. Libby didn't mind at all. Playing the flirt to the hilt, she plastered a breezy smile on her face. "I'll leave the eight-foot one to you."

"Suit yourself." Holden cut down one, then the other. Together, they dragged them toward his pickup.

"Since we're already here, we'll put mine up first," he said.

Libby knew it was imperative to get the tree in water as soon as possible, to keep it fresh. She was standing close enough to see the quarter inch of beard on the underside of his jaw that he'd missed when he last shaved.

Inhaling the scent of man and soap, she asked, "You want to decorate it, too?"

"Can't." Holden put his tools in their case and shut the tailgate of the truck. Pressing his hand against her spine, he walked her around to the passenger side. "I don't have any more UT stuff to put on it." He took two bottles of her favorite sparkling water from his truck and handed one to her.

Pleased by his thoughtfulness, Libby uncapped her beverage and took a long drink. She studied him over the rim of the bottle. "You're really going to decorate your Christmas tree in burnt-orange and white?"

The mischief was back in his eyes. "It'll be unique," he claimed, toasting her silently. "And it will match the wreath on my pickup."

"Well—" Libby walked around to take another look at the Christmas wreath attached to the front grille of his pickup "—never underestimate the powers of coordinated decor."

Holden chuckled. He lounged against the truck and clapped a companionable hand on her shoulder. "What are you going to put on yours?"

Libby stalked off through the calf-high grass. In the distance, she could see some of Holden's incredibly beautiful quarter horses grazing contentedly in the pasture.

She could understand why he liked living on a ranch. It was so peaceful out here. So pretty and still so wild in places, too.

She whirled around and walked toward him, not stopping until they were toe-to-toe once again. "I'm not sure yet."

He peered at her curiously. "You don't have any decorations at the house?"

She sighed. "I do, but...Percy's mom was all about symmetry. Her trees had to have one color ribbon and one type of ornament, and that was it."

Holden winced. "I remember."

Libby reached out to pick off some pine needles that were stuck to the fleece lining of Holden's jacket. "She varied it from year to year, but..."

"Doesn't suit you?" he guessed.

Finished, Libby stepped back again. "I'm a very disciplined person, but not in that area."

"What about decorations you used growing up?" Holden cocked his head playfully. "Still have any of those?"

"Aunt Ida liked glittery ornaments. Unfortunately, they are all so old the exterior is constantly flaking off."

"Not good," he commiserated.

"Not at all." Libby looked in his eyes, surprised at the banked desire she found there. "So I've been thinking, while we were traipsing your entire property, Holden McCabe, that maybe it's time I got new decorations, too." She lifted a hand in warning. "Before you get too excited, no burnt-orange and white."

His eyes crinkled at the corners. "Traditional all the way, hmm?"

Not always, Libby thought, considering the rebound relationship she had agreed to have with him. "We'll see. I think I want to look around first," she confided, more eager for a fresh start than ever. "I think I'd like to get something really special to start my own collection with."

"Sounds nice."

It did, Libby thought. But what was even better was the joy she felt being there with him.

IT WAS JUST STARTING TO get dark when Holden and Libby arrived at her place.

She hopped down from the cab before he'd even cut the motor. Her long legs eating up the drive, she circled around to the back. "You don't have to carry my tree in, Holden. You can just leave it on the front porch."

He knew she could manage the tree on her own. The question was, why did she want to?

Frowning, he hefted the pine onto the ground. "Is there some reason you don't want me to come inside?" Was she afraid he was going to put the moves on her?

Despite his own desire, he'd managed to control himself thus far....

"Well, now that you mention it—" she pulled her keys out of the pocket of her jeans "—the place is a little messy."

Holden shrugged, not sure where this sudden tension and evasiveness was coming from. "I'm a guy. Mess is my comfort zone."

Still Libby hesitated.

Had he done something? Said something? Holden thought worriedly. Everything had been fine up to now....

Finally, she shrugged and said, "You're going to find out, anyway."

Find out what? Holden wondered as she led the way inside.

He got the tree just past the threshold, when he stopped in shock.

The Lowell family photo gallery that had lined the stairs and the foyer had all been taken down. The frames were stacked on the dining-room table. Additional boxes littered the floor.

A hammer and a jar of nails sat midway up the stairs.

Libby laid her clump of "his and hers" mistletoe on the foyer table, took off her vest and hat, and hung them on the coat tree next to the door. Flushing, she gestured. "That's as far as I got yesterday morning before I had to leave for the Community Chapel bazaar."

Holden was glad the photos of Percy and his ancestors had come down. It was yet another sign that Libby was ready to move on.

"What made you decide to do this now?" he asked, carrying the tree on into the family room at the rear of the house, where she had said she wanted it.

"Several things, actually," she murmured, opening the door off the kitchen and going into the garage.

She returned with a Christmas tree stand.

"Jeff Johnston is sending over a bank appraiser and broker on Monday afternoon, to evaluate the property. The local broker I had here on Friday morning said if I was serious about selling and getting the best price possible, I should start stripping the home of personal memorabilia."

Libby put the stand where she wanted it.

Holden set the tree inside. "Is that the only reason?"

"No," Libby said quietly. "I've been meaning to do it for a while now, I just haven't been able to figure out what I should do with all the pictures."

While she held the tree, he knelt to tighten the screws that would hold it in place.

"Normally, in a situation like this, the thing to do would be to return the photos to Percy's remaining extended family," she murmured.

Holden saw her dilemma. "Only there aren't any."

Her shoulders slumped. "I thought about taking them over to the dealership, but many of them—like the ones of him catching a fish or climbing a mountain—are far too personal for that. Plus—" she exhaled, her inner turmoil evident "—they don't have anything at all to do with tractor sales. Any of the Lowell family archives that do are already at LRE."

Holden kept his eyes locked with hers. "You could distribute them to old family friends."

Libby sighed, looking even more vulnerable. "The question is, who would get what, and how would I go about it?"

No question, it wouldn't be easy. "Do you want me to help you with that?" Holden asked her gently.

She shook her head, withdrawing emotionally again. "That's something I should do, as Percy's widow. But there is one thing you could help me with, if you're so inclined?"

He straightened, his own feelings turbulent. "Whatever you need," he told her sincerely.

Libby flashed an appreciative smile. "Help me finish removing all the photos from the frames, and take the picture hangers out of the wall."

For the next hour and a half they worked side by side, pausing to look at the photos they removed. Eventually, after studying one particularly poignant shot of Percy and his folks at his college graduation, and another one of all four of them on her wedding day, Libby shook her head in consternation and murmured, "I know it was just ten years ago, but this seems like it was from another lifetime. One that's getting harder and harder to remember."

Holden knew what she meant. His own marriage seemed light-years ago, too.

Their circumstances were different, though. He had

opted out; she hadn't. He covered her hand with his own. "Does that upset you?"

"It used to." Libby leaned into his touch. "Now what I feel is more like relief." She swallowed and turned to search his face. "Does that make me a bad person?"

"No, Libby, it makes you human. And ready to move on." He wrapped his arms around her and hugged her fiercely. "And those are both good things."

"YOU'VE BEEN HARD TO GET ahold of," Miss Rosa told Libby at nine the next morning.

Libby blushed. She had been really busy.

"Anything you want to tell us about?" Miss Mim winked.

"Actually, yes." Libby sidestepped the subject of Holden and the fact that they had recklessly spent at least part of the night together yet again—at his ranch, in his bed.

She still couldn't bring herself to ask him to stay the night in her house yet. There was still too much of Percy there.

Libby went to her desk and got two copies of the fundraising letter she had drafted. "Read this…and tell me what you think."

"It's fantastic," Miss Rosa said, when she had finished.

Miss Mim enthused, "You did a great job explaining how much the institution means not just to Laramie, but all of Laramie County. We'll get it sent out right away."

"You're welcome to use the computer and printer here in my office," Libby said.

Miss Mim hesitated. "Are you sure we won't be in the way? We compiled a list of one hundred charitable foundations in Texas we want to try. So it's going to take a while…."

"That's fine," Libby assured them with a smile. "I'm going to be at the house, anyway."

Libby left the librarians and headed toward the exit. As she walked past the break room, she overheard a group of male employees talking.

"What do you think our annual bonuses will be?" Manny Pierce was asking the dealership accountant.

"Depends, but at five percent of the current profits, you can each figure on taking a very nice vacation…"

Her nerves jangling, Libby kept going.

Her aunt Ida had always said it was very bad luck to count your chickens before they hatched.

Libby had found that to be true.

As she reached the exit, Jeff Johnston was pulling up in his Maserati. Four more vehicles turned in right behind him.

The two men and two women congregated alongside Jeff. He introduced his attorney, bank appraiser, chief financial advisor and real-estate broker.

Libby hadn't expected an entourage, but she refused to let it rattle her. Smiling, she said, "Let's get started, shall we?"

The tour of the dealership, inventory and warehouses commenced. Finished with that, they headed across the road to the Lowell home. And it was there that the trouble began.

Frowns abounded as they toured the premises. Although he had been there briefly before, with no complaints, it was pretty clear today that Jeff was not impressed with anything he saw.

He returned to the living room, where the toddler section of the Laramie Public Library was now set up. "This is going to have to go—immediately," he said. "And the same goes for the information and help desk set up in the corner of the dealership showroom."

"Neither of those things are going to happen until we find a solution for the library crisis," Libby retorted.

Concerned looks passed among Jeff's team.

He paused. "You know, for tax purposes I want to close on this deal before December 31."

Libby nodded. "That still gives us twenty-one days."

"That's not a lot of time," his attorney remarked.

Jeff continued looking at Libby. "Mrs. Lowell is right," he said carefully after a moment. "That's plenty of time for me to get everything I want."

HOURS LATER, HOLDEN and Libby were roaming the stores in San Angelo's Sunset Mall, looking for decorations for her tree. While they shopped, they talked.

"So Johnston and his group made you uneasy today," Holden gathered, when Libby had finished relating the morning-long tour.

She left one shop and headed for another, Holden right beside her. "It wasn't anything he said or did precisely."

Holden slid his hand beneath her elbow and brought her in close to him. "Just a feeling."

Libby nodded and continued walking. Once again, his hand kept contact, this time pressed to the middle of her spine. "I think the info your dad scouted on Jeff might be right." She sucked in a breath. "He probably is going to play hardball with me. He just hasn't started yet."

Holden leaned down to whisper in her ear. "If you want backup, I'm here. And so is any other McCabe you'd like to bring along."

As tempting as it was, Libby knew that relying too heavily on Holden would not be good. Using him as a

sounding board was one thing; employing him as protection another. "Thanks. But I think your aunt Claire
can handle this for me." It was, after all, what her attorney was paid to do.

"Say, what do you think of this angel?" Libby paused
to admire a particularly beautiful tree-topper.

Holden studied the dazzling ornament. "I think she
looks like you. Seriously. Honey-blond hair, gorgeous
face, emerald eyes."

They were flirting again, Libby noted, and she was
enjoying Holden's teasing more than ever. She wrinkled
her nose playfully at him. "So does that mean you think
I should get it?"

He shrugged, pretending to misunderstand the question. "Unless you plan to sit atop your tree as the lead
decoration."

Libby chuckled at the ridiculousness of the idea. "I
meant, should I get an angel or a star? Because these glittery gold and silver stars are awfully nice, too."

"I see what you mean." Holden rubbed his jaw as he
studied them gravely.

"And…?" Libby moved close enough to inhale his
special scent.

He stepped even nearer, the heat from his body en-
gulfing her. "I have no clue. I'm not an expert on interior design."

"What are you an expert on?" she asked.

Holden paused. For a second, she thought he was going
to say something romantic to her. Instead, he pointed to a
display of college ornaments and said, picking up a box
for himself, "All things Texas, of course."

Chiding herself for wanting this fling of theirs to be
more than they had agreed upon, Libby moved farther
down the aisle, past the Western-themed decorations,

toward the next grouping. Without warning, she found herself standing in front of a display of baby's first ornaments. Next to that was a selection of porcelain bride and groom and wedding-bell decorations.

She stopped to briefly examine both, before she was swamped with such wistfulness she had to turn away or risk bursting into tears.

"It's going to happen," Holden told her. He shifted the box to his other hand and cupped her face with his palm, stroking her cheek tenderly with his thumb. "Maybe sooner than you think."

Libby only wished getting what she really wanted for Christmas—a husband and a baby and a completely new lease on life—was that easy.

Holden's gaze probed her slowly and deliberately. "You're going to get the baby you've wanted for so long," he said.

She gestured listlessly, feeling tears threaten once again. "Not without love and marriage and all the traditional things that go along with it." Why was she suddenly feeling so moody? Up one minute, down the next...!

"Including courtship." He gave her shoulder a reassuring squeeze.

"And a man who doesn't view me as an unwanted burden or responsibility."

"You'll get that, too," he promised softly.

Would she? Holden seemed so sure. Fighting off a new wave of emotion, Libby swallowed and moved on to yet another aisle of decorations, these more her current speed. "I think I know how I want to decorate my Christmas tree."

She pointed to the row of individual ornaments, of every theme and variety. "I'm going to make a completely asymmetrical, one-hundred-percent-whimsical tree. As a symbol of my moving on."

Holden smiled and caught her hand in his. "Sounds good to me."

Chapter Thirteen

"I'm surprised to see you here—alone—again," Emily remarked when Holden sought her out on Thursday evening. As usual during the holidays, his baby sis was working late. Hence, even though the Daybreak Café had officially closed after the lunch rush, Emily was back in the restaurant kitchen at eight that evening, making some of the dough and batter that would be baked and served the following day.

Usually, though, her husband hung out with her. Holden took a seat at the stainless-steel work counter. "Where's Dylan?"

Emily shaped dough into candy canes. "At our ranch, hosting a 4-H Club workshop on the best way to get a green horse used to the saddle. So what's up?" She paused to wipe her hands on her apron. "Are you just here to see if I will feed you dinner—as you know I will?" Her expression gentled. "Or is something else on your mind?"

"I've already eaten, thanks." Holden rested his forearms on the table. "I came to get some advice."

Emily lifted her eyebrows. "This is new."

"Go easy on me." He scowled. "I'm struggling here."

His sister poured him a cup of coffee and brought out a platter of cookies for him to peruse. "Obviously, this is about Libby and your crazy rebound deal with her."

Holden selected a thumbprint cookie with a strawberry center. "We're past that." He munched on the delicious confection.

"Oh?" Emily started shaping Christmas coffee cakes.

Holden worked to contain his frustration. "We agreed it would just go however long it goes. Into the spring, or before the holidays end." Realizing their affair could be over even sooner than he'd thought caused him to worry. And Holden wasn't used to worrying about romance.

Emily slid the dough into the oven and paused to set the timer. "Is that why you and Libby haven't been buddying around together the last three nights?"

Was it that obvious he was getting the heave-ho? Deciding maybe he was overreacting, Holden stuck to the facts. "I saw her Monday evening. We went shopping in San Angelo to get ornaments for our trees."

Emily cut peanut-butter fudge into neat one-inch squares. "What about Tuesday?"

Holden helped himself to a frosted sugar cookie. "She had an appointment with the outside accounting firm auditing her business, in advance of the sale."

"Wednesday?"

"A meeting with her attorney."

Again his sister lifted an eyebrow. "Tonight?"

Holden tensed. "She said she's not feeling well."

Emily mulled that over. "And you're not buying it?" she guessed.

He shrugged. "It is flu season. We both had our shots last weekend, but the pharmacist said it takes two weeks for them to become fully effective."

"I haven't heard of anyone being sick here in Laramie just yet, but that doesn't mean she didn't pick up something when you were in San Angelo the other night."

"So you don't think she's just making excuses to try and cool things off between us?"

His sister paused. "Is there some reason you think that might be the case?"

Holden wasn't sure. "Things have been moving pretty fast."

A knowing smile crossed her lips. "Too fast for her?" Emily asked pointedly. "Or too fast for you?"

"Too slow for me," Holden clarified. He threw up his hands in exasperation. "I'm not sure about her."

Emily patted him on the shoulder. "Well, then, brother dear, there is only one way to find out."

LIBBY WAS HALFWAY through changing the sheets and comforter on her bed when the doorbell rang.

She glanced at her watch. Nine o'clock? Who would be stopping by this late? And without calling first!

Swearing at the inconvenience, as well as her dishabille, Libby stepped over the pile of discarded linens and headed down the stairs. A glance through the peephole in the heavy wooden door gave her the answer she needed.

Feeling equally thrilled and dismayed, she opened the door. Using flirtatiousness as a shield, she propped one hand on her hip and approximated her best Southern belle voice. "Why, Holden McCabe, is that you beneath the red-and-white Santa hat?"

He grinned, then bowed to her like a courtier. "It is indeed."

Her glance drifted to the items in his hand. "What's with the wreath and the bag?"

"The wreath is for your front door, since you don't have one yet. You'll notice it's very traditional,"

Meaning, Libby thought, it didn't have any sports memorabilia or university colors on it. Instead it was adorned with red and white berries woven throughout, and a big, red velvet bow.

She smiled at his teasing and accepted the gift gratefully. Together, they used the hook provided to hang it on her front door. Libby centered it just so, then stepped back to admire it. "It's very nice, thank you." Shivering in her yoga clothes, she ushered him in.

"As for the other…" Holden stepped over the threshold, shut the door behind him and handed her the bag. "I brought you some chicken soup from the Daybreak Café."

Normally, that sounded great. Tonight it made her want to barf. Again. Just catching a faint whiff of it made her hold up her palm and back away. "Thanks, but…"

Holden shrugged out of his jacket, and tossed it and his Santa hat on the coat tree next to the front door. He peered at her closely, his expression concerned. "You really are ill, aren't you?"

Libby knew her skin was an odd grayish color again; she could feel it. Wishing her heart would stop racing and her knees cease trembling, she clapped a hand over her abdomen. Working to sound a great deal more matter-of-fact than she felt, she explained, "I've got tummy troubles. I'm not sure why. It may have something to do with the chicken-salad sandwich I had at lunch. It tasted odd, but I was so hungry I was weak-kneed, so I ate it anyway, and have been paying for it this evening."

"Bummer."

"No kidding. I made it only halfway through my yoga workout when I upchucked all over my mat. So…that's why I begged off seeing you tonight." She hadn't wanted to go into the gory details.

He walked with her to the family room. Saw the bags and boxes right where they had left them on Monday evening. "Still haven't decorated your tree?"

Libby sighed. "No time."

He leveled an assessing gaze on her and kept it there. "What can I do to help?"

Libby pulled in a stabilizing breath. "Honestly? Nothing. I was just changing the linens on my bed. I was going to take a shower and go to bed." *And hope I don't throw up again.*

He gave her a long look that spoke volumes. "I can help with that," he offered.

She swallowed around the parched feeling in her throat and made a joke to lighten the tension between them. "The shower?"

"The bed-making," he replied in a humorous way that made her heart skip a beat.

Their glances met and held.

Wishing she felt well enough to spend the evening with him, Libby sighed.

He clapped a hand to her forehead and frowned. "No fever."

Without warning, she felt weak-kneed again. Dizzy and trembling all over.

The last time she had felt like this had been in the first months after Percy died.

Libby swore silently to herself and closed her eyes. She could not go through this again.

IT DIDN'T TAKE A MIND READER to know that Libby wasn't telling him everything, Holden thought, as he accompanied her upstairs and helped her finish changing the sheets on her bed. Clearly, she was worried about the way she was feeling. He studied her pale skin and slightly shaky demeanor. "You sure you're okay to get in the shower by yourself?"

She scoffed, "I wouldn't do it if I didn't think I could."

A mixture of gallantry and tenderness surged through him. He touched the side of her face, not sure when he had felt such overwhelming devotion or responsibility for another human being. "Okay." He decided her color had almost returned to normal. "But I'll be right outside the bathroom door. So if you need help," he told her sternly, "you just call me."

Libby picked up the nightclothes she had already laid out, and cradled them in her arms. She took a moment to scowl at him. "I think I'll survive."

Heaven help him, he wanted to make love to her, here and now.

She slipped inside the bathroom and shut the door behind her.

Holden heard the water start.

By the time she emerged, her hair wrapped in a towel, prim and proper flannel pajamas on, he had her bed turned down and all ready for her. Wishing he could climb under the covers with her, Holden kissed the top of her head. "In you go."

She huffed in exasperation as he drew the covers up and tucked them in around her. "You're really overdoing it, you know."

Finished, he rested a palm on either side of her. "I'm also spending the night," he confided gently. "On the family-room sofa downstairs."

"You don't have to do this," she protested weakly.

He caught her hand, brought it to his lips and kissed the back of it. Still holding her eyes, he whispered, "I want to. And I'm not taking no for an answer."

LIBBY WOKE TO SUNLIGHT streaming through the windows. It took her only a moment to realize that the nausea and dizziness she had felt the night before were gone.

The desire she felt for Holden, when she walked downstairs and found him puttering around her kitchen, increased by leaps and bounds.

He looked incredibly attractive with his shirttail hanging out, the morning beard lining his jaw, his dark hair rumpled.

Turning, he regarded her with tenderness. "How are you feeling?" His voice was a sexy rumble.

"Much better, thanks."

Surprised by the emotions sifting through her, Libby sat down at the kitchen table. If she had been attracted to Holden before, it was nothing compared to how she felt now, after experiencing his kindness and consideration.

This was what an intimate relationship should be like. Two people caring for and depending on each other. Putting the other person's needs ahead of their own.

Holden set a plate of toast, a cup of her favorite peach tea in front of her.

By the time they had finished eating breakfast together, Libby knew she was well enough to go to work, so he decided to head out to his ranch.

She walked him as far as the front door. Taking a page from the man's playbook, she decided to try and line up their next date. "Want to come back tonight? It's Friday. I'll fix you dinner. You can help me decorate the tree."

Holden's face fell. He gave her a look more potent than any kiss. "I'd love to, but I already promised to deliver a couple quarter horses to a ranch outside Wimberly today. I won't be back until late." He smiled. "Rain check? For Sunday evening, maybe?"

Libby had missed seeing him this week on the days they had been apart. Missed having time to talk to each other. Missed making love even more. "Sunday evening sounds good." Even though she would have preferred it to be sooner.

Holden paused, looking as if he wanted to say something, but wasn't sure he should.

Following a hunch, Libby drawled, "You may as well come out with it. Otherwise, I'm going to be wondering all day long what's on your mind."

He exhaled. "You know the bowl games start tomorrow."

It took her a moment to follow what he was saying. "Football?"

He chuckled. "Yeah. Football."

Or in other words, the sport that was so popular it was almost considered a religion in Texas. It was all the guys at the dealership talked about when they weren't with customers. "I thought the Rose Bowl wasn't until January," Libby said.

"It's not."

"And UT is in that, right?"

Holden nodded. He came close enough that she could feel his body heat. "But the rest of the games are exciting, too. And my brothers and I have a tradition of placing bets with each other, and watching as many of the games as we can together."

"Sounds fun."

"It really is," he said with a grin.

Libby nodded. If there was one thing she had learned at an early age, it was how to be a good sport. "Then I wish you luck."

"Actually, I was hoping for more than that." He took her hand in his and clasped it warmly. "Tomorrow it's my turn to host the gathering at my ranch. There are three games—the first is at 1:00 p.m., the second at 4:30 and the third begins at 8:00 in the evening."

That was a lot of football, Libby thought. And though she'd never been all that interested in it, she was interested in Holden. "So you are going to be busy."

"Very. Given the fact that my brothers and sister and their spouses and kids, plus our parents, will all be there for the party. So I was wondering…" Holden tightened his grip on her hand and gave her a look that caused her heart to flutter.

"If you think you're up to so many televised sports and McCabes in one day…would you be my date?"

"THE KEY TO ENJOYING YOURSELF is to place bets on the games, too," Emily told Libby, as the two of them set out platters of wings and veggies, supplied by her café.

There was only one tiny problem with that, Libby thought. "I don't know anything about the teams that are playing."

Emily smiled mischievously. "Then do what I do, and bet against whoever your husband—or love interest—is backing."

Libby flushed self-consciously. Sex and friendship weren't the same thing as love. "Holden and I aren't exactly…"

Holden passed by with a tub of beers and soft drinks on ice. He paused to kiss the slope of her neck in a decidedly possessive way. "Yes. We are." He winked at them both and took off.

Emily's eyes gleamed with a speculative light. "Wow…I don't think I have ever seen my big brother that smitten."

Still tingling from the tender warmth of his caress, Libby looked in the direction the handsome rancher had gone. "We're just…" she sputtered.

"Falling in love."

Libby was so startled she practically dropped the blue-cheese dip. "No."

Emily chuckled. "Deny it all you want." She set out a fruit platter and yogurt dip, confidence radiating in her low tone. "I know what I see. And don't forget to sign up for your teams on the sheet and put ten dollars into the pot. The winner gets to donate the sum to the charity of his or her choice."

Her excitement mounting, Libby did as ordered, making sure her picks were the opposite of the ones Holden chose.

And Emily was right, she soon found out. Ribbing Holden, and getting teased in return, garnered a great deal of enjoyment.

Unable to stop smiling, she headed to the kitchen between the first and second games.

Holden was pulling out trays of barbecue and all the fixings from Sonny's Barbecue Restaurant.

She marveled at his multitasking hosting skills. "How can I help?"

"Says the woman who whipped my ego in the first game," he told her flippantly.

She came closer and taunted him with an impudent smile. "The day is young, or so they're saying out there."

"They're right." Holden paused. He favored her with a sexy half smile, his eyes roving her face. "Have I told you how pretty you look today?"

Libby swallowed at the rough note of possession in his voice. He made her feel beautiful whenever he looked at her like that. She met his too-innocent gaze head-on. "You look mighty fine yourself, cowboy."

He grinned wickedly. "Come closer and say that."

Curious, Libby took two steps forward. All the humor left his gaze, replaced by something much more dangerous. She sent him a level look, aware her heart was racing again.

"Holden...your family..."

"I don't care," he whispered ardently, fitting his lips over hers. "I need you. Need this."

And so, it turned out, did Libby. Their days and nights apart—had been excruciatingly lonely.

And that pent-up passion came forth in their kiss.

How long it would have continued, had the wolf whistles and clapping not sounded behind them, Libby would never know.

Flushing, she pulled back. Turned to see that they had quite an audience. The McCabes chorused their approval with huge grins.

"And here we thought you were the least romantic among us," Jeb drawled.

"Clearly, not anymore," Hank ribbed.

Even Shane McCabe, who usually chose not to weigh in on matters of the heart, smiled. "Looks like congratulations of some sort are in order," he declared.

"Stop gloating," Holden teased hours later, when the games were over and everyone had left.

Thanks to the use of disposable dinnerware, and the McCabe habit of pitching in, cleanup was left to a minimum. That mostly consisted of straightening a few throw pillows and carrying the bagged trash out to the cans.

"You beating me every single time was merely a matter of beginner's luck."

"Or," Libby retorted, enjoying the bantering and camaraderie as much as she loved his kisses, "as your brothers put it, your inability to keep your besotted mind 'in the game.'"

Holden winked and lifted his hands in a humorous admission of defeat. "I am a little distracted these days."

No kidding. So was she. "Speaking of which," Libby chided, still feeling a little embarrassed at the memory of their recent public display of affection, "you didn't have to kiss me like that in front of your family."

Holden scrubbed a hand over his jaw. "You're right." He leaned toward her, planting a palm on the counter on either side of her and trapping her there. "I shouldn't have kissed you like that." He fitted his body to hers, hardness to softness, until she sighed. "I should have kissed you like this."

The next thing Libby knew she was in his arms. Holden took her lips with a rush of passion, kissing her long and hard and deep. And heaven help them both, she was clinging to him and kissing him back with the same need and intensity.

It had been a mistake thinking she could ever tame or restrict this man with a rebound-romance agreement, Libby thought, when she really had a tiger by the tail.

But maybe it was best this way. To not overthink this. To just feel….

Reveling in the euphoric feelings rushing through her, she let him lift her onto the counter and step between her spread legs. "Now, where were we?" he teased, palming the weight of her breasts through her knit shirt, easily working her nipples to aching peaks. "Oh, yes, we were talking about what kind of kisses are suitable to give you in front of company." He kissed her cheek, her chin, the hollow of her throat. "How about these?"

A shallow breath soughed between her lips. "Good," she murmured back, kissing the strong column of his throat in turn. "All good…"

"How about this?" Holden demonstrated a very potent lip-lock with a lot of heat and pressure.

Libby's heart fluttered in her chest. Body pulsing, straining for more, she wrapped her jean-clad legs around his waist, scooting forward until his arousal pressed against her.

"Very nice, too…" She gasped as he slid his palms beneath her buttocks and pulled her even tighter against him. "But I'm not sure it's the kind of thing that's good for a PDA…."

"You're right." He swept his tongue into her mouth and kissed her so deeply and rapaciously she moaned. Grinning with masculine satisfaction, Holden slowly ended the kiss. His gaze lovingly roved her upturned face. "We should keep this just for us."

Holding her masterfully in his arms, he tugged her off the counter and carried her up the stairs to his bed.

He paused to turn the two battery-driven hurricane lanterns on low, infusing the room with a soft, ultraromantic glow. Then he returned to her side and gave her the kind of nothing-held-back kiss she had been wanting all evening. His mouth moved on hers effortlessly, demandingly, until she was lost in the sweet, wild wonder of his embrace.

Murmuring his name, Libby dragged him closer still, burying both hands in his hair, opening her mouth to his, every feminine inch of her aroused by his unswerving resolve to possess her. Need swept through her, until her nipples budded and her knees weakened treacherously. They undressed each other and she started to sink onto the bed.

Holden, she soon discovered, had other ideas.

Kissing her all the while, he backed her to the wall

and positioned her against it. Once there, he looked down at her with such intensity she almost couldn't breathe.

No longer content just to kiss her, he bent his head and moistened the delicate areola of her breast. Suckled it gently. Then turned to her other breast, delivering the same patient adoration until she trembled, unsure how much she could take.

"Holden…" How was it possible that someone so big and strong and male could have such a tender touch?

"Let me love you, Libby," he whispered as he replaced his lips with the pads of his thumbs and rose to kiss her again, deeply and erotically, as if she were his and always would be. "The way you were meant to be loved…"

Kneeling in front of her, he gently parted her thighs. Libby closed her eyes and moaned as he found her in the most intimate of caresses. Making lazy circles, moving up, in, out again. Just when she thought she could stand it no more, she quivered with pleasure and catapulted head over heels into bliss….

She'd barely stopped shuddering when he rose and situated himself between her thighs, pausing only long enough to sheathe himself, before kissing her on the mouth, lifting her and parting her, pushing past to the welcoming warmth inside.

They locked eyes and she offered herself to him completely, giving him the kind of access to her heart and soul she had never permitted before.

She knew there were no guarantees in life; the past had taught her that. She knew that the chance to be with Holden like this might be as fleeting as the rebound-romance deal they had initially made with each other.

But if she didn't take advantage of the chance they were being offered, she knew she would regret it for the rest of her life.

Christmas came but once a year.

The chance to be loved like this, and love in return, even less frequently.

This man, this moment, were her holiday gift.

And she didn't intend to squander it.

Wanting to draw out the moment as much as possible, she explored his back and hips and thighs with questing caresses that had him arching in passion.

He surged into her, entering and withdrawing in slow, shallow strokes that soon had her moaning for more.

Trembling with her need, she let every part of her adore every part of him. Rocking against him, with him, urging him on until at last she surrendered to a wild, untamed pleasure unlike anything she had ever known.

HOLDEN MADE LOVE to Libby two more gloriously satisfying times before they finally cuddled together, half-asleep.

"Holden?" she asked softly.

He loved the way she felt, so soft and warm and completely feminine. "Hmm?"

She rose slightly and propped her chin on her hand. Looking delicious ravished, yet heartbreakingly vulnerable, she continued, "You know what you said when Emily was teasing us about us being involved?"

He nodded, recalling the "announcement" to his family.

Libby raked her teeth across her lower lip, her uncertainty apparent. "Why did you make it—us—sound so serious?"

Her question was tentative, testing. Holden sensed one wrong move would have her dashing in the other direction. He could feel how wary she was. How unwilling to be hurt.

Determined not to let her shy away again, he said, "They can all see the same thing we can—that our relationship is likely to extend past the holidays." *Well past, in fact.* "I wanted them to know this was no longer a six-week matchup. That it was more serious than that."

And if he had his way, Holden thought, cuddling Libby close, they would soon be even more serious....

Chapter Fourteen

"Something sure smells good in here," Holden said on Sunday evening.

Someone sure *looked* good, Libby thought as she ushered him inside and took his coat. Instead of the usual jeans and shirt, he wore a pair of wool slacks and a V-necked sweater. His hair was clean and attractively rumpled, his jaw freshly shaved, and he smelled of a woodsy cologne. His handsome face bore the flush of the brisk winter wind.

Grinning in anticipation, Holden closed the distance between them with sensual grace. "My mouth is watering already."

So was hers. But for a much sexier reason than the dinner she had so lovingly prepared.

Forcing herself to concentrate on the hunger of the man in front of her instead of on where she secretly wanted the evening to lead, she took his hands in hers. Her feminine intuition told her this evening could be a turning point for them. Take them out of rebound territory and into the future. So she wanted everything to go perfectly—which, under the current circumstances, could be a problem. Especially if the way to a man's heart really *was* through his stomach. She tilted her head to one side. "You're not just being polite?" she queried uncer-

tainly, enjoying the way his fingers immediately tightened around hers. "You really think dinner smells good?"

Still holding her hands possessively, he gave her a lazy
once-over. "Yeah. Amazing, actually. Why?"

Her heart rate picking up another notch, Libby
shrugged. "My sense of smell has been a little off since
I was sick last week. Same for my sense of taste. Things
that normally appeal to me, like coffee with cream, don't.
In fact, I haven't had a taste for coffee at all since then."
The last time that had happened was during another very
difficult time, just under two years ago....

Oblivious to the reason behind her concern, Holden
tucked her in the curve of his arm and pressed an affectionate kiss on her temple. "It's probably better for you,
not having all that caffeine."

Libby sighed in relief and leaned into the warm, strong
curve of his body. "That's one way to look at it."

The other was not something she wanted to even consider. Not when her relationship with Holden was starting to go so very well....

Glad they were finally about to have dinner alone,
after days of juggling and rescheduling, Libby led Holden
past the temporary "children's library" room toward the
rear of the house.

She had taken pains to set the table just right—with
festive holiday dinnerware, cranberry-red linens, an in-
tricate holly centerpiece and candles.

A vanilla-cream-filled dark chocolate Yule log chilled
in the fridge. A hearty, homemade chicken potpie with a
sage biscuit crust was keeping warm in the oven.

It felt pleasantly intimate, having him here this way.
As if they were a real couple, and not just having a temporary fling.

"So. How was your day?" Libby went back to rinsing the salad greens, which she'd been in the middle of when the doorbell rang.

"Busy." Holden lounged beside her. "I had a lot to get caught up on at the ranch." He watched her snap the lid on the salad spinner. "How about you?"

She gave the handle a whirl. "I spent most of the afternoon with Miss Rosa and Miss Mim. We targeted another hundred charitable foundations to approach for help."

His gaze tracked her movements as she reached up into a cabinet for the champagne vinegar. She felt his gaze on her breasts and ribs as surely as she would have his touch.

"Any luck with the ones so far?"

Admiring the way he looked in her kitchen, so big and sexy and male, Libby got Dijon mustard from the fridge and shut it with her hip. "We've heard back from only about fifteen of the original one hundred thus far."

He studied her compassionately. "Not good, I'm guessing?"

Trying not to let her frustration bring her down, Libby measured vinegar, mustard, salt and pepper into a bowl. "Apparently, they all have local charities they support." Which was, she told herself realistically, perhaps the way it should be. For who better to know the most deserving, than people who lived and worked in the community?

He moved slightly to the left as she reached for the tool jar. "Even the ones in Dallas and Houston?"

Emily whisked the ingredients together. "Especially those." She paused to flash him a resigned smile. "It seems there are no shortage of worthy nonprofits doing good work, in need of funds to survive."

"You can't get anyone to help you?" he murmured in concern.

"The universal response so far is that this is the Laramie County commissioners' issue. And should be solved by them." Slowly, she whisked in the olive oil. "We've explained that waiting for that to happen will mean the library will likely be closed well over a year."

Holden leaned against the counter, arms folded. "Let me guess. Not their problem."

She affirmed it with a nod. Satisfied the dressing was properly emulsified, she dipped a spoon in and tasted it. Not sure if it was spicy enough, she offered it to him. "What do you think?"

His lips closed over the spoon with sensual reverence. Eyes locked with hers, he savored the taste. "Delicious."

Libby flushed at the husky, intimate timbre of his low tone, and the desirous look in his eyes. She had the feeling he wanted to forgo dinner and take her to bed. Funny thing was, she wanted that, too....

The buzzer went off.

Jerked from her reverie, Libby went to get the potpie from the oven. Holden gave her plenty of room to maneuver as she moved the piping-hot dish to the trivet on the table.

"So what next?" he continued.

Libby mixed the salad and set the bowl on the table.

She had a few ideas brewing. But she was reluctant to disclose them, for fear they wouldn't work out any better than her idea to appeal to all the existing charitable foundations.

Cautiously, she said, "I'm still working on it. But enough about me and my problems." She guided him to a chair, feeling glad he was there. "Let's talk about you."

"You're not going to tell me where you put it, are you?" Holden drawled three hours later.

Libby laughed, a soft, silky sound. Her sea-green eyes

sparkling, she admitted, "I figured you'd have more fun finding the mistletoe than just standing under it."

"Uh-huh." He let his gaze drift over her, liking the way the trendy skirt and coordinating pine-green sweater gloved her slender form. Lower still, he liked what the black tights and the square-heeled shoes did for her show-girl-sexy legs.

Ignoring the fast-building pressure at the front of his slacks, he countered, "Well, it's not anywhere down-stairs."

A saucy smile tugging at her lips, she planted her hands on her hips. "Are you sure?"

Holden considered kissing her again—without stand-ing beneath the holiday greenery. Deciding it might be more fun to wait, he shrugged. "Unless you anchored it under the sofa…?"

"No." Coming closer, she regarded him in a deliber-ately provocative manner. Color flamed in her cheeks. Her breasts rose and fell with every excited breath she took. "It's up high. Tradition, you know."

The only Christmas tradition he was interested in at the moment was kissing her. Long and slow. Deeply and passionately. And every way in between.

He held her eyes and prodded, "High meaning the second floor?"

Libby winked at him. "I guess we'll just have to see."

This was a big deal, Holden knew. Prior to this, the only time she had allowed him to go upstairs with her was when she was sick. But now that the Lowell family photo gallery and a lot of other artifacts had been packed away and put in storage, it felt more like her house. And it looked more like her place, too, with fresh flowers and other feminine touches everywhere.

"You sure you want to do this?" he asked her quietly.

"We could go to my ranch." The way they usually did when they wanted to make love.

Libby shook her head, looking happy and relaxed. "I want to be in my house tonight. Playing by my rules. So start searching, cowboy."

Holden liked the mischief in her voice. It was a side of Libby he'd like to see more often. "Okay, then…" he teased back.

He headed up the front staircase, checking every nook and cranny in the high ceiling as he went. Down the hall, to a bedroom he didn't recognize at all. The feminine furniture, the ribbon-bouquet bedding and the flowery, pastel rug on the floor all said Libby.

With satisfaction, Holden noted that she had finally made the changes she should have long before, making this into her life, her house, her domain. Best of all, in front of her bedroom door was a sprig of mistletoe hanging in plain view. He touched the velvet ribbon holding it pinned to the door frame.

"Found one."

Libby leaned against the portal the way a high-school girl leaned against her locker. Hands folded behind her, she tilted her chin up and taunted softly, "Seems like you owe me a kiss."

Grinning wickedly, he positioned her beneath the green leaves and white berries and indulged, until she was arching against him.

Curious to see what would happen next, he released her.

Taking her role as seductress seriously, she said, "Keep going."

Three steps into the bedroom, he found another. Holden kissed her again, the scent of her perfume waltzing through his system. "Mmm." He sifted his hands through the silk of her hair. Dropped his lips to the soft skin of her throat, the hollow of her collarbone. "This is fun."

Libby sighed and wiggled her body sensuously. "You're right," she murmured, enjoying the chase as much as he was. "And keep looking, 'cause there's one more."

Holden glanced in the one direction she was avoiding. "Here it is." Right over her brand-new brass bed with the very sumptuous-looking mattress and linens.

Playfully, she wreathed her arms about his neck and stood on tiptoe to better align their chests and thighs. "Finally," she whispered, every bit the temptress. "We're right where I want to be...."

Right where Holden wanted to be, too.

He planted one hand at the base of her spine, the other at her nape. His mouth covered hers. Daring to put his feelings on the line, he kissed her, and felt her respond with an immediacy that stunned him. He shuddered as her tongue plunged into his mouth, hotly and passionately. With a soft moan, she threaded her fingers through his hair and brought his lips closer still.

Satisfaction roaring through him, he twined his tongue with hers, drinking in the sweet feminine taste of her lips. She trembled as his hands moved to her breasts, and he realized how much he needed her. And how much she needed him, too.

"Holden..."

He slipped his hands beneath her sweater and cupped the soft weight of her breasts. Her nipples tautened in response, and she swayed against him. His need to be close to her as overwhelming as it was inevitable, he continued kissing her, long and hard and deep. Then soft and slow. Until the world narrowed to just the two of them once again, and he drew her toward the bed.

They undressed each other slowly, kissing and caressing as they went. All layers of restraint fell away, and Holden drew Libby down between the sheets.

Ever so delicately, he traced her curves, delighting in the way her flesh heated beneath his palms. Bending his head, he caressed her creamy breasts and kissed her peach-colored nipples, sucking and caressing them until her hips rose off the bed to meet him.

"Oh, Holden," she whispered, clinging tight, "I want you so much."

"I want you, too, sweetheart." His own body shaking with the effort to contain his desire, he parted her legs, then rubbed and stroked. She caressed him in turn, bringing him to readiness.

"Now," she demanded, pushing him onto his back and climbing astride him. He throbbed against her surrendering softness. The connection turned even more reckless. She drew him in lustily even as he found the soft, sensitive spot with his thumb. And then he was going deeper still, filling her to overflowing, as she rocked against him. She moaned and clung to him, kissing him even as she climaxed. He followed, hard and fast, taking everything she offered and giving her everything in return.

Knowing, if they were as smart as he intended them to be, that it would always be this way. He would be hers. She would be his. And together they'd find a way to have a satisfying future.

But for now, Holden thought, it was enough just to lie here with Libby wrapped in his arms, clinging to him, as if she, too, knew this was the way it was meant to be.

LIBBY HITCHED IN A BREATH, aware that, as always, Holden made her feel so warm and safe. Even when she was trembling and falling apart. And she knew, even if this wasn't the pact they had made, that it was what she wanted. Not just now, but forever. Holden. In her arms. In her bed. Making hers a life worth celebrating to the max.

Knowing that gave her the courage to ask the kind of thing she'd never been brave enough to venture before.

Libby rose up on her elbows.

Affection glowing in his eyes, Holden sifted his fingers through the mussed strands of her hair. "Something on your mind?" he asked quietly.

She nodded. "This isn't the way I had planned to do it, but…" Usually, when it came to relationships, she let the man make all the moves, rather than risk rejection.

But she'd gone after what she wanted just now, in the bedroom, and succeeded. So maybe she could do this, too.

Misunderstanding her hesitation, Holden stroked his hands over her hair and teased, "Sweetheart, we can make love any number of ways…."

Libby chuckled. She knew that, too.

"It's not that," she said.

"Then…?"

She gathered her courage and pushed on. "I want to invite you to the dealership Christmas party next Saturday evening. It's going to be a much bigger fete than usual, and definitely the last one I will ever host. So…"

"You're still feeling a little nervous?" he guessed.

Libby nodded in relief. "Even though I know everyone is pretty much on board with the sale now, there's still a chance the party may not go all that well."

"And that being the case, you'd like a little backup on hand."

Actually, she thought, it was more than that. But not sure how she should say it, she drew in a long breath and continued, "Anyway, I was wondering if you'd be my date for the evening."

He looked deep into her eyes. "Officially?"

"Very officially," Libby affirmed.

A slow, sexy smile crossed his face as he took her hand and lifted it to his lips. "Then it will be my pleasure."

"YOU'RE SURE THAT'S what you want to do with the proceeds from the sale of the dealership?" Claire McCabe said, after Libby had discussed it with her at length on Tuesday.

"Yes." Libby sighed, relieved to finally know what she was going to do with the million dollars she would garner from the sale of the dealership. "As long as it's legally viable, works out taxwise…and we can accomplish it by the end of the year."

"It is. And we can."

Libby gave her attorney a thumbs-up sign. "Then let's go for it," she said, encouraged to find she was no longer confused about what she wanted to do with the rest of her life—professionally, anyway. Personally was another matter.…

The paralegal stuck her head in the door, interrupting Libby's musing. "Jeff Johnston and his team are here for the meeting."

Claire held the copies of the contract they were proposing. "Ready?"

Libby nodded.

This was a good thing, she assured herself firmly. The right thing.

For Percy and his family, and for her…

Short minutes later, the two teams were seated opposite one another.

It was a little lopsided. Libby had opted to appear with

only her attorney, and the compiled financial data and appraisals. However, Jeff Johnston had brought along the chief financial officer for his entire company, a commercial real-estate broker, a private real-estate broker and two attorneys.

So there were six people on his side of the conference table, two on hers.

Libby immediately saw it for what it was, as did her attorney.

Intimidation.

"Let's get down to business," Claire said, with a brisk, matter-of-fact smile.

Jeff had insisted upon delivering his offer in person. He handed them his written bid.

It didn't take Libby long to spot the glaring omission in Jeff's proposed contract. "There's nothing in here stating the current Lowell Ranch Equipment employees will keep their present salary and position. And nothing at all about the five-percent share in annual company profits you've promised them."

Jeff gestured broadly. "I gave them my word. I'll keep it."

"Then why isn't it in writing?" she demanded.

"If it's part of the proposed acquisition, it has to be spelled out in the contract," Claire insisted.

Libby noted that no one on Jeff's team was surprised by the omission—or her reaction. Which probably meant it wasn't the first time it had happened.

Keeping her composure, she rose. If they wanted to play these games, so be it.

She looked at her attorney. "Clearly, this is not a serious offer. So it's not worth my time or yours."

Her posture militant, Libby headed for the door.

"Now, hold on there a minute," Jeff said. Leisurely,

he kicked back in his chair. "We can proceed on a hand-shake."

"No," Libby said, with as much steel in her voice as there was amiability in his. "We cannot." She glanced at her attorney, leaving no doubt about the strength of her resolve. "And we will not."

"OBVIOUSLY, JOHNSTON LOOKED into my background, too, and decided he could push me around," Libby fumed less than an hour later.

From the meeting, she had gone straight to Holden's ranch, spotting his pickup in one of the fields. Cursing her lack of boots, she had driven out to find him.

He'd stopped repairing fence to get a blanket and spread it on the bed of his truck. Then, hands on her waist, he'd lifted her up so she could sit with her legs dangling over the side.

"You don't look like much of a pushover now," he observed.

Libby tried to tug the skirt of her trim black business suit to her knees, but gave up. Savoring the feel of the winter sun on her shoulders, and the warmer than usual afternoon breeze, she retorted, "That's because I'm not! But two years ago, and long before that, all I cared about was trying to live my life as nonconfrontationally as possible."

Holden went back to the fence he was repairing. "Because you were orphaned," he guessed.

Gazing out across the pasture, Libby reflected, "To be perfectly honest, it probably started way before then."

He pulled the split post out of the ground, then regarded her curiously.

Aware they had never talked about their childhoods,

Libby confessed, "My parents were both very single-minded. As an only child, all the emphasis was on me."

Holden, who'd had three siblings, made a face.

Libby sighed and continued, "I learned pretty quickly as a kid that whatever outfit my mother wanted me to wear was the one I was going to put on that day. And the same went for my dad. He expected me to keep my toys and books picked up and put away, just so, and I did," she recollected wearily. "Because if I put my books on a different shelf than the one he had in mind, I was just going to have to do it all over again."

His shirt stretching tight across his shoulders, Holden pounded a new post into the ground. "Doesn't sound like there was a lot of room to negotiate," he observed.

No kidding.

Libby grimaced. "There was even less after they passed, and I went to live with Aunt Ida. She was in her late fifties by then, and had never married or had children. And she liked her life just so." Libby studied the herd of quarter horses grazing in the distance. "It was easier to go along with what she wanted than to fight anything."

Holden pounded in another post. "And Percy, God love him, wanted everything his way, too."

Libby gestured helplessly, recollecting that her husband, too, was an only child. She frowned. "His parents indulged him terribly, trying to keep him happy. Having me cater to his every need only perpetuated that."

Holden stripped off his leather work gloves and strode back to the truck. "But now you're different." He picked up a bottle of water and drank thirstily.

Libby tore her eyes from the strong column of his throat and neck. "You know I am. The last two years have made me think long and hard about who I am and what I want out of life."

Holden wiped the moisture from his lips with the back of his hand. "Do you think Johnston was trying to cheat you?" He offered her the bottle.

Finding she was thirsty, too, Libby took it and drank deeply, before handing it back. "Initially, yes. But since he doesn't have that reputation, I'm more inclined to believe that what went on today was all just a negotiating ploy."

Holden could not disagree with her assessment. "So you're still interested in doing business with him." He hefted himself up to sit beside her on the bed of the truck.

Although she could have shifted over, Libby stayed where she was, letting their hips and thighs touch.

Absorbing the warm masculinity of his body wedged up against hers, she shrugged. "More than ever, oddly enough. Jeff has some great ideas for expanding the business and taking it into the twenty-first-century internet sales and service in a way that, to be perfectly honest, I could never do." She shifted slightly, to better look into Holden's eyes. Her stocking-clad knee nudged his denim-clad thigh in the process.

Swallowing, Libby continued, "Under his guidance, I know the dealership will be a success and continue on in the tradition of excellence that the Lowell family was famous for." She paused briefly to reflect. "It will be a way of keeping Percy and his family alive, even though I'm still planning to move on." *Here, hopefully, with you...*

Holden rested his hand on her knee. "So where do I come into all this?" he said softly, intuiting there was more.

Glad they were on the same page, Libby smiled and looked deep into his eyes. "That's what I wanted to talk to you about."

"LIBBY IS REALLY OUTDOING herself this year, isn't she?" Emily remarked to Holden, one week later, as she parked the Daybreak Café catering van at the rear of the dealership.

He smiled at his sister. "By giving a Christmas party for all her employees and their families…not to mention a few reporters and any and all customers and library patrons who want to attend? I would have to say so."

"I think it's nice that she wants to go out in such a big way. Not that I've seen the two of you together all that much this week."

That, Holden thought, was his one regret. "Libby has been really busy," he said as he helped his sister load desserts onto a cart. "She was in meetings with Jeff Johnston and Claire on Wednesday and Friday."

"She was in Claire's office all day Thursday, too, wasn't she?" Emily brought out plastic-covered trays of appetizers.

Holden nodded. "She had to sign more documents this morning. At the bank and in Claire's office."

"Well, at least financially she should be set when all this is done."

That was true, Holden thought. Libby would have the means to settle wherever she wanted, in style.

"Do you know what her plans are for after the holidays?"

He refused to let his lack of information frustrate him. He knew Libby wanted to make her own decisions and prove she could handle this, all on her own.

He shook his head. "I know she's weighing her options."

Beyond that he had no clue whether she planned on staying in Laramie County, or even if she wanted to continue seeing him.

Although he knew what he wanted. Libby in his life, from here on out.

"What has she said?" his sister probed.

"Not a lot," he admitted reluctantly. "She's afraid she might disrupt the negotiations if she says much of anything before the contracts are all signed."

Emily sighed. "That's understandable, I guess. Especially given how upset the people in Laramie County were about her selling the dealership to begin with."

Holden pushed the cart, warning, "There's still a lot of uncertainty." Everything could explode if the deal Libby had brokered ended up not being all that it was reputed to be.

Emily held the door. "I know. I hear ranchers worrying every day at the café." She paused, her voice lowered in concern. "How is she doing emotionally?"

Aware that his sister was watching him carefully, Holden stated, "Libby's okay." On the surface, anyway. "I can see her getting stronger, more determined to go through with the sale of the Lowell family business and the reorganization of her life, every day."

But at same time he felt that she was definitely keeping something from him. Something personal. He just didn't know what.

I CAN GET through this, Libby told herself firmly as five o'clock—and the start of the Lowell Ranch Equipment Christmas party—approached on Saturday evening.

I am not going to do what I did before, and imagine

all sorts of things to be true just so I won't be alone. I'm fine. Honestly. And that slight indigestion in my gut, and the wobbling in my knees, is nothing more than yet another ridiculous physical reaction to stress....

To prove it, Libby stood and picked up the notes for the speech she was soon to give.

A second later, Holden walked in. Smiling, he shut the door behind him and he closed the distance between them, draping an arm across her shoulders. The warmth of his nearness spurred her heart to beat a little faster, even before he pressed a brief, tender kiss to her temple.

His eyes darkening with possessive intent, he told her in a low voice, "I am going to be so glad when this party is over and I can take you home."

There it was, the trademark McCabe orneriness that Holden employed whenever he felt her spirits needed a boost.

Glad for the diversion from the huge step she was about to take, Libby let her gaze drift over him. "That sounds so great... You just don't know..."

His expression grew tender. "I think I do. I've missed you this week."

"It'll get better soon," she promised, curling into the warmth of his embrace. "We'll have more time for each other."

"I like the sound of that," he murmured, tucking a lock of hair behind her ear.

Just then a rap sounded on the door, interrupting the moment. With a sigh, Libby eased out of his arms and stepped away. "Come in."

The door to her office opened and Claire stuck her head in. "Hey, Libby. Holden. Everyone is here. The microphone is set up."

"Thank you. I'll be right there."

The attorney waved in agreement and took off. Libby turned to Holden, all the emotions she had been holding at bay surging to the fore. "When this is all over I will give you a proper thank-you for all you've done for me this week." In addition to moral support and errand running, he had taken over the library hours at her home.

He returned her hug and lifted her hand to his lips. "Just goes to show what a good team we make," he murmured huskily. "Now, go get 'em, tiger."

Feeling newly confident, Libby walked out into the dealership showroom, to take the stage that had been set up.

Gathered around were all the LRE employees, the library staff and many patrons, and many ranchers from the area. She also saw Jeff Johnston and his team, and Claire. But most of all, there was Holden, patiently waiting, believing in her....

Her nervousness dissipating despite the task at hand, Libby took the microphone and thanked everyone for coming. "Before we start the party, I have a few announcements to make. First—it's official. This afternoon, I sold the dealership to Jeff Johnston. Everything Jeff has promised LRE employees—including the five-percent share of annual company profits—is in the sales contract."

A cheer went up.

Libby smiled, glad to see so many happy faces. Knowing the next part was going to be a tougher sell, she forged on. "In exchange for Jeff's generosity, I have agreed to a change in the name of the business. From here on out, the dealership will be known as Jeff Johnston Ranch Equipment."

Silence fell.

No one looked enthused about that.

In fact, just as Libby had expected, a lot of people looked downright ticked off.

She held up a hand to stave off any boos or negative comments, and continued sincerely, "And while I'm happy for Jeff, this makes me sad." She paused, looking audience members in the eye.

"For generations, the Lowell family served this community and served them well. Which is why I have taken the proceeds from this sale and created a charitable foundation in my late husband's name.

"The Lowell Foundation will serve Laramie County and its residents. And my first project, as director and chairman of the foundation, will be to get the Laramie Public Library back up and running, the way it should be."

THE NEXT FEW hours were filled with tons of questions, even more congratulations and a lot of celebrating. Finally, four hours later, the dealership was empty, except for Libby and Holden.

She returned to her office, where several empty boxes waited.

Looking unbearably sexy in a dark suit and cobalt-blue shirt that brought out the hue of his eyes, Holden undid the knot of his tie. He lounged in the doorway, one shoulder propped against the frame. "So I guess this means you're staying on in Laramie?"

Nodding, Libby slipped out of her high heels. She flexed her aching feet against the plush carpet, working out the kinks. Exhausted, she took off her earrings, too, and set them on her desk. "This last week has given me a lot to think about. I figured I had to leave Laramie, and all the trappings of being Percy's widow, to move on. When the truth is that experience—all the good and bad of it—made me the woman I am today." Pausing, she gazed up at him reflectively. "I can move on, right here. Honor my past, while at the same time pursuing my future, because if there is one thing all this has taught me, it's that Laramie is my home."

Holden came toward her. "What about the house?"

"I'm keeping it—at least for the time being. That was one of my bargaining chips in the marathon negotiation this week. I told Jeff I would lower the overall price on the sale by removing the house. In return, he said he'd put everything he'd promised the employees in writing…." To her consternation, Libby began to feel a little wobbly again.

Gosh, darn it!

Holden's brow furrowed.

Libby steadied herself by putting a hand on the file cabinet, then went to sit on the edge of her desk. "If I… agreed to a name change of the dealership. Which I think was what he was angling for all along."

Holden walked over and sat down next to her. He took her hand in his. "Then why didn't he come out and say it?"

Libby stared down at their linked hands. "Because when we started talking, I wouldn't even consider selling unless we kept the Lowell name on the business. It was only later," she admitted, tightening her suddenly damp fingers in Holden's, "that I realized what the real purpose of this windfall inheritance could be."

Holden nodded, listening, seemingly unable to take his eyes from her face. Although he looked worried now.

Doing her best to hide her symptoms, Libby forged on. "This way, Percy's family will continue to do a lot of good, and they will be remembered always." She paused to acknowledge quietly, "And I'll be able to help a lot of people, too."

Holden searched her face. "You have always been quite the problem-solving crusader."

She smiled and withdrew her trembling fingers from his, discreetly blotting the moisture on her skirt. "And now...I'll have the funds to..." Libby swore as the room tilted sideways. Or at least it seemed to. That darned dizziness again!

"What is going on with you?" Holden demanded in concern, taking her by the shoulders. "You're white as a ghost!"

And that was the last thing Libby heard.

Chapter Fifteen

"This is ridiculous!" Libby argued as Holden escorted her into the Laramie Community Hospital. "I do not need to go to the emergency room."

"It's Saturday night," Holden stated firmly. "You are not waiting until Monday morning to see your family doctor."

Before she could respond, Paige stepped out of an exam room and approached them. "Hey." The scrubs-clad physician and mother of three paused to put down a chart at the nurses' station, then turned back to them. "What's going on?" Her glance swept over them both, taking in the tender, protective way Holden's arm was clamped around Libby's waist. "I heard you were bringing Libby in."

Relieved to have medical help at long last, Holden confided to their mutual friend, "She hasn't been feeling well since she had a virus a couple of weeks ago."

Paige grabbed a new chart and pen. "Is this true?"

Libby waved off the intermittent bouts of nausea and dizziness, combined with the ever-present urge to curl up somewhere and take a nap. "It's just fatigue. And stress."

And a menstrual period that was nearly three weeks late, causing the physical commotion. There was no way she was going to let herself be prey to another hysterical pregnancy, or even the hint of one, Libby thought grimly. It was bad enough she had allowed that kind of melodrama to happen once before. This time, she was doing the rational thing and keeping her suspicions to herself.

Unfortunately, her lack of full disclosure, to either Holden or her best friend, had Paige's radar on full alert.

Her expression concerned, the physician steered them toward an exam room. "Describe the symptoms."

That, Libby really did not want to do. So instead, she stalled and said, "Aren't you a pediatrician?"

Paige flattened a hand against the door and ushered them inside. "It's the holidays. We're shorthanded tonight. At this moment, the internist on call is busy stabilizing a coronary patient. And the other physicians are busy, too. So unless you want to wait until another doctor can be called in…"

Holden lifted his palm. "We're grateful for the help."

Meanwhile, Libby *was* feeling a little wobbly. Actually, she thought, putting a steadying hand on the gurney, make that a *lot* wobbly.

Holden grabbed her by the waist and lifted her onto the bed. Still holding her, he peered at her face. "Are you going to pass out again?"

Paige broke out the smelling salts and waved the aromatic scent beneath Libby's nose. "You fainted?"

Libby jerked back from the hideous smell. "Just a tiny bit," she admitted grumpily.

Not bothering to hide his concern, Holden told Paige, "She scared the heck out of me."

The pretty physician smiled knowingly. "And you are not a guy who scares easily."

He was gallant, though, Libby thought. Sometimes way too gallant for his own good.

"You'd never know that by the way he's been acting

this evening," Libby grumbled, knowing much more of this tender loving care from him and she would be tied to him emotionally—for life.

Paige reached for a clean cotton gown and handed it to her. "We're going to examine you and see what's going on. Do you want him in with you? Or out in the waiting room?"

Libby didn't even have to think about that, as she admitted reluctantly, "In here." Turning to Holden, she tapped the middle of his broad, strong chest. "I want you to hear it firsthand when they tell me this was just exhaustion."

Because she was definitely not pregnant. It didn't matter how much her mind was trying to trick her into believing it was so.

"Get changed. I'll be right back." Paige eased out. The door shut behind her, leaving Libby and Holden alone again.

"Want help getting into that gown?"

Libby felt so shaky and weak she wasn't sure she could manage. However, there was no need to let her handsome companion know that. He'd only use it to torture her with kindness later. "If you must. And stop smiling."

"Can't help it." He playfully tugged on a lock of her hair before helping her off with her sweater. "You're really pretty when you're cranky." He stepped behind her to allow her some modesty while her bra came off and she eased the polka-dot, green-and-white-cotton gown over her shoulders. "And that temper of yours is working to bring the color back into your face." His fingers brushed her skin as he tied the gown in back, then helped her to her feet.

A short time later, she was relaxing beneath the sheet.

Holden kept up the chitchat until Paige returned with an E.R. nurse.

Libby answered a ton of questions. Endured a physical exam and gave blood and urine samples.

After an interminable wait, which in reality was only twenty minutes, but was more than enough to tempt Libby to fall asleep, Paige returned.

The auburn-haired physician studied them both, the hint of a smile in her eyes. Finally, she looked at Libby and announced with candor, "The bad news is there's a reason you've been feeling the way you have. And it's likely to continue."

Holden turned and gave Libby an I-told-you-that-you-needed-to-come-in-tonight look.

Paige continued, with a warm smile, "The good news is…you're pregnant."

For a long moment, the mixture of shock and surprise rendered them motionless.

For Libby, this was all too reminiscent of a very similar event—with a very different outcome—two years prior.

She stared at her friend, hardly able to believe… "Are you sure?" she finally gasped, clapping a hand over her heart. "Because we used condoms! Every time!"

Paige smiled.

Holden, Libby noted, couldn't stop grinning like the proud papa-to-be he was.

"No method of contraception is one-hundred-percent fail-safe," Paige said.

"But…" Libby sputtered, still unable to fully comprehend.

"The blood work confirms it. I'm guessing you're due in August. But of course, you'll need to follow up with your ob-gyn." Paige rattled off a few more instructions, then gave Libby a prescription for prenatal vitamins and a list of dos and don'ts for mothers-to-be.

She congratulated them again. Then, leaving them to absorb the news in private, she slipped out of the room.

Holden grabbed Libby and hugged her fiercely. "Can you believe it?" he murmured, every bit as stunned and happy about the news as Libby was, deep down. "We're going to have a baby!"

It was, Libby thought, still struggling with a myriad of emotions, almost too good to be true. For her to suddenly be getting everything she had ever wanted—save love…

"Of course, we'll have to get married right away," Holden stated.

The confidence in his tone snapped her out of her lethargy. "Whoa!" She held up a palm, wishing she had on something other than a hospital gown, which left her feeling far too vulnerable. "You've already had one shotgun wedding," she pointed out, forcing herself to be practical. "You can't do another."

Holden's brow furrowed. "That was different."

Deliberately, Libby ignored the mixture of disappointment and hope on his face. "Yes, you and Heidi had been dating longer than you and I have. And your marriage still failed."

Resentment flashed in his eyes. "*Our* marriage won't fail."

She studied his suddenly poker-faced expression. "Why not?" she demanded impatiently, wishing he could reassure her.

He kept his eyes locked with hers. "Because I care deeply about you and I know you care for me."

Care, Libby thought. Not love…

Unwanted emotion welled up inside her. Wistfulness

and hormones combined, leaving her all the more out of sorts. "Listen to me, Holden." Her temper spiking, Libby folded her arms across her chest. "I know your instincts are noble and that it is very important for you to do the right thing in all situations. But I can't—won't—be a ball and chain to anyone again."

Holden smiled at her in the same indulgent way she had seen other men gaze at their pregnant wives. Gently, he placed his hands on her shoulders. "You wouldn't be a burden to me."

"You say that now," she countered. Doing her best to remain immune to the warmth in his grin, she added, "But as time goes on, you're going to feel cheated. And when that happens—" she swallowed hard, forcing herself to go on "—whatever affection you have for me will diminish."

She held up a hand before he could interrupt. "Maybe only a tiny increment at a time. But it will happen. And then you'll look around and see the kind of deeply loving matches everyone else in your immediate family has made, and you'll regret rushing into this the same way you now regret rushing into that union with Heidi." Tears blurred her eyes. "And I couldn't bear that."

Holden stared at her, his hurt and dismay evident.

Libby mourned, too, but knew the pain he felt now was only a fraction of what he would endure if they continued recklessly down this path.

It didn't matter how she felt, or would always feel, about Holden, Libby thought sternly. It didn't matter that she would marry him in an instant, if only she thought he could love her. She had to do what was right for him. And ultimately, their baby, too. And that meant facing the facts, no matter how harsh.

"I'll share custody of this child with you, and we'll

raise him or her together with all the love and tenderness we have to give." Hoping to hang on to the passion for as long as possible she blurted, "And we can even keep the physical side of our relationship going, as long as it works for both of us." *As long as you still want me...*

A flicker of interest appeared in his eyes.

"But I won't let you marry me as a point of honor, or enter into a sham of a marriage, just so everyone else around us will be happy."

As Holden realized how serious she was, his expression grew stony. "You're asking us to settle for only a portion of what we should have."

Feeling as if her whole world were crashing down on her once again, she edged closer, looked deep into his eyes. "I'm trying to protect us," she told him softly. "To create a situation we both can live with."

Holden braced himself as if for battle. "No, Libby," he argued, "you're *protecting* yourself. And that's not fair to either of us, never mind our baby!"

"What are you saying?" she whispered, afraid she already knew.

With his jaw clenched, Holden laid down his ultimatum. "If you don't care enough about me to even consider marriage—after everything we've been through together...after the incredible way we made love—then it's over, Libby." He grimaced and stepped back. "It has to be."

"Is this a good time for us to talk?" Greta asked, several days later.

It was and it wasn't, Libby thought.

Determined to avoid the subject of her broken heart, she ushered Holden's mother out of the wintry gloom.

The forecasters were predicting snow, but Libby wasn't expecting that to happen.

She smiled at Greta. "Tomorrow is Christmas Eve. Shouldn't you be getting ready for the big family dinner you're hosting?"

The older woman inched off her leather driving gloves. "I wanted to make sure you were still planning to attend."

There it was, the maternal concern that she so longed to have in her life.

Libby swallowed, figuring she owed it to both of them to be honest. "I didn't think…under the circumstances…" She decided just to come right out with it. "I presume you heard our news?"

Greta smiled, looking overjoyed. "That congratulations are in order? Yes. We do know." She paused to give Libby a warm hug that spoke volumes about the affection and inclusiveness of the McCabe clan. "And we are *so happy* for you and Holden both."

"But—unless I miss my guess—probably not so happy that our rebound romance is officially over."

Looking more thoughtful than upset, Greta allowed, "We're still hopeful things will work out, over time. But that said, the invitation to become a member of the McCabes is still on."

"Because of the baby," Libby stated, needing to know where they all stood.

Greta shook her head. "Because you're you. You're a wonderful young woman, and you need family. And we would love to include you in ours. The same thing goes for your baby, of course."

Libby bit her lip. "Even if Holden and I don't ever marry?"

Greta took her hand and patted it gently. "Our offer is not conditional. There is no pressure to do anything any one particular way. Love isn't a one-size-fits-all sort of thing."

She continued thoughtfully, "You've seen the different paths it has taken with Holden's siblings and even some of his cousins. Kurt and Paige loathed each other for years before the triplets that were abandoned on his doorstep brought them together."

Libby grinned, recalling, "Hank and Ally came together because of the ranch she inherited."

Greta nodded. "Dylan and Emily tamed each other."

"And Jeb and Cady let a two-week babysitting gig for her sister turn their years-long friendship into something more," Libby recollected.

"And then, of course, there's my beginning with Shane," Greta reminisced fondly. "A late-night mix-up landed us both in the same bed, with our mothers' entire bridge club looking on."

And what a scandal that had been, or so the story went. "The two of you decided the only way to fix it was to get married."

Greta chuckled. "So we eloped to J. P. Randall's Bait and Tackle Shop. And then did everything possible to prove to our matchmaking families that we were not meant for each other."

Creating more legendary scandal in their wake. "And fell in love along the way."

"Very much in love," Greta confirmed, the corners of her eyes crinkling contentedly. "And four children and thirty-six years of marriage later, we're still very much in love."

She leaned forward earnestly. "The point is, we all found love in different ways, and took different paths to get where we are today. So don't feel you have to marry or not marry to get the McCabe stamp of approval, Libby.

You already have that." She smiled kindly. "We will love and support you and be there for you no matter what path you-all take. Just make sure whatever path you choose is true to the feelings in your heart."

SHANE MCCABE WALKED INTO the stable and stood looking over the stall door at the foal and mare Holden had just brought in from the pasture. "Is that the Willow I've heard so much about?"

Holden surveyed the breathtakingly beautiful filly with the dark gray mane and tail. "It sure is," he said proudly. He paused to check out the little one's hocks and hooves, gave the filly and her mama a pat, then stepped out of the stall and headed for the tack room to mix up the feed. "She's already got great speed and agility." Which were key traits to an outstanding cutting horse.

Shane nodded in approval. "She's going to make a nice addition to your quarter-horse bloodlines."

Holden thought so, too. His dad stood by while he opened the airtight containers and measured crimped corn, cracked oats and soybean meal into a feed bucket.

Shane handed him the big jar of vitamins, minerals and protein supplements. "Amazing, isn't it," he drawled as Holden added the additional ingredients and a dollop of molasses—for taste—to the feed. "How a mama and a sire that should not have been able to come together and produce a viable heir could not only have done so, but be as happy and thriving as that."

Holden shot his dad a look of muted resentment. "I feel a parable coming on." One relating not to a foal that had survived hemolytic disease, but to him and Libby and the baby they both wanted so very much....

Shane fell into step beside Holden and walked back to the private stall where Willow and her mama were quartered. "Your mother and I know people who did everything 'right.' They followed the prescribed, traditional path of courtship, engagement and marriage, and they still ended up getting divorced."

Holden stepped into the roomy stall and poured mixture into the high and low feeders. "No one in our family really stays on the straight and narrow when it comes to romance, Dad."

Shane watched as he led the filly to the feed mixture. "And you know why that is?"

Holden hunkered down beside Willow as she nosed and nibbled the grains. "I have a feeling you're going to tell me." And it had nothing to do with the fact that Libby did not love him—and apparently never would, Holden thought dispiritedly. Slowly, he got to his feet.

His dad continued, "Because we have all figured out that loyalty to tradition, or really to anything, can take you only so far." Bluntly, Shane stated, "Doing the right thing—the gallant thing—is important."

Holden knew that. He'd been raised on that sentiment.

His dad came closer and clapped a reassuring hand on his shoulder, looking at him man-to-man. "But chivalry is not enough to build a marriage and family on, and never has been. Any more than trading one life for another ensures happiness or parity in the universe."

Heaven help him, Holden thought, biting back an oath. They were talking once again about Percy. About the accident that had claimed him. And Holden's promise to help Percy's widow.

Shane mused soberly, "Fate, destiny, God's will—whatever you want to call it—plays a part in everything that happens and we have no control over that part of our lives, son." He paused, letting his words sink in. "None whatsoever. It's what we do with the hand we are dealt that counts."

THE SNOW STARTED AT two o'clock in the afternoon on Christmas Eve. At first it was just a flake or two, fluttering down from the white sky overhead. Then a light smattering. By four o'clock, it was coming down hard.

Libby gazed out the window, marveling at the miracle and praying it wouldn't be the only one to happen that day. Then she grabbed her coat.

She was just slipping it on when her doorbell rang.

She went to answer it and saw Holden standing there, his hands thrust in his pockets. Snow dusted his Resistol and the shoulders of his shearling-lined suede coat.

Libby wasn't sure what was sexier, the determined look on his handsome face or the fact that he was there at all. She only knew she wanted him in her life. And she hoped—once he heard her out—that he would reconsider and want the same.

She drew a deep, bolstering breath and looked up at him, her heart in her throat and her emotions on the line. "I'm glad you came by."

Silence stretched between them. He stared at her, an undecipherable emotion in his cobalt-blue eyes. "I thought you might like a ride to the gathering at the Circle M tonight."

Although there wasn't a great deal of snow accumulation, the roads were slick. She could see chains on the tires of his all-wheel-drive pickup.

Was that the only reason he was here?

"But," Holden continued in a rusty-sounding voice, still holding her eyes, "before we go…I'd like to talk to you."

Her heart racing, Libby stepped back and ushered him inside.

He took off his coat and hat, and hung them on the coat tree. Libby removed her coat, too, then took him back to the family room, where the Christmas tree had been set up. Too nervous to sit, she turned to face him.

"First, I want to apologize." His expression gentling, he closed the distance between them. "I never should have thrown down that ultimatum." His lips took on a sober slant as he gazed deep into her eyes. "Whatever feels right to you is fine with me."

There was such a thing, Libby realized, as too much latitude in a relationship. She peered at him, struggling to understand. "Does this mean you're taking back your marriage proposal?" Her voice sounded throaty and uneven.

Holden grimaced. "It was more like a marriage *assumption*, but…yes." He caught a lock of her hair and tucked it behind her ear, the gesture so tender it made her want to weep. "I want to wipe the slate clean. It was a thoughtless idea," he confessed huskily, "delivered in a meaningless way." He shook his head regretfully. "I have always thought you deserved better, Libby, and I still do."

Not quite what she had been expecting. But, Libby told herself sternly, it was still a step in the right direction.

She cleared her throat and pushed on with her own much-needed apology. "As long as we're on the subject, Holden, I think you deserve better, too." The longer they stared into each other's eyes, the more her heart thawed. "I haven't been careful with your feelings, or true to what I want in this situation, either."

I haven't been exactly honest. With you or with me.

Holden clasped her hands in his. "If it's more space you need…"

It was time to take the risk, to act based on what was in her heart instead of what would keep her safe. "It's anything but that. The thing is, Holden, I've had a thing for you for quite a while now. I'd like to say it started a month ago, but that would not be true. I was always aware of you, way too aware of you, even back in college when we first met—which was why I had to constantly keep my guard up. The more time I spent with you, the more I liked you." She released a quavering breath. "And I became even more drawn to you after Percy died. You showed me what kind of man you were deep down, and you were so wonderful to me in those few months, so kind and so understanding and tender and caring."

His eyes darkened with emotion. "Since we're being honest here…I felt the same way you did, Libby. And it was not only a forbidden attraction on my part, it was for all the wrong reasons."

Libby nodded, glad he understood. "I knew nothing could come of it because of our mutual guilt. It was like yearning for something you had always wanted and knew deep down was exactly right for you, but never could have." She sighed, remembering. "My hysterical pregnancy and the embarrassing aftermath, our near kiss, was a wake-up call in so many ways, because it all combined to give me the impetus to stay away from you. To get better and wiser and stronger all on my own." Which was something she had needed to do.

"And you have." Holden gave her an admiring glance and brought her all the way into his arms.

Libby splayed her hands across his solid chest and mustered up all the courage she possessed. "And it's because I reached this good place in my life—where I was finally able to separate duty and obligation and people-pleasing tendencies from my need to do what was right for me—that I was finally able to pursue my true feelings for you.

"Of course," Libby continued wryly, feeling the steady beat of his heart beneath her palms, "I went about it all wrong…out of fear of being hurt again."

"Oh, Libby," he whispered hoarsely, planting a kiss on her forehead and waiting for her to continue.

"But—" she gulped, her pulse racing all the more "—maybe because the universe says I am finally due for a little happiness, and because it is Christmas…I ended up where I was supposed to be, just the same. In your life, in your arms…in your bed."

Tears clouding her eyes, Libby took the final leap of faith. "I love you, Holden," she whispered emotionally. "So much."

She wreathed her arms about his neck. Their kiss was long and slow…soft and sweet.

"I love you, too," Holden told her tenderly, then kissed her again even more passionately. Finally he drew back, his resolve as apparent as the depth of his affection. "Enough to do this or not do this in whatever way feels right to you."

From a McCabe man, it was quite an admission. "So," Libby clarified, her heart taking on a happy, excited rhythm, "if I said I never wanted to ever get married again…"

Holden's gaze was steady and sincere. "I would stand by you," he promised.

Delight bubbling up inside her, she said, "But what if I said I wanted to get married—so our baby would be born legitimate—yet not live together?"

He remained unruffled. "I'd be okay with that, too."

Libby looked deep into the eyes of her strong McCabe man and took another deep, bolstering breath. "And if I said I know there will be those who won't approve, and who think you rushed me into bed. Or that I seduced you. And others who assume we are only together because of some outdated notion of shotgun marriage..."

He raised a brow, but patiently heard her out.

She paused to take a last innervating breath. "And yet, what if I say I don't give a hoot what anyone thinks. That I want to marry you anyway. Right here. Right now. *Today.*"

Joy radiated from every fiber of his being. He hugged her close and gave her the confirmation she had been waiting for all her life. "I'd be okay with that, too."

THANKS TO THE WINTRY weather, the drive to J. P. Randall's Bait and Tackle Shop took an hour and fifteen minutes instead of the forty-five Holden had estimated. But Libby didn't mind. It was Christmas Eve. She was pregnant with Holden's baby. He had asked her to marry him, and she had said yes. Life didn't get any better than this. At least that's what she'd thought until they turned into the single-pump gas station.

The squat, flat-roofed building with the peeling white paint was out in the middle of nowhere. Just run-down enough to make it disreputable, not dangerous. Libby'd heard of this place—it was, after all, the stuff of McCabe legends. But she'd never actually been here. "Are you sure this is a wedding chapel?" she asked in bemusement. "'Cause it sure doesn't look like one!"

Holden grinned, looking handsomer than ever as he came around to help her down from the cab. "Positive." They swept through the falling snow to the front of the building. "Says so right here." He pointed to the sign next to the door. "'Bait, fresh and frozen, for sale. Tackle, all kinds. Groceries, beer, coolers and ice available.'"

"'Hunting knives sharpened. Spare tires repaired,'" Libby read, impressed. "'Marriage licenses issued, ceremonies performed.'"

The only problem was a closed sign on the door. Shivering in the cold, Libby rested her back against Holden's chest and leaned into the warm, comforting circle of his arms. "I hope someone is here," she said.

"It would be disappointing as heck to drive all the way out here, wedding rings in hand, only to discover…"

"One way to find out." Grinning, Holden let go of her long enough to pound on the door. And then again.

Finally, fluorescent lights switched on in the store. The door opened. A young man in jeans and a Brad Paisley T-shirt beckoned them on in.

"J.P. Jr.!" Holden greeted him with a warm handshake and a slap on the back.

"Howdy, Holden." The young cowpoke with the spiked haircut and tattoos rocked back on his heels. "What brings you out this way?"

Holden grinned, looking every bit as excited and happy as Libby felt. "We need a marriage license—and a ceremony."

"Following in the folks' footsteps, huh?" J.P. Jr. teased, getting out the paperwork and a tray of rings.

There was something special, Libby thought, about eloping to the same place Greta and Shane McCabe had. It seemed like a good omen for their future.

Holden took Libby's hand securely in his and winked. "Or making our own."

Epilogue

One year later...

Libby had just taken the pecan and cranberry-apple pies out of the oven when Holden appeared in the doorway of the kitchen, three-month-old Cooper cradled in his arms. It was a sight that never failed to warm her heart.

Their son had his daddy's blue eyes and her honey-blond hair. And a quick cherubic smile that could have lit up all of Texas.

As usual, Libby noted fondly, both of the men in her life looked as happy as could be. As was she.

Under her direction, the Lowell Foundation was doing great things all over Laramie County and serving as a coordinating agency for other local charities. The tractor dealership was thriving and the public library was open again. And life as one of the McCabes was better than she ever imagined.

It had been a magical year, and she knew her future with Holden and Cooper and the rest of her new family would only get better.

"You can come and look now," Holden told her. "Coop and I are done putting the finishing touches on the holiday decor."

Contentment flowing through her, Libby walked over to give them each a kiss. "I can't wait to see."

Holden handed her their son for a cuddle, and wrapped his arm around her shoulders. Together, they walked into the family room.

The eight-foot-tall eldarica pine was topped with a shining gold star and threaded with shimmering white lights. The branches were adorned with a wide-ranging selection of ornaments. UT sports, *Sesame Street* characters and the beloved *Peanuts* gang hung next to all the whimsical, one-of-a-kind decorations Libby had picked out the previous year.

Stockings with their names embroidered on them hung on the mantel.

Beneath the tree were presents waiting to be opened.

Mistletoe they had picked themselves was hung strategically throughout the house.

Holden grinned. "Is this a great family Christmas or what?"

"It's spectacular," Libby admitted. "Especially the tree. It beats the his and hers versions we had last year hands down."

"That's what I was thinking. The question is," Holden murmured with another adoring look at her and their son, "what is Cooper thinking?"

Libby looked down at the infant snuggled into the warmth of her breasts. His head was turned slightly to the side, and his eyes were shut in peaceful repose. Soft, rhythmic breath soughed out of his Cupid's bow lips.

Parental tenderness swept through her. "Not much, apparently. Looks like he's just fallen asleep."

Gently, Holden touched the baby's cheek. Then hers. "What do you think?" he whispered. "Should we put him down?"

Libby nodded in agreement. "It's probably a good idea for him to have as much of a nap as he can get. He's going to need his energy for the Christmas Eve dinner this evening, at your parents' ranch."

They took him up to his crib, covered him with a soft blue blanket and turned on the monitor. Then they tiptoed back out again, and adjourned to their bedroom for a little quiet time of their own.

Holden stopped her beneath the mistletoe. "Have I told you how much I love you?"

"Many, many times." Libby grinned and wound her arms about his neck. "But that's okay." She kissed him passionately. "Because I never get tired of hearing it, and I love you, too, Holden. So much."

He kissed her back.

When at last they drew apart, he looked deep into her eyes and said, "It's time I showed you, too."

He withdrew a velvet gift box from his dresser drawer.

Libby undid the ribbon and opened it up. Inside was a beautiful diamond solitaire, which he slid onto her finger. "It's the engagement ring you never got. The one you would have had if we hadn't eloped...."

Libby couldn't think of a better present. "Oh, Holden," she breathed in delight. "It's beautiful! I love it!" Beaming, she said, "And I have something for you, too!"

She went to her dresser and brought out another small box. Inside was a note that said simply: "IOU a baby girl."

"So whenever you're ready, too, we can get started working on that," she teased, having learned that time was the most precious commodity of all. And never to be squandered. "Or even have a practice run..." Because she and Holden were never ones to put off until tomorrow what could be accomplished today.

"I like the idea of that as much as I enjoyed eloping

with you. So…" Holden brought her intimately close, all
the love she had yearned for reflected in his eyes. "How
about right now, Mrs. McCabe?"

Libby smiled. "Sounds good to me, Mr. McCabe."

And together they went about doing just that.

* * * * *

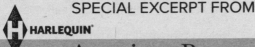
Read on for a sneak peek at
HOME TO WYOMING
by Harlequin American Romance author Rebecca Winters,
available September 2013.

Buck Summerhayes and two of his buddies started the
Daddy Dude Ranch as a way to give back to children who
had lost a parent in the war. Alexis Wilson is overwhelmed
by how wonderful Buck is with her young ward Jenny—
and how rugged and handsome he is, too!

Alex felt as if she was falling into space when Buck emerged
from the shadows of the barn, leading a saddled horse by
the reins. In his hat and jeans and wearing a Western shirt
that accentuated the size of his chest, he looked sensational.

He raised his head, causing their gazes to collide. Buck
had to know she'd been staring at him, because he'd caught
her before she could look away. One side of his compelling
mouth turned up, giving her senses a jolt. "This is Blossom.
She's a mare you can trust."

Don't touch me, Buck. Don't come near me.

But it was too late, because he steadied the horse while
she climbed into the saddle, and his hard-muscled arm
brushed hers, sending liquid fire through her body. "Thank
you," she said in an unsteady voice.

"You're welcome."

While Alex attempted to recover, he went back to the
barn and rode out on a dark brown horse.

Jenny made an excited sound. "What's his name?"

"Dopey."

The little girl laughed. "No, it isn't."

"Buck's just teasing," Johnny explained. "His real name is Dynamite. Can we ride to the new house so Jenny can see it?"

"Sure. It's midafternoon. The workmen should be gone by the time we get there. Why don't you lead the way?"

"Okay. Let's go."

Alex hurriedly drew alongside him with Jenny on his other side, and they were off. Buck brought up the rear. It had seemed like a good idea to go ahead with the children, but she couldn't forget that he was right behind them. Alternating thrills and chills bombarded her as they left the sage brush and entered a forested area filled with the sound of insects and birds whirring about.

The children talked incessantly, but their voices couldn't drown out the sound of her own heart pounding mercilessly in her chest. Alex breathed in the fresh smell of pine and simply absorbed the wonder of her surroundings, made more intoxicating by the man trailing them.

Watch for
HOME TO WYOMING
by Rebecca Winters

Available September 2013
from Harlequin® American Romance®!

WIN *Vegas*

A **TRIP** TO

& **TICKETS**
TO CHAMPIONSHIP
RODEO EVENTS!

Who can resist a cowboy? We sure can't!

You and a friend can win a 3-night,
4-day trip to Vegas to see some real
cowboys in action.

Visit
www.Harlequin.com/VegasSweepstakes
to enter!

See reverse for details.

Sweepstakes closes October 18, 2013.

NO PURCHASE NECESSARY TO ENTER. Purchase or acceptance of a product offer does not improve your chances of winning. Sweepstakes opens 7/22/2013 at 12:01 AM (ET) and closes 10/18/2013 at 11:59 PM (ET). Enter online at www.Harlequin.com/VegasSweepstakes. Open to legal residents of the U.S. (excl. Alaska, Hawaii, Overseas Military Installations and other U.S. Territories) and Canada (excl. Quebec, Yukon Territory, Northwest Territories and Nunavut Territory) who are twenty-one (21) years of age or older. Void where prohibited by law. One Grand Prize available to be won consisting of a 3-night/4-day trip for winner and guest to Las Vegas, Nevada (12/05/13 to 12/8/13); tickets for winner and guest for two single performances at championship rodeo events; and $700 USD spending money (Total ARV: approx. $3,990). Odds of winning depend on number of eligible entries received. Full details and Official Rules available online at www.Harlequin.com/VegasSweepstakes.
Sponsor: Harlequin Enterprises Limited.

Home to the Cowboy
AMANDA RENEE

It seems as if all of Ramblewood, Texas, is far too up-to-date on Tess Dalton's love life, or rather, recent lack thereof. She thought the trip home would help heal her heart—instead, it just puts her face-to-face with the first man to crush it.

Cole Langtry is determined to fulfill his father's dream and he doesn't have time for distractions, especially of the heartbreaking brunette variety. But when one remarkable little girl finally brings Tess and Cole together, it's hard to remember why they've stayed apart.

**Available August 6, 2013,
from Harlequin® American Romance®.**

HARLEQUIN®

American Romance®

ROMANCE THE ALL-AMERICAN WAY!

Use this coupon to

SAVE $1.00

on the purchase of

ANY

Harlequin American Romance book!

Available wherever books are sold, including most bookstores, supermarkets, drugstores and discount stores.

✂ -

SAVE $1.00

ON THE PURCHASE OF **ANY** HARLEQUIN® AMERICAN ROMANCE® BOOK.

Coupon expires February 28, 2014. Redeemable at participating retail outlets in the U.S. and Canada only. Limit one coupon per customer.

52611113

CANADIAN RETAILERS: Harlequin Enterprises Limited will pay the face value of this coupon plus 10.25¢ if submitted by customer for this product only. Any other use constitutes fraud. Coupon is nonassignable. Void if taxed, prohibited or restricted by law. Consumer must pay any government taxes. Void if copied. Nielsen Clearing House ("NCH") customers submit coupons and proof of sales to Harlequin Enterprises Limited, P.O. Box 3000, Saint John, NB E2L 4L3, Canada. Non-NCH retailer—for reimbursement submit coupons and proof of sales directly to Harlequin Enterprises Limited, Retail Marketing Department, 225 Duncan Mill Rd., Don Mills, ON M3B 3K9, Canada.

5 65373 00076 2   (8100)0 11879

U.S. RETAILERS:

Harlequin Enterprises Limited will pay the face value of this coupon plus 8¢ if submitted by customer for this product only. Any other use constitutes fraud. Coupon is nonassignable. Void if taxed, prohibited or restricted by law. Consumer must pay any government taxes. Void if copied. For reimbursement submit coupons and proof of sales directly to Harlequin Enterprises Limited, P.O. Box 880478, El Paso, TX 88588-0478, U.S.A. Cash value 1/100 cents.

[8] HARCOUPWBLCGT